New White Sands City Cyberpunk:

SHADOW'S FALL
STREETS of FIRE
The LAST HERCULES

More Titles Forthcoming....

SHADOW'S FALL

NEW WHITE SANDS CITY CYBERPUNK

Book 1

RON BENDER

AlphaTek Global Publications
Calgary

AlphaTek Global Publications

Calgary, AB
Canada
www.thecyberdeck.com

Pull-quote by Tghu Verd (Amazon Reviewer)

Editorial and interior design by Ella Beaumont

Cover image elements by ostil, Tithi Luadthong, and woodoo007
Cover design by Ella Beaumont

First Print Edition

Printed and bound in the United States of America
Published simultaneously in Canada

ISBN 978-0-9952643-7-3
(e-book ISBN 978-0-9952643-0-4)
FICTION / Science Fiction / Cyberpunk

To my dad.
Who always told me to do something with my stories.

New White Sands City was built on the bones of an eroding age . . .

In the face of rising sea levels, a decaying ozone layer, shifts in rainfall patterns, and resulting natural disasters, displaced populations sought housing, services, and security from wild weather and, increasingly, from each other.

Now . . .

Byzantine rules, hidden costs, and tiered services are the new normal. Everything is datamined, manipulated, and controlled. The ever expanding opportunities for the rich and well-connected are inversely proportional to the growing social disparities for the poor. Glittering towers soar high above the turmoil. Corruption, erosion of free press, riots, elitism, and the wealth gap form the basis of the Pile: the multi-tiered strata of New White Sands City.

SHADOW'S FALL

1.01

Raven and Brios

The lunch crowd left as I arrived, and now the Siffre's on Seventh is empty except for the sweet barista who smiles at me from the far counter. On my table, the miniature holographic waitress stands frozen, waiting, just like I am….

Brios is late, and he's not the type to be late for anything.

I catch myself checking my reflection in the café's mirrored back wall while I sip my drink. Keeping one eye on the flirty barista and the other on the rainy street, I try not to get twitchy. My palmscreen flashes ads for counseling, stress medication, and heavy-g yoga. I hit the *clear all* tab.

I stifle a yawn. The coffee isn't doing squat aside from tasting excellent. Last night had been busy and not in the way I liked. It started with a mugging and ended with me killing a guy. Between running around town avoiding a carload of bully boys and dropping the goods off in my stash, it was a late night. When Brios called, I was barely conscious enough to set a meeting time and crawl into the shower. Definitely not the best start to this girl's morning.

I'm tired and pissed that I have to sit on the stuff I lifted off the body last night. Having to wait for the heat to drop before I can make a profit slowed my hustle down to a crawl.

I'm hoping Brios' job tip proves solid, or I'm going to be bored and broke. Two of my least favorite things.

It's hard to miss him when he finally appears; he's a head and a half taller than the salarymen who part around him as they head back to the Corporate Core.

He sees me through the window. I nod at him as he steps through the projected ads that crowd the front door. He ignores the barista's interested hello and slings his wide frame into my booth, squeezing himself onto the bench seat.

The shoulders of his black jacket are painted with a seeping darker tone from all the rain. He looks like he's been out in it for a while. It's a new coat, and it looks good on him, kind of cute. I'll never tell him that; he probably bought the damn thing just to impress me.

As I tap the console for a second black coffee, I reward his style efforts with a sidelong flash of a smile. Yeah, just as I suspected, he catches the smile and puffs up a bit, trying to look bored.

He'll never learn. I'm not going to sleep with him again, no matter how hard he works at it.

To make sure he remembers that fact, I sit straighter and stare at him, one eyebrow arching.

"Nice jacket, but we're not dating."

"Right." He looks away, watching the rain distort the holo-ads that line the street.

It's been the same deal for years. He tries to woo me and I shut him down. It's our little game, and he always looks away first.

I can't fault him for wanting to sleep with me again. I look really good today.

I have a mental list of all the local coffee shops and diners where the lighting works with me, and this is one of them. There are a lot of reasons to like this place.

"You're late." I take the coffee out of the table dispenser.

The projected mini-waitress smiles and cheerfully reminds me to be careful and that the coffee is hot.

Brios clears his throat. "I had to turn down a job offer. This other one I've got is more important. So, have you heard the one about a guy who stole from the rich and gave to the poor?"

"Yeah." I slide the cup over to him. He's got my attention. Brios rarely calls a job 'important.' "Some guy named Robin Hood. Had the worst business plan ever."

I peek past Brios' wide shoulders toward the door. Two guys have ducked in out of the rain and are casually giving us the once-over. Construction workers on a break? I start a mental map of all the building sites I know in the area. It's possible they came from a site up the street.

Brios falls silent at my distant gaze, his expression switching from friendly to patient killer. He isn't always the smartest guy, but he is my favorite go-to-gunslinger. He leans forward to take the sugar bowl, his free hand easing his pocket-cannon into his grip.

The two guys sit at the counter. They can cover the front door and kitchen entrance from there. They place an order for coffee with the smiling barista and look around the place.

Real coffee is expensive. Real coffee served by a svelte French barista is a novelty that costs considerably more. It's the only way to order it at the counter. We'd be sitting there too, if we weren't talking business.

So these guys are well-off construction workers?

The helmets they set on the counter are blue and shiny, not beat up and covered in stickers. The helmet liners look new.

There's the tell. They're going to be trouble.... Just not the kind of trouble a girl might want on a rainy afternoon.

One of them catches my stare. I ease my shoulders back as I look away.

Maybe he likes my new top. I bought it on my way here, and it hadn't been cheap. It's this season's newest look, a skin-tight dark burgundy rig that does nice things for my cleavage.

I refocus with my new eyes so I can keep the two jokers in line of sight without tipping them off.

I love my new installs. I went to a Doc Ripperkin's clinic for the upgrade last month. I always buy the best, and Ripperkin's is the best TopSide has to offer. Short of going directly to

Japan, you can't get any better. I'm not going to die out here because I didn't spend the cash on basic gear. Not if I had the cash to spend.

Of course, sometimes that's the problem….

The one guy keeps his attention on me. I *do* look really good today. Or maybe these guys followed Brios. In that case, I've just been tangled in the fallout from the big dummy screwing up his exit plan.

I want to sigh. Instead, I answer Brios' unspoken question with a bored frown and a lopsided shrug.

"Robin Hood?" Brios picks up our conversation like it never stopped. "That's not the tag of the guy they found dead in Nu Hong district." He tries his coffee, his eyebrows going up at the result.

"Please tell me you've heard of Robin Hood." I'm not surprised, just kind of disappointed with my partner's newly revealed level of ignorance.

"Nope." He points with his nose at the cup. "This is really good coffee."

"Yeah, it costs a shit-ton more, but the coffee's real. The owner has a mysterious connection to a grower across the Gulf." I lean back and catch a glimpse of myself on some reflective signage. I fight the impulse to go shopping.

I'm too slow.

My palmscreen blinks with a dozen really good deals within walking distance of the café. Crap.

Brios hasn't even gotten to the details about his job tip, and some of these deals are timestamped. Again, crap.

Brios snorts. "How the hell do you save enough money to eat?"

"Hey, would you rather I turned into an airship-shaped balloon?" I would've said Hindenburg, but I'm sure he wouldn't catch the reference.

He gets sullen. Part of me wants to smooth down his damp hair. I didn't notice earlier, but he got a new haircut. It's the same one we saw on a billboard last week. I'm pretty sure I made a favorable comment about how it looked on the model. I decide not to mention it.

I have another sip of coffee and tap open the lunch menu. The mini-waitress flickers back into existence with a cute little curtsy and points out the deals of the day.

Brios looks past me. His eyes flick along, following something going by on the street.

"Truck." He fills me in. "Billy's Fish."

I get back on topic. "I can't believe you don't know Robin Hood," I mutter.

Brios growls. "Not all of us had the pleasure of a misspent youth. Hanging out in libraries and schools wasn't a privilege of mine." The guys at the counter get twitchy at the sound of his rising voice.

I shrug. "So tell me what's so special about this guy? People die all the time in Nu Hong, and it's not exclusive to that part of town. In case you haven't noticed, it's the middle of summer; UnderCity smells like a morgue with no power."

"Well, this guy didn't go by Robin Hood. Get this, his tag was Shadow." He snorts louder. "These wannabe guys from uptown are such a joke."

"With a name like that, he should've just hung a lumiotarget on his head," I say. I don't want to let on, but I've heard of Shadow. He swam in a way bigger pond than Brios and I.

Brios nods. "It would've been better for everyone if he'd just gotten shot. You know, a nice ranged-in rifle round."

Something registers in my brain. A red flag on the play.

"What do you mean?" I lock eyes on Brios, a sinking feeling hitting my gut. I'm not interested in breakfast anymore.

"My guy at the police station says this Shadow got himself carved up pretty good." He keeps his head down like he's reading the menu, but he lifts his eyes to meet mine. "Carved up like you like to carve."

The guy I tried to mug last night drew down on me and things went sideways from there. I hadn't known who he was. Now I do....

Brios has his I-knew-it face on.

Before I have a chance to process how any of this relates to Brios' job tip, everything changes. The software running my peripheral vision triggers a warning and amps my augmentations into overclock mode.

In slow motion, I see the construction guys at the counter reaching for guns.

I cut off Brios' smart-ass comment before he can say it. "Gun. Gun. Gun."

The guys still have their hands under their jackets as my boost system hammers me full of synthetic adrenaline.

I surge out of the booth. Electricity pulses along coated graphene nerves and flashes into augmented muscles.

The guys turn to face us, but they're too slow.

My beloved Italian-made double barrel double cylinder dial-a-round .45 roars. The barista inhales to scream as my rounds rip her last clients of the day to jelly.

It occurs to me that I'm not going to get to the deals on my palmscreen. A new pair of pumps would've been nice.

Brios pushes up and out of the booth. His gun swings to cover me as I crouch and bull rush the counter, pulling a pop-up as I move.

"Get down," I yell at the barista.

She listens well.

I get to the end of the counter and cover the kitchen and front door. At my nod, Brios moves down the hall to the bathroom doors.

I catch my full reflection in the mirror. My ass looks awesome when I crouch like this. JabbaJeans cling to every curve. My palmscreen lights up with local denim sales. The delivery truck, also in the reflection, bearing down on the windows behind me looks way less awesome.

"Truck," I yell as I move for better cover.

"Goddamn Billy's Fish."

It has to be the same truck as before. I kick myself. There's no Billy's anywhere near here.

A big truck from a big franchise means bigger players pulling strings. What kind of shit was Brios into to draw this kind of heat? No time now.

My Doc Ripperkins are linked to muscle manipulators and my trigger finger. It's the first of a list of highly illegal aftermarket modifications I can't live without.

I see the driver, flick my desire for his death into my arm, and the rest is hi-tech perfection.

As I'm diving behind the counter, my arm tracks him and squeezes the trigger. Plate glass bursts onto the street, and the bullets pound through the truck windshield. The driver's head explodes as pedestrians scatter.

Killing the driver makes no difference; the Billy's Fish truck tears through the pop-up bollards and slams into the building. What's left of the windows, glittering fragments and tumbling shards, hurl toward the counter front. The explosion of noise is impressive.

The truck lurches and stops.

Two more construction-commandos come through the kitchen door, zipper guns firing as they run the length of the café. I know Brios has this. I fling myself flat to escape the hundreds of ricocheting, super-light, hyper-fast bullets.

The barista looks up at me from her prone position.

"Stay down," I yell over the gunplay. I half-climb-half-slide over her. "They aren't here for you."

As cute as she is, I bite my tongue about her need for a better bra.

I scramble, cutting my angle of fire to get the drop on the guys I suspect will come through the front door.

My palmscreen lights up once more.

Brios lobs a hand packed grenade into the path of the submachine gun wielding construction guys.

The detonation shakes the counter front. Another reason I like this place: solid granite countertops and fronts. A girl never knows when she'll need dependable cover.

The zip guns stop shooting.

"Sweetie, watch your door," Brios calls as he heads to the back of the building.

I hear his cannon go off twice, then twice more. That means the exit to the alley has been breached. These guys are getting an 'A' for effort but an 'F' on timing.

I pop up long enough to grab a chromed creamer off the counter and drop back into cover. Yet another reason to like this place. It has practicality and high style. I lift the container over the lip of the counter and peek at the doorway in the curved reflection.

On cue, three skinny boys in ninja pajamas shove their way through the front door, the holo-greeter flickers as they run through him. Yakuza? What were they doing here?

I pull Little Tommy out of my back holster. The backup gun looks small beside the hulking .45's metal shrouded length. I shove the big gun over the counter's edge. I fire twice to suppress with the Double-Double and rise up to snap fire my off-hand.

Little Tommy rips a smoking line through the air. The ninja on the receiving end is instantly on his way to the floor, his chest making a perfect landing pad for the two stage micro-rocket.

The .45's blind fire dropped one ninja for bonus points. That leaves the third to come at me.

I don't wait around. I duck as the micro-rocket's second stage kicks off inside the one guy's chest. The flechette payload fills the room with an eerie noise, like a kid pull-starting an old gyroscope. It only takes a second.

I stand and look over the counter. Meat puree.

"Job's done here," I call as I eye the street for more trouble.

Brios doesn't answer.

"Brios, sound off." I yell louder.

No answer. Cop drones will be here soon. I frown as I jump over the prone barista. "Stay put."

As I move, I sneak a peek at the wicked deal on bras at the Uptown Lingerie. Nice. But I just launched a kBit worth of cash to wipe out the pajama boys. I need to make money today, or I really am going to go hungry.

The short run to the bathroom is cluttered with bodies. Three of four are missing limbs. Brios' cannon did its job.

I hear sounds of a fight from inside the ladies' room.

Just to be sure I'm not going to get flanked, I head to the backdoor and do a poke-check: head out, around, and back. Little Tommy tracks with my eyes.

A getaway van is parked tight to the building; the side door is open. No driver. What I can see of the alley through the rain looks clear. No surprises there at least.

Behind me I can hear the smart mirror in the bathroom.

"AlphaTek Global Security has individualized contracts to keep you safe. An altercation has been detected. Would you like to speak with an intake advisor about a new contract or a service upgrade?"

I mule kick the bathroom door open in time to watch a burly son of a bitch use Brios as a sheath for a long tapered blade. He shoves hard to get it through Brios' body armor.

I send a destroy signal to my gun-hand.

The .45 keeps firing into the guy long after he drops.

I rush over to Brios.

"You frak-headed idiot." I crouch and pull the now ruined jacket away from his injured side. "I'm the hand-to-hand on our team. Now look at you."

He lies there breathing shallow.

"Would you like to speak to an intake advisor now?"

"No," I bark at the mirror.

The ad cycles back to a VR-travel advert for high-end yachts in Ibiza.

"How do I look?" Brios' eyes meet mine. This time, he doesn't look away. "Is it gonna leave a sexy scar?" He tries to fool me with his pretty-boy smile.

"Nope. Because I'm going to get you fixed up." I shoot him a tight smile of my own as I double-check him for other injuries.

A heavy gouge runs down his right forearm, exposing the cyberware beneath. The sleeve of his new jacket is ribbons of faux leather twisted up with sliced synthskin. I ignore it. Biological trumps mechanical.

"Besides, you know I hate scars on my men."

"Yeah, because it means they're wannabes, or they're too poor to get'em removed." The tension goes out of his spine.

This is bad.

I glance at the dead guy's knife. It's a special ops hypo-knife. The injector is open and spent.

"Brios, that blade was pressure filled with anti-coagulants and maybe something worse. We have to move you fast."

I think about getting a medical screening; my palmscreen scrolls. A mobile medical clinic is two blocks away doing inoculations for a new outbreak of some shit or another.

"Ugh." His voice is sluggish. "Sure thing, Sweetie. Just give me a minute to get up some steam. I'm right behind you."

I leave him and sprint to the wall by the sinks. I tap three quick sales. A handful of eBits draw from my account. I yank a tampon and two pads out of the dispenser.

I make it back to Brios, cut the straps of his armor, and flip it away from the hole in his side.

"Hey," he says softly, "why don't you ever want to go out with me?"

"Shut up, Brios." I tear his shirt open, ignoring his gasp as I rip the packaging off the tampon and insert the foam plug into the wound. I pack the pads over the outside.

I rummage Brios' pockets and find a single shot of Suspend. I push the discharge tip against his neck and thumb the switch. The drugs vape through his skin.

"Why is that, Raven?" He drifts as the Suspend kicks in. His heart rate drops. "We never go to movies or for dinner anywhere nice."

"Goddamn it, Brios." I yank the belt off dead-guy's pants and loop it around Brios' chest. "Breathe out, you dumb mother."

He tries his best, and I reef the belt as tight as I can over the pads. At least there's hemostatic pressure on the wound.

He moans, and his eyes swim.

"You pull through this and I'll take you to dinner," I say loudly. "TopSide, someplace nice."

"Deal," he whispers. "Be straight with me, Raven. It was you who carved up that guy last night wasn't it?"

"Crap and Jesus, Brios. Talk later."

I struggle to get him upright enough for me to dead lift him to my shoulder. My muscle augmentations kick in. The system burns a lot of calories. I really am going to go hungry today.

We borrow the getaway van, and I get us to the MobiMed in under a minute. The med-techs on board are surprised to see me as I shoot the lock off the rear door and heft Brios inside.

"We're doing inoculations here, not treating street savages," the lead EMS declares as I kick the privacy screen aside.

I shut him up, the Italian Double-Double .45 pressed hard under his chin.

"Everyone else in this crap wagon likes money, right? There's 5kBit in it for each of you if you patch him up."

The rest of the medical team starts working. The lead EMS looks ready to argue. I grab medical tape, shove him down into a chair, and wrap him into it.

"See, they earn money and get to live," I say angrily into his ear as I work. "You don't get money and I'm still thinking about the living part."

"What's this guy's name?" a nurse asks.

"Brios," I answer. "Who's the driver of this rig?"

She points to the one team member seated behind me. I turn. He looks up at my face. His expression changes fast, but not before I notice how much he's enjoying the view. I wear JabbaJeans just for that reaction.

I look back at Brios. His color is better. I promised him dinner. He'll think we're dating....

A whole different level of crap.

I vent. "You drive this vehicle?"

The guy's slow to answer so I keep busy yanking open the service panel above his head. This is the same type of medi-vehicle Brios and I jacked behind enemy lines in South Am. Thank God for standardization.

I hunt around and tear out the tracker. As I throw it into the disposal unit, I remember Brios' favorite line during that whole conflict. "Good times…," I mutter.

"Um, yeah," the driver finally answers. "I'm the driver."

Cute accent, even if he is a little slow; he sounds Aussie. Easy on the eyes too.

"Are you ready to do your job?" At his nod, I rattle off an alphanumeric string. "Roll us to that address but use the alley when you park."

He climbs into the front seat, loads in the data, and stares at the transit screen. "This address is for a lingerie shop."

"You can drive, or you can join him." I point my Double-Double at the bound EMS.

"What are you going to do when we get there?" the driver asks over his shoulder. The MobiMed pulls smoothly away from the curb and heads for the TopSide causeway.

"Well, your friends are going to keep earning money and as for you…." I glance back at Brios. He's going to be fine. "You're coming inside with me."

"What?" He jerks his head around.

"Eyes on the road, cowboy." I wave the gun barrel toward the front. "I figured since you were staring so hard, you'd want to help me pick out a few things."

I have a promise to forget and some steam to blow off; a little action would be just the thing.

1.02

Warning Signs

The medical team puts Brios back together, and I get his drugged up ass to his MidTown safe house. I bully his neighbor, a South Am vet buddy, to keep him under lock and key. Only after he's promised to convince Brios to lie low do I leave.

I'm restless and frustrated, and I'll die trying to not shop … but I have a solution to all that.

I keep myself out of trouble and stem the boredom by jumping Mobi-boy.

Two weeks later, the novelty wears off.

I need to get back into the hustle, and Mobi-boy's not cutting it anymore.

He likes looking good, knows how to play rough, and spends his money like water. He's the same as me. And that's the crux of the problem. I'm the pretty one in any relationship.

Even Brios could've told him that.

We have a semiprivate implosion at a crosstown bar and part company. I lift all the hardfold out of his wallet before he leaves with a skank who could be his sister.

My palmscreen lights up with a sale on 'I hate your guts' cards and 'Please take me back' ones, both from Emoto-san's ECards. I feel like I don't need either.

I drink my way through his cash-money between rounds of nasty dancing with bunches of guys and even a couple of women. I figure it's a good indicator of how well I dance, or at least how hot I look doing it. All the best-looking people in the place find their way to me.

Just before sunrise, I slam my last drink, tip back a scotch for Brios, and leave.

I'm alone and oddly happy about that fact.

The sun's on the horizon. I like TopSide. I get to see the sun most days. Problem is sunlight's a privilege not a right. It costs money to be up here.

My palmscreen shows me a short list of finance companies willing to work with me. It's a good reminder that I need to get back to business. Coasting on Mobi-boy's kBits had been an easy way to pass the time while I waited for the heat to drop but enough is enough. This girl needs to shop. To shop, this girl needs money.

If the guy I killed really was Shadow, it certainly explained the high-end gear. I knew it was a good haul, but I hadn't had time to put a value on any of it. Assessing my prize is where I'm headed next, but first I need some sleep.

When I get home, Otto, my kitchen unit's AutoChef, has a bowl of ramen waiting. As I eat, the countertop extrudes coffee into a small carafe. Belly full of noodles and caffeinated goodness, I sleep like the dead until noon. I dream about blood on my fingers and wake feeling like shit.

I roll out of bed, toss back a second carafe of coffee, and I'm back at street level.

I jump into a Googlecab.

The service is ancient, but they keep their cabs clean and the collision ethics algorithms are still biased toward passenger survival.

"We regret to inform you that due to civil unrest in various areas of the city, this cab is no longer capable of traveling into certain UnderCity districts. For your safety, please refrain from visiting these affected areas…."

I glance at the screen as the city map segments out and rotates, illuminating the relevant areas in red and orange.

Most of the districts along the eastern edge light up, and Nu Hong is a fiery shit-storm. Thankfully, the district I need is South Central. I can use my CitOne card to get past the checkpoints, and I can spoof the GPS if I need to.

An old boyfriend showed me how to bump the sensor arrays both inside and out. It lets me keep the cab in service and running without me being inside, and I can bump the location tracker a few blocks in any direction.

Whenever I jack one of these cabs, I wonder if Stephan is still running his scams in Italy, or if he's come over the pond.

I tap my fake ID against the screen and swipe through the legal warnings to confirm my intent to travel into a dangerous area of town.

I almost laugh. UnderCity is always dangerous.

The cab makes its way down the long causeway ramps through the layers of New White Sands, burrowing like a metallic tick into flesh.

After I set the software for an hour long loop, I take a few minutes to clean up from last night. With a Streaming News service playing in the background, I use a shower in a can, comb out my hair, and check my make-up.

There's a blurb on the wire about a yakuza gang war spreading across UnderCity. Something about an attack on a clan controlled bathhouse in TopSide that sparked the violence a few days ago. I'd already put the flameout at Siffre's behind me. The crap happening now wasn't on my radar. I don't do news. I do deals.

As for Brios, he could figure out his own shit. I could count on him to keep his head down until he was ready.

I pull a bundle of wires from under the plastic dashboard and flatten them out until I find the hidden data port. A quick look at the passing scenery tells me I have time before I need to chip-in. I keep an eye on a line of cop cars and an armored van rolling slowly along on a cross street. There's definitely more security than normal.

I check the overhead mirror. I look as tired as I feel.

An ad scrolls across my reflection.

The best rest ever on a Cloud Nine interconnected mattress. Lease rates start at fifty eBits a month, standard data collection and privacy terms apply. Tap the screen to get connected and finally achieve the sleep you need and deserve!

I opt for a chemical solution and dig through my handbag. I peel out a mil-spec pick-me-up stim and wrap the patch around the underside of my arm. It's my last hit. I'm going to have to find my pharmacist to score a refill.

The cab stops at a light close to where I need to be. I plug the stick into the wire harness port. Chipped-in, the cab will cruise around and its black box will show it has an occupant the whole time. I'll grab it on the return leg a few blocks from here. I jump out and start walking.

Water condenses off the underside of the city complex overhead and drifts down as a pseudo-toxic fog. Summer drives up the humidity in UnderCity. It will drip brown water till winter when the real rain starts. The bigger puddles of this stuff are great places to dispose of bodies. Chopped up and thrown in, all the flesh and bone dissolves in a few days.

I flip up my hood and slip a respirator out of its case on my hip. I push the seal over my mouth and nose.

I considered getting nasal filter implants, but the technician at Doc Ripperkin's told me I should wait until my eyes took all the way. "Besides," he said, "people still get head colds, and a cold with filters means drainage work and maintenance." Then he tried to sell me on a self-draining unit that cost a hundred times what I paid for my mask.

I just can't find a mask I like the look of, and all of them leave an itchy reddish line for hours where the seal bonded. Ugh, so ugly.

The stim kicks in. The ends of my bones feel like polished chrome, and my eyes keep switching to tight focus when they lock onto anything for more than a second. I know that, even with an hour booked on the cab, I need to keep moving, but moving is easy. The ground seems to fly by.

I shove my way through a hole in the chain-link fence, and then I watch, timing the movement of the automated forklifts before I slip across the loading yard. The automated loaders are so low-powered and efficient their visual arrays only work in one direction. That and they follow a buried cable path. I make sure I stay behind their direction of travel until I close in on a nondescript looking outbuilding.

My stash is the best investment of time I've ever made. The gang I hooked up with after South Am buried two international cargo canisters, one on top of the other, under one corner of the outbuilding. We put them in as the yard was being built. A few of the girls slept with the site manager, and he turned a blind eye for a while. When he got to be a problem, the boys arranged for a car accident. Problem solved.

I've outgrown that life, and the rest of the gang is either dead or in jail. So I'm the only one using the place. If the interior were sexier, I would use it for things other than dumping, stashing, and crashing.

I climb down the ladder and flip on the low volt system.

As the lights come on, I lift my lockbox to the grimy tabletop and open it up. It's time to assess my prize.

Some very nice looking pistols are the first items out of the box. I realize they have no ejector ports. They're caseless. Formed charges burn up as they fire. No brass left behind for police to find, or for me to have to hunt for after a messy takedown. The price per round will be higher, but the cool factor outweighs the cost.

I rummage through a drawer on the hunt for a ballistic rated diagnostic handset. I plug the first pistol in. It's spotless. I whistle as I take a closer look at the link software. It's custom and, from what little I understand, it's coded better than my current setup. I'll rip copies for my other guns when I find some time.

The second gun is identical to the first. God bless America. I'm now the owner of a pair of expensive, matched, and unregistered firearms.

Shadow's rep made him out as a killer, thief, and local hero. I know he was involved in some big jobs. These pistols are probably connected to a lot of very serious crimes. I try to imagine what a leaked police ballistics report will do for my cred. It feels like my birthday.

I pull the plugs on the diagnostic unit. The guns are elegant art pieces, even pretty. The grips and scrollwork match an outfit I have at my apartment. Into the jacket they go.

I find myself grinning as I reach back into the lockbox.

"Next up," I say aloud as I pull out a thumb-sized hardware unit. It looks like a common security tap. Taps like this sell for an even kBit on the open market.

I plug it into my computer to see what software it's running.

Smoke pours out of the system's grills so fast I flinch. I yank it out of the port. My system's memory core fuses itself into a solid mass.

My hands twitch as my body deals with the excitement and sudden action. The stim has me feeling tweaky and nauseous.

Crap.

That was an expensive experiment.

This isn't a normal security tap, and I still don't know what the hell is on it. I know a guy who can help me figure that out. I might be able to fence it to him, and, if I haggle him higher, I could afford a new computer.

What a waste.

I slide it into my coat pocket with a sense of regret.

Next comes the kCard. I know it's empty. I pulled all of the eCash into a blockchain account the first night I got it. That cash flow offset my payment for 'Brios' Big MobiMed Adventure.' Anything leftover was already spent, and not just on shopping. I have side projects that require constant funding. I sigh and drop the kCard back into the lockbox.

"First in, last out." I lift up a portable data core.

It's a silvery metal slab the size and thickness of my palm. I've seen one like this before. It paid out big, maybe this one will too.

I struggle to remember the name of the guy who helped me last time. That unit turned out to be a high density data storage setup: an expensive custom build.

This one, unlike the other, weighs way more than it should for its dimensions.

I turn it over in my hands, seamless, no screws, rivets, or even glue lines to be seen. At one time there may have been something stamped on one end, but it's been thoroughly gouged off. There's a gap for a tiny plug dead center on one narrow side. The hole is a shape I've never seen before.

My eyes hyperfocus. I stand there staring, watching the overhead lights flicker off the gouged-up edge as I try and fail to hold it still. My heartbeat throbs through my fingertips.

Military stimulants are the best.

I don't have a plug that will fit, even if my system hadn't turned itself into e-cycling. The slab joins the rest of the items in my pocket. I'll take it to my guy in East End UnderCity. He'll have the name of the guy I can't remember.

As for the nameless guy, I don't even remember where he works from.

Red flag. Why the hell can't I remember this jerk-off? I'm pretty good with names. Even as I wonder, I feel it slipping away; I have bigger issues.

I know Shadow was a regular feature in East End. Maybe my guy was a contact for Shadow. Maybe he was going to see my guy same as I'm going to do now. Maybe my guy will be pissed I have the goods Shadow was supposed to be bringing.

I catch myself and chuckle. The mil-spec stim is hammering me with a load of paranoia. The drugs are designed to work on three-hundred-pound infantrymen, so the dose is way high on little-ol-me.

Keep it simple. Get to my guy and figure it out.

My Googlecab is due back soon, and I want to get the most out of the stim. I kill the power and lock up.

It's easy to make my way out to the street. I timed my walk to coincide with the shift change at a small manufacturer in the next block. I blend in with dozens of other people going the same direction.

A couple of guys ahead of me grumble about police checkpoints and something about an apartment block getting torched. A lot of people just got homeless.

I keep my head down and slump along the same way they do. No one notices me or even cares that I'm mixed in with them. I have a 'down in the brown' vibe as I slow my pace to let everyone move past me.

By the time I hit the corner, I'm at the back of the pack. They go straight, but I turn right and pick up speed.

A quick time-check looks good. The hack in the cab says it's en route.

A thundering noise makes me glance up.

Two bone-white twelve-ton VTOL APCs descend out of the thick overhead fog. They're not sporting ID tags anywhere, and I know enough about military cutting edge to know the white paint is actually an active camo system.

Both VTOLs come in hot, arcing overhead in a full fuel gulping burn. The bomb bays swing open. Their belly guns swivel in their direction of travel.

The big craft come with full electronic countermeasures. With the flip of a switch they can drop into electric motors and pretty much vanish from sight. If everyone down here can see them, it means whoever owns them is more interested in making a show of force than ambushing their target.

If the intent is to scare the locals, it works. I'm not even local and I fight a surge of panic.

Homeless types melt out of garbage piles all around me and run in every direction. I run too. The last dozen yards are flat out.

I go to ground next to a smashed transit booth and make a futile wish that the VTOLs didn't catch me on their cams. A top down angle doesn't flatter my face. My cheekbones always look way too high.

The back ramp on one of them slides open as it slows.

I can't help it, the stim and my new eyes focus right onto two guys in combat gear and a third one in a full-length black leather coat. I see all of them perfectly. The two regulars pull on combat respirators. The last guy flips a long pale queue over his shoulder and draws a pair of hip-howitzers from under his coat.

The hulking taper-nosed craft fling into full braking mode. I don't have to see where the commandos drop. The VTOLs are hovering over the warehouse where my stash is buried.

1.03

You Know that Job Tip?

The VTOLs hold position, and the regulars exit on zip lines.

The guy in the long coat just steps off, falling feet first, arms wide, pistol in either hand, a batshit crazy grin on his lips.

I mentally kick myself. Did I trigger a silent alarm on the way out? Would they know to look for my stash? All I know is if they find it, I'm screwed. My DNA, along with all kinds of other stuff, has been collecting down there for years. I've gotten lazy and now I'm in panic mode.

My Googlecab arrives at the lights on time. I sling myself through the side door and program a new destination just outside the district.

I need to change transportation and direction fast.

While the cab moves, I use my last shower in a can and wipe down everything I touched. I hunt for stray hair I may have left on the seats and curse as my eyes keep overfocusing.

Whoever owns those VTOLs will have access to Big Data feeds. This cab would be on my list if I were the one looking for anomalies.

Maybe I'm still acting paranoid because of the stim, but I don't think so. I'm not taking any more risks. Until I earn a payday from this stuff and maybe disappear north someplace, I'm running silent and deep.

I reach up to my neck to turn off my palmscreen.

The screen lights up as my finger finds the hidden skin button. There's a great deal on tonight's VIP Nightlife Pass. All of my favorite clubs scroll by on the list.

A VIP Nightlife Pass is an invitation for select purchasers to see and be seen in TopSide's hottest clubs with New White Sands' sexiest 'A-listers.' All red carpet stars, mega-rich business types, and huge money.

I've gotten some of my best jobs by hanging out and rubbing elbows with those people. Sometimes we rub other things, but never for money. I'm not that kind of girl.

Crap.

I switch it off.

The cab slows and then pulls over to a stop. It's close enough to where I need.

I shove a handful of hardfold into the slot and the door unlocks. I watch a police cruiser speed past. A second later a massive truck whips by on the same route. A huge AlphaTek Global Security logo blazoned on every angle.

"What the hell is going on down here?" I mutter.

The whole place went to shit while I wasn't looking. It's only been two weeks….

I book it the rest of the way on foot to the rundown utility pillar. These things are everywhere down here. City services, which don't drop straight through the ceiling and into a building, route through them. I cross my fingers and lift the steel door as I pull. It springs open.

"Nothing for it." I step in, pull the door closed behind me, and dial my optics.

I spend the better part of forever climbing the spiral stairs into MidTown. I keep reminding myself it's better than going through a checkpoint. Just over a thousand vertical feet later, I'm starving after pushing my augmentations to make it in a reasonable timeframe.

Back on the street, I sweet talk an old Japanese guy into extending his bike rental for me. He looks surprised and then excited by my little speech.

As I pedal away I realize I may have asked him to help me shave my privates. I can't be sure. I suck at languages and the guy who taught me had a weird sense of humor. But hey, whatever, it worked.

It's been years since I rode a non-powered bicycle and my ass is on fire by the time I lock the old man's bike in front of the Pan-Asia Mall complex.

Ignoring the maze of shifting holo-ads, I cut through the mall and head for the food court. I've burned more energy than I was planning, and I ignore the people staring at me as I order three full noodle pad Thai with vatbeef on my available credit.

I devour my food and then shuffle through the fashion outlets to convince the Big Data feeds that I'm not just passing through. Part of me wonders why I torture myself. I don't even have the eCash to spend on clothes, and my credit's blocked on most fashionista outlets anyway.

This is turning into a shitty day.

I limp into line for the Pan-Asia Mall maglift. The mall security attendant who runs my ID through the scanner gives my outfit a once-over. I know I look good, but if you wanted to live in TopSide, you had to look the part. I flash a smile at him, and he waves me through.

Out in the warm tropical air, I walk the last dozen blocks to my apartment. As casually as I can, I use the utility door to get into the building and take the stairs even though every inch of me strains with the effort.

I slap the palm lock and trigger the number key. I don't look at the mess in my flat as I toss all of my newly recovered goods onto the coffee table and drop onto the couch.

My ass has barely stopped burning when my crappy doorbell rattles. The stupid thing was a gift from Brios; he hung it on my door as a joke last April Fools' Day.

I roll behind the couch, my heart pounding, one hand braced against the hidden plate of steel I screwed on under the fabric. I draw my pistol, waiting and counting.

It chimes again on my five count.

Just to be sure, I open my wall screen to the view from a pin cam hidden in the hallway. The wide angle view shows Brios leaning against the doorframe.

He looks exactly the same as the morning of our gunfight. He even has a fresh haircut.

I open the door a little quicker than I should. He might get the wrong impression, but I don't mind so much. I've missed him.

"Hey," he says all casual, still holding up the doorframe with his shoulder.

"Hi." I step back and motion for him to come in.

He's been in my apartment exactly four times before this. There's a part of me that wonders why he's making a point of showing up now, but I let it go.

I'm glad the mil-spec stim has worn off; I hate the idea of being paranoid about Brios. He's the only person I really trust. Being junked out right now would taint that for me.

He hands me a tiny bunch of real flowers as he walks in.

"We're not dating, Brios." I hope my tone offsets my eagerness. I had no idea Brios knew where a flower shop was. I've never told him I like flowers let alone which blossoms are my favorites.

I try not to look excited as I head into the galley and crack open my last bottled water. Even as I put the flowers in a glass, the cooler asks for confirmation of a re-order. I tap the *yes* tab and hide a smile as I put the colorful bunch on the counter.

"You're welcome." He looks around the mess and makes his way to the couch. "I figured you might like them. They're just a little something to show my appreciation for you hauling my ass to that MobiMed."

I look around. Signs of my last few rounds with the Aussie are everywhere. Weirdly, I feel self-conscious that Brios is seeing so much of my private life scattered around.

His eyebrow twitches as he sees the ball gag. I wince, but I'm determined to be an adult about my lifestyle choices.

He sits, putting his foot on the table after carefully moving this morning's ramen bowl to one side.

"So, what brings you to Casa del Sweetie?" I try for casual. I am happy to see him, but it's been a long day and I'm beat.

"I figured you were finished with that MobiMed driver and were looking to get back to work." He leans back and glances out the windows, the Corporate Core towers are lit in fiery orange by the setting sun.

"How do you know he isn't coming over after his shift?" I'm irritated that I'm so predictable. I start to hide items around the room, kicking them under chairs, pillows, and piles of clothes when I think Brios isn't looking.

He laughs. "Is that what you want to go with, Raven? Because I can leave."

My fist closes around the ball gag. I cross my arms and stare at him. At least he has the decency to stop laughing.

"Seriously, I've known you since the South Am Uprising. I've never, in all this time, seen you keep any guy around longer than two weeks. Ever." He leans forward, frowns, and picks up a bottle of chili-pepper-chocolate flavored body cream. "Since he didn't strike me as a keeper, I figured you were done. And yeah, you're that predictable. We talked about this before too." He sets the container down and leans back again; his eyes meet mine for a second.

"Go screw yourself, Brios," I snap at him.

He shrugs, stands, and walks to the door. "I'm going to the MetroCafé down the street. I'll wait an hour." He steps into the hall. "If you want to pick up where we left off, show up. If not…" He pulls the door shut.

I glare after him. Why does he have to be so cocky? He knows it drives me crazy.

I pull on fresh clothes and dig out a matching handbag from a pile of them. All of my EDC items go in first: lipstick, eyeliner, spare clips for Little Tommy, skinseal, hairbrush, fighting knives, and speedloader cylinders for the Double-Double. I go to the coffee table. The silver slab is missing.

"Motherfucker."

Brios.

What the hell is wrong with him? Stealing my shit right out of my apartment. I work myself into a frothing anger and jerk the door open.

Brios slings himself off the opposite wall and goes through the motion of checking his embedded watch. "That has to be some sort of record."

I swing for his jaw.

His military boosted reflexes let him catch a glancing blow.

"Whoa there, Sweetie." He grapples my arms and pins me to the wall.

His hand clamps over mine and he pushes the data core into my fist. "Whatever's on this thing, you figure it's worth a lot of money?"

"Brios, you bastard." I breathe against his chest and force myself not to squirm against him. I love him and hate him so hard in that moment.

"Yeah, I'm a bastard," he whispers as he presses his cheek to the top of my head and smells my hair. "You've known that since South Am."

"You took my stuff." I let my frustration over his bullshit come out a little too weak. I kick myself.

Always Brios. He's the only one who pushes my buttons so hard that I lose momentum.

"It got your attention." He keeps me pinned as he almost whispers, "That was the point."

"Well," I snap, "you have my attention." Part of me likes that he hasn't pulled away from our contact while he does his speech. "Why don't you tell me what the fuck you're talking about?"

"The yakuza at Siffre's...." His voice stays low. "They were there because I dropped out on their job."

"Yeah, I knew it was your shit that stank up the place." I smirk into his shirt. "Why d'you want to work for those ghosts?"

"The pay. Why else?" he says. "They hired me to find whoever has their goods."

I look up at him, a bad feeling starts to grow in my gut.

"They know Shadow took their stuff. They have his corpse. But not the items he stole." He grimaces. "When I dropped the job, they figured I knew more than I let on. They laid on a tail. That's why I was late meeting you."

The yakuza ops team in the coffee shop came there following him on a hunch.

No matter that he was careful, he'd led them right to me, and whether or not they made the connection, something triggered a full-on corporate paramilitary search of my stash.

Lingering paranoia tickles me in an ugly way. Brios had known it was me who killed Shadow just from a description of the guy's corpse.

I remind myself that anyone else would've sold me to them but not Brios. He'd rather drop their contract, take the heat, and deal with the consequences. I chew on guilt for a second and can't meet his eyes.

He squeezes my hand around the slab. "If this is what you took off Shadow, somebody wants it back. They're willing to pay good money and they've leveraged the yakuza to do it."

"So I'm the job?"

"Yeah. Sorry."

1.04

Something Big

We roll back into UnderCity an hour later. Most of our time is spent driving around TopSide looking for a down ramp without a huge police presence. The bribe is a little high, but Brios is the one spending the hardfold.

UnderCity isn't like the rest of New White Sands; it oozes a dangerous energetic vibe that amps up at night. The daytime crowds are gone and the streets are full of my kind of people. All the extra killing makes the energy pop.

The club we pull up to is one of the biggest in East End and the crowd out front is even bigger than usual. I slide off the back of Brios' bike, open my hair clip, and shake my hair out. The party crowd thronging up and down the street gives us space.

I know I look fantastic.

Brios looks all right.

He gets points for parking our ride under the flashing faux neon sign above the door for Pluggz Triple X. The light glitzes everything it hits. He gets bonus points for his taste in bikes. The gloss black Briggs & Valiant Ej 300NFC hogs the curb lane. The bike bristles with angles, wings, and tapered fairings that curve around its fat tires.

Brios swings off the saddle, the Electro-jet turbine generator whining evilly as it shuts down.

The alarm pips as he joins me on the curb.

After our grand entrance nobody cares. We get lost in the movement of the crowd, hidden in plain sight by hundreds of ads floating in front of our faces. Strip clubs, illegal weapon implants, and escort services all compete for our attention.

I lead the way toward a sleazy looking alley mouth.

It's always dark in here. Dark and narrow. Alternating rows of trash bins and cardboard squats are stacked along its walls. You have to weave side to side just to walk the path.

The alley is choked with people whose business flourishes in the darkness next door, conveniently located but separate from the 'real' world. We ignore a mix of solicitations and make our way straight to the back.

Brios sweeps his gaze left and right, trying for a casual disregard. It's his unspoken way of sarcastically commenting how nice a place is, as shit-holes go. His gun hand stays close to the grip of his cannon. I trust him completely to keep me safe.

The crowd thins as we approach the dead end. The buildings vanish upward into the dark. Two city maintenance helos lumber overhead. They drift a few meters above the roofline of the fifty-plus stories on either side of us. Their marker lights flicker through the upper level brown haze.

We make a slow approach on the heavy steel door in the back wall.

My tech guy's bodyguard steps into view with her favorite weapon in hand.

I know the innocuous short barreled shotgun has a mixed load of explosive, solid, and flamethrower rounds waiting for trouble. This end of the alley is always nice and quiet.

"Vicky." I nod. She's more done up than the last time I saw her.

I admire her tattoo. She's been working on it for the last year. It suits her seven-foot height perfectly.

The blazing red dragon coils around her left leg and crawls over her torso culminating with its head, jaws wide, curving along her right cheekbone. The dragon is completely visible except where it slinks under a tiny pair of crimson short shorts and a gold bandana top.

The tattoo glows, illuminated by bioelectricity. It's cutting edge, and set against her dusky brown skin, I'm frank when I say, "The ink looks fantastic."

The shotgun doesn't come off Brios as she nods her thanks, then asks, "He okay?"

"This is my backup, Brios." They eye one another intensely for a moment. I tip my head at the door. "Is he seeing clients?" Having crowds at my back makes me twitchy to begin with, and here everyone is at my back. I glance over my shoulder, the hair on my neck starting to stand.

"I'll let him know it's you." Vicky's face gets the thousand-yard stare of someone who isn't used to having a built in com-link. There's a heavy clank as the lock disengages, and she turns to open the steel door.

We're barely inside when she pulls the door shut behind us. It feels hasty, and, coupled with my uneasiness in the alley, I clench up.

Brios never misses a beat with me. It's like we have a wire hooking our reactions together. He pulls his cannon.

My Doc Ripperkins dilate, flip filters, and in less than a heartbeat it's as bright as a clear afternoon TopSide.

We move deeper into the shop and find a narrow beam of light illuminating a worktable.

"Hey Sweetie," my guy says as he stands, pushing a lamp and lens affair out of his way. Half a dozen manipulator arms slide back into rest mode.

I relax a little, and Brios holsters his gun.

"Hi Ishacc. How are things?" I saunter over to where he squeezes his bulk out from behind a low wall of boxes. The cardboard is marked with some of the biggest names in tech and labeled with strings of number letter combinations that are meaningless to me.

Ishacc has been rewriting and hacking my software for years. He specializes in code cracking and software mods. He learned his skills while working for City Utilities. His specialty is electronic locks and the control software for them. He'll unlock anything for a price, but fencing electronics and code strings are his hustle.

About three years ago, I took Ishacc out shopping to set him up with some sort of style other than skater shoes, sweats, and a smelly tan colored fishing vest. I graduated top of my class in fashion design with a minor in fashion direction and trend prediction. He was looking to impress a girl, and I was the only one he knew who could help him. I took the job and it worked out. Now he slaves away even more to pay for her and their kids. I wonder if he likes the way his choices turned out for him.

"Well, you know. It's okay." He leans in to kiss my cheek. "Not great, never great. A couple weeks back, a local enforcer turned up dead. He was the one keeping a lid on things around here. Now the streets are a mess."

I shrug noncommittally. "You're right. It's just a pain in the ass right now to get honest work done."

He nods. "Now that's the truth. So, honest work? What's that look like for you and I?"

"I need your help with this." I fish the security tap out of my pocket and turn it over in my hands. I watch Ishacc's pupils tighten and widen again. The low key neon backlighting of his shop glitters along the black enameled edges.

Ishacc wipes his mouth with the back of one meaty hand. "Can I see that?"

There are kBits spinning in his head. I can't see them, but I know Ishacc and I know they're there.

"Sure." I hand it over slowly. "It comes with a warning. It fried my rig in under a second."

"Come on, Sweetie." Ishacc spins it in his grip as he lumbers back to his work station. "You know that kind of talk just makes me hungry."

Brios and I move closer to his tech covered worktable. Ishacc drags a few pieces of seemingly discordant equipment together and runs handfuls of clips and plugs back and forth between them.

He lifts a large silver cylinder from a rack and sets it carefully in the middle of the workspace. When he eases the top off, a thick white vapor crawls over the lip, swirls to the table edge, and spills down to the floor.

Brios lets out a subtle grunt. Since I'm prompted, I ask, "Ishacc, what the hell is in there?"

"Liquid nitrogen." He smiles as he finishes tweaking all the raw cabling. "It'll slow the unit down so I can get a better read on the software and trip my system if it looks dangerous. It may take more than one pass to skim it all."

He delicately connects the tap into a lone bundle of wire leads. He gently lowers it into the smoking canister, and with the flip of a switch, his monitors start pulsing data.

"We may not have time for that."

My comment is lost on him; Ishacc is enraptured.

Code streams along in ever thickening amounts until it pours along like water.

"What the hell is this shit?" he mumbles as he sits. "Where did you get this thing?" He speaks louder but doesn't take his eyes off the scrolling lines.

A coil spring thermometer with tinfoil mounted to the needle tracks the climbing temperature toward its mate. They touch. His system trips. An old fashioned Frankenstein-style bladed relay switch clicks off.

The connection ends.

Ishacc dials back the whole file and starts re-reading the event log from the beginning. His eyes go wider. At one point he clasps a hand over his mouth and lets out a gasp of horror and delight.

He lifts the tap out of the smoking cylinder and lays it on the table. He sits in silence for a few minutes, watching the frosty condensate slowly fade.

Brios gets restless and starts looking around. "Is this normal for him?" he asks me quietly.

It isn't. In fact, I'm getting worried just standing here, like I'm waiting for God to throw a bolt of lightning at my head.

"Oh yeah. This is fine," I reply.

"This is not fine," Ishacc says in a whisper. He continues, his voice rising, "This thing is bigger than I can handle."

"You're just saying that," I say, rolling a hint of mockery into my flattery. "You're the best code analyst in UnderCity."

"No, Sweetie. I'm good at software, but I barely scratched the surface of what this tap is running. I can't tell you where it's made, or by who. But the only people who could get their hands on this are top level players." He slides the unit around with a steel probe. "You've heard the term 'bleeding edge?' This tap exists a fraction of a second before the blade hits. I could make a fortune pulling fragments of code out of here and recycling them. That," he says as he points with his probe, "in one tiny custom unit, coded as it is, will open any door in the city. It's worth a fortune."

I snort. "So it's a good thing I'm not a thief or some sort of criminal?"

Ishacc laughs. "You could walk into AlphaPlaza One and straight into AlphaTek's data core with that thing overriding all their security."

"Interesting," I say, trying not to sound too excited as I pick up the tap. The black metal is still cold.

I gotta play this next part cool. With what was on the security tap, maybe Ishacc will be too freaked to hand over his contact. "Hey, on a separate note, I have a chunk of hardware I need to have valued. What was the name of that guy? You know. The guy you sent me to a couple of months ago when I had that other hardware for sale?"

"Larus?" Ishacc is distracted, scrolling over code and chewing on a fingernail.

Even as Ishacc drops the guy's name, it slides around my memory like a slippery piece of fish.

"Yeah, that's right. Larus." I mentally repeat it a dozen times to get it to stick.

Ishacc flicks his eyes over me. "I haven't seen him since he worked with you. I heard he moved shop. He's somewhere in the Ganglands, hiding."

"The Ganglands?" Nobody simply walks into Ganglands. Moving there is certifiable crazy. "Wow, I did not see that coming."

It occurs to me the last data core I sold to Larus could be the reason he went into hiding. An uneasy feeling hits me again. I hope Ishacc won't make the connection between me, my hardware, and whatever scared his buddy.

Ishacc is sometimes smarter than he looks.

"Well," I say as I slip the tap into my pocket, "you go ahead and sell that code, Ishacc, and pay me my standard cut later."

"Fine." He hardly looks up from the screen. "But if you get caught by anyone with that, do me a favor?"

"Sure," I say.

"Blow your brains out so they can't brain hack you to find me." He says it deadpan.

"Um. No." I look at him like he's a plague carrier. "How about we don't get caught?"

Ishacc snorts and says, "Say hello to Larus for me, if you find him alive."

We push our way back out to the street.

I catch a vibe from Brios. He's probably thinking about the money we'll make with the security tap.

I'm thinking about wild five-finger discounts at all my favorite shops. I'm also worried about the Ganglands. Nulls are, by nature, style deficient. They have as hard a time wrapping their craniums around a person like me as I do them. The only thing I've ever agreed on with a Null is that violent deaths sometimes need to happen.

We move through the flow of people and the crush of holo-ads. Directed sound drops in and out as we walk.

Brios rumbles the B&V to life, and I make a show of getting on the back. I know it'll distract him temporarily from the idea of where we have to go next.

I push it by sliding my hands around him a little lower than I should, but the crowd likes the overall aesthetic. People stop to watch. I can see it as an ad for my leathers, or the bike. You know, big ugly guy, superhot girl, his awesome equipment, i.e. his bike, gets him the girl to the rousing adoration of the crowd.

At one time, I'd strongly considered leasing a Lifestyle Capture Drone to follow me around so I could sell the footage to media outlets as advertising. Then I remembered that most of my clients would not appreciate being on camera; one revenue stream open, another one closed.

Brios doesn't say anything about my hands. As we accelerate away from the crowds, I move them higher on his hips. I feel his disappointment through his spine.

By unspoken agreement ,we roll out of New White Sands and across the Jumble. The remains of the old city are picked out here and there by homemade lights and heavily armed squatter camps.

Brios kills our headlights and flips the bike into nano fuel cell operation. The jet spins down into silence. The only sound we make is the crunch of our tires over gravel.

The city of New White Sands looms behind us; a glittering mountain, a seething anthill of struggling life and countless death set against the backdrop of an endless hum of data and flowing money.... Maybe I should sell poetry.

Somehow we find our usual place and Brios shuts the bike down. We stay silent as we slip past the stacked rubble barricade and through the tarp doorway of the makeshift bar.

There's never a sign out front. Only South Am vets have any idea how to find this place. It moves randomly across the detritus of a different time. And now we're here. The items in my pocket make me feel dangerously obsolete.

It's the kind of tech that turned uptown wannabes into real players.

Brios nods at the few faces spread out around the low roofed room. We find a table under an archaic work light and pull up mismatched kitchen chairs. The waitress recognizes us. She doesn't ask; she just brings over three beers. The bottles look cheap and dusty. The product is top notch though. We wait politely until she's out of earshot.

"Now what?" Brios asks.

"Well, I figure we wait until sunrise and go see Larus."

I'm not a South Am vet. I just happened to be there when the pre-existing condition liquefied into the shit that was the Uprising. I'd have died there if it hadn't been for Brios.

All the regulars in the room know me, but a few others see me as an interloper.

I keep my head down and avoid eye contact. I know my discomfort will fade. The faces I recognize will fill the others in on my story. In the meantime, I figure it's best not to push it.

Brios, the big dummy, doesn't notice these kinds of things. Even if he does, he never changes how he acts. He takes a long swallow of beer and then says, "So this butt-clown, Larus, is holed up in the Ganglands."

"Yeah." I know Larus by the work he's done, so I try to defend him a little. "And he's not a butt-clown, he really is talented."

"He's voluntarily living in the Ganglands." Brios shrugs. "He's gotta be some kind of a butt-clown."

"It could be he's a genius." I sip my beer. "Maybe he's letting the Nulls be his protection. No corporation is going to chase him in there. It's just too much of a hit to their bottom line." Brios looks like he still doesn't get it, so I continue, "No company wants to lose money and resources like that. All the Nulls would come out to fight just because it's a fight. And for them, having him there is a win-win. Anyone comes for him, they get a fight. No one comes for him, they get their hardware modded and fixed for free."

"Huh." Brios finishes his bottle and slides the empty aside. "He's still a butt-clown, because we have to go in there just to talk to him." He pulls the spare over, cracks the cap, and takes a draw.

I can tell Brios isn't happy about any of this. He's going through his beer faster than normal.

"The joke's on us for actually going in there to find him. He *is* an asshole though. An asshole for making this harder than it needs to be."

My palmscreen itches. I wonder what deals I've missed.

The sooner I dump the goods, the sooner I can get back on the grid, the sooner I can shop.

Unfortunately, the Jumble is a huge dead zone for shopping or style unless a girl likes dirty fatigues, unshaven-ness, and man-stink, even on the women.

"You good with moving on this in the morning?" I ask.

"Yeah." He nods. "Not a good idea to interrupt a wild night of blood sacrifices and hunting human prey."

"I agree." I hate the Ganglands just as much as he does.

"I got a guy who owes me big time." Brios has more beer and watches my reaction.

I keep it cool.

He continues, "This guy is good at what he does. I think he could keep the Nulls off us until we finish with Larus."

"Are you saying you can't keep me safe?" I ask, flashing him a smile.

"I'm say'n, I'm one man and I'm real good at kill'n." Brios dips the bottom edge of his bottle in and out of a wet ring that has formed on the table. "But in the Ganglands, everyone's a killer and there's an endless supply."

"So, this guy coming on board." I widen the focus of my eyes to watch more of the room. Drinking makes Brios' Texan drawl slip out and, veterans or not, there might be people in here who will take offense to sitting with a Texan. "What's that look like?"

"I know you don't like pay'n if you don't have to and I agree with you. It's good policy not to leave a trail of hardfold or kBits anywhere if you can help it." Brios speaks slowly. I always take that to mean he's thought about what's coming out of his mouth. "He owes me enough that I could call it all in. He'd help out if it made us even. We find him tonight, rest up, and do our Ganglands fishing trip in the morning."

"Okay. But I have final say."

Brios relaxes as I answer.

"If I don't like this guy at all, for any reason, he's not playing in our sandbox."

"Sure." That's all he says. It's an unusual enough thing, him not blah, blah, blahing, that I wonder who this guy is he's talking about.

I thought I knew all of Brios' friends.

I finish my beer and we leave the bar with a fraction of a plan. "So where does this guy of yours live?"

"He hangs out with the Rafters, but he isn't one." Brios flips the bike on and mounts up. "I think he just likes the lifestyle."

~ ~ ~

We pick our way along roads cleared by corporations for whatever purpose.

The concrete gets rough as we approach an old bridge. My eyes amp a blend of starlight and ambient spill-over from the city behind us, and I spot manned barricades.

Rafter country.

Rafters are itinerant crop workers who use the old canals and river systems to get around. They have a retro style, are loyal, and slow to anger. A deliberate sort of people.

They're river hippies.

A few years back, a small corporation didn't pay them for their work. That company's head office was a smoking hole by sunset the next day. Love, peace, and happiness, but on their terms. They're hippies with guns.

I've heard they breed really good snipers out here.

Brios rolls onto the bridge deck and shuts the bike down. "We walk from here, until we talk to them. After we get approval, we can move into their perimeter."

At the barricade, Brios speaks quietly to three men: hunters on guard duty. He motions for me to wait. The riflemen look me up and down while Brios pulls the bike behind the barricade, dismounts, and comes back. "Stay close and don't say anything."

I nod.

We go down to the river bank, following one of the guards who guides us.

Along the river's edge is a clutter of different kinds of boats and rafts tied off to form a floating community.

I never knew so many Rafters were down here.

An antique looking PBR sits roped off but ready to go, gun tub uncovered. A handful of burly men huddle in the stern playing cards under a hissing white lamp.

Lamplight glitters softly from decks, railings, and out of quaintly decorated windows. The smell of cooking food drifts with the breeze along the valley. The whole place is neat, tidy, and organized.

I stop as kids run by with mini lights. They're playing a chase game with one another. Key word here is playing.

I thought only CitOne kids had the luxury of playing. Everyone else I know with kids has them working. It isn't cruel; it's an economic reality, another indicator of how advanced we are as a civilization.

The few adults who lift their heads from evening work, repairs, sewing, or tinkering with mechanical parts, nod and smile at our guide but give us wary looks.

The breeze picks up along the river valley and the air turns clean and smells intensely sweet. Something pulls at my chest. I shake my head. There are no shops out here. Plus, I remind myself, I look huge in plaid flannel which seems to be THE fashion du jour.

I turn and stare at the glowing towers of the city in the distance. That's my home, filled with shops, people to bilk, and money to make and spend.

"Is he here?" I hear our guide ask.

I look back. He's speaking to a woman perched on an old water drum. She's dressed in jeans and cross laced knee-high boots. She looks fit, and hot, like this year's trending supermodel hot.

I tamp down my jealousy. If I spent everything I'd ever earned, I could look like her. Where is she getting cash like that out here?

As she stands, her old air cavalry jacket swings open exposing a stripped down flight harness, a short cropped one button vest, and no shirt or bra. I catch a fleeting glimpse of the flawless pale skin on her belly and an eyeful of glorious underboob. She could hit any club in the city and fit in perfectly. The name tape on the jacket has been re-stitched at some point with a newer badge, one that reads *Angel.*

As Brios requested, I keep my mouth shut.

She nods. "He's just finishing dinner. Probably getting ready to go."

She lifts a weather flap from a window with a long delicate finger. "Wolf, you've got some friends here."

A deep voice responds. "Let them in."

We step onto the sturdy raft and enter the small cabin.

If Angel wasn't enough, Wolf is wide shouldered and taper-waisted. There's a lot of Spain in his features, but his voice is unaccented. He's an awesome middle-aged specimen of male.

He looks at us a moment and stands from the small table. He silently clears his plate to a counter in the tiny galley.

"I want to propose a job." Brios jumps right in. "One that would make us even."

Wolf's eyes drift over me. I don't know why he's bothering. He has a blonde supermodel for a door guard. I let him look. Maybe he's just being polite.

"Right to the point," Wolf says, "That's what I like about you, Brios. No waste. No fat to our conversations. The downside is you sometimes forget your manners."

Brios shuts his mouth and steps aside.

Wolf's eyes finally meet mine.

I try to stare him down like he's Brios.

He doesn't look away. "I'm Wolf. I've known Brios since before South Am," he says as he leans forward to shake my hand. "His manners haven't changed."

"You can call me Sweetie." I almost use my real name as I take his hand. His gaze disarms me. His eyes are dark grey, set over good cheekbones and a wicked jawline.

I slap myself mentally and make note to be extra vigilant around him.

Weird thing is … I feel like I've seen him before, someplace in the city.

His smile widens. "I've heard of you, Sweetie."

"Whatever you heard, it's probably a lie circulated by my detractors," I answer. This far out of the city someone has heard of me? I want to call 'bullshit,' but Brios is sure we need this guy.

"I think it's noble of you to pay for Mr. Quan's youngest daughter's piano lessons." Wolf's eyes soften. "I hear she's improved at least tenfold."

I sit heavily on a chair.

Only a handful of people know about that arrangement.

I stare. This handsome face with its disarming gaze, this Wolf; his is the face of danger.

1.05

Fresh Wounds

Brios has launched into a distilled version of what we need while I sit in a daze. As he finishes, I stand.

"Sure, I'm in," Wolf is saying.

"Nope." I cut him off. "No, you're not. You think you can bombshell me with my own secrets and then have me trust you?"

Brios looks at me sharply. "Sweetie, I told you, he's good at his job and we need him."

I turn on Brios. "And you agreed I had final say on who plays in our sandbox."

Wolf interrupts me. "I was working near a piano shop and wondered about the little girl in handmade clothes arriving in the back of an old armored car twice a week like clockwork." His expression is neutral. "I thought it was an interesting question, so I looked into it. I heard her play a bit while she waited for her instructor to finish with another student. She's very good. She also spoke highly of you. She told me she was grateful. I promised her that your secret would be safe and that she and her father would be safe."

I casually remove my hands from the grips of my fighting knives. Forcing myself not to kill this guy sends a trickle of juice into my brain via my pleasure center. I get a low down thrum, and I breathe out to steady myself.

Somewhere in my chemically blocked memories is the origin of the pleasure-tap. I guess the idea was to connect a lot of different primal joys to the act of killing. In this case, I have it set to reward me for good behavior.

To distract myself, I look at my palmscreen. I wish it was on. Then it could show me some sale someplace and give me a reason to leave.

Brios sighs. "Sorry to bother you, Colonel. We should go. We still need a place to sack for the night."

"Stay here. I'm going out racing tonight." He nods to the bunk. "It's wide enough you two won't even touch unless you want to."

Brios says nothing. Wolf turns and pulls a worn looking racing jacket off a hook. I see a homemade holster tacked under one arm and the Special Forces badge hidden on the inside of the right chest.

Red flag.

Colonel? This is the colonel who managed to get so many troops back to the U.S. after the Uprising.

Twelve years ago, the big multinationals ran an end run that threw everything into a decade long freefall. Some people say we're still falling. Those companies stepped into the power vacuum they created. Then they put themselves in charge, spun themselves as community minded.

It's the stuff from fiction. Ideas from books, seventy or eighty years old, suddenly twisted into a bad life imitating art scenario.

The cataclysm on the home front stranded military personnel in dozens of hot zones without rescue, recourse, or relief. Some soldiers never made it home. They maintained their capability in hostile territory until eventually they were overrun. Rumors still pop up about soldiers working as slave labor in some rat-hole country or another.

I look at Wolf once more. He doesn't carry himself like a blood-soaked hero.

Crap.

I just made Brios look like a shitheel in front of his old CO. One who owes him a pretty big favor. Brios even asked me to keep my mouth shut.

I catch myself with a finger on my palmscreen's power button. I let my hands drop to my lap.

"Okay. Listen up," I say as I stand. "I'm exercising my God-given right as a woman to change my mind."

"What?" both of them say in unison.

"I've changed my mind. Wolf can play in our sandbox." I look from Brios to Wolf and back. "He can watch our backs while we look for Larus."

Brios comes over to me. "Sweetie, are you sure? Your argument's still valid."

"I'll find my own cot space," Wolf says. "You two can camp out here and sort out what needs to happen. I have a date, and I'm behind schedule."

Without another word, he leaves.

Brios and I stare at each other and then turn to look at the wide, but obviously single, bed.

I start in on him. "Why didn't you tell me he was your old colonel?" I can't stop my hands; they wave about emphatically, matching my state of mind. "THE colonel."

"Who he was in the past isn't as important as who he is now." Brios makes his practical-and-stupid face. "Neither of us is in the military. The fact that he can help us now is what matters."

After how much he's gone on about the guy to suddenly drop all their history like it didn't matter?

"Crap'n Jesus, Brios. As much as I don't like the fact that he follows me around—"

Brios cuts me off. "He didn't follow you around. He asked the girl who was helping her out, and she answered him. It's what polite kids do."

My mind flies. How many of the people I've helped will just blab if they're asked?

"I need to find Mr. Quan and explain to him that—"

Brios' anger erupts. "Explain what? That all adults are paranoid? That his little girl's a leak in the information chain and should be silenced? Then what? Are you going to be the one to silence her?"

I punch him. His sudden anger surprises me. My fist lashes up and out. The automated muscle manipulators do the rest. The software works, using everything in his 201 profile automatically. This time there's no warning. He drops like a sack.

After my own surprise, I realize I've suckered him right where he was stabbed.

"Oh shit, Brios, I'm so sorry." I drag him over to the bed and flop him onto it.

"What the hell was that for?" he asks around wincing breaths.

"Why the hell didn't you get a full rebuild on your stab wound?" I glare at him.

"I needed a new jacket to come and see you," he answers with a hint of protest. "I spent the money on that instead. I figured I'd heal the rest of the way for free."

"You spent your money on a jacket?" Then I catch myself.

First, the jacket barely registered. But I know I would have laid into him if he'd shown up in a wrecked coat.

And second, I would've done the same thing if our positions were reversed.

"Dumbass." I pause. "I'm sorry I slugged you."

"Apology accepted." Brios slowly nods. "I'm sorry I flipped on you for wanting to kill a kid."

I choke down my anger.

He chuckles at my expression.

"Screw you, Brios," I say quietly and beat a hasty retreat off the bedside.

"The bed's wider than it looks." He grins and pats the space beside him.

"I'm. No. Just no, Brios."

I don't wait for him to get all noble and I-won't-touch-you. I leave the cabin.

In the dark, I try to clear my head. I'm too worried about my software link to enjoy the sweet smelling breeze coming off the river.

I've been that mad before. That mad at Brios specifically. But I've never lost it to the point that my limbs kicked into automatic action. Maybe I need to purge old data, flush a mem-cache or something.

I scratch at my palmscreen. A growing sense of desperation at being isolated and out of the loop hits me. I need deals and shops. The truth is that I need food and sleep. Cut off from the first three items, I curl up in the nook of the doorway and drift off.

I wake before dawn and freak out a little; I'm in bed with Brios' arm over my hip, and I've been stripped down to my basics. I panic and get ready to slide out from under the covers. I poke a leg into the cabin.

It's friggin' cold in here.

I pull my leg back under. There was a time when I didn't care about how cold or hot it was. I've turned into a city girl.

Brios' arm is heavy and warm like the rest of him. Nothing's happened between us that I can tell, so I ease myself deeper under the covers, feeling his warmth press against me.

He wakes a short while later, and I pretend to sleep to see what he'll do.

I want some kind of a reaction. I tell myself that if he tries anything, I'll have a reason to keep him at arm's length and enough fodder for a year's worth of arguments. If he just lies here, I'll have a broken heart.

Instead, he gets up, hunts around the galley, and makes us coffee.

I get dressed.

We don't talk about the fight, or how I ended up in bed.

"He's got good taste in coffee," I mumble over the lip of the cup.

"He's always got good coffee." Brios doesn't meet my eyes. "Good coffee, good intel, good guns."

"Maybe that should be the tagline on his business card." I chuckle. He joins me. Everything between us clicks back to normal.

We hear sounds of the community coming to life. Mothers call children to breakfast, gruff sounding men discuss the weather on the water, and the smell of real bread and the sizzle of pork product draw us back to silence.

This is what neither of us ever had, even as kids.

"This place is dangerous, Brios," I whisper. "I need the edge. Staying here will get me killed the next time I go to work. I'll be soft."

Brios looks at me. "Let's head to the bike and figure out what the hell we're doing."

I nod and we share an awkward moment as we get ready to leave.

"I'll make the bed, you do the dishes," I say.

We don't get far after that. As we make our way off the raft, a kind looking lady on the raft next to Wolf's intercepts us and makes sure we eat. She's sweet, motherly, and a million years old. Her English is terrible. But that doesn't slow her down.

She treats us like we're a couple.

I file all those feels away as we finish, say our thanks, and go. If Brios is affected by our breakfast experience, he doesn't let it show.

We both become all about the job as we drive to the edge of the Ganglands and park. Wolf calls Brios and tells him he'll be joining us momentarily.

The sun is already scorching bright, even through my filters. I look up, my filters dialing to max.

The ozone layer is thinner over cities. It gets thicker again as you move away from civilization. New White Sands and a couple other places are lucky; a near earth orbit blanket floats high overhead.

It's a full-time, man-made ozone layer that also generates tons of electrical power for the city's industry and transportation systems.

I squint and can see the huge sheet of darkened fabric hanging in the air.

How did we screw up an entire planet? Oh yeah. That's right. The same sort of greed and fear that keeps me moving did this.

It's part of the human condition to want. If there's money in it, business will provide. We all want only for ourselves and mess it up for everyone, remembering too late that we're a part of everyone. Since we can't hold one another responsible, we all agree to point at the past and say the people before us are to blame. It doesn't fix anything, but it makes everyone feel better.

Crap. The memory of the Rafter community and its emotion laden breakfast has me musing.

I push it all as far down as I can and refocus on the job, the pay-off, and what that cash will net me.

Brios opens one of the B&V's fairings and under-hands me a zip gun. I hook it onto a quick sling.

We watch as a thundering antique car careens toward us on the dirt road.

I arch a brow. In response, Brios shrugs himself off the fender of the B&V.

The car is a rich metallic blue with a white roof. Galloping chrome horses are blazoned down either side.

I've never heard a gasoline engine before. This one rumbles straight out of some gearhead's wet dream as it pulls in beside us, cascading fine dust in a rising cloud.

Wolf gets out and makes his way to the trunk. He pops it open. I peer in, trying to be casual. The colonel drives around with a ridiculous arsenal. I look away before I start to drool. This is more my taste.

"I had time to think between heats." Wolf speaks quietly and without speed. "You realize finding one guy hiding out in Old Core, sorry, in the Ganglands, is a tall order."

We nod. Old Core is the official name for the old downtown core of the original city. Between growing hurricanes, rising sea levels, a sublimating coastline, and a tsunami or two, the place ended in an ugly mess. New White Sands City was built next to the ruins of the century-old buildings that had gone to crap and then worse than crap. Now only Nulls live out here, and everyone just calls it Ganglands.

"At the very least I'd like to look at the item this Larus-the-butt-clown is supposed to help you with." He picks through an assortment of guns, grenades, and ancillary items stowed in the trunk.

Brios shoots me a look that says butt-clown told-ya-so. I roll my eyes and pull the silver data core out of my pocket.

Wolf takes it and turns it over in his hands. "And you found this?" He looks at me. "Just lying in the gutter?"

"The body I took it from was in the gutter, so close enough." I try for casual urban bland.

He meets my eyes. I feel my knees loosen. The Wolf at my door. I look away.

"Okay." He hands it back to me. "At the race last night, I ran into a friend of mine. We got to talking." Wolf hefts out a heavy combat vest and settles it over his shoulders. He tugs it into place and slaps the tabs closed. "He pulled a few strings and got us this…."

He reaches into the car and brings out a rumpled sheet of honest-to-God paper. He closes the trunk, unfolds the page, and smooths it across the wide tail fin.

"What am I looking at? Yesterday's comics?" I feel a little lost as Brios leans in and, in an apparent case of military ESP, begins to nod at the page. It's covered in thin colored lines that are scattered everywhere across its surface.

Wolf points at a spot as if the convergence of squiggles holds a dramatic and important purpose.

"I say again, what the hell am I looking at?"

"This is an EM map." Wolf cocks his head to see if I get it.

I do. "Oh, okay. You had someone make a map of the electromagnetic fields in the Ganglands," I say in my most polite tone.

"Yes." Wolf nods. "I figure, if this Larus character is as much a tech-head as you say, then one of these convergences has to be him, or at least his shop."

"Of course, you know that Null gangs use maps like these to trap fools who use them. And you know the Nulls have EM projectors pointed at the heavens so corporations stupid enough to come on their turf will get their asses handed to them in kill zones." My tone is ice.

The colonel talked to his friends about my job. Who else listened in while sitting around the trackside?

I feel justified in my anger. "Of course, you know all that and came here with a backup plan. Of course, you have a backup plan, right?"

He stares at me blankly.

Maybe it hasn't happened to him before; attractive women like me would rarely have a reason to call him an idiot over a military plan.

I'm pretty sure I hear Brios sigh behind me.

Stepping back, I look between the two of them. Ex-soldiers: always thinking in straight lines.

If Wolf is pissed at me basically calling him an idiot, his expression doesn't change much. He turns and walks out of earshot with a brick of a datavice jammed against his head. All I catch is that he's speaking fast and in some kind of code.

Brios purses his lips. "He's just trying to help. And hey, at least we got a topo map of most of the area we need."

"Yippee. A topo map. One copy. On paper." I'm disgusted. "Useful for both of us in a pinch if we get acid rain later or we get separated. On top of that, he talked about our job to his friends. People we don't know jack squat about."

Wolf stalks back and yanks open the trunk. He digs around and pulls out a couple of field-portable map projectors.

"Here." He points as the equipment displays a copy of the paper map. "All of the non-fluctuating signals have been removed. The remaining signals were amplified and the data cross-imaged with ground penetrating radar which was used to fix distances inside or below ground. The image is overlaid onto a real-time satellite visual of the whole area. There are Nulls patrolling here and here." He points with a stylus. "Satellite also indicates concentrations of heartbeats in these dozen zones. Those Nulls are inside thin roofed or damaged structures."

"Where are you getting this from?" I'm stunned.

The show-off is choked that I called him on his crappy paper map, and now he's pissing everywhere trying to make a point.

Brios nudges me with his elbow as he grabs one of the map-boxes.

"If it were Brios and a squad of men, the first map would have been sufficient." Wolf locks his eyes on mine. "But you're right, Sweetie. You're a civilian, and as such, I need an elevated level of information available, both for your safety and your psychological well-being."

The bastard, to prove his point, lays the paper over the map-box and shows me where he first pointed. As he pulls the paper away, I can see he nailed the location. The most likely spot to look for Larus is under his finger.

"I don't mind providing the data, or the additional resources and equipment, if it makes you 'feel' safer."

"Can I hate him now?" I ask Brios who just frowns at me.

I imagine that Wolf is mistaking the flush across my face for embarrassment.

I wait a moment for my pleasure-tap to quit juicing me. He has no idea how close he just came to playing a game of shallow grave.

Wolf looks across the sprawling wreckage of the Ganglands. "Are we going to stand here much longer? Because I have other places I need to be today."

I pluck the map-box off the car and stomp toward the first row of crumpled buildings. If the map is accurate, then Larus will be three blocks northwest of Old Core's center and forty-five feet below ground.

I scratch my palmscreen. It's going to be a long day.

1.06

Disputed Territory

As Brios and I slide from cover to cover, we alternate the task of scanning for threats as the other person moves.

In the heat and humidity, the tension builds up fast. If I didn't have so many bad memories chemically blocked, I'd be suffering flashbacks.

The holes in my memory rattle their cage doors. Whatever I've chosen to lock away fills me now with a different fear, the fear of not knowing what each cage holds.

I point to a Null tag painted onto a slab of concrete as we creep by. We're deep in Slammers territory.

Both of us know we're in it now.

Slammers eat and drink every kind of combat stimulant ever made. The stims make the less crazy ones incredibly dangerous and the real crazy ones almost unstoppable.

We slow our pace even more. Scattered across our line of travel, mixed with the blown in trash, layers of debris, and gravel, are tiny flat grayish disks.

Landmines.

These are just the ones we can see.

We look around for a trail or path.

Before he found me, Brios was an urban hunter, a specialist of sorts, and now he works his skills. I watch the ruins around us as he makes a slow looping circuit of the terrain.

"We have to fallback to the third building on the right," he says as he joins me. Neither of us look at the location he refers to. "Then we hit the second story window off the roof of the burned-out bus."

He uses military hand sign to let Wolf know about our shift in approach to target, and we're off. I can't spot the colonel, but Brios seems confident he's back there, watching, making me 'feel' safer. Cocky bastard.

The building we climb into was once an office of some sort. Everything that could be hauled off and repurposed has been stripped. Holes have been chopped, shot, or blasted through most of the walls, and thick layers of graffiti cover every surface. We make our way to a stairwell but find it blocked with debris.

We retreat to a side passage and creep along until it widens into what may have been a reception area.

Brios freezes mid step. In a most primal way, I understand.

We've screwed up. I gesture to Brios: *Situation?*

He signals back. I was never in the military; I know what hand sign I need to, that's all. He motions again, and I look at him with my I-don't-get-it face.

He makes a picture-taking motion with his hands and points to a hole in the wall behind us. *Camera.* We walked right by it.

I slink to the doorway and poke-check the room, darting my head in and out.

It's there. An ancient hunting unit. Back when there were still wild animals, people used to strap these things to trees. Easier than watching the trail in person. The better ones had night vision and auto-alert features in case it ever went off.

I look a second time, easing my head back into the room. The cam has a glow coming from its backside. It's got power and is on.

"Fuck it," I say, "if they're coming for us, there's nothing we can do except run or fight."

Distantly we hear yells, cat calls, and echoing bellows.

"Move." Brios hustles us back toward the center of the building.

It's counter intuitive, and I hesitate.

He yells, "Sweetie, let's go."

I catch up with him as he finishes buckling a slip harness and two loops onto an old elevator cable. He's forced the doors open just enough to slide through.

I slip my foot into a loop, thankful that my boots aren't new, and then I push out into blackened space.

Brios joins me.

The buckle creaks as he leans back and pushes the door closed with his cyberarm.

We slowly spin in the harness. I don't care what he thinks, I cling to him. He stiffens with a soft grunt.

Instantly I loosen my grip, and he lets out a breath.

"Sorry," I whisper at him and move my arm away from his wound.

"It's okay." He slips his arm around me. A glow flows up from an integrated cufflight on his jacket.

We hear Nulls swarming the landing we came off of. I train my zip gun on the door.

Brios connects a power pack from his belt to the buckle. Silently the motor unit pulls us higher, one slow story at a time. He kills the cufflight as we continue to rise a few more stories. The yelling recedes below us.

The Nulls are going to figure out what's happened.

We have a closing window of time to get to where we need to be.

Crap.

The floor we come out on is cleaner than the one we left. Trouble is, there are scattered nests where random people have short-term camped. Some nests are fresh. Most aren't.

We find one that contains most of a body. It's maybe a week old. Blood is splattered everywhere, and the limbs have been stripped of flesh.

Brios narrows his eyes.

I share his feelings.

I don't like cannibalism. When you work with a cannibal, it affects your relationship. You catch them looking at you sidelong like they're wondering how you taste.

We make our way to a blown out window and step out onto the ledge.

The drop is long and the view is nice. I remember my airship tour of Europe from a few years past. Usually I had a guardrail this high up. Even a light wind up here makes my feet sweat with thoughts of falling, or just stepping off, just to see what it would be like.

"Come on," Brios says as he eases himself along the narrow ledge.

We shimmy around a corner of the building and crouch down. "Now what?" I ask. My voice shakes, and I curse under my breath.

"We're two blocks off target." He lifts out his map-box. We watch in real-time as tiny figures comb the streets a block over, searching for us.

"Where's Wolf?" I scan high windows and rooftops.

Brios points across the street. I dial in my optics and see Wolf crouching as he makes his way along the edge of a roof line. He has a huge sniper rifle over his back.

As we watch, he stops and looks at us with his scope. He waves once and he and Brios signal back and forth by hand.

"He says his side is better for us to move on than ours."

"Well no shit." I look at the map-box. The street is still crawling with Nulls. "Okay, what's his recommendation?"

"Get to ground level." Brios points for me to look. "Bolt the few blocks using the east side for cover."

I turn my head to look at the recommended path. There is a lot of good cover and only a couple of areas where we'll have to really run. Wolf won't even have to change position to give us overwatch.

Part of me hates that he's right.

I look at the drop. "And how are we getting down?"

"You didn't pack your rocket boots?" Brios looks at me in surprise.

"Screw you, Brios. I'm serious, how do we get down?"

Catlike, he spins, walks a short distance to the next broken window, and passes a loop of fine cable around the column.

"That'll hold us." He tosses the spool off the edge and peers down. He has a wild look in his eyes. Brios loves heights. He'd been air cavalry before he got into Special Forces.

He hands me a clamp rig from his pack and shows me how to hook it on.

"Got it?" he asks. I can see he's concerned, but we don't have a lot of choice.

"Yeah. Yeah, I got this." I give him a smile.

"Good." He leans backward off the ledge and gives me a tiny wave. "See you at the bottom, Sweetie."

I watch his flawless repel. He makes it look so easy. I scan the street around him and look up at Wolf.

Sniper in hand, he's watching the street too.

I hook on following Brios' instructions and lean out.

My boost system cuts in on automatic when the medical monitor picks up on the fact that I'm stressing.

"Fuck, fuck, fuck," I say as I try a little kick off.

I drop too far too fast. I bounce into the wall and slide an entire story, scuffing my leather jacket all the way up my arm.

I hang there a moment, catching my breath and getting my feet back under me. I push out again, farther this time, and I manage the speed better. I almost eat my kneecaps as I meet the wall.

The push off after that has me swinging all Tarzan-like into the setback for the building's ground floor doorway.

Brios snags me with one arm and sets me down.

He doesn't say anything as he lets me go.

I have plenty to say to him, but it's a waste now that I'm down. Excess energy from my boost makes my hands twitch for a dozen heartbeats.

The flat metallic taste of sour adrenaline floods my mouth.

Inside the building we can hear Nulls howl and scream. It won't be long before they come out to the street.

With impending violence pressing on our backs, we push our way down the street to the target. It's an old parking garage at the cross-end of a T-intersection. The sides of the structure have been completely boarded over with a mash-up of corrugated steel, old billboards, and automobile hoods.

As we reach the cluttered intersection, hunting Nulls pour onto the street behind us. Brios pulls me down with him, tight against the fender of an ancient burned-out vehicle.

The Nulls surge up and down the street, trying to flush us out. I tighten my grip on the zip gun as Brios motions toward our next piece of cover.

We silently hop-scotch our way across the intersection. We know it's just a matter of time until we're spotted and it all goes to shit.

We reach the base of the parking garage as the Nulls behind us fall eerily quiet.

Brios points at a slab of fallen concrete leaned against the building. A different gang tag is sprayed there in a mix of paint and blood. We've crossed onto a border street.

The fact that this area is clear of cover suddenly makes sense. It's a friction point between Null bands, a disputed territory and no-man's land. The border also explains why our pursuers have gone quiet. They don't want a brawl with their neighbors. They want a quick meal and our gear to fight over later.

"There?" I whisper to Brios and point out a jumble of collapsed concrete and garbage midway along the building's front face. "The sheathing they've got goes over that pile not behind it. There might be a crawlspace we can get into."

We both look at the parking ramp entrance gaping wide and black, grimed with soot and splatters of other unknown liquids.

"It's better than the front door." He nods at the ramp.

I glance back up the street.

Our pursuers are milling together at the edge of the intersection, but their numbers are growing as I watch.

There's a hissing spark overhead. An orange signal flare lofts from an upper story of the parking garage.

A rising roar of voices echoes out of the ramp entrance. The Slammers coalesce behind us, waving their weapons and fists in the air. Answering calls and yells fill the rubble strewn street.

"Move," Brios snaps. "Move now."

We move together. The time for a careful approach is gone. Brios and I dash for the rubble I pointed out.

The inhuman sounds around us have the hairs on the nape of my neck stiffening. I can't help it; I turn and look.

The Slammers are mid-charge. Some of them have seen us. A group has broken off from the others and is sprinting toward us, screaming their anger.

There's a sharp crack, and the ones in the front cartwheel into headless bloody ragdolls.

Wolf.

The parking garage entrance seethes as the new gang comes pouring out to defend their turf against what must look like an all-out attack by their neighbors.

Badges of flayed human skin, covered in the tattoos of their enemies, are stitched and pinned to clothes and living flesh. Nasty looking limb replacements, bad hair, and yelled obscenities seem to be the fashionable norm. Then I see one of them wielding a human thighbone as a club.

The two bands start shooting.

Brios and I don't slow for cover. We're in a flat-out sprint over broken ground.

The colonel continues to lay down a steady stream of destruction, pouring out cover fire, aiming into the group closing with us. The Nulls drop in ones and twos. The rest hesitate and slow in their rush toward us. As merciless as Wolf is, a few Nulls continue to make their dogged way forward.

By the rampway entrance, the Nulls' gunfire gives way to screams as the two bands make contact.

I skid into cover. Brios turns, stands in full view, and drops our last three pursuers in quick succession with his cannon.

"That's our window," he says as he crouches into cover beside me. "Start digging in."

1.07

Trouble at the Door

We poke into the pile of rubble and find a likely looking hole to shimmy into. Two false starts later, we find a gap that angles downward and opens onto one of the lower floors of the garage.

Brios and I drop into the below-ground parking level. It's dark, damp, and it stinks. As I dial my optics, Brios turns his cufflight on low. We look around.

It's uglier with the light on.

Piles of gnawed on human bones, spent ammo, nasty smelling heaps of cardboard, and rags covered with filth have been tossed everywhere. It's a different kind of minefield, and it extends far past the beam of our light.

Sounds of shuffling, punctuated by ragged breathing, random coughing, sniffing, and a soft metallic clicking all seem louder with their sources unseen in the distance.

Brios abruptly kills his light. We may be inside, but we're far from safe.

Larus is somewhere near the center of the building, on the lowest level, living here, surrounded by Nulls as his full-time neighbors.

Brios leads us through the darkness to a concrete block that forms the support for an old stairwell. We walk around it until we find a battered but intact steel door.

While I wait at the corner, Brios riffles through the supplies in his pack. He comes up with a snake cam and shoves it under the door.

I link my eyes into the feed.

It's a simple stairwell in all respects except for the reinforced steel strapping bolting it from the inside. "The door's been strapped horizontally. It looks like a simple breach," I say.

"Got it," Brios whispers.

The feed goes dead. I blink. I'm still linked.

"Um, Brios?" I don't like the hint of panic in my voice.

"What?" he asks. I hear him readying charges; to do that he must still have access to the feed.

My vision hasn't kicked back on.

I feel him press against me. The sound of the steel door buckling inward is startling.

"Brios," I say against his chest. I fling my hands out to him. "Fuck, Brios, my eyes are dead."

I hear muffled sounds of movement around us. Brios' left hand goes around my waist, and he pulls me tight against him. "Brace. I'm going to open fire."

His silenced zip gun lays down a sweeping arc. The sound of movement becomes muffled scraping and low moans.

"I've got you. Come on." He guides me over some debris. "We got this." His tone is flat so I know he's at least as worried as I am. "I'm right here."

We travel down a flight of stairs.

His breath comes against my ear as he says, "There's another door. I'm using the cam again. Try to tap into it, maybe that'll reset your system."

"I'll try," I whisper. Everything sounds impossibly loud. Suddenly I see his face, lit up dimly by his cufflight.

"Try to disconnect now," says Brios.

My frustration borders on tears as I try to unlink. "My eyes won't disconnect from the cam."

I breathe out to steady myself. I can see, awkwardly, and for now that's better than nothing. I'm about to say something sweet to lighten the mood when Brios slews the cam around and under the door I fly. I yelp at the sensation of movement without moving and grab onto the wall.

My new perspective is showing me a very clean, bright tech workshop. I see Larus puttering at a counter. Then I see what he's looking at.

I turn as best I can and face the concealed cam pointed at us. I wave while seeing myself wave on Larus' monitor.

"Open up, Larus. It's me, Sweetie," I say.

I watch his reaction.

He hesitates. The bastard actually hesitates.

"Oh come on, man, I'm not that bad a client that you want me eaten, am I? This is my friend, Brios. We really need your help, and I don't want to stand out here waiting to be eaten by your neighbors."

He makes his way to the door. As he jacks it open, Brios kills the cam. He must have meant to stow it, but my inarticulate protest makes him pause.

"Sorry, Sweetie." Brios flips it on and hands it over to me. I try to hold it casually in front of me as the door opens.

"Hi Larus." I angle the cam up from his rumpled lab coat.

His feathery blond eyebrows are drooping in suspicion. Larus hasn't changed much. He's lost weight and his clothes are a little dated, but hey, it's not like there's any place to shop around here.

He ushers us inside. The view of the room bumps and jogs strangely as Brios and I step through.

I keep blinking in the hopes that my eyes will reset.

"Why the hell are you here? How the hell did you find me? And what the hell is wrong with you?" Larus runs a hand over his face.

"Whoa. Relax, Larus. I need your help with my eyes."

He snorts. "If it's warranty work, then you should talk to your installer."

"I would, except that's kind of hard to do when there's no Doc Ripperkin's in the Ganglands."

I watch him make his way toward a tool rack. Brios moves subtly to cut him off.

I shrug. "I don't know what happened, Larus. They died on me when I switched to the snake cam."

"If I fix your eyes, you will leave?" He sounds lonely.

"I still have something for you to look at. Ishacc sent me. He says 'hi' by the way."

I fumble forward, making it look worse than it is.

"Ishacc, huh?" He comes over and takes my arm.

I cling to him for the sake of drama.

If he feels manly, he'll be more inclined to help us.

"Nice of Ishacc to keep my secret location a secret." His voice softens as he gently guides me through his shop.

I reward him by pressing sideboob against his upper arm.

Damsel-in-distress always works on tech-heads. I have a theory that it's something buried in their collective cultural subconscious. Some old console game they can all reference where they're heroes rescuing a princess. Every tech-head I've ever met responds to it. Pavlovian I think is the term.

"Well, I had to bring Brios and one other guy into the fold." To dissuade a return to his anger, I switch to a more conversational tone. "You buried yourself pretty hard, Larus. What's up with that?"

"I had to hide. The last portable data core you sold me turned my ass into a heatsink for an uncomfortable amount of aggro." He doesn't sound mad, just nervous. "There's still a lot of data on it that I haven't been able to crack. A lot of conceptual stuff without context or details."

Larus eases me against an old style barber's chair. As I park my svelte ass into it, my cam catches him checking me out.

Larus is a leather lover. Or maybe he just likes my ass. It's good to know either way.

He pokes around with some hardware and gets ready to wire me up.

Brios watches, his concern coming across as a twitch of his gun hand. When Larus isn't looking, I wave him off.

Brios takes to pacing the workshop.

"Don't touch anything," Larus barks at him.

I jump. Brios doesn't.

"Sorry, Sweetie," Larus mutters. "I don't get visitors who respond to polite instruction."

"Don't lie, Larus," I say, keeping my tone light and tinged with flattery. "You're a popular guy. I'm sure a lot of people from the city make the trip."

He snorts. "Don't push it. Where's your optical port?"

Lifting my hair along my temple, I trigger the grafted skin panel. He inserts a cable bundle and taps around on a screen.

"Nice setup. Very clean edges. Is this a new install?"

"Yeah." I relax a bit. "So, what do you think, Doc? Will I see again?"

"Hm? Yes," he mumbles as I watch him scroll through diagnostic settings and default modes. "Interesting. This is really nice hardware in here, expensive."

I beam with pride at the acknowledgment of my good taste. "Thanks, Larus."

"My point is, if they're this new and this expensive, they shouldn't be doing this. A simple link shouldn't have caused a glitch. Weird."

The angle I have on Larus feels odd, and I can't decide if he's checking out my tits.

"It looks like a redundant system activated and then failed. I'll cut the remote link and override the code if you want."

Brios steps up to my side. "What do you mean activated and failed, and why would it need to run a redundant system anyway, if the primary software is okay?" I watch him lean into my field of view. I see the concern in his eyes.

"As soon as I know, I'll tell you." Larus wheels a set of manipulator arms closer to me.

I watch in third person horror as he sets them in motion over my face. Hair-thin wires grope the air, descend, and then slide under my eyelids to link his rig directly to my optics and other hardware.

"Oh I see. That's well and truly redundant. Beyond the typical failsafe, you have a secondary set of connections for your palmscreen, processor, medical monitor, and a private wireless channel. That redundant system seems to have malfunctioned and overridden the failsafe. Beyond that, I'm not sure why your eyes are even connected to your palmscreen."

"Makes sense to me, Larus. I do a lot of shopping. The optics connect to the Lets-Find-A-Bargain network and they push ads to my palmscreen for stuff in my profile that I might want."

"You know, that's the same as selling your soul." He doesn't look away from the monitor.

"You have to believe in that stuff for it to matter, Larus. Just fix the problem please." It's unnerving to feel the wires sliding around my eyeballs and hooking into different sets of micro-ports behind them.

"The encryption on this system is really robust." Larus looks confused. "I've never seen anything like it. It's not Ripperkin's usual fare, that's for sure. I'm not even sure I know what I'm looking at."

Brios leans over me again.

The angle shows he's definitely staring at my breasts. If the situation were different, I'm sure I would laugh.

His eyes move to my face, and his voice becomes serious as he says, "Why would your optics have anything other than typical high-end encryption? Did you get them upgraded?"

"I don't know, and no, I didn't," I say defensively.

All I know is I'd rather be shopping in an empty secondhand store than sitting here moments from a panic attack. I just want to use my eyes.

I can feel my system amping up to auto-respond again. Not good.

I take a deep breath and hold onto the edges of the seat.

"If I can't override the code, then I'll just physically disconnect the secondary connections. The entire system will reset, and it should be fine. We won't know what all that other programming and hardware is doing unless we turn it on and trace it back."

"Leave it off," Brios and I say in unison. My vote is louder.

"Okay."

I can tell Larus is curious, but screw that, I just want this part of my day over.

He deftly uses his manipulator rig through a remote hand and a keyboard to prep for the disconnection. A second thicker manipulator undulates into view. I see tiny pincers flexing just before they ride up under my lids. I take another deep breath.

Brios squeezes my shoulder.

A moment later I'm staring at the roof from my own eyes. Metal arms hang over my face, and I can see the robotic wire descending toward my eye sockets.

"I'll make a copy of what I found and what I've done. Someone else can look at it later."

"Please do."

Larus lifts the manipulators away from my head. The sensation of tiny fishnets skimming off my eyes has them watering.

"Some of the features of your installs may not work as supplied, and before you ask … no, I don't know which ones. But at least they shouldn't cut out anymore."

Brios looks as relieved as I feel.

Larus doesn't let me sit in the afterglow long. "Why are you really here?" He makes a display of cleaning the wires, as if to remind us that he really is a doctor.

"Well, Larus. This object d'art may look familiar," I say as I fish the silver data core out of my coat and hold it up. "Since I don't know what the hell is on it, can't plug it in to check, and am not that curious, why don't you buy it off me for a flat rate?"

Larus takes it from my fingers. He studies the outside. His expression becomes hesitant.

"This is almost identical to the last one you sold me."

"How about I sell it to you for the same price as the last one? That's a good deal when you consider you're getting the device *and* its contents. I'm sure a guy like you could use the data for your own purposes and pull in even more profit. Just like last time."

He shakes his head, and his eyes harden. "I'm not saying anything until I see what's on it."

"Or you could just buy it because the last one you bought off me generated profits." I smile.

Larus frowns. "You know why I'm out here in this rathole, right?"

"Ishacc said someone got to you," Brios comments as he looks over a rack of jars filled with circuit boards, nano vacuum tubes, and other electronic components organized by size and function.

"You could say that, yes." Larus glances at me.

I distract him by swinging my legs. His face goes blank. I almost laugh.

He drags his eyes off me. "This is a puzzle box, Sweetie. Watch." He pops the core into a cube reminiscent of a microwave oven and runs in some power. "This should do the trick," he mutters as he peers at a monitor above the cube. His hands adjust some kind of wavelength tuner. "You see, this data core is built with its own shielding. I can't see anything inside. In fact, by scanning it … it seems to be charging—"

Control and indicator panels across Larus' workbench pulse with light. Larus loses his slouch. He looks up and down the length of his gear.

"What was that?" Brios and I ask.

The screen above the cube switches to static. Larus gets an 'I'm-not-buying-this' look on his face.

I know I have to scramble for a quick sale before he completely shuts me out. I lean forward, hoping to get him back on track with a cleavage pump. Larus ignores me.

His screens flash red, then blue. And then the room darkens as every screen in his workshop goes dead.

"Oh," he says. "Shit."

1.08

Company's Coming

I know enough about Larus' line of work to understand that what's happening isn't a good thing.

"Oh shit, what?" I ask.

Lights across the ceiling flicker. Larus is silent as he pulls the silver data core from his scanner and slaps it back into my palm.

It's disconcertingly warm.

"Not interested," he says. He tries to look casual as he moves along his workbench uncoupling wire harnesses.

He stares at the ceiling as more overhead lights flicker.

Since I've lost the sale, I go for the intel. "What's the 'oh shit' about, Larus?"

"Nothing." Larus smiles weakly at us then pulls out a box stuffed with bags. He shakes them all onto the tabletop. He looks around his workshop with a sigh. "It's nothing."

Brios and I look at one another. His expression fits my feelings; we're screwed.

I hop off the chair. "Listen, Larus, I need your answer, but I think I already know it."

"Someone followed you here. This has to be your fault." Larus' tone is accusatory. "Every time I'm around you, there are people wanting to kill me."

"Piss off, Larus. What the hell is going on?"

The lights flicker a third time.

Larus hands me a thin electric yellow data-ribbon; he looks flustered. "Here's the business with your eyes. The work is on the house. No charge."

"Someone is busting in here, aren't they?" Brios' delivery sounds more statement than question.

"They aren't here yet. My neighbors are very territorial, if you hadn't noticed." Larus keeps loading his bags with electronic goodies.

"They?" I'm not wasting any more time. I ask point-blank, "They who, Larus?"

"I don't know who. Probably the same corporation you keep stealing those units from. After you sold me that last data core, people I didn't know started asking very pointed questions. They paid a lot of money to anyone who had the right answers."

I took the first core off a yakuza courier and this one off a philanthropic street thief, both in completely different districts. I'm not ready to buy that there's a connection.

"Wait, if you thought they were from the same source and these guys were after you before, then why did you plug it in, Larus?" I narrow my gaze.

My tone must have sharpened because his smile freezes on his face: part mask, part rictus terror.

"It should've been fine. The last unit didn't have a refined trap built into its programming. I didn't expect this one to commandeer my system and send out a traceable electromagnetic signature when I tried to copy—" He shuts up.

"Larus?" I keep my anger in check as a spasm of distracting pleasure slides into my brain and down. I take a breath."You tried to copy the data and not pay me?"

"You can't really be mad at me, can you? I mean I've had to hide out here because of the last damn core you sold me."

"Screw you, Larus," I snap. "You made money. It was a business exchange."

The flickering lights seem to jog Larus back into motion.

He lifts out a system memory core and sets it into a padded messenger bag.

"I have a question." Brios jerks his thumb at the lights. "How long do we have?"

"That pulse indicates my secondary defense system is holding them off for now." Larus plugs in a spare monitor and turns it for us to see as he goes back to packing.

I watch as a team in tactical gear move toward the stairwell in a tight staggered column. Suddenly it looks like they're in the worst dance contest ever. They flail around and drop to the floor, arching and twisting.

"What the hell is that?" Brios asks Larus.

"The trade-off for living in this shit hole, thank you very much," he snaps. "Micro-robotics. The design concept was on the first data core you sold me. The design is far more advanced than anything I could do on my own. I modified them, crudely, to lie dormant until someone comes through the door to that stairwell. Well, I also tweaked their hardwired commands." He pulls a second memory core from his diagnostic unit.

He stashes the last items in various sacks and starts hanging them around his body. "I built a couple of buckets of them. I was in the process of building more to fill the second stairwell, but oh well."

"If we'd come through the first stairwell, that would've been us?" I ask quietly.

"But you didn't," Larus answers, then frowns. "How did you get in?"

"We fell down a rabbit hole, Larus. More to the point, that could have been us?" I ask again. I have to focus on the moment. I'm still pissed he actually tried to steal the data. My product.

"Well, yes." Larus grabs a bag in either hand and looks around his plundered workshop. "The micro-robotics can't distinguish between friends and enemies. They're far too small to have truly complex programming. Networking them would make them vulnerable to interference, or even reprogramming. Species specific is about as good as it gets. They don't go after dogs and cats, or rats either." He sounds disappointed by their failings. "The original design allows them to bypass air filtration systems, like masks and built-ins. They attack the lungs and bloodstream directly. In essence, these men are drowning in their own blood. It's been a very effective deterrent."

We watch on the monitor as more men come through the upper door. These ones make it a little farther.

Larus frowns. "Oh dear, they are determined."

"Yeah, they are," I say.

Brios shakes his head. "There's no back door to this place. How the hell does anyone live in the Ganglands without a backdoor?"

"Larus, how were you planning on escaping? Just in case they make it in here?" I ask.

He looks worried as a third wave of men appear on the monitor. "Well. Obviously, I assumed I'd be alone."

Brios is busy on a com-link with Wolf as the ops team on the monitor gains the second stairwell only to find it conveniently breached.

"What's the plan again, Larus?" I ask, readying my zip gun and yanking out my Double-Double.

We hear movement on the other side of the door.

Brios opens fire. The metal door takes a beating, holes popping through in quick succession.

There's muffled yelling from the stairs.

Gunplay follows, and I duck into cover. Larus scrambles across the floor to join me behind a tower of consoles and shattered mainframes.

"I'm going to activate my AlphaTek account. That was my plan," he says as he pushes a skin button on his forearm. "And since I'm suffering through another helping of your mess, I'm not inclined to help you leave."

"Fuck you, Larus." I aim at the door around the end of the console stack. "You wanted that first data core so bad, you walked around with a hard-on for twenty minutes while we negotiated a price."

The door rapidly fills with fist sized holes and bullets keep coming from both sides.

"Well, that was before I found out I'd be killed for owning it." He shakes his head. "You set me up. You knew it was trouble and sold it to me anyway."

"I didn't set you up, Larus."

Maybe shooting him is a viable option. He blames me for his problems, tries to steal my product, and threatens to leave me and Brios behind; I should shoot him.

If AlphaTek didn't have a reputation of exacting permanent revenge on behalf of dead clients, I'd do it right now.

"I haven't seen sunshine in six months," Larus mutters as he hides beside me, bullets ricocheting off the floor around us. "I eat crappy prepack, limp hydroponic vegetables, and questionable meats left on my doorstep by my neighbors. I had to build a recycler for my piss just to get enough water to stay alive."

"You drink reprocessed piss?" Brios asks from another block of cover to our right.

Even I have to admit that's pretty desperate.

I lean out and drop a few rounds into a figure I see rushing the door. I can't really call it a door anymore.

There's a clatter as a cylinder gets lobbed through the gap.

"Gas," I yell.

Brios and I pull on rebreathers; our hands are fast and practiced.

Brios lays down a burst of cover fire as the swirling pale grey cloud obscures the doorway. Someone on the other side screams through a mask.

Larus is fumbling around in his bags. He finds his mask and struggles, choking, to get it on. He's too slow.

His arms drop, and he lists heavily to one side. I reach over to yank the clear plastic mask over his face. His body shakes a couple of times. A thin line of blood seeps from his nose.

"Larus is down," I yell over to Brios. "He's gonna need a medic pretty quick."

These guys aren't screwing around. They want us dead, and they want their shiny box back.

"How long?" Brios asks as he joins me.

I tug Larus' sleeve up. The skin switch, a rapidly blinking golden AlphaTek logo, is all I need to see. "He's got a premium account. I'd guess they'll be here any second."

Larus coughs hard. The corners of his mouth have crimson lines beading downward.

"Hang in there, Larus." I pull the security tap and the data core out of my pockets and shove them to the bottom of one of Larus' bags. "Not long now."

A grenade from the top of the stairs blows the remnants of the door inward. We tuck our heads. Shredded metal buries into counters, equipment, and other furniture.

From the doorway, the ops team times their rush.

Brios' timing is better. He lobs two anti-personnel sticky charges onto the floor inside the doorway just as the guys are coming off the last step. The first three men vaporize in thunder and crimson rain. The next three hesitate, stunned.

Brios triggers the second grenade. It detonates as they stand there. The results are the same as the first.

We don't have a monitor left to show us if there are more coming, but we don't need to wait to find out.

Deep throated gunfire chews up the edges of the console stack, shrinking our cover by sizable chunks.

Their heavy weapons support has arrived.

Brios drags Larus deeper into cover.

I pop up to rip the air open with my zip gun.

The bullets keep streaming past. There's a heavy clang, and I hear Brios curse behind me.

"Brios?" I call.

I glance back as I crouch.

Brios is examining a hole in his cyberarm. He flexes his hand. "We're good."

"This is an AlphaTek security detachment. Drop your weapons." A big chunk of tech is using the ceiling overhead as a low frequency speaker. The generic sounding burly-boy voice thunders around us and hijacks every available com channel on our built-ins. *"We're here for Doctor Larus. We're counting to three and coming in."*

I only count to one.

The ceiling behind us explodes and a wide disk of sheared cement drops into our room.

I hold up my guns.

A security team, blazoned with the AlphaTek hex-shield logo, swarms over and around me. One guy takes my guns as another one pats me down.

"Whoa, hey, we're with him. With Doctor Larus." I shake Larus a little.

His eyes flutter, and he manages a nod. I'm not sure he knows what he's agreeing to, but I'm not going to set him straight.

A contingent of men breaks off and heads for the stairs, gunfire already echoing in the confined space. As Larus is being parceled up and evacuated, I pick out the AlphaTek squad leader and get his attention.

"Hey, tell your boys to avoid the main stairwell. Larus has a nanotech booby trap up there. It'll kill all of you. Mask or not."

The guy eyes me once and then passes the news along on a subvocal channel I only register by the physical actions of the troops around us.

While one of them clips me into an escape harness, I turn to Brios and ask, "What about Wolf?"

Brios hands me the end of a powered zip line, and I'm reminded of the day's earlier repelling adventure.

"He's got his own way out."

The leader calls in a confirmation and then Brios and I are whisked up and out through the roof of the parking garage.

On the way up, I get an opportunity to look around the neighborhood.

A VTOL APC sporting a camouflage paint job and no other markings is nose down and on fire, buried on impact in the side of a building half a block away. The big belly gun of the white VTOL we're tethered to is busily hosing down swarms of Nulls who are firing on us. Chunks of concrete are spalling from buildings, crushing anything below. Chaos reigns the streets for blocks around.

It's awesome.

My brain rattles cages. South Am memories fight to get out.

The AlphaTek VTOL shimmers as we close the last dozen feet to the cargo ramp. Its active camouflage turns it as blue as the surrounding sky, and waiting arms reach out of nothing to drag us on board.

Red flags fly. A pearlescent bone-white VTOL APC with active camo….

Crap.

Our feet are barely inside the fuselage when the VTOL drops its nose and vectors away from the fighting.

Troopers in full gear push me into a jump seat along one wall. Brios finds his own way to me.

We continue with our steep nose down acceleration as the ramp buttons closed. Since we aren't the ones with the account, we have to sit still. The medical team seals Larus off from us as they work on him. He looks like shit, but, with the gear on board and the treatment he's getting, I'm confident he'll be fine.

A figure steps out of the command area in the middle of the craft. I recognize the guy in the black leather long coat with the hip-howitzers.

Crap. Double plus crap, this is definitely the same VTOL.

Leather-coat-boy flips on a com-link and says, "Ops to Control. Picasso reporting all clear. We're done here. Clock this counter incursion and extraction." He doesn't look at me, and I force myself to breathe normally.

The narrow gun-port style windows show a flash of New White Sands, the TopSide Corporate Core filled with towers clawing at the clouds. The APC turns northwards, out past the Jumble and toward the Feral Lands. We level off and pick up speed.

I'm a passenger on this flight. I'm grateful to be rescued, but pissed I'm heading away from the city.

Screw AlphaTek.

To choke down my frustration, I ask into the silence, "No stewardess on this flight?"

Brios shakes his head.

The Picasso guy glares at me. His eyes have emoto-projectors built into them. Huge leaping flames flare over the curves of his eyeballs.

"So does that mean I pissed him off?" I ask Brios. I don't bother to whisper.

Brios shoots me a look. "Maybe we should be quiet until we touch down."

1.09

New Haven

The AlphaTek VTOL sets us down on a paved slab surrounded by carefully tended grass. The ramp opens and we walk into a green space bordered by trees, flowers, and a low white picket fence.

I burst out laughing. "So we died and went to heaven?"

"Follow me," the guy named Picasso barks as he stomps away. His voice is rough.

I watch him walk for a second or two before I do as he requests.

"Where are we?" I ask.

"New Haven," he grunts.

I heard New Haven was a private get-away-bedroom community for AlphaTek's top level CitOne employees. I look around. What a difference a ton of money makes.

Behind us the VTOL thunders away, shifting its skin back to pearlescent white.

A cobblestone walkway leads us to an arbor gate. We come off a low hill close to the center of town. Houses, like I've seen in old kids' books, are set in tidy rows along a clean street. Flowers grow in rows and plots everywhere.

My jaw loosens as I watch a guy walking down the street. He's hand-delivering old-fashioned letters door to door. A mailman. The first mailman I've ever seen; I'm so excited.

"Don't get comfy," Fire-eyes says to me as I gawk like a tourist. "We need to settle the bill for your extraction. Doctor Larus has an account, but you two have to pay up."

"Or what?" Maybe my tone is too cheeky.

"Or." His black coat flares wide as he turns sharply to look at me. "We strip your gear and drop you and him back in the Ganglands."

A hefty round of juice flows off my pleasure-tap. I smile at him and pull in a deep breath.

What's being alive worth? I catch myself answering that question. I'm already carrying a debt for my eyes. A little more isn't going to make a difference.

I snort; I just played a sales pitch for AlphaTek services in my head.

The pitch works. I'll pay whatever I have to.

We're shipped off to a low roofed house. Inside, it's a fortress. We're separated and directed to wait in holding cells.

A bored looking guy in uniform joins me.

I'm a little nervous; these are the people who came looking for my stash, and I only have a hunch as to why.

I switch my medical monitor so it cuts off every automatic response it can access. No pupil dilation, no blush response, no galvanic temperature shifts. They aren't even going to get sweat from me.

They don't really need any of that shit anyway. They have access to the best scanners imaginable. The kind that actively track all of your brain waves.

The guy sitting across from me doesn't care if I'm nervous or not. This has got to be a formality for them. But I'm not going to make it easier.

His line of questioning is dry: How do I know Larus? How do I know Brios? Why was I in the Ganglands? What do I know about PharmaComp? What do I know about the yakuza? How did we get access to the map-box data? Why are PharmaComp after us?

I don't answer.

If their fancy sensors are monitoring my brain activity anyway, they can tell if I'm thinking the truth, or thinking about lying and to what degree. Instead I make up fairy tales in my head about why I'm here. I daydream about deals, shopping, and having sex with Fire-eyes on the table right here, right now.

I let the guy go on and on because he might reveal more about what AlphaTek knows.

PharmaComp is the only bit I get that's new and solid.

That and it occurs to me AlphaTek swooped in after I plugged the black security tap into my rig, which probably means the damned thing is useless to me.

It does give me a hint about how they operate. They were onto Shadow. His operations were either tracked, permitted, or soon to end. Interesting, but not overly valuable news on the market.

Crap.

In good conscience, and because I like him, I have to let Ishacc know. He's going to be pissed that the code he's been working on may be rigged with a trace. I hope not, because he'll want me to pay him for services rendered if it is.

My interrogator ends our one-sided conversation with the bill for my extraction.

The numbers on the contract he shows me are huge.

How had Larus kept up a premium account with these guys? I'll be flat broke inside a few days between making payments and maintaining my lifestyle.

"This isn't a payment plan," I snipe as I review the numbers in detail. "It's aggravated financial assault."

It teaches me one thing. I'm undercharging for my bodyguard services by at least half. I'll keep that in mind when signing future gigs.

"Unless your corporation is in the business of making people homeless, who can afford this?"

The guy is about to reply when his dv chimes.

He answers the call. "Yes. Oh? Oh, of course, I understand

completely, yes. Yes sir, I'll do that right away."

He cuts the line and, without a word, starts packing his paperwork. His silence works on my curiosity.

"So, what was that all about?" I ask.

"Your bill's been paid in full." He doesn't meet my eyes. "The others from your group will join you in a moment. You'll all be free to go."

"Paid?" Now I'm really worried. "Who paid it?"

"I'm not at liberty to say." He opens the door. "Thank you for your time."

Crap.

I hate the idea of owing someone. Favors are a different kind of debt. They're the kind that get you killed.

But there's no choice in the matter, it's done.

I push aside those ugly feelings and distract myself by thinking about everything else.

Shadow walked into someone's covert laboratory, used an uber-powerful security tap with a trace on it, and swiped a data core. He had to have had a buyer in mind for the goods. Maybe he was under contract to steal the data.

Now, the owner or the buyer wants it back. And AlphaTek's in the mix.

Selling the thing is going to be a bitch. Larus tried to make a copy and a couple squads of corporate soldiers showed up. That's a hard sell right there. 'Buy this data core and let your worst enemy get a hold of it. Let them plug it in.' It's the only pitch I can come up with.

My mind drifts and something else pops.

I've seen the PharmaComp brand name someplace important, and recently too.

Red flag.

It was someplace relaxed, someplace with no stress, no weapons: someplace I spent money.

I snort, that place could be any S&M shop, shoe store, or lingerie outlet from TopSide to UnderCity.

The door opens, and Brios is shunted into my room.

"So what do you owe?" I ask.

He drops into the chair across from me and tips his head back to stare at the ceiling.

"They didn't get that far," he says. "Someone covered my bill. You?"

"Same. But I saw the numbers, and I'm pissed." I draw a breath to calm down and settle in for a wait.

Brios shifts in his chair and looks around. He knows we're being monitored.

To take my mind off all the bullshit, I ask, "How'd that new compound chemical work in your cannon?"

"Not bad. The rounds throw a lot more heat than I'd like. I think they'll be okay for your Double-Double, but anything with a high rate of fire…" Brios shakes his head.

"You're worried the casings might deform too much? Maybe jam?" This is our fallback chatter. We can keep this kind of talk going for days.

"Yeah. A lot of power for the size, but it would suck if it jammed an ejector on a zip gun." His fingers find the hole in his upper arm. He pokes at it, testing the edges.

"You still mobile?" I nod at his cyberlimb.

"Mostly. Doesn't feel like I've got full strength. Internal diagnostic's coming up with a warning but no errors."

"You want me to take a look?" I ask.

He glances at the ragged hole. "Sure."

I stand and cross the space to lean on his side of the table. He activates his cufflight. I angle his arm so I can peek inside.

"It looks like it missed the major mechanics. Maybe damaged some electromagnetic musculature. There's nothing completely severed that I can see."

"Then we're good I guess." He's pouting, I can tell.

"Hey, you said you wanted an upgrade, so here's your chance." I smirk at him.

Brios grunts.

They don't let us stew for long. We're ushered down a hallway, and Larus joins us. Silently we make our way outside.

The doctor looks kind of shaky, but he's moving under his own power.

"Good to see you survived," I say to Larus. He's sweating a lot. I don't ask him about what. "You wouldn't know who paid our tab would you?"

"No, I don't." He shakes his head. "I want to thank you though for getting my mask on. Apparently the gas was of a lethal variety."

"You're welcome." I grin at him. "So you want to buy the unit or not?"

"I'm being polite when I say this, Sweetie." His tone is deadpan. "Go screw yourself."

"Thought so." I nod.

We're hustled into an armored transport and actually driven back to New White Sands. Half a dozen flat-faced security guards stare at us the whole way.

I stare unblinking at the guy across from me. I tease him when he blinks or looks away. The drive feels long.

We get dumped out in MidTown close to the north end CitTwo managers' housing complex. E-cars zip by mixed in with smaller robotic delivery vehicles making their rounds. No mailmen here. Distant sounds of AVs climbing the wide air shafts echo along the narrow streets.

"PharmaComp is chasing us, you guys got that, right?" I ask them as I look around at the traffic. An internal map of the district lists my favorite shops in the area. All the deals that must be going on make my mouth water.

I scratch restlessly at my palmscreen.

"PharmaComp? They're the ones chasing us?" Larus stiffens and glances around.

Brios shrugs his typical so-what.

"Yeah, Larus." I'm back in my city and feeling cocky. "The domehead who asked me questions let it slip."

Since I know where I am, I start walking. The boys follow: Brios relaxed and vigilant, Larus winding up like an old spring ready to snap.

I stop on a corner and look at Larus. "I have to ask. Where are you going to end up, Larus?"

Larus looks at his sacks of possessions, his expression one of concern like a mother with her young. "I need a new home, someplace where I can work in safety without interruptions." He looks up and down the street. "I feel sniper scopes on me just standing next to you. I can't be here."

"Thanks," I reply in as dry a tone as I can.

Brios gives me a little head shake; we're clean for laser sights at least.

"Just remember." Larus keeps fidgeting. "Don't be around when your buyer plugs that thing in, or, as you say, bam, instant bad guys."

We both look at him. I nod. "Thanks for the tip, Larus. Are you leaving?"

"Hells yes, I'm leaving." He flags a cab.

Before he can get away, I grab his shoulder and spin him around. I find the bag I need and rummage to the bottom.

"What are you doing?" he asks, jerking away.

I hold him in place. "I knew AlphaTek would execute due diligence and pat me down, standard procedure for non-clients." I pull out the security tap and silver data core. "But you, you're a paying client, and it's all about the customer."

"Can I simply express how much I dislike you in this moment?" Larus glares at me.

"Yes you can, Larus." I grin as I shove my possessions back into my pockets.

He shakes his head. "If I see you inside the next year, it will be too soon."

I lean forward and smile at Brios, plumping my cleavage with my upper arms. "How quickly he forgets that I saved his life in a gas attack." I sigh. "Well, take care, Larus." I turn away with a shimmy of my hips.

I know Larus is staring longingly after me. I can hear him muttering to himself as he gets into the cab and slams the door.

I catch a glimpse of my reflection in the window as his

cab drives by. I think I look like shit, but Larus is pasted to the glass, eyes wide.

I sigh and glance at my blank palmscreen. I need coffee.

"He'll be fine," I say. "Let's find a café."

"Sure." Brios falls into step beside me.

We cover a block and a half before we get to the Vietnamese coffee and noodle house I want.

The news feed is streaming along as we push through the door. *"...after last week's violent fallout between rival yakuza clans, the Corporate Council has chosen to lift the mandatory checkpoint protocol throughout the city in response to confirmed reports..."*

I order coffee and pull out my kCard to pay.

The bored looking server flatly refuses my eCash. "It's taken care of," he says.

"What?" I look around the place. From the only corner booth, Wolf throws me a nod and points to the bench seat across from him.

"He paid?" I double-check with the server.

"Yep. Arranged a tab for food too, so I'd recommend—"

I don't let him finish. "Brios, how the hell did he find us?"

"Ask him," Brios replies. "I told you he's well connected."

To spite Wolf, and remind myself that I didn't ask for his charity and therefore shouldn't feel obligated for any reason, I order the most expensive thing on the menu: a gold-leaf wrapped Vietnamese fusion chocolate truffle cake made with authentic organic cocoa and African gold. Screw him.

As I drop into the booth across from Wolf, I think about all the cultural ramifications of a Spaniard buying me things. And then I hate that I've thought about it.

"I'm not dating you." My tone is wooden.

"I know," he replies in the same tone and throws down a 'whatever' shrug. I find I like him more for it.

Then I catch myself. This is not a trend I like.

"So what's the verdict on this job?" Wolf asks as I dig into the cake.

"Things went to shit the moment Larus plugged in the data core. He tried to steal a copy." I'm still pissed about that. "And bam, instant bad guys. Looks like PharmaComp's the one pulling the strings."

Brios steals a forkful of my cake, and I realize he's probably as hungry as I am. We burned more than our share of calories today. I slide the plate so he can reach it.

"PharmaComp?" Wolf asks, watching our byplay like a spectator at a cricket match.

"The domehead who asked me questions let it slip. It's going to make finding a buyer difficult. Not that it matters to you." I sip my coffee. The coffee isn't as good as I remember. I should have asked for a classic iced coffee over sweetened condensed milk.

Wolf's eyes narrow, and he leans back. "Meaning what, exactly? Where's the problem?"

"Meaning I'm not saying anything until you answer a few questions. First off, how the hell did you get out of the Ganglands so fast? And second, how did you find us?"

"I heard you have paranoid tendencies," he says dryly.

I stab at the cake and eat a mouthful. Part of me hates that it tastes as good as it does.

"Heard from who?" I realize he's messing with me and jump back to topic. "Don't answer that. I don't care who's talking shit about me."

"To answer your first question, I left the same way I came in." He meets my eyes and holds me there, trapped until he looks away. "I have combat skills, and I practice them often."

"And?" Damn it, I hate that he can mess with me so easily. I open the table menu and select the options for pho noodle soup. I order two bowls and leave Wolf to fend for himself.

"I contacted AlphaTek and asked them where you were being dropped off. The coffee shop was just an easy guess after that."

"Bullshit. AlphaTek doesn't just hand over information like that. That's bad for business."

Wolf cuts off my rant by saying, "They told me, because I'm the one who paid for both of your extractions."

I lock my hands onto the table edge, fighting the impulse to pull my knives. My pleasure-tap pulses me with a reward for not reaching across the table and slicing him to ribbons.

"Why would you do that, Wolf?" All my anger leaks out. Glad to be alive, glad to not owe a private security mega-corporation a shit-ton of money, but now I owe this cocky bastard more than I can pay.

Brios doesn't look surprised.

I'm not impressed. "How the hell do you have that kind of money?"

"My money is my business." The colonel gets brisk. "I paid his share of the bill because good soldiers are hard to find, and he's very good at his job. This gig in the Ganglands would have put us even, and I don't want to lose him completely to freelance work. As for you, Sweetie, I'll think of something."

Red flag.

Our noodles slide out of the delivery slot. I grab a spoon for each of us and take chopsticks out of the dispenser. I use the actions to distract myself from my rising anger. My temperature's up and I'm pissed.

I split my chopsticks apart with a crisp snap. Ignoring Wolf completely, I turn to Brios and say, "I have to tell you, Brios. As big a help as Wolf's been, he's cramping my style. We needed him to get into Ganglands, and he may have covered our tab for the ticket out, but I don't want him thinking he runs anything on our gig."

"I'm sitting right here." Wolf's voice sounds detached, all PTSD. He sets down his coffee. Maybe he's trying to scare me.

"Good of you to notice that you aren't part of our conversation," I say as I look at him with an arched brow. "You should take the hint." I turn back to Brios. "He's out of our sandbox as of now. I'll find a way to pay my share of 'Our Great Ganglands Rescue,' and that's it, over, finished, drop the curtain, we're wrapped."

Brios chews silently as he looks between Wolf and I.

Wolf says, "I have the name of someone who can help you with this PharmaComp thing."

"Like I need your resources," I snap. "I know people who can help with this too."

"Like who?" Wolf never turns his grey eyes off me.

I reach for the only person I know who might be able to help us. "The White Witch, that's who."

Wolf snorts. "Okay, go make your deal with the devil. Let me know if you need help, Brios." He stands, pulling on his coat. "The table's paid for. Eat till you're done." He throws Brios a key fob. "Your bike's out back."

Wolf leaves. I watch him go. He's still hot. Still has a great car and an impressive arsenal.

He's still a presumptive asshole.

"We're going to need him," Brios says around a mouthful.

"No. We aren't." I sigh and keep my concerns to myself. "Trust me, we're better off on our own."

"If you say so." Brios doesn't look at me. I know I've hurt his feelings somehow.

"Sorry for dissing your old boss," I say quietly.

"Whatever." Brios looks at the doorway over my shoulder. "Food's good."

We eat in silence after that, and I'm still fuming when we finish. I clear about a quarter of the menu into takeout bags. If Wolf wants to buy me things, then he can suck it up.

1.10

The Lair of the White Witch

"Do you even remember how to get to the Witch's house?" Brios asks as he lets the bike's Electro-jet turbine generator run a regular warm-up cycle. He's tucking our food away in compartments around the bike.

"Yeah, just look for a house covered in candy," I mumble.

You only needed to get caught trying a break-and-enter at her place once; most people didn't live through the experience.

"Trust me, I remember."

We ride down into Harbor District, UnderCity.

This is a built-up industrial area with transit hubs, warehouses, and kelp and seafood resource farms.

I've gotten over the idea that seaside air is supposed to be sweet. The stench of processed fish and rotting sea-greens taints the breeze off the Gulf. Even the horizon isn't a view in this district. Tidal Power Wall Number One stretches a couple of miles in either direction.

Over forty million people call New White Sands their home. Eighty percent of those are working poor CitFour citizens who live in corporately subsidized flats, their diets supplemented with mixes of different medications, birth control, and vitamins. If they can't get a job, they're entitled to a bare minimum support fund that comes through a traceable Corporate Monitored Universal Wage account.

Social engineering ensures they live in designated districts. The broken dreams of America all lumped into secure zones.

Harbor District is one such zone. Everyone born here is too poor to leave, too poor to get an advanced education. All of them trained from birth to be unquestioning consumers and pathetically grateful employees.

They're just people caught in a downward spiraling meat grinder of fear and greed. The fear is foisted onto them by the corporations, and the greed is an emulation of the successful people they see above them.

I'd weep, but I'm not one of them. I work a ragged edge. Blood, guns, and flash. And just enough day job to fudge my records at tax time.

As we make our way along the seawall, a huge electric powered Gulf Transport United ekranoplan heads out to sea. The engines on its wings churn the water as the ground effect builds. In a moment, it's racing along fifteen feet up and full throttle.

My palmscreen buzzes a brutal bio-feedback like a phantom limb. Maybe it's my brain's way of telling me it's time to run, a buzzing filled with imagined deals on one-way tickets to the United Yucatan. Maybe Merida Freeport.

I resist the urge to turn it on.

The late afternoon light glitters off the fish farm enclosures. Wild seagulls pinwheel overhead. It's such a great day except for all the crap that's happened and all of the crap that still needs to happen before it's over.

As we get close to the building we need, I tell Brios to switch the bike to full electric mode. The Witch hates loud noises near her place.

We slink the rest of the way to the warehouse.

"That's close enough," I say. I want to make sure we stay on her good side. "We'll walk from here."

The grunginess of the outside never seems to change. The structure, on the other hand, changes all the time. That's the candy coating.

Looking at the place, you know it has to be loaded with something valuable for the building to get modified as often as it does.

Sometimes, I'll come by and there'll be a new stack on the roof drifting one rank smell or another into the air. The next week the stack will be gone and solar collectors will take its place, or a spiral staircase leading to nowhere will be randomly bolted on.

It's that constant morphing of the building that had me curious enough to try my hand at an old school break-in.

The White Witch has a reputation for being a loner, being insane, and being so overeducated as to put some AIs to shame.

No one, not even me, has seen her outside in the daylight. She might be an albino. I say might, only because she's bone white and I know she wears contacts.

A loner? Yes.

Insane? Maybe, sort of.

Smart? She's the smartest person I've ever met.

I hate her as much as I admire her. She does what she wants, when she wants, and no one ever stops her. But the thing that pisses me off the most is that she's flawless: no mods and, other than data ports, no implants. If I didn't know that fudging DNA is so damned illegal, I'd swear her Russian parents built her piece by piece in a test tube.

I tell myself I'm not jealous. If she really is natural, I would be … but if not, then hell no.

Either way, her skin is perfectly smooth, and she's got perfect teeth and perfect hair. She's the full package.

"You okay?" Brios asks. "You look spooked."

"Me?" I laugh. "I'm good."

We make our way past several signs in multiple languages warning people away. The last one is a pictograph of a giant carnivorous plant using a tentacle to dangle a child over its jagged mouth.

My belly does a flip. "Nice." I try to sound casual. "That one's new."

Brios grins at the sign. "I wonder if that sign actually works on kids."

"That plant is real, Brios," I whisper. "I've seen it."

He stares, his face blank. He shakes his head in disbelief and pushes the buzzer marked *IF YOU ARE IN NEED OF ASSISTANCE, PLEASE GO AWAY.*

The *RING FOR SERVICE* part of the sign is scratched out, and the *GO AWAY* part is written on in black marker.

The penmanship is impeccable.

A speaker built into the yard light over the door comes on. *"You were told not to come back here."*

"I didn't expect to be so memorable," I say.

"How can I forget you." The Witch's thick Russian accent cuts the air. *"You did not become food for my plant. I was strangely disappointed."*

"I like your new signage, looks good. I have to ask," I pause, "you don't get many children coming around here anyway, so why bother?"

"The emotional context of offspring for weeks slowly dissolving in digestive juices of gigantic plant is unsettling to most corporate types. It steers them away from my doorstep by a statistically significant amount. Why are you still here? What do you want?"

"I'm here because you're the best person I know at solving riddles." I look sidelong at Brios. "I need your help."

"Say that last part louder and look up at sign."

I look up; wide, high cheekbones here I come. "I know you can't resist a good riddle, so let me in."

"No."

"Come on. I need your help." I repeat the line she's waiting for. I'm surprised she hasn't taken my bait already. She must be busy with something.

"Very good." The door pops open and the smell of fresh bread wafts out.

"That's not fair," I say to Brios, "I just ate and now I'm hungry again."

Brios chuckles and holds the door for me. "Maybe you can hit her up for a slice when we're done."

"Maybe." Personally, I'm wondering if she'll help us or not. Just because we're this far, doesn't mean her help is a sure thing.

I'm plagued by the memory of someone else's limbs being dropped into the belly of the plant. Another curious trespasser. Just another one of the faceless vanished.

The interior of the warehouse is as spotless as ever. The place is gleaming white enamel and high-gloss paint. If it's not white, it's chrome.

I see our hostess through a partially closed door. The White Witch is stunning in a floor-length crimson gown. She's all paper-pale perfection, and she's definitely busy.

The White Witch is in the arms of a tall chin-and-cheek-bones blond guy who's wearing about two years' worth of my paychecks in his suit alone.

The Leopold Geiger brand is not something Brios will ever afford.

Blond guy with the razor cut hair leaves her side, and I can't see where he goes.

"I apologize for my attire," the White Witch says as she makes her way to where we wait.

"It's all good," I say.

The sight of her up close, her perfume, all of her, makes Brios stand up straight. I swipe my jealousy away.

Stay focused on the job, I tell myself. Even I have a hard time not staring. Except I'm looking for a flaw, any flaw, anywhere.

It's futile. I'm screwed.

"You mention riddle?" Her manner is clipped. She's in a good mood.

"Um, yeah." I pull the silver data core out of my pocket. "This is a custom data rig. I would be ever so appreciative if we could get a valuation, and if you can see your way to giving us some possible buyers' names?"

"This is riddle?"

"The catch is you can't plug it in or scan it without inviting a strike team. Doctor Larus von Ganglands found that out for us. He also mentioned designs for nano-robotics in reference to a data core like this one. Not sure if that's what's on here, but it might be similar."

"Raven, you should have come here first." She sounds bitter. "Doctor Larus? Doctor? That is a joke."

"Vlasta, you told me not to come back." I make a quiet retort. "Besides, I never know if you're busy. It's not like your schedule is posted on a media site."

"Wait." Brios drops his shit. "You two are actually on a first name basis?"

"I was stuck in her ventilation system for a week, Brios." I try to play it cool, like she and I are old friends. I hope she picks up on social cues. "We had time to chat."

"Plenty of time." She starts off great. "I stood on chair feeding her low calorie sandwiches, and she cursed fact that there is no washrooms in ductwork." She fails the back half.

"Can I ask?" Brios shakes his head. "Why didn't you just cut the duct open and let her out?"

"Unacceptable. She was breaking into my home." Vlasta raises her voice like a nasty school teacher, green contact lenses flashing. "I saw no reason to assist in her escape at my expense. She needed lesson. She refused to pay for ductwork, so we waited until she lost enough weight to slip free."

"Robbing her made no sense at that point." I try to explain. It's hard to lie in front of her. She's a witch for sure. "Besides, she fed me by hand. Nitrile gloves aside. She makes killer sandwiches."

"Sure." Brios stares at the two of us like we're crazy. "So, about that data core?"

Vlasta extends her hand. I present the unit like it's jewelry and set it in her palm. She hikes up her gown and spins away, moving like a silken shawl in a breeze.

"Come. I will have answer soon."

Brios and I trail along behind her.

I catch a glimpse of one section of the warehouse that has been renovated into a full-on tea room. Two cups sit on the table amid roses, carpets, and freestanding woodcut panels.

Vlasta makes her way along a workbench, picking and choosing equipment for her task as she moves. She reaches over the table and runs her fingertips across a series of massive brass gears mounted on the wall. It takes me a moment to register that it's a huge open-faced clock.

"Is that new?" I look at the mechanism, exposed and vulnerable. "I don't remember it being there."

"It was recent gift." She smiles at it. "It is fitting reflection of realities of this world."

Brios leans close to speak into my ear. "Who would give the White Witch a gift?"

"Someone who feels indebted beyond payment?" I look up at him.

She isn't a bad person, just her redeeming qualities have to be looked for. Obviously someone looked.

"Jesus, Brios. I don't know."

He sighs and turns to look at the greenery.

"Don't go near the plants," I whisper.

I watch him squint and lean closer.

The plants completely fill the other end of the warehouse. One of them undulates in an imaginary breeze. Its scent is enticing. That one, I know, is the Witch's favorite.

I was here when she fed it. Rats, parts of trespassers, and every other living thing she would catch in and around her home, one bloody piece at a time. It ate quickly for a clump of vegetation.

Seeing it again makes me nervous.

She told me that one day it'll start moving, shuffling around the shop on its own, hunting.

"Simple design," Vlasta says.

She hasn't even hooked the silver case up to anything.

"I would say South African housing. But plug shape indicates it is United Korea internals. So, likely software is from there as well." She frowns. "Lee has not been active in months. That is because he is dead."

She starts to string cables to her system. It hums happily under the length of the table.

"I am curious, but I understand I should not ask how you come to possess this device."

"It was a botched mugging."

No point in lying. I'm sure we're being passively scanned, and I'll be damned if I lose her insights because of a screw-up maneuver like lying at the eleventh hour.

"I ended up killing the man who was carrying it. I think he'd just stolen it from a secret corporate lab in Nu Hong district. So manufacturer's dead?"

"Da." She nods slowly. "I received private notification from mutual friend last month. This data core is taken from PharmaComp facility in Nu Hong? Interesting."

"How do you know?" Brios turns to me. "How does she know the place was a PharmaComp facility?"

I shrug.

She ignores him. "Nice hardware, very clean. Some of Lee's best work. Such a shame. He will never be better than me now, but this is good attempt."

"Um, Vlasta?" I hate to interrupt, but her casual ease with how dangerous the slab is puts me on edge. "I know you heard me when I said it was risky to hook that thing up…."

"Risky for those who don't have correct equipment. An excluded virtual work environment is time consuming to build, nuisance to install, but necessary for my work. This core will assume it has sent its signal." She flicks me a dismissive brow and plugs the core in. "We are safe here."

The slab sits there on the spotless counter, making me sweat with its lone wire linking it into the system. I can feel Brios getting twitchy beside me. He's glancing for exits.

I have to trust Vlasta to be smarter than anyone in this end of the biz.

"What about the information on there, Vlasta?"

Her eyes unfocus before the data starts rolling across the big screen. "Pretty nanites," she murmurs.

It hits me. Vlasta's brain has to be bio-linked.

Damn near vat grown perfection for sure. If that's true, it makes sense that she's hiding. She's illegal everywhere in the world as a gene-mod, built one trait at a time. She might be 'all natural,' but she's not from nature.

"This is shade above nanotech. It can be better built. Sloppy delivery system. Perhaps it is prototype." She pauses a few screens for a heartbeat. "Tsk tsk."

I pace. "Delivery issues aside, what does it do?"

She stops her work and turns to look at me.

I know the look. It's her get-ready-to-listen face. Vlasta hates going over material twice. I mentally brace myself.

"After defeating air filter and purification systems." She holds up a finger for each point. "It forms nodes throughout host brain. Nodes grow glands. Glands manufacture complex neurochemicals."

I clench my jaw. She catches herself lecturing me and waves her hand dismissively.

It's a sore point she and I have been over before. I don't respond well to being lectured.

She must be warming up to me. Her monologue is an improvement on the style of communication we shared last time: I screamed, she mocked … it was generally ugly.

"To what end, Vlasta?" Improvement or not, I can feel my patience thinning. "What does it all do? What's the end result? And who am I going to sell it to?"

"This is cunning device." The tone of her voice changes, becomes curt. "Elegant, except for crude delivery method. In short, nanites create glands everywhere in brain. The glands have remote switching system. They sync with networked cyberware implants. When signaled, the glands release neurochemical load. Those chemicals cascade inside brain and body. It turns on or off feelings of love. It is more complex than that, but, in essence, this is what it will be used for."

"It can make you fall in love?" Brios doesn't hide his surprise. I'm just impressed he followed most of that.

"Da, love." She stares at him like she's noticing him for the first time. "Deeply and profoundly in love, to exclusion of everything but automatic functions."

"Why would anyone need that?" He doesn't get it.

"I can think of a billion reasons," I say.

"It is very potent biological manipulation," Vlasta says. "The letdown from such a profound emotion would have a devastating effect on mind of host. Depending on speed of reversal and duration of initial attachment, one might become suicidal. Or murderous."

"Shit," Brios says.

Vlasta nods. "Here are hypothetical uses. CEO floods shareholders meeting with the device to gain agreement from all who then vote as he wishes. Or terrorist leader sways World Court to back his actions. Cultists convert enemies to become followers who will die for cause without hesitation. Extracted corporate types could be given unbreakable version of Stockholm syndrome. Perhaps paired with RNA retro-viral memory triggers, it could be quite effective for spies or turncoats."

My oldest cages rattle in my head. I voice a hypothetical of my own. "Contract marriages could be turned on when you sign, then off when the contract expires."

"Kidnapped, trafficked slaves would worship their owners no matter how they are treated," she says. Like it's old news, something the world would simply do to thousands of unfortunates.

I start thinking about who will buy the data off me. Tech like this is going to be a hot item for all kinds of unscrupulous corporations.

I try and think through more humane applications.

Then it hits me.

This tech could buy instant brand loyalty for anything: lingerie, jeans, coffee, cyber implants, anything.

Red flag.

"Crap, Brios."

"What?" He has a stunned expression as he sees more ramifications on his own.

"There was PharmaComp gear all over Doc Ripperkin's." I try hard not to yell. "They're an exclusive component provider."

That was where I saw their brand name.

My stomach does a slow roll.

"Bah. Why do you go to those hacks?" Vlasta snaps. "Here I thought we were friends. I make implants better than best Ripperkin imports."

"First off, you told me never to come back." I look pointedly at her.

She doesn't share my immediate concern over the situation.

"Second, I only knew you designed gear, Vlasta. I had no idea you manufactured, or that you do installs. Third, I'm positive I could never afford what you do in here."

"You are right. You cannot afford me, my poor American friend." She sighs. "I have select client list who must prepay everything. Many high-end black operatives come here for installs and repair. Not so far as Japan, cleaner than China or South Africa, more advanced than Israel or Middle East."

Brios is looking at me, having caught up with my thoughts.

"You need to check her," he says, pointing at me.

"Why?" Vlasta frowns.

My palmscreen tingles under my skin.

"Please, Vlasta. My eyes are new Ripperkin installs, and they glitched out on me this morning."

"Perhaps it is coincidence?" Her frown doesn't change.

"Vlasta. I need to know I'm clean." I struggle to keep a pleading tone out of my voice.

I realize I'm scared. My blocked memories become more pronounced, their cages suddenly crystal clear, contents loud but obscure. My panic ramps up.

Vlasta moves closer and takes my hand. The contact makes everything slow down.

"If the nanites are there, they may not be easy to remove."

I reach into my pocket and fish out the data-ribbon from Larus. "Larus gave me this. It's the data about my optics glitch." I calm myself. "Just see if I have them or not. Do it before I change my mind."

1.11

Compromised

It takes a while to set everything up. Vlasta runs scans, fMRI, X-rays, ultra-sound, everything before she finally plugs me into her system.

"This will take time. I shall make you sleep," she says to me as I lie on the medical bed.

I'm out before I can reply.

My internal clock pings midnight as I wake. I feel stiff but refreshed. Brios rubs sleep from his eyes as he joins me at my bedside.

Vlasta sits like a statue at her worktable, face pressed into the viewing end of a really big microscope. A series of manipulators in front of her are barely moving, working on something.

"So, what's the news?" I look at Brios. I've seen him look worse, but he doesn't look great either.

"It's there." He squeezes my hand. "She can't take it out, can't undo the damage."

"Okay." My voice feels small.

"She's looking for options. Looking for a way to remove it without turning your brain into chow mein." His expression doesn't change. "She's trying to micro-modify the hardware, or at least rewrite the software on a few of them, to see if they'll undo their own work."

"And?" I ask, but I don't want to know.

He shakes his head. "Nothing yet. Up-note, she put in a kill switch. When it gets flipped, you won't be susceptible to the device's impulses." Brios squeezes my hand again. "For now you're stuck with it."

"Well that's awesome." I can't cry and don't want to scream, so instead I just lie there watching Vlasta work.

Eventually she unglues her face from the manipulator rig and comes over.

"You have early version in your head. Demo model." She taps my forehead. "You are like walking advertising."

"What do you mean?" I feel bile churning. "And use small words, Vlasta. Your big words scare the shit out of me."

"Okay." She hooks a rolling stool with her foot and sits. From my angle, the open-geared clock sits like a halo framing her face. "The device in your head is not from an inhalable nanite swarm, though there are plans for that application in the software package. This device was implanted to piggyback with your optics. It is linked through your palmscreen."

I clench my jaw and sit up. "Goddamn Doc Ripperkins."

She looks between me and Brios. "The clinic might not know that their goods are malicious."

"The real problem is PharmaComp," Brios says.

"Da. Very bad men." Her blunt tone tells me she's impressed with their tech but angry about its application.

Being forced to live with her for a week let me learn more about her than she suspected.

"I can fix, but it will take a long time, weeks, maybe months to design effective strategy that will not harm host in process. It is faster for you to find data from them on how to remove this system. It looks like one-way procedure, but that is not sound business practice. They must have workaround."

Brios grimaces. "So we go after PharmaComp and get the intel we need."

"I will keep this data core." She points at the metallic case on the counter. "It is safe here. Consider it my pay. You will become less a robotic slave to their evil plans with my help."

I can only nod.

How much would you pay?

I feel drained just swinging my legs off the bed.

Brios hands me the Double-Double and Little Tommy. "We still owe hardfold to people over this job," he says.

Vlasta shrugs. "Raven is alive. I have installed partial switch and monitoring system. Who you owe and how you pay is your business."

Brios and I exchange a look. No data core, no money. We're screwed.

Abruptly she stands and makes her way back to her work. "I am sorry this thing has happened, but it is good you come to me. I have more work to do to solve riddle. It is good riddle. Now, go."

We make our way back to the B&V in silence, mostly because I have nothing to say and Brios knows I don't want words right now.

He doesn't miss a beat. He takes me TopSide on an extended drive to my favorite vista points across the city. When I shift against him, he pulls over and parks.

We sit in mutual silence, staring up at the Corporate Core, its towers shining with brilliant lighting, silhouetted against the glowing night sky. Blinking AVs and speeding ground transports, their shells pulsing color, leave tracers in my vision.

I wipe angry tears from my eyes.

Life in New White Sands moves and shifts, uncaring, unceasing, and unstoppable around us. The MidTown Night Market, one city floor below us, is visible through the Grand Central Vent. Tiny looking people move under giant swinging red paper moons. Lights flicker around the edges from thousands of interactive displays.

It's a transient moment from which any second could be paused and framed on a wall.

That's how I know I'm scared. Poetic crap like that gets people killed.

I struggle and then flounder. "I need to go to bed."

Brios nods and takes me home. I walk into my apartment thinking I'll relax. I'm surrounded by all the stuff I own. And then in an instant, I realize I can't trust myself.

Did I buy these things because I really liked them, or was it an artificially induced hormone cascade making up my mind for me?

What made me want all this stuff? I never second-guess or even hesitate when shopping. Was I the ultimate consumer, a programmable one?

I sift through my belongings, desperately searching for something I feel I've lost.

Brios lets me do my own thing. He drops onto my couch, and his head bobs with near sleep.

The sky through the heavy blinds begins to pale, and I still haven't found what I set out to find.

I look at Brios. "Brios, come on." I pull him up and steer him to the bed.

"No, Raven." His voice is firm even as he wobbles with sleep. "I'm not having sex with you."

"That's my line," I protest. I keep him moving, pulling off his coat and his shirt. "I just. I just need to feel you near me. Can you hold me for a while?"

He's asleep the instant his head hits the pillow. I lie for a long time with his arms around me. Cages in my head rattle. In my heightened state of nerves, I poke at the locks. They're solid for now.

I wake with his arms still around me and my lips pressed to his neck. His dv is chiming in his coat pocket on the floor.

It rings a third time.

"It's Wolf," he says. He's instantly alert.

He reaches up, pushing his finger against his mastoid to answer the call.

"Go," he says. He's polite and doesn't subvocalize. "Got it. Clear." He drops his hand, cutting the line. He's moving before I start to sit.

It's like old times.

All we need is to be holed up in a burned-out school bus with the place reeking of blown open bowels and rotting forest. Rain and people shooting at us would've been the finishing touches. Instead, my apartment is a warzone on the home front. I've scattered everything I own across every surface.

I watch as Brios pulls on his shirt. He glances around at my life strewn over the floor, couch, and chairs.

"I never figured you for a pink panties kind of girl," he says.

I find a pair of said unmentionables and toss them at him, making a face as I do.

I move to the bathroom and tap the shower start. "So what did your old boss have to say? Let me guess. He thinks I'm a bitch."

The Water-Smart system begins my favorite preprogrammed cycle of cool mist, warm cascade, pause, and warm rinse.

Here is my rain. I ease into the tropically warm water and feel my body relax.

Brios steps into the doorway. If he watches me shower as we talk, I don't care. He's seen more of me than this over our time together.

Brios crosses his arms and leans against the doorframe. He shrugs. "Wolf's just wondering if you're calm enough to talk, that's all."

"That's crap, Brios. I don't need some Spaniard flashing his money around and pressuring me into some kind of relationship, working or otherwise. I don't owe him anything." I let my mouth fill with water and spit it into the drain. "Least of all a cut on our job."

Not that that mattered now....

Crap.

"See, Raven, I don't think he thinks like that. He's got enough cash for anything he wants. He pays for everyone. He's done that ever since I met him. Sure, sometimes he expects to be paid back. He's in business just like us. But if he wants payback, he'll tell you. And as for our job, we're going to need him if we have to get answers from PharmaComp."

I'm avoiding the PharmaComp in the room.

I know I've switched the target of my anger: I'm furious with PharmaComp, making it about Wolf, and taking it out on Brios. But knowing all of that, I know I'm more afraid of the shit going on inside my head than of anything else.

"Nice habit to have, if you have the money," I snap as I step out of the shower.

I force Brios, out of politeness, to step aside. I walk past him, naked and dripping wet, and hunt for a towel in the living room. Screw him, screw Wolf, screw PharmaComp; this is my apartment.

I watch Brios out of the corner of my eye as I towel off. He looks like a mistreated puppy, wary, anxious, and conciliatory for nothing he's done. A wave of guilt washes over me, and I don't feel as clean as I did a second ago.

"Okay. Damn it. Let's say Wolf likes to spray his money everywhere."

Brios shrugs. "He does. It's a thing with him."

"So my next question is this." I wrap the towel around my hair and scoop up a pair of panties. I make sure they aren't pink. "We have the intel from Vlasta and we got way more than we would've using Wolf's contacts." I grab a new pair of jeans from the middle of a pile of clothes. "What do we need him for?"

"PharmaComp is huge. Private army huge. Maybe some good backup on the outside, sitting overwatch, isn't a bad thing?" Brios moves into the kitchen and tries to get Otto to start coffee.

"I'm out of coffee," I say as I finish dressing. "The real stuff wasn't available to ship, and I can't drink the synth stuff."

He nods and tops up the water for my flowers.

I throw him a bone by saying, "And no, having someone sitting overwatch isn't a bad thing."

"So what's the problem?" he asks. He flashes me his best pretty-boy smile.

"Damn him, Brios. He's just so cocky. That kind of shit

makes me crazy." I slip my Double-Double out of its rig and check the loadout.

"Still need him. Crazy making or not."

I'm grateful Brios doesn't just point out that my brain's been hijacked and we need Wolf to get my problem solved.

Brios checks me out.

I can feel him looking, so I turn for him.

"You look good," he says. "Let's go."

~ ~ ~

I've never been to the VR Museum. Over the payment counter, all I can see is a big, empty, sunlit room.

"I got this," Brios says.

I wander around looking at the massive holo-ads for a lunar surface tour. In the background of other conversations, I can hear the woman at the counter asking Brios if we needed headsets or plug-ins. He takes the plugs-ins and pays.

A VR guide appears as a hologram and tells us to wire in or put on headsets. We stay close together in the morning crowd of tourists and jack into the museum's program.

The automated tour starts. After a brief title shot and floating roll in, the full immersion VR kicks in.

We're standing on a dusty Mediterranean hillside.

The tour guide materializes in front of us and leads us forward. As a group, we walk along the outside wall of the ancient Acropolis in Athens.

The VR guide starts her show. "The real Acropolis in Athens was destroyed by anti-corporate rebels a decade ago and is currently being rebuilt by the tourism ministry of the European Corporate Board."

Wolf shows up on time.

My vision fragments and re-forms. My internal com-link clicks on. Suddenly, we're standing in the sunshine on a power-yacht traveling across pale blue water.

A half a dozen models lounge on the bowsprit chatting and laughing. Wolf is in their midst wearing a crisp white linen shirt and canvas shorts.

In this reality I'm dressed in a bright pink halter-top bikini with a plunging neckline. Brios is staring. I glare at him and register the fact that he's wearing a wife-beater with Hawaiian-print swim trunks.

His shoulders look enticingly broad in the sleeveless undershirt. I set my eyes front.

Wolf disengages from the group of beautiful women and approaches us.

"Did you pick this?" I ask him as I wave at my level of undress. I look at Brios again. "I told you. I told you he's an arrogant dick."

"You aren't the only ones visiting me by VR." Wolf shrugs and motions toward the narrow bands of fabric. "It was either that, or we meet later today on a topless beach."

In my mind, my powered-off palmscreen is trying to send me deals on this season's latest colors and styles. The fact that it can't makes me even more moody.

I snarl, "Pink?"

"It complements your skin tone."

I can tell Brios agrees, but that's beyond the point.

Wolf walks by me. "We can talk privately on the stern." As he passes close to Brios, he says, "I thought you said she was calm enough to talk."

I'm not going to let him get to me. I'm determined to engage first, fast, and fatally. I hit him with my opener as he's turning around. "Look, I'm not going to apologize for a damned thing. I don't care if you spent a pile of money on me for the AlphaTek thing. Brios says you're the best guy he knows to keep overwatch while we chase the intel we need. If I didn't give a shit about Brios, I wouldn't be here."

Wolf's casual blank expression has me clenching my fists. He comments to Brios, "I think your definition of calm needs work."

Wolf leans against the railing. A wide frothy wash fans out behind the boat. Wind ruffles his hair and tugs at his crisp white shirt. The VR is really good. I can almost feel the wind he feels.

"Calm enough." Brios shrugs. "Either way, this conversation needs to happen. The intel we recovered uncapped a whole lotta bad. At a minimum, it'll screw up things for everyone in the city. The people running the show are bigger than we can handle on our own."

I glower, but I can see Brios' attack plan, and it's a good one. Wolf will give a crap if the picture is too big to ignore.

Wolf nods. "I suspected something was going on when PharmaComp muscled in so hard in the Ganglands. I took my own initiative and asked around to see what I could dig up on the situation."

He's doing shit on his initiative for my gig … again. I want to reach out and end him. I remind myself I'm in VR. I'm physically powerless to act. The bastard probably chose this meeting location exactly for that reason.

My pleasure-tap registers my desire and my inaction. It kicks in hard. It doesn't matter that my body is somewhere else; I can't escape it.

And I'm in a skimpy swimsuit feeling what I'm feeling….

The VR program is good enough to translate my body's responses into visual. I know I'm blushing because Brios glances at me and whispers a warning. "Sweetie."

I draw in a deep breath and keep my eyes on Wolf. The fact that the bastard doesn't even notice makes it worse.

Brios takes over for me as I squirm. "What'd you find out?"

"Not a lot." Wolf sounds disappointed.

In a way, that makes me happy. I let that feeling work on me to relieve some of my frustration.

"PharmaComp is buttoned down tight. They employ a couple of full-time mercenary units and are covertly connected to a company called Living Memories Inc., which I do know is wrapped up in some questionable corporate practices." He turns to me and crosses his arms. His tone stays flat. "One thing is clear, going against PharmaComp is not a job you two can do on your own. Which is why I called. You're going to need my help. The only thing is, I'm getting the sense that you don't like it when I offer, so if you want my help, you'll have to ask for it instead."

He knows he's holding all the cards, and he's rubbing my face in it. My pleasure-tap trickles in more juice. Wolf and I glare at each other. The models on the bow shriek with laughter, and I resist the urge to turn and look.

Brios drops his shoulders with a quiet sigh. He's sure I'm going to walk, and I sure as shit want to.

But Brios put himself out there with his colonel … THE colonel.

I make myself say the words. "I need your help."

Wolf narrows his eyes. Maybe he's figured out this is as far as I'll move.

"So here's the gig…." I explain the nanobots, the neurochemical switches, their uses and possible consequences. I end with, "PharmaComp managed to get one of their chemical switches into my head. My source—"

"The Witch?" Wolf comments dryly. "Sorry. Your source … she can't help you?"

I bite my tongue. His sorry is just enough for me to make the effort to play nice. "She says she'll turn my brain into Swiss cheese if she tries to fix me. She needs more information. Specifically, how they remove the implant."

"And now you want my help?" He watches me, unmoving and unmoved, goading me.

I hate him.

Brios draws himself up. "Respectfully, sir, you're pushing buttons here that shouldn't even be touched."

Wolf's eyebrow twitches.

Apparently Brios is breaking new ground in their relationship … because of me….

Damn. Now he's really gonna think we're dating.

I keep my anger in check, barely. I breathe through my nose and watch the rolling eddies of white water.

The pleasure-tap slowly eases off.

I realize that even though I hate the outfit Wolf picked, he had to have picked it to satisfy something. I turn a little and let the VR wind do its thing to my hair. I know I look good. Screw him.

When his eyes flick off me, I don't hide my smile.

Wolf clears his throat and turns to stare at the ocean. "As it happens, PharmaComp's head of research and development is making an appearance in New White Sands tonight."

"Perfect. If we kidnap him, Vlasta can pick his brain."

Given my circumstances, I'm all in. I have to be.

Wolf's lips tug into a sexy frown. I hate that he can turn my game back on me.

"We need to scope him out first and get some intel."

"What'd you have in mind?" Brios asks.

"I hear he likes dance clubs and dangerous women." Wolf chuckles. He glances at me. "Sounds like a match."

1.12

Chem-Cocktail Love

We spend the rest of our time in VR planning, nailing down contingencies, and setting communication protocols.

I reluctantly admit to myself that I'm impressed. We get to the end of the conversation and I've managed to contain most of my impulses. Brios looks a little harried by juggling our conflicting personalities, but I can see he's good with the plan we've put together.

As casually as we met, Wolf dissolves and the VR world flashes back to the dusty Mediterranean hillside.

Our tour guide cuts in. "… and that concludes our walking tour of the Acropolis in Athens. Come back next week. We'll be raising money for the old Kremlin in Moscow. As some of you may know, it burned down forty years ago. Half the price of your ticket will go to pay for the land purchase."

We log out before she finishes her pitch.

On the street Brios asks, "So what do you think?"

"Me? I think he's arrogant and a bastard." I meet his eyes. "But he can afford to be. He's got the money and the contacts, and he knows his shit."

We walk through the late morning sun along the Southern Lip to the viewpoint at Vista Park. At the railing we have a great view of the Tidal Power Wall and the desalination plant beyond it.

Brios and I find a spot on a park bench that doesn't charge by the minute rates.

I stare nervously at my palmscreen.

"You ready?" Brios asks.

"No, but this is where we need to go next." I take a deep breath. "Or we stop caring about PharmaComp's evil plan for world domination and retire to a Fijian island."

He looks down at his hands and then up at me. "So, this Robin Hood guy … he ever have problems like this?"

"Nope." I smile. Sometimes Brios isn't as dense as I think. "Different times. He has a run-in with a wicked prince. The prince pays to have the king locked up. Then the prince declares himself King. Robin dodges some firefights until he gets stupid and cocky. He gets trapped and locked up by the prince's cronies. Hood's gang, and the mob of locals who like him, break him out of security. Together they rob the prince to pay a bribe that gets the real king out of holding. Last of all, he marries a young woman raised by the real king. So basically, he's a slave to one duty or another his whole life and gets shit on all the time."

"That's all huh?"

I nod. "Yeah, the Raven's Notes, harshly abridged version."

"You think Shadow knew what he was doing?"

Brios stretches out his legs. Some women jogging by give him the once-over as they make their way past us.

He doesn't notice them ogling.

It's classic Brios.

"I don't know." I shake my head. "Maybe someone put him up to it, or he was freelancing, or he was bankrolled for the job." I watch the tiny white line of breakers roll over the seawall far below us, each wave adding power into the grid. "The only thing I know for sure is that he was an idiot for drawing down on me. Anyone else, maybe, but me, he didn't stand a chance."

We sit a moment longer, listening to the rumble of a Low Earth Orbital transport ascending over the Gulf.

His eyes meet mine. I look away and push the power button for my palmscreen.

Welcome Back Shopper! The words scream in curvy pink letters. *As an exclusive VIP member in the most elite shopping network in NEW WHITE SANDS we have special time-sensitive deals for your consideration.*

I feel a blossom of pure joy as secret algorithms riffle my customer profile and pump it through a customer retention subroutine. My palmscreen begins to ply me with great personalized deals. All of them are within easy walking distance of the free bench.

"How's it feel?" Brios asks.

"Oh God, it's so good. So good to be back in the loop." A giddy happiness pours through my psyche.

The palmscreen assesses my available credit and shows me how much I can spend today.

"There's a shoe sale half a block away from here. They have Milanos. They arrived today. Direct from the factory in Italy." I start to stand.

"We're working," Brios says. He puts his hand on my arm. "Have a seat."

The deals keep getting better as I sit for a few minutes. The GPS built into the hardware registers my lack of movement. That detail is loaded into the algorithm. The program desperately tries to find something I'll respond to.

Finally, after six minutes of blissful hellish torment, the item we need comes up. Tonight's VIP Nightlife Pass.

I look at Brios. I must look insane. I can feel my eyes bulging as I pant and squirm on the bench.

He sees the tickets onscreen. "Buy two."

It's better than sex when my finger pushes the purchase tab on the display.

PURCHASE CONFIRMED.

I jump up and caper around the bench like a wild thing, shrieking with delirious joy. More joggers slow and make a wide path around us.

I bend over, grab my calves, and breathe, trying to slow myself down.

Brios does the one thing he knows will crack my insane happiness. Standing up, he slides one hand over my ass and gives it a firm slap. "Nice ride, how much?"

Vlasta's implanted password hammers a reality spike into the software.

I slump, suddenly cast adrift. The palmscreen is still on, but all the euphoria oozing from its function is gone. Just another data stream in a world of streaming data.

I drop onto the bench, pull up my knees, and cry.

I don't know how long I sit there.

Brios goes over to the towering Hammerglass barriers that keep people from killing themselves or anyone below them. He stands there motionless, staring out at the Gulf, until I unfold my legs and turn my palmscreen off.

He glances over his shoulder and makes his way back to me.

"Thanks," I whisper.

"Anytime," he replies in a similar tone. "Well that sucked." He sits beside me.

"Yeah." I mope.

"There is an upside." He leans back and stretches out once more, lips pulling into a smirk. "Since I'm going out with you tonight, I'll need a new outfit."

"Oh, you bastard." I jerk myself upright. "You're a prick. You know that?"

"Yeah," he replies; his tone is all mock hang-dog. He makes his I-know-I'm-stupid-but-love-me-anyway look.

He keeps it up until I laugh.

~~~

It feels good to be spending his money.

By sunset we have a mix and match of two different outfits. Both make Brios look good. We retire to my place, work out
~~~

backstories, and pack and repack until we have the barest minimum of equipment to do a breeze by on our mark. Then we wait together in silence, sitting on the couch watching the mega towers as they light up the city's nightscape.

The VIP passes kick in.

We dress, then head over to a local bar. We switch into our roles as we walk. I watch to see if the locals are keeping an eye on us. It's the details of our backstory in case anyone asks around.

An hour later, two somewhat drunk and incredibly hands-on lovers tumble onto the street.

Memories spin forward from the not-so-distant past of the times we took out our release on one another across South Am.

We thrived inside that pressure cooker, counting on one another. Keeping each other alive. Over it all, every day a rage focused inside us. Rage against the circumstance we were in. Rage against what we were forced to stoop to.

Always afterward came a hollow sadness coupled with a crazy need to fling ourselves into even more danger.

We lived and breathed the ragged edge. Having to live it was why we fucked in the first place. Why we haven't since we got back. Why I pushed those memories down, and why I never had them chem-blocked.

They're too much a part of me.

I've done a good job forgetting how good a kisser he is and how he can move against me in a way that doesn't feel like movement at all but fires me up on all cylinders.

We grope our way to the corner and fall into a Googlecab. Brios has his hand halfway down my pants. As soon as we're moving, we look around the vehicle's interior. Wolf is as good as his word. Brios pulls a couple of flexible ribbons from under the bench seat. A low tech file drop.

"The pink one must be yours." He hands me the data-ribbon and grins. "Your favorite color."

I stick my tongue out at him and slide the contact edge into my wrist port.

Now our mark has a description, a corporate position, likes, dislikes, a bio, and choice bits of business news that will entice him to want more.

As the cab takes us deeper into the Corporate Core, I watch Brios, eyes slitted, head tipped back as he takes in the data. After our grope session on our way to the cab, I wonder if I'd been right to stop our relationship cold after we got back in-country.

He catches me looking, and I flick my gaze out the side window, letting facts fight feelings in my brain.

The first clubs on the VIP Nightlife Passes are a good time but not the kind of place our mark would go to. We just need to be seen in the food chain. So we are.

Brios and I dance with anyone who asks. He isn't bad and picks up a few new tricks as the night goes on. We drink a lot and build a rolling tab to carry from one party to the next. In the cabs between hotspots, we pop Killjoy pills and drink bottles of water to sober up for the next round. We act drunk, more than we are. We flash rolls of Wolf's money. We grope and make out in corner booths.

Everyone who's important knows me by reputation: a tour guide who's also a good-time girl and a killer. I let slip to the right people that Brios is a rich Texan looking to invest in the next 'sure thing.' It works because as he drinks his accent comes out, and he sounds hot.

People from the Grand Republic of Free Texas are typically hard to meet in New White Sands. There aren't a lot of them walking around on the loose. Texans are the stock bad-guys on late-night streaming shows. Between drinks, dancing, and girls stupid enough to try cutting in on my gig, corporate players drift out of the shadows to sit with him, make introductions, and prod gentle inquiries about what he's really looking for.

Brios brings his A game, which is good because we need it. He spends money 'looking for information' and verbally dances around enough that at the next place we go to we find that someone vouches for us before we even get to the door.

No further need for the passes or even lineups. It's expensive, and it's awesome.

We hit five clubs in eight hours and the last place on the ticket is a new private club called Black Stables. Two floors, one primary and four secondary dance floors, three balconies, five full-sized bars, and three automated shooter bars. The central section of the ceiling is retractable and tonight it's open to the sky from a hundred floors up.

I love it.

We find our way to a huge seating area clustered around a grouping of faux fireplaces. Brios sits, and I drop astride his hips facing him and playing with his hair.

He reaches up and strokes the hair off my temple. His index finger presses on my mastoid.

It's always weird having him talk to me through his fingertip, but, for an oddball piece of equipment, it has its uses.

"He just got here. He's three seats to your left facing us in the next row. The guy who vouched for us is with him."

I grind down a little harder on Brios' lap and then get up. "Why don't you want to dance? Are you done? So soon?"

"No darl'n, I ain't." The Texan drawl coming out of his mouth makes me grin. "My momma always said I should save a bit for the home stretch. So unless you're planning on takin me to bed right now, I'm gonna sit this round out."

"Fine." I lean down low and kiss him. "Stay where I can find you."

I retire to a shooter bar to find someone to dance with. Brios has this. Whoever is providing our boy with security will notice me hanging around. Between the persona Brios is running and my reputation, we look like a tasty bite. Now to make sure our target doesn't know it's bait.

I mingle my way along the far wall of the club, keeping an eye on Brios. A flash of black leather catches my attention. I let my gaze flick to the motion.

Fire-eyes skirts behind a partition wall and is moving with purpose.

AlphaTek. Why are they here?

I can't suppress my inner carnivore. I make my way over to where I saw him disappear.

Who wears a black trench to a club like this? This guy does. I look around; no one else shares his fashion choice.

I casually poke-check the corner and see him talking to someone in a private seating area.

The part of the table I can see is packed. I pick out a couple of models, a top flight lawyer, and more than one big shot CEO. Fire-eyes just walks in and sits down like he belongs there. I can't get a bead on who else is in the booth.

Fire-eyes turns his head my way.

I duck out of sight and make my way over to a hostess.

"Who're all the elites in the corner?" I ask.

"The owner of AlphaTek is sponsoring a private party." She shrugs. "And no, I don't know which one he is. Can I get you a drink?"

"No. I was just curious." I pout. "The guy I was dancing with vanished back there."

"Plenty of others around." She smiles.

"Yeah, it's a good thing too." I make a show of admiring the men around us. "This place has great music."

I make my way back to Brios. Our mark has just left him. I track his bodyguards by the fact that they're the only ones not moving to the beat. I file their faces away on removable mem-chip.

Brios is chatting with another business type. I decide to swing wide around him and see who jumps.

I stumble up the short staircase and beeline into our target's personal space. I dial my optics to maximum field width, and I spot three more partygoers who flinch on my approach.

I turn to our mark. Late thirties, early forties, tall, cute, short corporate-cropped sandy brown hair, blue eyes, and a wicked sense of style. A pretty good overall package with one big problem. Something deep in one of my chemical cages claws at the bars trying to get out.

"He's busy." I motion to Brios. "You wanna dance?" I say over the beat, trying to play it cool.

"Sure." He smiles. There's a hint of a British accent buried in his voice.

We dance. He's good at it. I almost wish it wasn't him. I hate losing dance partners who look good and can keep up.

Brios walks by and extends a hand. "I'm done with talk'n."

"I gotta go. It's been nice."

Our mark nods his farewell and Brios and I bolt.

We swap transportation partway and then walk a dogged path to a hotel. Only after we're in the room, showered, sober, stimmed, and our clothes locked on the balcony, do we speak about the job.

"So what's your take on things?" I ask.

The back of my brain is still firing off unsettled feelings I can't place. Bars of cages rattling.

"I think he knows a lot about the PharmaComp plan." Brios drapes himself across the bed. "He has more money than brains, and his security isn't local."

"I got their faces on a file."

I pop the micro mem-chip out from under my eyelid, pulling it free with my fingernail. I hand it to Brios.

"That'll take a few minutes." He slides it into a military-grade handheld computer. "He seems like a nice guy."

"What the hell is that crap?" I'm surprised. "A nice guy?"

"Yeah. Well, if I actually were my cover," he drawls sleepily, "I'd probably like him.... He says he's looking for investors to buy into a plan. He didn't mention nanobots directly but told me PharmaComp has developed a way to convert and retain clients."

"Nanites that build chemical cascades in your brain so you feel love whenever you spend money on specific products? Yeah, that qualifies."

Brios pauses for a moment and scrubs his face. "I'm wired and tired. Too many stims. I'll see you in the morning. We can fill in the blanks after we rest up a bit."

“Sure.” I feel myself getting sleepy just watching him.

The handheld comp chirps.

“We have ourselves a winner,” I say as I reach for the handheld on the nightstand.

It chirps another six times as I eject the mem-chip and look at the screen.

“Our mark’s crew is a blend of Tokyo toughs and South African mercenary types. They’re subcontracted by a corporation called Bijou Security based out of Baton Rouge.”

Brios mumbles something I don’t catch. He’s asleep.

Bastard, I don’t even get to tell him about AlphaTek being at the party.

I scratch at my palmscreen as I lie down next to him.

Blocked memories and the not knowing what warning they might hold, it all builds to a sense of dread. I tamp it all away.

I put those blocks in for a reason.

They keep everyone around me safe.

~~~

I wake up before late checkout still feeling hollow. Brios has ordered breakfast from room service. The coffee is still hot when I get to it.

I eat while he soaks in the tub.

I catch myself thinking about how much fun I had fooling around with him last night.

Stripping to my basics, I make my way to the bathroom door. My hand hits the latch and the door abruptly opens.

“Hey.” I suddenly feel awkward.

“Hey.” Brios stands there already dressed. “Just finished. It’s all yours.”

He slips by me on his way to the balcony. He picks up an Electronic Countermeasure kit. “I’m going to scan our clothes for anything nasty. Don’t be too long unless you want to pay for another night.”
~~~

"Got it."

I watch him a moment and curse under my breath all the way through my shower.

1.13

Blast from the Past

We meet Wolf in Rafter country to discuss last night's recon.

Our guide takes us along the river. Wolf is sitting on a rock by the water, fishing rod in hand.

"Is that get-up for looks?" I ask as we climb down the bank.

"These?" He points at his vest and the battered old fishing rod.

"I meant the vest, but the gear is even more dated." I stand beside him, watching his technique. "Are there even any fish in there?"

"A few years back, a fish farm had one of their pens bust open in bad weather. So yeah, there's a purpose to this other than nostalgia." He meets my gaze.

I drop onto the rock next to him and take the fishing rod. I don't ask. "We got the info about the security team. And Brios spoke to our mark. Sounds like he knows a lot about PharmaComp's plans."

The line twitches. I wait.

"So what do you want as next steps?" Wolf asks me.

Patronizing bastard.

"I think he's a rotten tooth."

The float bobs deep. I jerk the rod, setting the hook. I start playing the fish in. I've done this before. Let him wonder where I learned.

"You want to extract him?" Wolf asks. He watches me bring in dinner.

"Unless you have a better idea, yeah we extract him."

I see silver white flicking back and forth under the water. He may be bigger than the line can hold.

"We can hit him hard and fast while he's in transit from his office to his flat on Power Island Four. His security doesn't look good enough to stop us."

I let a bit of line out and take in even more.

I grin. "At least they aren't AlphaTek." I watch Wolf out of the corner of my eye as I sidle into my sore topic.

He doesn't react and doesn't remind me what I owe.

The fish fights his way up and skitters along the surface.

"So you'll need route maps," Wolf says, "a line on what he drives, when he drives, who's likely to be in the car, lead and tailing vehicles, deuce, and satellite coverage. What else?"

I laugh. "Deuce? I haven't heard air support called that in a long time. You're so old."

I watch him twitch.

There's a nerve. I file it away.

I find myself thinking about the cages in my head. I'm missing something.

I wrangle the fish closer to shore. "Brios," I don't say anything else; he has the net ready.

Wolf watches us tag team the fish.

"After you grab him, then what?" he asks.

"The Witch brain hacks him for us free of charge," I say. The fish comes out of the water, and Brios scoops the net under its flashing body. "It's just a matter of getting him to her. Or vice versa."

Wolf looks at Brios. "You have anything you want to add?"

My partner hands his old boss the net. "Here's your fish."

I stand.

"You have a lot more contacts than Brios and I do, old man," I say as I pat Wolf on the shoulder. "Let me know when you get your end of this sorted, and then we'll take him."

I sense a rising storm behind me as I follow Brios up the hill. I can't help but grin.

~~~

After we get back into the city, Brios drops me off at my building.

"I'm rolling back to my place to change and re-up my ammo," he says. "I'll call you."

"Sure." I watch him pull away.

Should I feel weird about not even hugging him?

I remind myself we're not dating.

The maglift whisks me to my floor. My palmscreen itches. I steal a glance at it. It's still off, and I resolve to keep it that way as long as I can. I sweat just thinking about how long that could be.

The doors slide open. I freeze and reach for my Italian Double-Double.

The telltale I bribed the janitor to wire into the light above my door is working. The bulb cycles output high low high. You can't notice it without good optics. It's another reason I spent as much as I did on my eyes.

I slip the Double-Double out if its holster and suck to the wall.

I try the latch. It's unlocked.

Red flag.

On a five count, I shove my way in.

I move through the living room, check the balcony, and poke-check the kitchen. My bedroom is next. Last up is the bathroom.

I slam open the door and lead with my gun.

"Goddamn it, woman. Whoa. Hold up, I'm not armed." The Aussie lifts his hands, exposing his soap covered self.

"What the hell are you doing in my flat?" I yell. The Mobi-Med driver is sitting in my tiny bathtub. His lanky frame fills
~~~

the small soaker. He's got a bottle of my favorite scotch, a cowboy hat, and a grin.

"You're drinking my good scotch, asshole," I yell.

"I was more of an asshole to you when we were screwing," the hunk in the tub shoots back. "You liked everything we did fair enough then."

I glare at him. "You know what? You *are* an asshole. In fact, you're last week's asshole." I holster my gun. "You're last week's asshole *and* you're too stupid to understand that when I say it's over, I mean it."

"Come on now, you don't have to do me that way. We can still have some fun." He pushes his hat back. He motions for me to join him.

"You're not staying," I snap. "And we're not screwing. Not now, not ever again."

"Well not with a welcome like that." The Aussie has the balls to look offended. It pisses me off even more.

"A welcome?" I haul my gun back out and shove it in his face. "You broke into my place. I should kill you and ditch the body. You know me well enough to know I can do that, right?"

He stands. "Hand me a towel, and I'll leave."

I throw the towel at him. "Dry off, get dressed, and get out. If you come back here, I will kill you. You have three minutes."

I ignore him and head onto my balcony. Sure, it's got high glass sides, but it lets in a fresh breeze. I stare at the towers in the Corporate Core. Air cars flash and sparkle in the sunlight against the panoply backdrop of neo-architecture.

I feel the Aussie shuffling around behind me. I check the time. "Time's up," I say.

I turn around.

"Crap."

It's all I manage.

Mobi-boy's in the balcony doorway, heavy stun gun in hand. It's a new model. The leads are fire and forget. They'll lock on automatically and chase their target.

In this case, the target's me.

I dodge as fast as my boost system allows, but the balcony is too narrow to do me any good.

The tips nail me high on the inside of my thigh. It must be on the stop-a-truck setting. The contacts arc a couple of times around my groin.

As I fall into the dark, I curse in my head about the fact that I didn't let myself kill him.

~ ~ ~

"You were out a long time," a smooth voice says from somewhere above my head. "How are you feeling?"

I'm totally strapped down. Head, torso, arms, and legs. I'm going nowhere fast.

At least I'm on a comfortable bed. Except for the fact that my clothes are gone, and I'm wearing what feels like a medical gown. I bet myself a hundred hardfold that it's a crappy powder blue color.

I open my eyes and look around. All I see is a glossy clean medical facility. No nasty concrete walls, graffiti, or bare light bulbs.

At least the gown is the right color.

I win.

Brios and I tried to make a contingency plan in case something like this ever happened. But that plan was built for very different parameters than what I see around me.

That's how I know the trouble I'm in is bigger than Brios and I expected.

The guy speaking to me leans over my head. "I know you remember me, Sweetie," our mark says. His smile is all charm. "You know everything about me. Or at least, everything I put out in the world for people to learn. But you also know the truth."

We were made, probably from even before we got near him at the Black Stables club.

"Well...." I flex against the straps. My muscle augmentations aren't enough to break free in one go. "What I *do* know is that you're in a lot of trouble young man."

"I always loved your sense of humor, Raven." He strokes my cheek with one finger. "I've missed it."

I freeze.

"Oops," he whispers in my ear. "That was far too personal far too quick. Forgive me."

I swallow hard. "Who the hell are you?"

"You honestly don't remember me?" He's cute enough that, if I met him before, we might have fooled around. He danced well enough I would've gone out with him.

I scour my memory. Either I've never met this butt-clown, or I have and then I chem-blocked him out of my past. I shake my head. "Nope, sorry. I met you for the first time last night."

He seems taken aback for a heartbeat. "Hmm." He looks over at a medical display. I can see one corner of it above my head. I'm not a doctor so nothing I see has context. "I believe you honestly think that. I'm going to spend a few hours setting everything straight for you."

He vanishes from my line of sight and pops back above my head a moment later.

"My friend, he's a pharmacist, he tells me this will help." He holds a multi-barreled syringe where I can see it.

One of the five cylinders is filled with a swirling silver liquid that looks alive.

Nanites.

I have an idea of what the contents will do to me.

"Phillip." I try to stall. "Your name is Phillip Townsend."

He's found the one thing I'm afraid of ... my past.

"That's not really even a lucky guess." He grins. "Because my real name is Phillip. To keep it simple I use my own name to get around. So, no points there I'm afraid, love."

He lowers the tip of the syringe to my neck. "Those nasty men in South America did this to you. And I'm here to get you back."

I feel the tip bite into my skin. No amount of thrashing can stall the flow of my blood. My medical monitor has been hot-wired, and I can't slow the process down.

The tiny mechanical bugs float around, finding every chemical cage I've installed since South Am. One by one, the cage doors are thrown wide. Every chemically blocked memory creeps back into the light.

At some point during the rounds of injections, Phillip knocks me out. My consciousness slips away.

When I come to, my throat is hoarse from screaming. My temples are damp with tears. All of the restraints have been tightened. The flesh under them is chafed. All the lights are set on low. The room has the tainted stench of vomit, urine, and sanitizer.

My head throbs.

I hear a door open.

"They made a right mess of you, Raven."

"I was fine." I can't hold back my sob. "You screwed up. You opened all of them."

He comes blearily into my vision. "Do you remember this?" He holds up a still frame.

I'm sitting on a bench holding an umbrella and a pink carnation. Trafalgar Square is in the background. I'm so young in the picture. Phillip is in the photo with his arms around me. I'm making a silly face.

We were contracted by our respective companies for ten years of marriage right out of college. It was raining on and off all day, and we just signed the paperwork that morning. He loved me. I was simply obligated by contract.

Then we had a daughter. Adel.

For her, I loved him.

We were transferred to Colombia for Phillip's work. He worked for PharmaComp. The real Uprising was months away, the first of the trouble only just beginning to appear in newsfeeds. The random attacks occurring across all the major cities were focused on foreigners.

Cascading memories: sniper fire hitting our car, flames everywhere, Adel gone, burning, metal and cloth, concrete under me as I crawl away, smoking bodies, being found and beaten by a mob, men laughing over me as they punish my flesh further. A sense of surreal detachment as they, in turn, are killed: my revenge taken from me.

Revenge. Revenge was all I wished for. I wanted to become a machine whose purpose was to exact revenge.

Bright lights and piano music, Strauss, I think it was. I wanted Adel to learn to play piano.

More memories: waking up abandoned in an automated robotic medical bed in an underground facility; Brios carrying me out as the place burned; Brios feeding me, cleaning me, sheltering me in the jungle; Brios helping me re-learn to walk, to survive, to fight.

Our shock at how quickly I would heal. How easily I could kill. How much faster I was.

The decision to go back to the burned medical center. The realization that it was an illegal cybernetics lab. Someone brought me there and left me to live or die.

He's the only one who really knows how little there is left of me. I alone know that my wish was granted. I was reforged to kill.

Then the psychotic breaks along the way to the here and now. Points where the violence is so extreme that my memories show them with an eerie third person clarity.

Those memories are still hard to look at.

Needles at a forward operations base and more of the same in a US army field hospital. Days of cognitive therapy, all of it computer controlled VR. Then a sense of normalcy, of purpose, lifting out of the fog and finding an edge. The Edge: ragged, slippery, sharp....

I recall my last psychotic break. I hunted people through the TopSide Eccopark as they were leaving a fireworks show. I didn't just kill them. I butchered them, ready to eat. Brios caught me and dragged me to his place.

When I came out of it a week later, I had the wire tap to my pleasure center reversed so it would reward me for not killing people in my anger.

All of that floods into my head at the speed of thought. I feel myself throw up.

I drift.

"Do you remember?" Phillip leans into view. He's holding the photo. I want it to be fake. But my mind finds a way to twist it into reality each time he waves it under my gaze.

"I just want it all to stop." I close my eyes tight.

"I know, love. Only a bit more of this, and then I can help you even more." He leaves me alone again.

I flex my forearms and try an arm curl. I feel the restraints stretch. Soon.

It feels like forever, but my CPU tells me it's only been twenty minutes since he left. But how long is forever?

I try to sort out what's happening to me. Second by second, more memories flood back. The context for so many things clicks into place.

A thought flashes into my head. I remember the big open-geared clock in Vlasta's warehouse.

Clockwork: none of this is real.

Phillip smiles as he comes toward me. I feel my heart ache. He was, is, my husband. We had a life together, a daughter.

"Help me, Phillip." I need to be away from here. I desperately need time to grieve, to adjust to everything.

"We're almost done, love." He squeezes my hand. "Just a little bit more." He injects me with another hypo. I cry, pleading with him to stop. The cool rush of chemicals floods through me.

Rinse, repeat. The dark swallows me whole.

I open my eyes and my loving husband, whom I've missed for years, is holding my hands.

"It's all over now, Raven. Come with me."

I'm grateful for his strength. He found me. He's risked so much to get me back and help me make sense of it all. All of my dreams since we separated have been nightmares. Those are fading even as I come awake.

Phillip helps me stand, and I shakily move to a wheelchair he's placed at my bedside.

"I'm taking you to a recovery room where you can rest." He smiles at me.

I reach up and stroke his cheek.

"Then we can go home."

All I can do is nod. Tears stream down my face. My eyes scan across the room where I have been reborn.

A screen at the headboard reads:

Primary Memory Implantation: COMPLETE.

Secondary Re-imaging/Overlay: COMPLETE.

Primary/Secondary Memory Reinforcement: COMPLETE.

Stage Three Retrovirus Dissolution/Infection: COMPLETE.

Neurochemical Switch Upgrade Bundle 8.1: ONGOING – *Eighty Percent Complete.*

None of that matters. I may be in a hospital, but I have my Phillip. I know I'm home.

Everyone in the hallway watches as Phillip pushes us by. They all have wide generous smiles and adoration in their eyes. I understand their feelings completely.

Phillip is an unsung hero.

"How can you afford all this?" I ask in a lucid moment as we ride a maglift to a different floor.

Phillip smiles. "Everyone at PharmaComp loves me. I run the advanced research department. Everyone has seen how important my work is. Everyone from the CEO down to the janitors, they all love me and want me to be happy."

1.14

Not a Tango

I'm alone in a room with comfortable furnishings and dim lights. Pictures of Phillip and I line the walls. Little Adel is in some of them.

The image of a huge clock flashes into my mind. A clock with open brass gears. Where have I seen it before?

Clockwork. This isn't real.

What is reality? And where am I in it all? A voice in my head speaking from a distant nightmare reminds me: *Good times....*

Brios?

My arms and legs go numb. The call button on the table is so far away. My eyes go grey with static.

Someone is using my eyes. My fear is eaten by the understanding that there's nothing I can do.

I see a brilliant white wall with the same open geared clock. A woman who has the smoothest most flawless skin I've ever seen steps into the frame. She holds up a large hot pink cue-card.

I pause as my brain slows. I'm forced to read what's written on the piece of cardstock. *Nice ride, how much?*

I drift and feel like I shrink down and ride on my own shoulder. I cringe inside. This is what my psychotic breaks feel like.

Part of my brain struggles for a moment to get the crazy under control.

Reality. *This isn't real.*

I need to escape. My processor, monitoring me, prompts a question. *What's a dance in Paris without a little butter?*

"Not a Tango," I whisper. The programming on my pleasure-tap flips into reverse and increases the trickle of juice. A splash of rage washes into me, the pressure building.

My muscle augmentations burn with the need to move, to kill.

I get out of the chair and check the room. The door is locked. I find a stylus in a drawer and dismantle it. The skinny metal refill gets shoved into the hinges, out pop the hinge-pins. I pull the door quietly out of its frame and set it aside. The gown is a hindrance to movement, but I have nothing else to wear. I drop the gown. I poke-check the hallway and step out, naked.

There are only two people at the reception area for this floor. I am a cheetah. I'm too fast for them and close the distance on silent bare feet.

Neither of them reaches the alarm button. Neither of them have time to scream. A stiff-fingered blow to the throat peels out a larynx. My other hand loops over the second one's shoulder. I brace her back against my chest, grab her face on the opposite cheek, and yank. Her neck snaps. She jerks and drops.

I feel myself getting aroused as the pleasure-tap rewards me for a job well done.

The first one is lying at my feet struggling, holding her throat. I feel nothing as I pin her to the floor with one foot. As her thrashing slows, I scan the on-floor security cams and rip through desk drawers. I find what I'm looking for.

I grasp the scissors and twist them apart. She stops moving.

The maglift glides open. A security guard with a surprised expression stands there.

My augmentations amp into high.

His right hand moves in slow motion reaching for his gun. His left hand moves toward his emergency call button.

I throw both blades.

I excel at what my body was spec'd for. Wetwork, adding to the body count using anything that cuts, slashes, stabs, or thrusts. It's my calling, what I'm purpose-built to do.

One blade sinks in up to the rubberized handle. It's on target, just to one side of his nose in the eye socket. The other blade, also on target, goes through the wrist of the hand reaching for the alarm on his collar.

He drops.

I can feel how flushed my face is. Three kills in under half a minute.

I'm damp as I vault the counter to recover my weapons. I take the guard's gun, com-link, and ID lanyard badge. I drag his body into the door of the maglift, pause to cut the skin from his fingertip, and return to the counter.

A second search nets me a spray can of skinseal.

I glue the guard's fingerprint over mine. The smartgun links with the chip in the guard's ID. The print matches, the smartgun unlocks.

The maglift bounces its doors into the corpse. Jamming the lift means one less access point for them which lets me control how I'll trap them as they come for me.

I push the com-link into my ear.

Favoring speed over elegance, I grab a fire extinguisher and coat every cam lens I find with a hint of Christmas.

I know the rooms on this floor are all empty, which is okay by me. It saves me from the business of silencing witnesses and prevents a host of other problems.

The private guards, the lack of corporate logos, the cheap off-the-shelf communications system, it all points to rented space in a regular hospital.

I move to the window at the far end of the hall. It's night outside, and I'm too high up to risk a jump even if I could shoot out the window.

A program running somewhere in the background of my brain pipes up: Based on the distant city skyline, the lack of lighting on the ground, and my angle of view, I'm on the thirty-fifth floor of the Bastion Medical Facility.

That information only changes how much guilt I'll feel later when I remember all the damage I caused in my escape.

The com-link starts speaking voodoo. It's a civilian grade encryption program for verbal communications.

The plan is to contain me on this floor. The maglifts are locked down, and the staircases to the floor are sealed. More private guards will be here as soon as they cut the indication lights by the maglift doors. They want to surprise me.

A squad is coming up in a service lift from the provisions floor. As the com-link chatters, I study the fire escape plans by the lift.

The laundry, kitchens, utilities, shipping, and the security offices are located in one conveniently avoidable area.

I strip the less bloodied scrubs off one of the nurses and pull them on. The fabric is designed to provide light protection from cuts, stabs, and chemical sprays. It's full-sleeved. It's also nasty and scratchy along the seams and only comes in white. I file those facts away for an online article.

I yank the oxygen tank off a crash cart and head to the service lifts. I choose the one on the left and force my fingers between the metal door and the frame. It succumbs to my efforts, and I open it just enough to see into the shaft to identify the lift moving beneath me. They're in this car.

I set the oxygen down in front of the doorway and then push the door as far open as it'll go. As the maglift rises to my floor and slows, I step onto the roof of the car. At the last second, through the narrowing gap, I shoot the regulator off the oxygen tank.

The noise isn't quite the explosion I'm hoping for, but the gunshot and the tank sailing around is enough.

I hear panic in the voices inside the car below me. The com-link bursts into confusion.

They think I'm premature in my attack.

Their doors slide open.

I can hear them firing to suppress and yelling loudly as they all storm out of the lift. I open the service panel at my feet. Looking into the car, I see the access keys hanging from the button panel.

Sloppy when panicked.

I have a few seconds on the roof. I cut the wires to the announcement system and yank the security cam feed.

I drop silently into the empty car. I push the button for the second sub-basement and twist the key. The doors slide shut, and I'm dropping into a different circumstance.

Listening on the com-link, I go fifteen floors before someone notices the elevator is moving.

They argue protocols.

Keyed as the lift is, they can't stop its decent, and because Bastion is a public facility, they can't even cut the power.

I whistle a happy tune as I pull myself back onto the roof and push the panel back into place.

Thin strips of dim horizontal light mark the tops and bottoms of each passing doorway. I time my departure from the roof of the car.

The lip inside the sliding door's frame is really narrow. I will myself to hold on with naked toes and fingertips.

I'm one floor above the lobby.

Bastion Medical serves truckers, outlanders, tribals, and pretty much anyone outside of New White Sands who doesn't want to go into the city for treatment. I've heard it's rough country out here. The place will have security features I can bypass by avoiding the maglift completely. The sub-basement button push is a ruse.

There's panicked chatter coming out of the com-link in my ear. I hear Phillip's voice.

"Phillip?" I gasp for air. Adel.

Clockwork. This isn't real. I cling to the doorframe with a scream choked off in my throat.

"Fuck, fuck, fuck." That's not good, that's not good at all. There's no way to tell how much time I have before Vlasta's implanted subroutine gets counter-hacked, shut down, and sealed away by Phillip's software and nanites.

I wedge the door open with my fingers. I remind myself that everyone on the other side will be a civilian. I hope they don't get in my way. I reset my pleasure-tap. Letting them live might be a rush.

The unit nurse and two others stare at me as I emerge. They wait only for a second. That's long enough for me to get the gun up.

"Touch an alarm and I'll kill all of you." The scrubs I'm wearing cause hesitation. The gun and gory scissor blades don't hurt either. "I've been kidnapped and held on the thirty-fifth floor. PharmaComp Corporation." I move forward. "No heroic behavior, okay? I need an outside line."

"There aren't any outside lines working," the oldest looking one says. "And you'd be the reason security cut everything outbound."

Crap.

Wait. My brain clicks. Bastion Medical serves the public. That means public protocols.

My way out.

"You have a choice." There's no tonal expression in my voice. "You can help, or you can stay out of my way. If you do anything else, I'll kill you."

I cut communications to the desk.

They grumble. I arch an eyebrow and they fall silent. They watch me.

I roll a cart over to the security cam and step up. I twist the view to face down a different hallway.

Cutting it would black out a monitor and raise suspicion, but how many people at first glance could tell if the view changed instead?

The body language of the head nurse changes.

I snap, "Don't think it." The gun swings up.

Three rounds later, I'm cursing a software glitch over a puddle of my own bile and three unexpectedly dead people.

Something Phillip shoved into my software is messing with my regular programs.

I breathe hard and fight for control. I'm being a good girl. I'm not killing anyone.

The pleasure-tap reinforces my control.

Finding a thermometer, I pry out its battery pack and slam it once or twice in a drawer to crush the top. It flares with a chuff of thick black smoke and then hot licks of flame. The patients on this floor are already jabbing their panic buttons from the gunshots.

I wave the burning battery pack under three separate smoke detectors around the unit nurses' station.

Public protocols. The 'in case of emergency' buttons can be bypassed by the hospital security office, but the smoke detectors themselves have to be wired directly to the local fire station.

Power across the floor switches to backup. Claxons sound, and amplified evacuation instructions echo. Guide lights start blinking.

I need more smoke.

I pull an oxygen tank off a cart and hold the last of the flames to the valve as I crack it open.

Fire leaps the length of the work station. My foot rolls on the arm of one of the dead nurses. I wobble for balance as parts of the injection molded desk start burning.

My shadow spins me into a nightmare memory. Wild gleeful dancing around a fire, the ground clustered with the corpses I placed as an audience for my performance.

The nurse call button panel lights up solid.

The battery systems for some of the gear on the burning counter start popping, adding to the flames. It reminds me of fireworks.

The ceiling panels overhead catch fire. I knock them down and toss them under carts, curtains, and chairs.

The fire suppressors cut in. Time to go.

As per fire protocol, all of the electronically sealed doors in the building are required by law to unlock. I thank the due diligence of insurance inspectors as I, in accordance to fire regulations, take the stairs down two at a time.

The chaos in the lobby and triage area has regular security distracted. There's no sign of private guards. I shove the gun into my front pocket.

No one notices my bare feet.

As soon as I'm out in the night air, I make my way to the emergency entrance.

The bays are filled with vehicles transferring urgent care patients out of the building. I keep going until I find what I need. A medical examiners' rapid response gyro.

It's small, with two seats and a cadaver transport rack. Usually the rack-space carries pedestrian road-kill, a traffic accident victim, or a dumped body. I furtively do a walk around the back end. I'm grateful the rack is empty.

Using the butt of the gun, I bust out the craft's marker lights, working all the way around.

The passenger side window shatters inwards with a few repeated blows.

Hot-wiring it is a bitch; there's so many circuits jammed under the smooth dashboard.

I panic as people begin to move into the landing area. I keep my hands well away from the gun in my pocket and breathe deeply, pleasure-tap keeping me in a happier place.

Evacuation vehicles begin to touch down.

I rip out the GPS locator and find the board with the starter circuits on it. The electric fans power up at the touch of the dashboard button.

A security guard sees me moving around inside the craft and waves at me. He starts to move toward me.

I drop the driver's side window just enough to yell out, "I'm clearing it off the deck. You can land another VTOL in here. I've let maintenance know these lights are out of service."

He slows and nods his gratitude. He turns around and thankfully doesn't see that I have no running lights at all.

I roll the gyro forward a few feet, testing the controls as I go. I've never mastered the art of taking off or landing these things. My relief grows as I find the controls marked *computer assisted liftoff.*

I'm up and following the road out for a hundred or so yards before I bank toward the city. I try to keep below fifty feet and fly without lights.

"Raven." My heart jolts in my chest. His voice comes out of the vehicle com-system. *"Raven? Why are you running away, love? I don't understand."* Phillip.

I check the time. No clockwork to save me.

"I made you who you are, and I will find you," Phillip whispers. *"I will find you and bring you home."*

Static erupts from the speakers. *"Sweetie. Raven, it's Wolf. I have people on the way just—"*

I'm in third person, sitting on my own shoulder. The ground spirals up toward me, warning lights and alarms sounding.

All I can think as the bad happens is that I really must love the dark. I visit there so often. I go there now.

1.15

Fallout

I come out of the dark screaming. I can feel clamps holding my legs down.

All over my body, wires, like hot nails, jab into my skin. I sit up. Now I have room to swing.

Brios blocks my blow, shoves me down, and grapples my arms to my sides. “Raven, you’re safe. Raven, listen to me, relax. It’s okay. You’re okay.”

Brios. Brios from South Am. The place all my troubles started. The place I lost Phillip and Adel. Adel.

“Hold her.”

Vlasta?

“No, nonono.” I struggle against his grip, his weight. Like the men from the roadside....

Cool liquid vapes through my neck. I go meekly back to the dark.

~~~

The sound of my own groan wakes me. The panic and craziness pumping through my brain has cleared.

I groan again. The image of a clock?

Weird....
~~~

I can feel heat coming from my CPU, snuggled up against my spine and flattened along the inside curve of my pelvis. It has to be running hard to throw that much heat.

"How long?" I croak. My internal GPS draws a blank.

I check my palmscreen. The status light isn't even glowing. It must be disconnected.

I can feel knitting braces on my legs, and my back feels like it's in traction. Wires and probes cover me and vanish under my skin at points across my belly, neck, and head. I'm a hot-wired mess.

"Two weeks," Brios answers from his perch on a stool at my bedside. I open my eyes wider against the lights.

Crap.

"Processor and medical monitor upgrades are complete." A woman comments briskly from out of eye shot.

"Is that Vlasta?" I ask.

"Yeah." Brios leans over me in an attempt to block the overhead light from my eyes.

"How does your head feel?" Vlasta, my treacherous caretaker asks.

"Why," I say with a snort, "so you can stick me again if you don't like how I behave?"

"You were irrational." Vlasta's answer drifts as she moves around, checking the equipment hooked into me. "Trying to move with all of the diagnostic cables still in place and parts of you in traction could have damaged equipment, both yours and mine. It was prudent." She dims the overheads, and both Brios and I relax.

I look around. "Where are we?" It looks like every other medical facility I've ever been in.

The room is so bright and clean behind Phillip as I plead with him to not use the hypo again. I scrub my face trying to wipe the memory away.

"We are in AlphaPlaza," Vlasta says. She swipes new data onto my mediscreen.

Red flag.

"AlphaPlaza?" Surprise never mixes well with fear. I have a tendency to kill first and kill again later. I'm glad she's out of reach and that I'm feeling better.

I feel Brios shift beside me, ready for action.

"Pleasure-tap appears to be working well." She nods. "Da, Tower Number One specifically." She keeps working over a diagnostic unit.

"How did we end up here?"

"Guess who?" Brios says. He's watching me, waiting for something.

"Wolf?"

And then I get it. "This is AlphaPlaza. AlphaTek…."

The white VTOLs at my stash, the extraction from the Ganglands, Fire-eyes at the Black Stables club, all AlphaTek, all Wolf.

My world view shrinks and bounces back.

Motherfucker.

I've been played, played hard.

"We're almost done, love." Phillip squeezes my hand. "Just a little bit more."

I'm crying, pleading with him to stop. The cool rush of chemicals floods in.

Rinse and repeat.

Black.

Primary Memory Implantation: COMPLETE.

Secondary Re-imaging/Overlay: COMPLETE.

Primary/Secondary Memory Reinforcement: COMPLETE.

I clench my fists into the sheets. What's real and what's not? The hair at my temples is wet.

I swallow it all down. And then comes my anger, a burning need for revenge.

"So where does that leave me?" I'm not really sure I'm asking or just wondering out loud.

Brios is blunt. "You've been stripped of all GPS and have no ID or public records. Wolf figured you needed to be Zeroed for the duration."

"Wow, I always wanted to have every trace of my existence electronically erased," I say. I'm aiming for normal. My sarcasm comes off more dejected than I want. I try again. "Hey, that means I don't have bad credit anymore. Oh yeah, I don't have any credit at all. I'm an outcast now. Worse than a Null." I definitely miss.

"Yeah. Reminds me of somebody else." He shows me his dv. *The Adventures of Robin Hood* is the title shot on his reading program.

It catches me off guard, and I laugh. "Bored much?"

"Two weeks downtime." Brios shrugs.

"Now, time is up." Vlasta bustles into view. She makes a shooing motion. "Leave the specimen alone, she must rest. Visit later. I am working."

"You mean patient." Brios corrects her English.

"No," she snaps. "Some of what I am doing is so new that specimen is better term."

Nice. Little-ol-specimen-me.

I think/feel the rattle of cages in my head like a phantom pain. I'm not even sure if the cages are there anymore.

Should I feel relieved or terrified?

The jury gets up and leaves.

Brios pats me on the shoulder and turns to go.

I hear the whoosh of the door and then, "Sir." Vlasta and I look over as Brios acknowledges the colonel and passes him on his way out.

"You have important company," she says as Wolf steps into the room. She sighs. "I will leave now. We will continue your treatment later." It's like she's upset someone is interrupting an engrossing experiment.

"Thank you, Doctor," Wolf says. He holds the door for her. He's wearing a classic cut suit.

Damn, and no tie either. He looks great. Bastard.

I glare at him. Why doesn't Brios ever wear a suit?

As Vlasta leaves, she hands Wolf an emergency call button stylus. "You may have need," she says.

He saunters over to my bedside, spinning the stylus along the edge of his finger. He takes the seat Brios just left.

"You have questions for me?"

"Nope," I lie, screw him and his expensive suit.

"None?" His eyes harden with suspicion. "None at all?"

I look away, my anger slowly building. "I'm not talking to you."

"Okay. Sure." He makes himself comfortable.

His whole attitude has me on edge.

"Why are you still here?" I ask.

"Because you have questions. Eventually you'll want answers. I have time."

"Fuck you," I snap. I'm rewarded for not killing him. I take a shuddering breath.

He sets the call button down, picks up Vlasta's mediscreen, and starts reading over my medical status.

"That's confidential," I hiss.

He keeps reading. "No, it's not. Not when I pay the doctor and own the building with everything in it."

"You *own* AlphaTek?"

"Yes." His nod is distracted as he keeps reading. "Yes, in fact, I do. I took over AlphaTek when the military collapsed." He looks up with a shrug. "Running this corporation exercised a similar skill set. I play to my strengths. Makes for an easy win that way."

"You arrogant bastard."

I'm struggling to stay still, not tear anything loose, not tear out his throat.

My pleasure-tap is feeding me a steady line of juice.

"So what if I am?" Wolf says with a shrug. "In this room, the immediate benefactor of my being an arrogant bastard is you." He tosses the mediscreen onto the table. "Phillip made a mess of your brain, Raven. Unlocked memories you had tucked away, highlighted anything he thought was useful, implanted others and manipulated the rest."

I stare at him. He doesn't flinch or look away.

"The problem, as Vlasta explains it," he says with a grimace, "is that the brain is very elastic. She can't tell which memories are your baseline ones and which ones were tampered with." He stands, pinning me to the bed with his gaze. "No one outside of PharmaComp and its subsidiaries has access to the technology they used on you."

I squeeze my eyes closed, trying not to remember anything.

"She worked with what was there." His voice softens a bit. "With what was left that made any sense."

...with what was left....

I refuse to let any emotion show. I can't trust him. He might try to manipulate me with those emotions later.

"Eventually, we'll have the ability to fix it all." He sighs. "I've got people working on the problem."

"I'm supposed to be grateful? Happy about it?" I glare at him. "It would've been better if you had let me die."

"Why?" he asks, but he doesn't look surprised by my words.

"Because Wolf, or whatever your name is, I'm a killer. That's all I am. Anything before that is patchwork or gone completely, and I can't let myself care about it."

"I'm sorry," he says quietly.

"Fuck you and your sorry. I don't want your pity." My pleasure-tap pulses into me in wild erratic intervals.

"I don't pity you, Raven. I led men into hell, lived there with them, and brought as many of them home again as I could." His face becomes stern. "I understand you. Broken. Scarred in ways no one can see. I understand you, and you hate me for it. Fine. Hate me. But I have something you need more than anything."

I stare at the ceiling, not caring that he's watching me get off on hating him, on leaving him alive.

"And what the hell is that?" I ask.

"I can get you a shot at Phillip."

Motherfucker.

My pleasure-tap turns off.

~~~

The next few days are hell as my memories fight themselves into something other than brutal flashbacks. I can feel myself growing colder and more detached as I struggle to come to terms with things I remember doing. It's the memories of Phillip, Adel, and normal life that I'm not okay with.

The only interruption comes when Vlasta sends me into the dark to tinker with the contents of my skull.

I'm learning to hate the dark. The idea of a medically supervised, chemically induced coma pushes buttons I didn't know were there.

I come around again to more darkness. I know my eyes are taped closed. I can smell the strange floral perfume that is unique to Vlasta, and I can't help but find it comforting after all that's happened.

"Vlasta?"

"I am here." Her accented clipped tone makes her sound angry even when she isn't.

She doesn't mince around and dives right into it. "Your procedure went well enough."

I feel her next to my bedside. I keep still as she un-tapes my eyes. The room is almost blacked out.

She passes me a bottle with awful tasting liquid supplements in it. I wrinkle my nose, but I know better than to argue with her.

She glares at me until I drink the entire bottle. Only then does she continue. "It was long process, but, with help of Brios, it went faster than expected."

"Brios helped put my memories back together?" Crap. I double-check to make sure we're not dating.

She pats my hand. "He made suggestions based on your time together as to which events should be blocked. You should now feel your memory voids returned to you. What did you call them?"
~~~

"Cages?" I offer my word for what I imagine them to be like. Cages to hold back the monster I am.

"Yes, your cages, where the memories are locked away. There may be some that persist unblocked, it is impossible to know for sure without proper tools. These you will need to be wary of. They are traps instead of cages."

"Right."

"You should be thankful." She continues checking medical and cyber repair displays. "You are incredibly in debt for my services."

I stare at her, my heart sinking.

She laughs at my expression and then abruptly stops. "I laugh because it is true."

"Is it true?" I keep my voice firm. I wonder what'll happen to all of my side projects.

"Yes. But Wolf has paid for my services to you." She smiles. "So, you now owe him. Premium rates. He is turning into good customer. He has asked me to move my home here. He has yet to answer my question about building a suitable conservatory for my plants on the three hundred and fifth floor balcony."

I don't answer her. I owe Wolf everything. I have no way to pay him back.

Vlasta picks up on my thoughts. "At least you are alive, and mentally intact. That is, intact enough to resume your life without overt difficulties."

"I love that line, Vlasta," I say with a chuckle. "Without overt difficulties."

"But it is true." She frowns. "You will have less psychotic breaks, less dissociative incidents. Those are good things to celebrate, yes?"

"Yay, more me, less crazy me." I'm still broke, without any hope of moving the needle on my life in a direction I want.

She shakes her head. "Who said you were not crazy on your own to begin with. It is a relative thing with you, with everyone."

I hide my impending depression by asking, "So, when can I go?"

She opens a portable closet and shows me my clothes.

"Brios brought some of your things yesterday. He is waiting outside. Checkout time is when you are ready. No rush."

Vlasta looks at her wrist. She's wearing an old school smart-device. "The cookies I am baking in staff lounge will be done very soon."

She leaves me to dress, and I hear Brios speaking quietly to her on the other side of the door.

"Did you tell her?" he asks.

"It is not my decision to make," she replies. "You are her friend more than I. Wolf has found reasons for not explaining anything to her, and he is paying."

Silence from Brios. I stop moving so I can hear.

"Still," Vlasta says, "you are not beholden to him are you?"

"Why? Would you tell her?" Brios presses.

"Da. I would. Secrets are dangerous things."

"But what good does it do?" Brios asks. "How will her knowing change anything, except for the worse?"

"It is up to you. It is not my place."

I finish dressing. They fall silent as I open the door. I'm curious, but I also don't want to be ungrateful by nailing both of my friends right now. I know I can work on Brios over coffee.

It may take a few more days for the guilt to build enough to have him crack, but he can't hold out against me for long.

"You look good." He hands me my Double-Double. The grip fits perfectly in my palm.

"Hey, you picked the clothes," I reply.

Brios did well picking this outfit. In fact, I look great. The Jabbas cling, my top plunges just so, the jacket skims around my shoulders and hangs open above my hips.

I do a weapons check on my gun, popping both cylinders.

Good to go.

I stuff the barrel down my back. "I'm just the clotheshorse."

"Okay." He snorts. "Nice horse."

"You want my job?"

"Nope. I only consult for friends."

I make a face at him.

I turn to the White Witch. "Thank you, Vlasta, for everything." I give her a hug. She seems startled, hesitant, and then pleased. She actually hugs me back.

I'm munching on a fresh cookie when Brios and I head for the maglift. As a bonus, I have one more in my pocket. We step into a lift and watch the doors close.

The floor numbers scroll silently by, dropping us to a parking floor in TopSide.

"How you feel'n?" Brios finally asks.

I take a measure of my emotional state. "Like a sack of crap without the sack."

He smiles. "So, better than you thought you would and way better than I thought you would."

"Thanks." I realize I can't decide how I feel about flirting with him. Things have changed.

I try not to get emotional.

"No problem." He shrugs. Brios never misses a beat with me. I know he's playing it cool, not pressing me for anything.

"Where's the rendezvous point?" I ask after a moment. Wolf promised me Phillip. Finding him with AlphaTek's resources shouldn't take long.

Brios leans into the back wall with his shoulders. "You're not ready yet."

"I'm done lying in bed with wires in every hole, Brios."

Brios hands me a shitty antique cell phone.

"Really?" I turn it over looking for a power button.

Brios nods. "Push and hold the side one."

"Does anyone even use this technology anymore?"

Brios shrugs. "Wolf will call when he has the intel. Then, if he thinks you're ready, we go right into the gig." I know Brios is throwing me a bone.

The maglift doors open and close on a dozen different floors. We mingle with employees and their families.

Through the open doors at every stop I catch views of interior parks, shopping areas, and residential blocks complete with schools. AlphaPlaza is its own vertical city. No one ever has to leave.

A gilded cage.

Finally the lift opens on one of the staff motor pool floors. Brios' hulking B&V rumbles to life as we approach.

We pull out of AlphaPlaza One and into the streets of the Corporate Core. I tighten my hands around his waist as we accelerate between towers slashed with adverts thirty stories high and sidewalks crowded with people. He whips us along, dodging through the late morning traffic.

We skirt the Eccopark, speeding south across TopSide. The sun blazes across my face, fresh air pulls my hair back. I'm alive, and I'm okay with that. I let the moment fill me.

Brios slows as we near the Southern Lip Vista Park. "You're a clone," he says. No lead-up. Just the bomb.

I jerk away and almost fall off the bike. He shuts down the engine and coasts the B&V to a stop. I scramble off the back, breathing hard.

"What the hell?" I ask.

"You needed to know, Sweetie," he says quietly.

I stare at him. "Who am I, Brios? Because if I'm a clone, I've been running around since South Am on my own. There's no way those memories are implanted. You were there." I stand in the sunshine in stunned silence. "Where's my original?"

"Vlasta says she expects you were active before you got to Colombia." Brios keeps his eyes on me. The suicide barriers are too tall for me to clear. But that's not an answer either.

All I can do is move forward.

"I can't remember much of anything before Colombia, Brios. Everything in my head that far back is a mess. I don't know what to believe." I let tears run. "I hardly even remember the lab."

Memories from Phillip's manipulations flood me. At least I can tell now those memories are implanted lies.

They're still better than nothing.

"I'm right here, Raven." Brios is genuinely sympathetic. He gets off the bike to stand near me.

I squeeze his arm. "Thanks." I look around at the horizon. "I'm going to walk home from here."

He glances in the direction of my apartment. "It's a long way. You sure you're up for it?"

I nod. He doesn't stop me as I turn and head toward the string of shops and businesses lining Parkway Boulevard.

It's sundown by the time I arrive. My legs ache, my feet are sore, and I'm starving. I walk up to the main door of the building and into the foyer. I hesitate. I'm Zeroed…. Will the lock matrices even let me in?

I don't have a home if they don't.

I take a breath and put my hand in the scanner slot. The glowing rim of the lock opening stays red.

I try it again. No change.

I try some kinetic maintenance and pound on the lock. The outer door opens behind me. I know I look crazy. A building maintenance program will be contacting security.

I turn to go.

"That's shitty." The guy from AlphaTek who's been dogging my steps since the beginning is leaning against the doorframe.

Picasso. His eyes are a low bank of twinkling coals as he says, "Things got busy. He probably forgot."

"Or he's a manipulative Spanish bastard who's fucking me over for assaulting his miniscule fragment of masculinity," I growl at him.

His smile is sardonic. "Yeah, or that. Doesn't change shit though. You still need a place to sack. You got any money?"

"What the fuck do you think? Someone left a stack of hardfold in my pants?"

My immediate anger is spent. I sigh.

"I got a safe house not far from here." He cocks his head. "You can bunk there tonight, and we'll go see him tomorrow to get it settled."

"No. No, I don't want a bunk right now." I feel wild and unchecked. "I wanna dance, drink. Go out. Not be here."

"You wanna go clubbing?" He looks surprised, then wary.

"Yeah, and you're gonna take me," I snap.

"Am I?" He holds the door open for me. Cocky bastard. Maybe he's Wolf's cousin.

"If you know what's good for you, yeah." I stomp past him and out onto the street.

There's only one ride on the parking slip that could be his, and I walk to it. I let my hips go as I do. I know he's watching, following along. I've seen my ass walking like this. It works for me, so I know it works for him.

I climb onto the saddle of the custom Indian Retro.

He saunters over to me and leans down. "You don't want to go there with me, Sweetie."

"Don't get all emo on me, you prick." I meet his eyes; licks of flame are scrolling upwards. "I'm not fucking you. I just wanna go out. You can back charge your idiot boss in the morning."

He pauses, then nods. "As long as we're clear."

"Shut up," I snap. "Drive."

1.1b

Zeroed

In the morning I wake. I'm stiff, and my head roars as I roll onto my back. I'm naked. I'm in a bed.

I keep my eyes tightly closed.

Memories flash. Loud music, nasty dancing, round after endless round of shooters, stims, yelling over music, glimpses of a bathroom stall, making out, hands groping under clothes.

Crap.

I reach for the other side of the bed. I feel the warmth of a body without having to touch flesh. Crap.

I turn my head and force my eyes open into slits. I breathe a mental sigh of relief. The hair on the pillow next to me doesn't belong to Picasso or Brios.

I lean onto my elbow and peek over.

Crap.

It's the supermodel from Rafter country: Angel.

She rolls over and sleepily opens her eyes. I notice how blue they are. She smiles at me. "Good morning."

"Good morning." I feel awkward, but I school my reactions into calm.

"I had a great time last night." She doesn't move any closer. Maybe she's waiting to see what I'll do.

"Um. Thanks." I pause. "I'm sorry. I only have flashes for, well, for any of it."

"That's okay." She's carefully neutral as she speaks. "After all, you were partying pretty hard."

I hesitate.

"It's all good. Okay?" Angel grins. "You were adamant this wasn't anything you'd ever done before."

"And?" Part of me hates having to go there, but I'll be damned if I remember anything coherent.

"I'll take it for what it was." She stretches out, yawning. "Besides, after you shut Picasso down so hard, you looked like you needed someplace to land."

"I see." I don't. I don't remember drinking that much ever.

"Picasso's safe house is anything but safe if you're a pretty girl who's been drinking," she says. She rubs her eyes. "We're at my place."

Angel gives me nothing else, so I have to ask, "Did you and I, you know?"

"What, fool around? Fuck?" She lifts the blankets and looks down at herself. "You might not remember, but I'm not offended. I had a really good time. So did you."

I know I blush. I don't think women have ever really been on my menu, outside of casual appreciation and dancing. I really try to remember. I draw a blank.

"I know you were having a good time because you kept telling me you were." She grins a wicked looking grin. "Right up until you passed out."

"Oh," is all I can muster.

She looks me in the eye. I know she's gauging my mental state. I'm not sure what to feel, so she gets nothing.

After a moment she kisses my cheek, tosses off the blankets, and goes to the tiny washroom. "There's a robe in the footlocker and coffee in the kitchen."

I can't help but admire the view as she walks away. Should I count myself lucky?

"Thanks." I sit up. My clothes aren't anywhere in the room.

I get up. It feels like my brain wobbles around inside my skull. The sensation takes my stomach and knees with it.

I lean heavily on the footlocker before I pop it open. I find the robe inside. Under it, I find a collection of naughty looking items. I pull on the robe and then hastily pat down the bed for any toys or anything else. Finding nothing, I do a half-assed job making the bed to hide my search.

She comes back out wrapped in a silk robe. "God, I'm feeling it this morning. You?"

"Oh yeah." I can't lie. "My head's a mess."

"Well, I have just the thing for that." She takes my hand and pulls me along. "Come on."

She leads me into a way bigger place than I thought it would be based on the bedroom size. We go down a hallway with three other doors before we drop down a set of steps.

"It's late." She nods at a clock in the kitchen. I stare at the timepiece.

My eyes well up.

"You okay?"

I drop into a fighting stance as Angel's hand on my arm jolts me back. She steps away; she's got training. She looks at me warily.

"Yeah, sorry about that." I suddenly want to be anywhere but here.

"You're not the first soldier with issues I've been with. It's okay." She turns around and starts making breakfast.

"I've never been in the military," I say. "No formal training or anything like that."

"I say again, it's okay." She nods at the table. "Let's eat light and get out of here."

I look at the time again. I don't really have anywhere to be, but I suspect she does.

She bustles together the rest of breakfast and joins me to eat. I try small talk to cover how guilty I feel at my earlier reaction. "This place is pretty big. You rent?"

"Yeah, me and a few others." She nods at the staircase. "It's all girls, so it gets a little crazy, but it's fun. I like it better than being on my own."

"I like my place…." Right now I have no place. I'm in the woods alone. The Wolf has me at his mercy.

I look into the common room. My clothes are scattered across the floor. I wonder if any of Angel's roommates were home to witness anything. Did they care? Should I care?

Angel leaves to get dressed. I pull on my outfit in the main floor half-bath. I smell like a night out clubbing.

We end up at AlphaPlaza One. Security doesn't bat an eye as I follow Angel into the complex. Leaving this place yesterday made me so happy and to be back so soon is all kinds of lame.

Angel stops on the way to one of the maglifts. "I'll, uh, I'll see you around?"

"Yeah." Neither of us want to make it awkward.

She heads off to whatever job she has.

I don't have any place to be.

Jobless and homeless, I linger in the lobby, watching massive holo-projectors fill the vaulted glass, polished marble, and high chrome space with ocean waves, then northern lights, and then swirling flower petals.

I sit in one of the lobby chairs. It's made of real leather, ostentatious, a reminder, just in case anyone forgets that AlphaTek is big enough to afford luxury on the mundane.

I toy with the idea of finding Wolf.

If I thought I had half a chance of getting past security, I'd try it. A good argument with the arrogant bastard would make me feel better.

Now that would be a twisted sort of therapy session. I might actually love to hate him.

I tell myself I'm not just crying wolf. Wolf is more than cocky and arrogant, he's dangerously overpowered. It's a good thing he's out of reach. Given how cornered I feel, I'm not sure I would fight the impulse to kill him.

Brios strides through the huge doors and past security. Brios, who keeps me from any rash action….

He looks around, spots me, and comes over. I don't even have to say anything; he knows I need out.

"Angel called and told me you were here," he says as he joins me. "You look like you could use some coffee." There's a tightening around his eyes that I read as concern. "You been waiting long?" He checks the time.

My eyes tear up, and I don't know why.

Brios says nothing as I wipe them dry. I can remember how often that dampness on my fingers was blood, and how often I would let it stay there until the stickiness would fade.

There are new cages testing their shape by the void they leave. I resist the urge to map the space or test the locks.

"As long as the coffee isn't courtesy of AlphaTek Global Security, I don't care. Let's just go."

~~~

We roll out of the Corporate Core, leaving AlphaPlaza behind, and it feels good. The B&V rumbles against my thighs, and Brios is as solid and steady as ever. This finally feels like something real, present, and in the moment, not part of a shifting memory or a lie.

"Brios?" My hair is flying around. The sunshine here on TopSide nudges me closer to normal.

"Yeah?" He rolls us to the edge of the Eccopark. We cruise, enjoying the greenery.

"Never let me walk home again." I tighten my arms for a second.

"You okay? Something happen?" He slows down to drag the view out longer. "What happened?"

"Picasso happened." I feel him stiffen. "Then I woke up at Angel's place."

"Oh?" I feel his anger rising through his back.

I try to head him off. "Picasso is a flamey-eyed prick. But I don't think anything actually happened with him."

"So…?" He draws the word out.

"Angel and I slept together." I say it matter of fact.
~~~

"Oh." He slows us down more. "And?"

I can't tell if he's turned-on by the idea or still mad. I hesitate. "I guess I just wish it was you."

There's a silence between us that lingers until we turn off Parkway.

He says, "Let's check out my new safe house. We don't even have to have sex."

I nod and lean into him as he guns the bike.

Brios' safe house is nothing like his apartment. It looks nice. Nice and bland. It's a two floor unit in a midlevel managers' housing complex in MidTown. It lacks the charm of his place in UnderCity.

We sit around for the rest of the day like an old married couple. I order small stuff for his place using his credit. We drink a bit, but my body is still suffering from last night.

We watch some old streaming movies, then order pizza. And like some old married couple, we go to bed together and nothing happens.

The next morning a small truck arrives and drops a pile of new everything onto the front step.

"It's Christmas," I yell as I tear open every box and gleefully greet all of his new possessions as though they were my own. Brios sits and watches, occasionally shaking his head.

The scattered mess makes the place feel homey.

As I push the same box of glassware this way and that for the umpteenth time, he suggests, "Let's go for that coffee we talked about and grab some food someplace."

"We need to find the local coffee shop anyway," I say in agreement. I arm up and pull on a jacket to conceal the firepower.

My palmscreen is dead weight even though I have the impulse to check it.

The place we find is no Barista Barb's or MetroCafé. I look around. It's obviously aiming at a high-end clientele and fails to hit the mark. It also has cams built into odd angles.

I sip on my coffee.

Maybe the extra security is meant to scare off bad people and give the manager-types a safe cuddly feeling.

If they only knew what kind of people were joining them for a cup….

"What do you think?" I nod at my mug. To me it's only a passable coffee.

Brios sniffs at his and takes a taste. I like to think I've raised his coffee palate above that of the everyman.

"Hmm. Well the other place, the one we shot up. The one with the granite counters?"

"Siffre's on Seventh." I'm pleased he likes the coffee there. I consider my experiment a success.

"Yeah, Siffre's—"

A random client at the counter turns, sees me, drops his kCard, and bull rushes our table. His screams are incoherent.

My knives are in my hands ready to eviscerate him.

He almost gets to me.

Brios half-stands from the table and jabs a single blow to the guy's jaw. The guy drops.

His jaw may be broken. He's breathing, but he's not moving.

"What the hell was that?" I sheath my blades as we both sit back down.

Brios has more of his coffee. "Dunno. Did you date him?"

I glare. "No."

There's discordant panic as the staff call the cops.

We can't bail because the cams have got us. Plus, Brios paid by credit. They'd freeze access to his accounts and find us eventually for questioning. We wait and try to enjoy the somewhat disappointing coffee.

The cops that arrive are thorough, not like the ones in UnderCity.

When they leave, they drag the guy out to EMS. He fights them to get to me. I watch through the window as they cuff him to the gurney.

"I'm calling Wolf," Brios says first thing when we get back to the safe house.

I don't like it, but I can't argue the logic.

He lets the colonel know what happened and fills me in when the call ends. "The guy was taken to Midvale Medical Center. AlphaTek already has people on the inside who will examine him. As soon as he hears anything, he'll let us know."

"Great, more waiting." I roll my eyes.

Brios checks out what's in the fridge.

We couldn't bring ourselves to try the food at the coffee shop. I know he spent calories on moving as fast as he did. I'm not sure if he has the kitchen on auto-stock.

He talks from the kitchen as I sit on the generic cream colored couch, "You should stick around here for a while until this settles out."

I'm determined not to let one psycho get me down. "The furniture in this place is lame. It needs to change. Want to come with me?"

"I dunno, Raven." He comes out with a sandwich.

I push a few more boxes around on the carpeted floor. Before I'm done picking through stuff, he's finished eating.

~ ~ ~

We get jumped twice more. Once as we cross a street, a guy in a car tries to run me over, and the second time the sales guy at the furniture place leaps at me. We bail on the cops both times.

The second time, I call Wolf.

"Go someplace, not home, and lie low," he says. *"I've got people looking into the situation."*

"Wolf, the guy in the car I didn't know from crap. But Lance?" I'm heartbroken. "I know Lance. He's been my go-to-guy for my decor furniture for years."

"You're on a first name basis with your furniture salesman?" I'm sure he'd be laughing at me if the situation wasn't so serious.

"The old me, you know, felt a profound need to stay extremely fashion current." I try to defend myself. Maybe if Wolf thinks that I think my knowing Lance was part of my crazy past, then my relationship with the furniture salesman won't seem so weird. "You understand that right? Of course I knew the guy at the store."

"Okay. Let's go with that." He's about to say something else.

"Wolf, I just want Phillip dead." I finish the sentence in my head: *so I can go back to living.*

"We all took a number. As soon as we find him, you're first in line for the job." He cuts the line.

"This sucks," I say to Brios as I throw the antique phone onto the cheesy living room table. "I can't go anywhere because random people might try to kill me." I'm pissed. I wipe angry tears. "How am I going to shop for new shower curtains with you?"

Tears. It hits me.

Doc Ripperkins. There are franchises all over town. They had PharmaComp gear all over the backroom. I'm not the only one who has evil implants.

Crap.

I call Wolf back. "I think I have a connection."

I fill him in.

"Good tip, I have to go." He hangs up on me.

Then the phone rings again. There's a very polite Russian man on the other end.

"Wolf is busy chasing your information in and around other meetings. It seems that last night all of the Ripperkin's franchises reported a massive data breach. There are no surviving client lists. At all. A third party is investigating in an undercover capacity on our behalf."

"Oh." I'm useless, and I hate the feeling. "Okay. Can I do anything?"

I say the words in my head as he says them, *"Go to a safe location and wait there until we contact you with more information and instructions."*

~ ~ ~

The security cam mounted by the door shows Brios walking up the short sidewalk.

I've been camping in his new safe house for the week while Wolf tracks down Doc Ripperkin's clients.

Brios comes in. "Hey, you're up."

"Sh sh sh." I shush him and pat the couch beside me. "Don't interrupt my morning show. Leah's in the hospital about to give birth. She's excited because she thinks it's her husband John's child. But it isn't, see? I have this nailed, I remember them saying John was rendered infertile due to a radioactive leak on the old test site he was excavating. He believes the medical reports but, because he loves Leah so much, he drugged her and let his best friend, Sam, have sex with her to get her pregnant. Sam is secretly in love with Leah and has been since they were kids. But what no one knows is that, in Sam's family history they have—"

He cuts me off. "You're watching this shit again?"

"I'm under house arrest because Wolf can't solve a software problem with Doc Ripperkins. What else am I going to do? Besides, look at the production value. Look at the story arc. I never get adventure and romance like this."

At this point he realizes I'm messing with him. He crosses his arms. "Wolf says he's got an update for us."

"If he's giving *you* updates, why do I have this piece of crap?" I shove the cell phone off the table with my foot.

I get a good look at Brios as he leans on the doorframe.

Something's off, his shirt doesn't hang right. He looks a little lopsided across his shoulders. More street tough than ex-soldier.

"Something's changed. You look different."

"My limb upgrade came through. Improved armor plating." He flexes. "Shouldn't have a problem stopping bullets now." He comes over and drops onto the couch beside me.

"Who paid for it?" I ask him.

"You know who," he replies.

"Yeah, watch out for that." I wag my finger at him. "What the company giveth; the company can taketh away."

"Where'd you hear that crap line?" he asks.

I point at the show. "John found out the hard way when the company auditor discovered he'd paid for an upgrade to his penile extension. They were claiming—"

"That's it." He cuts me off. "Let's go." He drags me from the couch and wrestles me to the front door. I mock protest all the way.

"So, where are we going?" I ask as we head up the street.

"Out." He takes his eyes off my ass. "We're supposed to meet Wolf in the Jumble. I'm buying."

"We're not dating, Brios."

"Yet." He grins.

"You've been hanging out with Wolf too much. It's affecting your attitude."

"Okay. Sure, Sweetie."

I follow him over to a low-end, lime green, e-car.

I shake my head. "And we sure as shit aren't dating if this is your new set of wheels." I climb in beside him. "Where's your bike?"

He stares at me. "You lapsing?"

Crap. "Oh yeah, I guess this makes sense." Phillip's psychos jumped us while we were together. They'll be looking for his bike to get to me. The big B&V is too obvious. This ride is pure vanilla.

I keep my thoughts to myself.

We pull into midmorning traffic. As a game, I count cars of the same model and color. I stop counting when I hit twenty-seven.

We drive out to the Jumble. Both Brios and I relax as we leave the city behind. No one out here can afford Ripperkin anything. It's noon by the time we get to the migrating South Am vets' bar.

I don't know how Brios unerringly finds this place. I've wondered about it before.

It reminds me of stories of migrating birds. There used to be millions of birds. Most died or got killed off by the rapid pace of change, kind of like old vets.

I enjoy my beer right until Wolf rolls in with the sound of gasoline powered thunder. Everyone in the place stands and salutes as he ducks through the canvas door.

I'm the only one not standing. It's weird.

Brios sits, and I down my beer completely. I order another one, wishing they carried something stronger.

Wolf joins us.

When the waitress comes over and sets bottles in front of the colonel and I, he looks up at her and says, "Put everyone's tab on here for the night and keep the rest for the widows' fund." He palms a couple of kBit chips to her.

She nods and moves off to tend other tables.

He's blunt when he turns to address me. "Vlasta says there's a facial recognition program that dumped a kill command into the Ripperkin hardware, and well, you know what it looks like so I'll skip that part."

"So, how are we going to deal with it?" I slug another mouthful.

He tries his own beer. It must be good because he turns the label and nods with sudden understanding.

"You mean how am I going to deal with it?" He flashes a rogue's smile.

I scowl at him. I know he's hot. I know it even more now that I'm drinking. I pour back my beer and wave for another.

"Ripperkin's is a legitimate franchise business." He keeps his voice low. "They're posting a news release tomorrow. They'll be requesting their clients contact them immediately to check if their hardware has been tampered with. I have some people running a shell around their system through the net. That will let us track in and out data flow. We'll have pop-up clinics doing emergency warranty work."

"That's a pretty sweet setup," Brios comments.

"Like that? That was Alexander's idea." Wolf smirks. "There's a nasty virus packet waiting for anyone who tries to hack back in, full trace and sabotage."

"And Phillip? Where the hell is he?" I sit on my hands to keep from punching him. My pleasure-tap sends me flutters of approval for my good behavior. "Have you even looked for him yet, or am I just sitting around like a used-up girlfriend waiting for you to call back?"

"I need to wait for PharmaComp to show their hand." Wolf sounds calm. "The media is eating them alive over the Bastion Medical incident. They'll move inside a few days. Then we'll look for him."

Red flag.

"Then we'll look?" I grab my beer and finish it, hammering the bottle onto the table. "You are a piece of work, you son of a—"

Brios cuts me off. "She's a little on edge. This is the first time in a week she's been—"

"Don't you dare." I glare at him and then back at Wolf. "This waiting around is crap. You could find this guy with barely a fraction of your resources. Stop being a dick and find him."

I stand, yank his beer from his fingers, and down it in one swallow. "Brios, I'm done sitting here. Let's go."

As Wolf gets up to let Brios out of the corner seat, I step forward and deliberately bump into him.

I back up hard, snarling, "Watch it."

He lifts his hands and lets Brios go by.

As I duck under the canvas door, I shove Wolf's wallet deeper into my coat.

1.17

Done Waiting

Brios doesn't say anything as we head back into the city. He knows I'm not happy.

I know I'm not happy.

Finding Phillip and popping a couple of bullets into him would be a great way to start being happy.

Wolf has his agenda. Corporate Council bullshit was too slow. I know he's not allocating his resources to my benefit. So screw him.

"Take me to see Ishacc." I'm done waiting.

"You sure you want to go anywhere but home?" He looks at me, the e-car bouncing along on the crappy roads.

"You're so cute when you're concerned." I pat his cheek.

He fires me a lopsided smile. Brios is like a puppy. A big cute cuddly puppy that's really good at shooting people.

"I've got an idea," I say. "We need to stop at a drugstore."

We pull into the Come & Buy Drugs, and I send Brios to do my shopping. Medical supplies still have to be bought in person. Thankfully I'm sure they'll have what I need.

He goes into the store, and I use the car's built-in dv to place a drone delivery order to my location.

Two drones show up. The first one is the payment drone. It lands on the sidewalk. I shove a bunch of Wolf's hardfold into the top.

The extra fee for a cash payment is big. It's not me taking the hit, so I have no problem with the surcharges.

The second drone drops my order at my feet.

I duck behind a dumpster in the service passage and change into my new outfit.

Brios comes out and looks at me.

"Like it?" I ask. "I couldn't stand smelling like the vet bar. No offense. It's just those two guys in the corner...."

"None taken. They're always a little manly, even for me." He looks around. "Your old stuff?"

"Dumpster." I shrug. "Did you get what I need?"

He hands me the box.

"Perfect. Let's go."

We park the e-car close to the alley leading to Ishacc's place. I'm dressed down, and my face is hidden by the medical mask from the drug store.

The cheap plastic mask is designed to treat chemical burns.

A lot of CitFours, gangers, and homeless folks end up wearing these eventually. Part of the joy of living outside full-time in the UnderCity fog.

For now, it hides my features well enough to walk down a street and not trigger murder.

The second I step into the narrow passage between dumpsters and crap-shacks, Vicky comes off the wall she's been holding up. The lighting in her dragon tattoo flickers in the perpetual twilight.

"Vicky, it's me, Sweetie." I'm hoping the Ripperkin implant problem is only visual or based on my entire identity. I've seen Vicky fight. I don't want to be on the receiving end of anything she's serving.

"Sweetie?" she says. "What the hell happened to you?"

"Who did your eye implants, Vicky?" I cut her off.

"My eye implants? Why?" She shuts down, switching to street-person-all-suspicious mode.

"Please just answer the question." The pleading in my voice is real. "It's important."

"If you say so." She blusters a bit and then relents. "They're Nikon Opticals. I got them on a discount."

"Okay good. Is he here today?" I pull up the mask. "I caught a killer case of mistaken identity. Ishacc can tell you about it when I leave."

"Brutal." She looks past me to the street. "Yeah, he and Larus are busy planning to take over the world."

"Larus is here?" I look at Brios who shrugs. "We wondered where he'd gone."

Vicky sighs. "He was camped in the alley for two weeks before Ishacc found him out here, hungry, in the rain. He's been living here ever since." She opens the door for us. "Doesn't bother me, extra body, extra pay."

"Nice," I say to her. I reset the mask.

"Gentlemen," I announce as I walk in. Both of them turn. They look like giant bugs with all the headgear hanging over their faces. "I have a question about your eyes."

~ ~ ~

"I can't believe that's what PharmaComp is doing with that nanobot design." Larus still looks stunned by my Strange Tales story. "I mean, it's brilliant, immoral, and illegal, but you have to admire the audacity of the plan."

"Yeah. Before you keep gushing over it, remember the immoral and illegal bits." I scratch my face. I don't even have the mask on anymore and my face is itchy as hell. "How does anyone wear those things for real?"

"The itchiness is the least of their worries," Ishacc replies.

"Good point." I glare at him. "Thanks for keeping it real, Ishacc."

"My pleasure." Nothing fazes him if he feels in a cheeky monkey mood. "So, you bring with you a tale of sorrow and woe." Ishacc purses his lips. "Usually, that means you want me to do something to help you. I'm right, aren't I?"

"Well, yeah."

Larus narrows his eyes at Ishacc's assessment of the situation. He turns his beady gaze at me like I'm the problem.

I ask, "You hear about that mess at Bastion Medical?"

Ishacc leans way back in his chair. "You were involved?"

"I was kidnapped. When I escaped, the hired mercs employed by PharmaComp made a mess of the place." I lie my ass off.

"And?"

"And the guy in charge of that party is named Phillip Townsend." I lean on the desk. I know my flirtatious efforts aren't lost on Larus. Ishacc, however, is going to want a better explanation. "He's the one who came up with this whole evil implant scheme."

Larus lifts his eyes from my thighs. "What can we do to help?" he asks.

"Whoa there, big guy," Ishacc mutters. "I smell a lot of work. What is it you think we can do for you, Sweetie?"

"He tried to brain hack me while I was in Bastion. I want to find him."

"Find him and kill him?" Ishacc gets blunt.

"I'll pay you." I get blunt back.

"How much?" Ishacc is giving Larus a business education.

I know I'll regret Larus seeing this. It'll give him ideas about how he should do things, and the price will go up for his services.

Brios clears his throat. I ignore him.

"I'm asking because I'm not a hacker, Sweetie." Ishacc crosses his arms. "I'll decrypt stuff. I'll write programs. I'll corrupt all kinds of software, and I know Larus here will do the same to hardware directly, but hacking isn't our thing."

"Come on guys." I put on my lost princess face. "I really need your help with this. This guy is like, on the top of the list for needing to be dead, and I can't find him on my own."

The moment I meet his eyes, Larus is in. I wipe a tear.

Ishacc is unmoved.

"If … I say *if* … we were to look for this guy. We'll both be outside our fields of expertise. On an hourly rate, and then with margins, it'll cost you."

I whip out the rest of Wolf's hardfold and drop it on the desk. "Will that cover it?"

Brios sucks in a sharp lungful.

Larus pokes the pile into a wider fan. He starts to nod.

Ishacc picks up the money. "I don't know where you got a stack like this and don't fucking tell me." He counts the amount. "We'll call you when we find him."

"Done. Except call Brios on his dv." I get them Brios' alphanumeric with a smile. "I know you boys have got this. Oh, and don't do anything stupid with that PharmaComp information, like try to sell it. Even passing around Phillip's name might be trouble in the wrong corners of the market."

"I knew it," Larus mutters, staring at me. "Helping you always leads to trouble."

"I'm serious." I look between the two of them. "There are people out there who are screwed up because of this implant. They might come looking if you aren't cautious. You won't even see it coming. Don't make your kids fatherless, Ishacc."

Ishacc shakes his head. "Way to keep it real, Sweetie."

Brios and I leave them to their work. We pass Vicky on the way out.

"They'll be busy for a couple of hours at least," I say.

"Nice. Last night they were bored, so they got drunk." She frowns at the closed door. "It wasn't good."

"You're welcome. See you later." I take a deep breath and put the mask back on with a sigh. "Those boys had better work fast."

Brios finally asks as we drive back into MidTown, "Where did you come up with that chunk of hardfold?"

"I have resources too, you know." I glare at him.

He shakes his head. "You stole it from Wolf, didn't you?"

"Maybe."

His disapproving look pierces through me.

"Okay. I took his wallet. Not like he's going to miss the money though."

Brios frowns, but he doesn't argue.

Later that evening, Brios gets the call on his dv. "Larus and Vicky will meet us in MidTown at JoJo Moe's in an hour. They traced Phillip and have the data for us," he says as he cuts the line.

"Score one for the boys."

Brios is watching me try on outfits in the living room when the crappy cell phone from Wolf vibrates on the coffee table. I'm digging through a bag of clothes Brios recovered from my apartment. Nothing in the bag makes a full put together look. He didn't pack accessories.

"What?" I snap into the phone.

"Wolf would like his wallet back."

Crap. It's the polite Russian guy.

"He is busy at a council meeting. You have it?"

"I do. Tell him I'll only give it back in person." God, it's like being on a school playground.

A memory pops: a dreary cluster of cell-like rooms, RNA retro-viral drips, and droning VR headsets. I guess no school playground for me.

"And tell him I got tired of waiting. I found Phillip. If he wants in on the action, he can meet me in half an hour."

"I will let him know."

I hang up and look at Brios. "That went well."

"You didn't tell him where to meet us." Brios frowns.

"It's Wolf." I pull on a new pair of Jabbas and hunt for a top. "He'll find us."

Brios shakes his head. He slings his holster over his shoulder followed by his jacket. "Let's go. We'll want to catch Larus before the theater show starts."

I'm halfway to the car when he says, "Sweetie?"

"Yeah?" I smile at him. Things are finally starting to go the way I want.

"Don't forget your mask."

~~~

We meet them on the sidewalk near the doors. Larus looks happy, Vicky looks pissed.

JoJo Moe's is an odd sort of fetish dinner theater.

I've never been inside.

Watching creepy fully anime-sculpted Adherents going in and out of the place settles it for me: I'm not ever going in.

I'm getting more stares than the freakers because of the mask. My face itches.

I hate this.

"Here's your information." Larus passes me a blue data-ribbon while Vicky grimaces every which way around him.

"Thanks."

I'm not going to ask him anything about anything. I never knew he liked freaker stuff. Maybe hiding in the Ganglands wasn't such a weird choice for him.

"Can't chat. Show's about to start." He nods once and goes inside. Vicky's frown gets deeper as she trails along behind him.

We get partway to the e-car when Wolf rolls up in his rumbling soft top racer. At least no one is looking at me anymore.

Wolf doesn't get out. The window drops into the door.

"Wallet?" he asks.

I hand it to him. "I spent it all."

His eyes flick to Brios and then back to me. "Right."

"I'm Zeroed with no access to cash. What did you think was going to happen?"

He hesitates like he's going to answer and then nods. "Right. And the data?"

"If it checks out, we move tonight or I won't look for anything from you ever again."

"Fine."

I give him the data-ribbon from Larus.

"I'll call you before midnight," he says. I'm about to answer, but he peels out with a shriek of tires. People around us cheer.
~~~

I hate him. But he proves as good as his word.

By midnight we're back in the e-car and heading to our rendezvous point.

We get to the northern outskirts of the city and follow a patchy piece of rain soaked pavement a few miles into the Jumble. The debris on the roadside opens into a flat space that tonight is passing as an airstrip.

A long range transport is sitting between a couple of support vehicles. A flash of headlights guides us over to Wolf's car sheltered under one wide delta wing.

Brios lowers a side window, and Wolf greets us. "Why don't you two come over to my car and we'll get started."

"Shotgun." Brios calls the front seat. He heads around to Wolf's passenger door.

I walk over to the driver side and wait. I could get in on the passenger side, but I'm more interested in pushing buttons.

Wolf stares at me for a second. The air is thick and heavy, reminding me of nights in jungle canopies. My grin is predatory. He gets out and I climb past him.

Wolf sits and slams the door. "About the intel…"

"I told you I was done waiting. So you're welcome." I sprawl across the bench seat, smugly enjoying myself. I wonder if he's ever tumbled Angel back here.

Brios shoots me a look over his shoulder.

I know Wolf is thinking up something snappy. I want him off balance, so I shoot first. "My contacts got clean intel on Phillip before you did, huh?"

"There's a lot of data about where the different assets of PharmaComp are heading." Wolf half turns to face me. "But yes, we traced the lead you gave me and the intel is clean."

Through the rear side window, I watch a guy in fatigues get into our crappy little e-car and drive off.

"Great. Let's get this over with. Where's Phillip now?" I kick myself. Now he'll know I didn't even look at the data.

Wolf doesn't bring it up. "He's on a privately chartered airship heading toward South Africa."

"What?" I quell my shout. "He's left already?"

"That's why we're meeting next to this plane." Wolf looks at me. "We're too late to hit him on the ground, but that might be for the best. Catching him in the air gives us more room to act."

"Okay. How's this going to work?" I ask.

"Air travel has different rules of engagement for corporations. Especially ones as big as PharmaComp." Wolf explains the subtle nuances of in-air-assassination. "Aircraft traveling in international airspace remain under the laws and regulations that govern the corporation which own or charter the craft. We hit them in international airspace and it's the same as if we launched an assault on their head office in the Corporate Control Zone. It's treated as a private dispute. If anything slides sideways, we'll have plenty of options for deniability."

"Nice."

He hands me a single sheet of paper. The bottom edge is perforated. I tear off the strip and push the contact end into my wrist port. An ops sheet scrolls up on my left eye.

"Is Brios on my dance card?"

"Of course. You're going to need backup you trust. Vlasta has a one-off chipset for your use and Operations has provided information and craft schematics for each of you."

Wolf adds, "The controller on this drop is Moro. Brios has worked with him before. The equipment's waiting on board. Good luck."

Brios and I get out of the car. The wind has picked up and spray squalls off the wing overhead.

Massive engines thrum to life.

Wolf starts his car, and we head for the loading ramp.

As the ramp buttons closed, I watch Wolf's convoy vanish into the night rain.

1.18
The Drop

Once we're in the air, I can feel myself slipping mentally into business mode. I can't help myself.

We move to the cargo hold. Brios tosses me a duffle full of gear and points at two more sitting on folded down jump seats. We suit up.

The familiar feeling I get from going through the motions is elusive. I sort gear and visually check pistols, ammo, and grenades. I fit them onto my combat webbing, letting the self-adhering action hold everything in place. I tack on a few essentials: pin cams, external monitor, backup com-link, and ECM.

When I try to recall anything about my life before South Am, my past runs off into a fog that's filled with an endless nothing.

I watch Brios as he checks his kit, gear, and loadouts.

He wasn't the one who killed the men on the road that night long ago. He doesn't know who brought me to that lab or who owned the place, or why I was left there. Was it even real, or was it a rebuilt memory?

The latest information I trust says the lab may have been run by the Triads. All that money in South Am brought them to the jungle. Illegal drugs, guns, human trafficking, and legitimate shipping to launder the money: it all merged in

South Am. Brios and I fought with them, and against them, as we made our way home.

Phillip tore down so many memories of my partner that I'm not sure if I love Brios or not. All I feel at this moment is that I trust him.

I try not to look too hard at where any of those feelings come from.

Everything he did for me after getting me out of the lab, all of that was real; he's my only constant.

Brios checks his mission brief again and strips out some redundant gear. I catch him looking at my ass. I make no comment. I don't react in any way except to let him look.

Brios grins as he finishes his gear up and clips on a wing pack. "Good times."

"Hell yeah," I say as I follow his example.

A balaclava wearing sergeant-type comes out of a sealed front area and makes his way toward the cargo ramp.

"Satellite footprint is an ongoing concern for this drop," the guy says. "As a result, this craft will *not* be reducing speed for your egress. Your target will be below us by thirteen thousand feet. Vector and trajectory will appear on your visor displays. If there is a critical failure with your equipment, or if for any reason you miss the target, don't bother slowing down; better for the paperwork, understood?"

Brios looks at me. I ignore him. I'm running through a map of the airship's interior in my head.

Some things on a drop are still better to memorize.

Brios nods for the both of us.

Distantly I register balaclava-boy saying, "Okay. Masks on. Helmets on. Visors down." He pulls on a mask of his own and hooks himself to a safety strap.

My feet start to sweat in my boots as I follow the directions.

Something about heights gets me every time. With my scrambled past, it's useless to wonder why that is. Maybe it's primeval. I cling to that idea. At least then my reaction is an honest one.

The cargo ramp unseals and lowers. The noise of wind and engines fills me. The plane bucks as the tail-end of the cargo section depressurizes into the night sky.

We capitalize on the rush of out-going air, sprinting forward. I plant my right foot on the end of the ramp and fling out into a vortex of chaos.

Flailing around at this speed will kill you. I pull myself into a cannon ball: knees to chest, arms in, elbows tight, and fingers wrapped behind my neck.

Squeezing my eyes shut, I let my processor count. I fall for six seconds.

I unfurl into a head-down glide, and my pack springs open its wings. Only now do I open my eyes.

I gawk at the endless stars in the sky around me. I've never seen it so clearly before. The swoop and line of the Milky Way glows like the lights of a million distant shops.

Looking down, my belly flips and threatens to stage a rebellion. I slow my breathing even as I deepen it. I spot pinpoints of light far below us, freighters and tankers plying across the southern Atlantic.

At this distance from our target, my visor display only shows a rapidly decreasing number string next to tiny glowing crosshairs. All I can do is count on the fact that some faceless programmer did his job well enough that I won't die.

Brios is ahead of me to my right. Our suits and wings, designed to absorb or diffract radar, make us look like evil birds of prey.

I think about killing Phillip. My mind slips around on memories of him. Does that make it any easier? I can't decide.

We fall, like the last bits of sand in an empty hourglass. Time drops away with that thought. The rolling numbers on my visor get smaller even as the crosshairs grow.

Brios spreads his arms wide, landing clamps held in each hand. I pull mine from my belt and stretch out, the safety tethers tying the clamps to my harness bow upwards against my wings. We have become avenging angels.

I would have thought the airship was huge if I'd seen it on the ground. Dropping at terminal velocity onto it in the dark makes it seem impossibly small.

Suddenly we're slowing on approach, then racing along the airship's spine. The computer controlled wings glide us up its length and then flair once.

Side by side we drop flat onto the semi-rigid skin. There's a moment of scrambling to clamp on as our wings fold in. We fight against a two hundred mile an hour wind. We end up sliding a dozen feet before we can lock on.

I see Brios' face through his visor; he has a wild look in his eyes and a grin on his face.

We shimmy over to each other, and, using one hand each, we roll out a strip zipper. As we press it into place, it heats under our hands, bonding to the airship's skin.

Brios pulls the fat zipper fob from one end to the other. The blade built into the zipper makes easy work of the airship's skin, and the action folds a layer of fabric over the sharp edges as he pulls it open.

He holds me by my harness as I release the safety lines. I shove a silenced pistol, my arm, shoulder, and head into the slit and hang upside down from the ceiling. The opening is a tight fit.

We hit the target perfectly; the zipper opening is right above a maintenance gantry.

I look for crew who may be working in this section.

No one's around.

I grab onto a cross brace and let my body slither in. I lower myself over the gantry and land catlike. From my crouch, I zoom my optics along the walkway from bow to stern and signal Brios an all clear.

Our Electronic Countermeasure units have quelled any systems that may have heard or seen us.

Brios slides inside and hangs from the girder one-handed. He pulls the zipper closed.

I hand him a com-link signal booster.

He sticks the booster onto the airframe and plugs it into the end of the fob. Our zipper becomes an antenna, a way to get a signal through the skin of the ship.

Brios drops down beside me, draws his pistol, and thumbs a short static burst on the com-link through a scrambled and mixed channel. He signs to me that the link is up.

Our controller, Moro, now knows we are in and safe.

We keep watch for each other as we shed our helmets and wing packs. Hooking them to a line, we lower them into the darkness, dropping the packs between two of the huge helium lift cans. If the plan works, we'll need them for our escape. I dismiss the idea of failing.

We check our re-breather masks. This area of the airship isn't pressurized. It makes sense from an engineer's standpoint, but it makes breaking in unnoticed a real bitch.

At the mid-ship ladder, we drop one level and split up.

My Doc Ripperkins have had a full treatment from Vlasta. I pull up an augmented reality overlay of the helium compressor pumps.

Starting with the tank farthest astern, I attach an explosive pack and combination remote override, and then I clamp on the wire leads. I repeat the process at every tank until I've made my way to where Brios has come from the bow section. He finishes by locking on remotes for the engine speed and steering modules.

Our controller can now fly the craft if we need him to. Or he could blow the whole thing with us inside. Trust.

Brios taps another static burst on the com-link.

It's been a cakewalk so far.

Someone told me a lie about a cake once. My mind edges away from the memory as a failed training exercise. Was that even real?

We continue to our next objective: gaining access to the crew area. We know it's impossible to get through the airlock undetected from this side. The plan called for us to get help from the crew.

Of course, they're not going to know they're helping us until it's too late.

Together we find the passenger cabin water controls. The AR shows me the primary and redundant circuits that control the water to the airship's luxury kitchens.

We replace the redundant circuit with a failed one and then fry the primary one. Someone from maintenance will be coming soon to look at the water controls.

We move to the security door that separates the lift and mechanical section from the passenger compartment. It's the closest door to the water control circuit. We're counting on the maintenance crewman choosing the path of least resistance.

Brios leans in and presses his ear against the door. His built in system amps up the sounds from the other side and software eliminates the base sounds. He nods.

We barely have time to hide in the service conduit bundles overhead as the door cycles open.

As the crewman moves under us, Brios nails him with his dart thrower. He's out of the overhead and catching the guy even as he's falling.

He's opted to leave the guy alive. It's a good reminder of the mission parameters … my impulses tend to be a lot more basic.

I help Brios stuff the bound and unconscious crewman into the overhead.

As we go through the pressure lock, I hand Brios another com-link booster module to mount above the lintel.

The crewman's ID lets us cycle the inside door. We slip into the sealed part of the airship.

Our ECM units twinkle with glowing colors. In this case pretty rainbows are not a good thing. We freeze.

Brios lifts his mask and guards me while I check the ECM for information regarding the light show. I pull off my mask, ignoring the sting from the adhesive peeling off my skin.

Somewhere aboard ship a computer is trying to find out why a series of cams in the maintenance area have failed. It will have tried default resets, then full system restores. A light will begin to glow on the lead flight engineer's console and another on the shipboard security officer's panel.

Our equipment is good, just not good enough. The cakewalk is over.

I shake my head at Brios. His expression doesn't change. I know he's checking the time.

Someone would be dispatched to look into the cam failure and find nothing wrong. The cams would come back on after we moved out of range. It may or may not trigger a detailed security sweep.

Strike one. We need to move quickly.

Brios taps out one long and one short static burst on the com-link: *security triggered.*

With an increasing sense of urgency, we ghost our way out of the crew section and into the passenger area.

The door we go through has a sign on it that reads: *Full dress uniforms only beyond this point.*

The inside of the airship is more beautiful than I could've imagined. Once again, it's the money that makes the difference. Golden toned nightlights shine along burnished African mahogany walls. Hand tied silk carpets cover the floors and are so thick I could be a stampeding elephant and no one would hear me. Expensive art is tucked tastefully in alcoves down both sides of the hallway.

We get to a secondary lounge. The whole room has a viewport floor. My feet break into a sweat as we make our way to the other side. Moonlit clouds drift by beneath us. I can see ships far below; the glow of their mega lights spill across a star filled ocean.

Our goal is the steward's station. Brios slides a snake-cam along the floor and checks the cubicle.

He touches my mastoid bone. *"Three men. Unarmed. Playing cards. Only one facing the doorway."*

I nod. I touch a button on my ECM. Instantly the switchboard system and the cubicle's security cam are jammed.

I step out.

The three guys playing cards don't notice the lack of lights on the panel beside them. The one facing the door sees me. I can see in his eyes the exact moment he realizes I'm not dressed like a passenger.

He starts to say something.

I fire three tranquilizer rounds out of a dart gun. The only sound comes from the thumps of unconscious bodies hitting the floor. After the tension of just getting to this point, the pleasure-tap juices me for all three. Congratulations, you didn't kill anyone.

It's the most business-like and unsatisfying climax of my career. I catch my breath for a second.

I signal an all clear to Brios as I pull out the drawer with the guest services interface.

The fact that this system doesn't have a wire conduit in the maintenance area is the only reason we had to come inside where we did. This is the closest interface to a door.

Now I stare down at a board covered in unfamiliar keys and icons.

Brios stashes the night steward and his friends out of sight as I whisper, "Okay, Vlasta, show me how good you are."

Since we don't have a nettie with us, I brought the next best thing: a piggybacked hack loaded into my processor via the one-off chip Wolf gave us. The keyword pops a program open, and I relax.

Vlasta's program, written on a simulator of the identical console, takes over. I feel a tingle in my eyes as the software borrows the view. Muscle manipulators in my arms pull my hands up and move my fingers over the keyboard.

I watch as my fingers open and close windows and access information at a rate I didn't think was possible on such a chunky keyboard. This is how Vlasta moves. I'd make a face at Brios, but I still have to pay attention for the sake of the program.

The screen floods with data. In seconds everything we need is on the display. My eyes screen-cap all of it while my hands take a moment more to wipe the inquiry from the access log record.

I know where Phillip is supposed to be lodged. I also know he's switched rooms for the night and is currently in a young woman's suite with two other passengers attending.

Thirty minutes ago, Guest Services delivered some late night snacks and champagne.

Vlasta's program closes everything, moves my arms away from the panel, and lets me have my body back.

I sway at the sudden return of control, and Brios puts his hand on my shoulder, eyes questioning. I brace myself on the counter and nod.

He narrows his eyes.

I sign the room number we need.

Mentally I struggle as we move. Phillip, the father of my child, my husband, is at this moment cheating on me with three women at the same time. He never showed me that much vigor.

Betrayal turns to rage, but my anger only gets me so far.

I try for a different set of controls by reminding myself of a few things: He's my ex-husband. He's my kidnapper and torturer. He's my target. One who is currently distracted and doesn't know about his impending death.

There can only be resolution and satisfaction at the completion of the job.

Despite my efforts, I can't separate all of it, one feeling/memory twists into the next, and my turmoil continues as we find the door.

Brios puts his hand on the sterling silver door latch and looks at me.

Security will be here in a minute or less after we force the door open, without a key, from the outside.

What's a dance in Paris without a little butter?

Silenced pistol in one hand, blade in the other, I answer the mental question with the command keywords for my pleasure-tap. "Not a Tango."

Brios pushes the go button on the ECM unit at his waist, twists the latch off with his cyberhand, and shoulders the door open.

The suite has three large interconnected rooms. I'm inside as time begins to dilate. My augmentations ramp into high.

Brios steps into the room and turns to cover the hallway.

I cross the first room in a blur. The first woman I meet is naked. The fact that she's naked barely registers with me.

She looks up from her knees by the coffee table. Her eyes lock onto mine. An injector full of illegal drugs falls from her fingers.

I don't feel my pistol recoil. She slumps forward, scattering drug paraphernalia across the beveled glass of the tabletop.

The room service cart is near the door to the bedroom. A feminine voice asks from the next room. "Hey, are you okay?" I reach the cart in the same instant she does. I snap a round into her throat. She stumbles and drops, thumping into the wall.

I catch her midway and lower her to the carpet.

The third woman rolls over and sits up in bed, sheets in a jumble around her waist.

I stare into my own eyes. It's me, younger, but she's me.

In the frozen eternity of that second, our eyes widen at the sight of each other. Realizations get built up and torn down. I watch my face in a mirror. My feet get sweaty as a precipice widens under me.

The moment passes. She screams, and I cut off the sound with two shots through her heart.

Phillip calls jovially from the bathroom, "Don't start without me, ladies. Or go ahead, and I'll catch up…." A pause. "Is everything all right out there?"

I hesitate and laugh awkwardly. "Sorry. We just dropped ice cubes in the bed."

There's a longer pause. I know I've screwed up.

Phillip's voice comes out of every speaker in every room on the airship; *"The intruders are here. Kill them."*

The yelling I hear starts as human voices, and by my third heartbeat, it's become the roar of animals. All of them rushing into the hallway.

Red flag. Back in Bastion Medical, Phillip said everyone in PharmaComp loved him.

We've stepped into the corporate beehive.

I hear Brios swear and start firing quick single shots.

I kick open the door to the bathroom.

Phillip drops the ship's com-link and stands defiantly naked in the bathtub, water dripping off his toned body. His voice is quiet and firm. "You know that killing me won't end this, don't you? Because you love me, and somewhere inside you, you know I'm right."

The feelings I had for him in the medical center rush back. Vlasta's mind tricks give me just enough distance that I can make a decision. It feels like the first real choice I've had in a long time.

Part of my mind goes blank. I'm sitting on my own shoulder, but it's a different angle somehow. I lift my gun and fire three rounds into his head. Pain. Loss. Satisfaction.

My relief lasts for a second, and then it dies too. Sadness and regret catches in my throat. I make a strangled sound and lean one-handed onto the counter, catching my breath.

Phillip's words cling to the edges of my mind.

I struggle to push aside my feelings. So many of my questions may never have answers. I have to live with that.

Brios yells, "A little help here."

I storm back out to Brios and crouch against the opposite side of the doorframe to cover the second approach.

PharmaComp employees have flooded the passageway wearing everything from flannel pajamas to full-on lingerie. A few are nude, and some are in house robes. They're all rushing forward with murder in their eyes.

The instinct to survive replaces my tangle of feelings.

I burn through a full magazine as single shots then toggle a grenade to flechette mode and toss it into the hallway.

We both pull back and use the gap to reload.

The muffled whump is followed by screams and moans.

"Sweetie." Brios points with his chin as we move back into the opening.

I see the wounded. They're crawling forward, limbs missing, faces mutilated and bloody. They're trampled by the able-bodied, all of them pressing toward our doorway.

1.19

Higher Love

There are two hundred and fifty passengers on board, add to that number ninety crew less four, and we have ammo for two hundred and thirty of them if we use one round per head. Even using tranquilizer rounds, we only bump our potential count by another eight.

The math takes my processor a fraction of the time it takes to drop another body.

It's a grim statistic.

Reloading becomes our primary concern and a losing battle. We cover each other, taking turns to dump magazine after magazine. The mob edges closer. They have to climb over their own dead to keep coming. But they do it.

They do it out of love.

It's morbid and unnatural. It creeps me out even as I get juiced with each pull of the trigger.

And they don't stop coming. It's the worst apocalypse VR game ever because it isn't a game.

A tiny part of my mind acknowledges that these people are innocent. They just happen to be the live experiments for Phillip's mind-fuck system. I'm one of them.

I keep firing down the hallway. I fight a growing nauseous guilt over how good the pleasure-tap is making all the mayhem feel.

We hear banging behind us. I glance back to see the head of a fire axe come through the wall from the next suite.

"I wish we'd packed zip guns," Brios says, echoing my thoughts.

We pull back into the room. Brios shoves the door shut and leans heavily against it. The moment he moves we'll be swarmed.

I activate my com-link. "Control, we are pinned down in room thirty-nine. There is high risk of being overrun by mind-controlled passengers. Looking for a little help."

There's a pause as our controller, Moro, absorbs what I've said. I'm glad it's a short pause. People howl and pound against the door.

In the break, I shoot the two guys making the hole from the next room. I look through the ragged opening, firing at single targets as they come into view.

"Brace yourselves on aft bulkheads only. I say again aft bulkheads only." A crisp Russian accent gives us our instructions. I recognize the voice as the same operator who sometimes fills in for Wolf. *"The craft is about to perform a drastic maneuver."*

I know Brios hears the message on his com-link.

"Brace now," Moro says.

We fling ourselves to the appropriate wall.

The door bursts open.

People flood in. Their faces twisted into bestial expressions of raw hatred.

The airship lurches as the nose of the craft pitches up at two hundred miles an hour. The airframe of the ship groans loud enough to be heard over the internal sound suppressors.

I roll out of the path of the room service cart as it flies sideways. Glassware and food scatter.

Phillip, it turns out, had expensive taste in caviar.

Pictures come off the wall that is now a ceiling, furniture drops toward us and slams into the new floor, pinning attackers until they free themselves.

The sustained damage to the airship takes its toll; the lights flicker and go out. Emergency lighting glows to life, casting a crimson hue over everything. The lighting hides the blood but makes the people closing on us look demonic.

PharmaComp employees surge forward, biting, punching, kicking, and spitting in endless scrambling movement. We're ground fighting, hand-to-hand, with the insane people who have fallen on top of us. A woman clamps her teeth down on my thigh, and Brios grunts as he loses part of his right cheek to the teeth of a mousy-looking secretary type.

Groping fingers gouge at the flesh around my eyes. Light flickers off a wedding band. The hand stops moving as I fire the last of my magazine into the writhing, fighting bodies.

Fists hammer my torso, slapping my body armor against me until I find it hard to breathe.

Someone tears part of my left ear away, and a moment of panic floods me. Muscle augmentations and manipulator controls fuse into harmonious movement. My blades flick, cut, slice, and stab completely of their own accord. I am an unthinking whirlwind of death.

Then we find ourselves alone, poised in fighting stances, our eyes checking every opening into the room.

My belly and legs quiver as the pleasure-tap finally catches up to my actions. The reaction makes my knees weak. Both of us are covered in blood. A lot of it is our own. I moan. It's the sound of guilty pleasure.

We stand motionless amid the carnage until I reach for our medical packs.

Brios squints his right eye closed as I spray skinseal onto his bloody face. He skin tapes the remnants of my ear to my head and sprays skinseal over the whole thing.

"Control, can we get to our wing packs?" I ask. "Or are we looking for alternative exits. Please advise."

"Standby."

The screaming, groaning, and shuffling movement from the hallway sounds exactly like how I imagine hell sounds.

I pick out dozens of voices sobbing for Phillip over and over again. My emotions rise in a sickened wave and then go flat. Vlasta's reverse brain hack is tested as cages rattle.

I lean furniture against the wall and pull myself onto the sideways doorframe. I look over the edge. It's like looking down a mineshaft whose bottom is a seething mass of twitching limbs and bodies. I watch, knowing what I see should horrify me.

The survivors struggle on top of one another and start to organize themselves for a climb to where we are.

"Crap'n Jesus." My brain, as messed up as it is, still has a hard time processing what I'm seeing.

"What?" Brios comes over.

"They're coming," I say. The terrifying implications for the technology Phillip developed become very real.

We trade places, Brios levering himself onto the lip. He looks down. "Give me one of your grenades."

I hand one up. He sets the dial to frag and drops the grenade into the hole. The explosion shakes the walls. The screams become moans. He sits on the frame, watching, assessing. "We need to move, some are still coming."

I check my ammo. He catches my concern and does the same. I know he's done the math just like I have.

Pulling out two thick combat food bars, I shove one in my mouth and toss the other to Brios.

My augmentations have stripped a lot of energy out of me. The fuel cells are scavenging for glucose. I can feel the weakness in my limbs slowing me down.

Moro's voice clicks in. *"The craft cannot maintain integrity in this position for much longer. Its safety overrides are hardwired in. It will soon level off. Recommend use of an alternative exit."*

Control recommending a different exit isn't good. I can guess where this is going....

"There's an escape pod bay," I say to both Brios and Moro. "We can get to it through a side door in the secondary lounge."

There's a reason I hard-memorize things like map details. It's quicker than bringing it up on optics.

Our controller's voice comes on once more. *"Your alternative egress is confirmed as the closest survivable exit. Situation report?"*

His words sink in.

Brios looks up the hallway's length to the bow. "Control, there are an unspecified number of attackers in both stern and bow positions who are actively attempting to engage. We have sustained light injuries and are both fully mobile. We have limited ammunition remaining."

Passengers and crew from the bow section are now above us. They're more likely to reach us by dropping down than the others who are trying to climb.

Five of the crewmen are cross-trained as shipboard security. There's a strong chance they're still above us somewhere. Security means guns.

I bring up an operating log for this craft. My marquee display rolls the stats. It specifies two standard issue handguns per security crewman, with two magazines each. So far we've been lucky that none of the passengers packed extra firepower.

"The craft has stopped all forward movement and will level off in sixty seconds. I have forwarded a request that Alpha-Wolf Actual authorize mission containment."

Crap. Mission containment. My guess had been right. If we don't get off this thing, we'll go down with it.

I look up at the bedroom doorway. "Brios, give me a boost."

"Why?" He turns his head, staring at me from his perch on the doorframe. He's still spraying skinseal onto bloody injuries across his hands.

"Just give me a fucking boost." I give him a look.

He drops down and braces to give me a leg-up through the doorway. I pull myself into the wreckage of the bedroom.

My alternate me was flung free of the bed and is crumpled along the wall/floor. I haul her onto my shoulders. She smells like me. A dead me. A dead me after sex. It's disturbing.

I jump back down carrying myself.

Brios' eyes bulge. "Who the hell is that?"

"It's me, Brios." I turn so he can see her face. "Or my twin sister, or a clone, I don't know."

"You shot her?" Brios asks as he lifts hair off her forehead. "Or was she dead already?"

"She screamed." I watch his expression and then add to my weak defense by saying, "It was reflex."

"Holy shit, Raven." Brios shakes his head. "I'm sorry."

"Don't be." My voice sounds distant, even to my ears. "Through my death may come my salvation."

"What?" He looks at me oddly. "Vlasta's been in your head one too many times."

I lift myself higher onto my shoulders. "She's coming with us." I know he wants to argue, but I stare at him.

He stays quiet and doesn't look at either her or me.

We hear louder sounds coming from above. Crap. People are chopping holes through the wall/floors to reach us. The chorus of voices yelling Phillip's name gains volume.

The airship starts a slow nose-down rotation.

"Here we go." I push off the stack of furniture and get onto the doorframe. By the time I make the climb, the floor is at a sixty degree angle and declining quickly.

The yells take on an excited tone. The mob can feel the floor shift. Doorways above us hold faces filled with insane hunger. We pick off the overzealous ones in an effort to thin the resistance along our direction of travel.

Gunplay drowns out our com-links as we're fired on and return fire. The expensive wall paneling splinters around the doorframe.

"Say again, Control," Brios says loudly. "Say again."

"This is Alpha-Wolf Actual. Green light for mission containment. Green light for mission containment," Wolf says on the line.

It might be the last time I hear his voice. The idea of that pisses me off.

"Green light for mission containment. Forty seconds from my mark." There's a short pause.

"Mark."

My processor starts a countdown. The number shrinks faster than I'd like.

I flag the door we need on my optics.

We launch ourselves into the hallway. I rush to the far side and keep my gun hand as free to move as possible. The bloody carpet under my feet is slick; the walls are scored from blow-through, smeared and streaked with gore.

Brios fires past me. Falling, rolling, bodies turn the first dozen yards into a life or death dodge and hurdle.

The voices behind us surge louder.

"Grenade out on our six," Brios barks.

Faces appear in doorways above. A guy in flannel pajamas half-runs half-falls toward us. We don't have time to sidestep as he plummets, arms wide and grasping, his eyes blazing murder.

"Brace," I yell as I fire. My shot hits him square on the bridge of the nose.

Brios leans against my back. "Got you."

The dead man's body slams into me. Brios must be braced on a doorframe because, aside from the impact, we don't move. He pulls me closer to the wall, and I shove the dead guy aside.

We both burn power into our augmentations to get moving again. Speed of movement and controlled violence are all we have. Too slow and we're dead. Miss a target and we're dead.

The glowing visual marker I've painted on the door pulses between orange and purple. The pulsing increases in urgency as we close the distance.

The steward's station has two armed men in it who are both trying to get a bead on us....

"Guns," I say over Brios' steady firing to our rear. "They have cover."

He's down to his heavy pistols. He swings his arm past my head and squeezes two shots off. His rounds blow through the wall the men are hiding behind.

The angle of the floor is leveling out and more passengers crowd the hallway ahead of us. I can see the entrance to the lounge. First class passengers are coming in from the bow staterooms....

As I pass the last suite on my left, the door opens and two people grab at the body over my shoulder. Off balance and nearly dropping her, I spin into the center of the hallway and snap fire two rounds. The shots aren't kills, but it buys us some space.

Software monitoring my peripherals flashes a warning. In the center of the lounge, the captain of the airship is in a low stance, gun in hand. He's got a bead on me.

I act on instinct, swinging my dead body into the line of fire, using her as a shield. I hate the extra damage that dead-me soaks up, but I'm grateful she's there because he's a good shot.

I can't let the bastard keep firing.

"Shooter," Brios yells. "On our six."

The wall by my head shreds to splinters. The smell of shattered wood and heat-melted varnish fills my next breath.

"Switch walls," Brios says.

As I move, I present another clean target to the captain. The rounds he fires aren't wasted. My light torso armor slaps tight, and the impact vibrates my insides. My medical monitor floods in more drugs to keep my insides stable, my blood pumping, and every part of me cranked with synthetic adrenaline.

Brios takes out the armed crewman behind us.

I get my gun on the captain, marking my target and firing just as a swarm of people crowd between us. An older guy with wild eyes gets in the way. The bullet drops him. The emergency lighting and the color of his crushed velvet smoking jacket hide the gush of blood.

The press of bodies forms a living wall. It's a barrier that works both ways. The captain can't hit me, and I can't hit him. But he still has the advantage; I'm chewing through rounds keeping the mob at bay, and he only needs to move to a better position to take another shot.

My shot counter tells me I'm down to a single round in the pipe. I squeeze off the last one, throw the pistol into the face of a passenger, and pull my secondary weapon.

I tell Brios, "On my back up."

"Down to my last two magazines," he replies. "More targets closing from our six." Brios' tone is calm, unexcited.

I recognize his detachment. He's come to terms with the idea of not making it.

The drugs and the technology I'm packing can't change how fast time moves, and we're almost out.

We enter the lounge. The view from the glass floor spirals out beneath us, the blood smeared clouds taking my breath. I don't have time to feel my feet sweat.

Brios shifts his fire from the people behind us to those blocking our immediate path. He keeps up his steady aim and fire, taking the legs of the first and second rank of people. He forces the rest to scramble over or around their injured and flailing comrades. The blood on the glass floor smears wider as they slide, fall, and go still. Maximum impediment, minimal round count....

I'm trying to track the captain through the press of people.

There. My optics flag him as another bullet zings a hot line across my cheek.

"Brios," I say. "Clear a line."

His grenade toss flashes past my head. "Grenade out."

It's a heavy concussion, and it knocks enough people flat that I get two shots off at my intended target. The captain crumples. His brimmed hat rolls on its edge into the carnage.

The viewport floor isn't designed to have a grenade detonate anywhere near it. Fat, long cracks radiate out from the blast point like red tinted lightning, creaking outward through the glass.

"Run," I yell.

We try for an all out sprint. Even over the howl of voices, I hear the sharp hissing and popping of the cracks as they extend under our feet. There's sweat slicking down my back, and a warning blinks on my optics about an empty glucose power supply. I've got five seconds left of amplified boost, and we're down to fourteen seconds on the clock.

Shit, shit, shit. I slip on the gore, lurching my way to the emergency escape exit.

Brios is two long steps behind me.

I punch the emergency door open. It slides aside, and a wrench, swung heavily by a crewman on the other side, bounces between my cheek and the hip of the body over my shoulder. I execute a knee strike kick. The crewman falls with a scream. I fire into his head as I push past him.

There's a loud *snap* behind me. I hear the sound and for an instant my world unhinges.

The glass floor drops away with a shattering roar.

Brios….

I spin in place. The scene is complete mayhem; swirling glass fragments, fluttering napkins from the lounge bar, leaves torn from plants, and people … everything swept away by the immense decompression.

My heart hammers back to life when I find Brios amid the wind and chaos. He has one hand on the doorframe. The rest of him is hanging partway through the hull. He's fighting to hold on.

It's a fight he's losing.

I amp up, burn through my power, and dump dead-me to lunge at Brios.

My fingers wrap around his tac vest.

Straining, I feel muscles in my back that haven't worked this hard since South Am. My boost system shuts down. In desperation, I throw my weight backward.

Brios is dragged with me, and we slam to the floor.

The physical weakness hits and my hands shake, nausea turning my stomach.

Nine and a half seconds.

"Go." Brios flings me forward, barely on his feet. "I'll get the body. Go."

I stumble past my battered corpse and into a hallway lined with dozens of escape pods. I toggle the first one open. The hatch whisks aside. I duck through and collapse into the nearest seat.

A voice blares instructions in a dozen languages. *"Remain calm. Seating arrangements will be made by the attending crewperson. Please stay seated. Evacuation protocols have been activated. The automated system will detach this pod in thirty seconds."*

Thirty seconds.... Screw that. The emergency release lever is on the wall by my head. I lock my restraints and put my hand on the lever.

Brios piles in, tosses dead-me into one seat, and crams himself into another. "I'm in." He slaps the restraints button.

"Launching," I yell as I yank the lever.

The hatch snaps shut. There's a rush of compression, and the pod vibrates as the locking bolts explode. Chemical rockets hurl us away from the hull.

The auto restraint system is still locking Brios in even as we fall away from the airship.

My clock times out.

Mission Containment....

Across the ceiling viewscreen, we watch the carnage unfold. Fireballs rip along the entire airframe. The whole craft turns itself inside out, ribs inverting and curving upward along its spine, and then it breaks into sections. Flames race outward and roil into the night sky. Helium doesn't burn, but the fuel cells for every other powered system burst into wide orange fireballs.

I grip the armrests in the throes of a wicked string of climaxes; the lag time on the wire isn't meant to cope with consecutive kills in huge numbers.

The rescue pod's parachutes deploy, tangle, and then burn in the wake of flying, fiery debris. We plummet down and away until the secondary chutes pop. We bounce hard and lose some speed.

Our pod has lost a lot of altitude, and we're still coming in fast. Alarms ring and automated voices tell us to brace for impact. We slam into the ocean, submerge, and bob sickeningly back to the surface.

The alarms switch off one by one as the pod's systems work toward a new normal.

"Pod integrity: ninety-eight percent. Buoyancy: stable. Stay seated and remain calm." The instructions echo and fall silent.

Green interior lights flicker to life. I'm sure the designers meant for the effect to be calming, but it just makes the gore we're covered in turn black.

There's a lot of it.

Moro's voice fills my com-link, *"Prepare for immediate recovery."*

"Well," I say, after a moment of quiet introspection, "that could've gone better."

"You're kidding, right?" Brios stares between me and dead-me. "We got out alive...."

"Yippee. Mission accomplished. We took out Phillip and laid waste to an evil mega-corp. Maybe after a beer, we should go find Wolf and Moro and kill them for being jerk-offs. Now that's a mission to accomplish. Who the fuck sets a mission containment for forty seconds?" I can't help that I'm yelling. "Who does that? No one sane, that's who." I think killing them is a great idea. Blood everywhere ... a lot of mayhem. End this party before it gets started. "What do you say? You in?"

"I like the beer part of the plan." He reaches into his webbing and throws me his last food bar. "As for the rest ... not so much."

1.20

Back on the Grid

The day after the drop, I get a follow-up invite to dinner with Wolf like it's a friggin' consolation prize. Brios isn't invited, and that has me wound up long before I get there. Brios doesn't seem concerned, which is the only reason I agree to go.

The sunset has just finished, and the evening wind is shifting through the Corporate Core.

I'm at the restaurant on time.

The La Fleur de la Croix d'Or is so expensive it's never been on my radar. I step inside and am seated at what is apparently Wolf's usual table. I wait for twenty uncomfortable minutes before he arrives.

A security guard walks him into the restaurant. He's dressed in a damned expensive suit; he looks amazing.

The hostess greets him with familiarity. "Good evening, Mr. Ferdinand. I believe your other party is at your usual table." She leads him over, and he smiles his thanks as he sits across from me.

He waits until we're alone.

"I'm glad you're up and around." He smells good too. "How was revenge?"

"Screw you, Wolf. I'm alive. That's all I am," I snap. "I'm Zeroed, broke, homeless, and not even a person under the law. I may as well move to the Ganglands."

"Wait," he starts.

"No, I'm not going to wait." I can't check my rising voice. "I owe you what must be a cubic fuck-ton of kBits, and I have no way to pay you back." I drop into a whisper and look around. "On top of that, I'm a bloody clone. The duplicate me is kind of hard to ignore."

He sits still, staring at the table in front of me, waiting.

I continue, "I don't know if that means I qualify as human even if I had ID, since clones are so illegal, the Council used to issue bounties."

He meets my eyes and raises his head as I run out of steam. Ever the patient Wolf.

"There was nothing left of the airship," he begins, as if my outburst never happened. He's giving me a recap of the operation outcomes. "There's no evidence of anything, other than the fact there was an explosion. No leads, but lots of motives that point to various companies. Companies other than mine."

He spins a menu on the table and picks it up. He sets it down again without looking at it. "You did good work, and you got out alive."

I watch him. He's intense, controlled.

The menu is the only bone he throws me that tells me he's irritated.

"What about the Ripperkin's client list?"

"We recovered what we believe to be a full list. A subsidiary I control will be loaning them the money to get mobile units out to every client we may have missed." He has a sip of ice water. "It'll be a dog and pony show for the general public. Pretty soon, it'll only be the holdouts who want to kill you instead of everyone you meet."

I make a face at him.

He sighs. "I don't expect you to pay me, Raven. In fact, I don't want a goddamn thing from you. In fact, I'm paying you for the work you've already done."

That hits me by surprise. "What?"

"PharmaComp Corporation, in particular the nanite system developed by their R&D head, the late Phillip Townsend, is, in my opinion, far too dangerous to allow to exist."

"So what does that mean?" I have to hear him out now.

"It means I took the initiative and eliminated what I saw as a potential threat to a lot of people. Now I'm actively suppressing the information about the very existence of that threat." He speaks quietly, with resolve. It's stupid hot. "It also means I've covered your medical expenses as I would for any other operative in my employ."

"I don't want—"

"You had your turn." He cuts me off. "Now it's my turn, so shut up and listen. Here is your new clean ID." He slides a stack of monobond over to me. "Here's the chipware to back it up. You have new accounts; everything is set up. I also started a separate account for pay drops from me."

I'm belligerent by nature, but Wolf brings out the best in me. "I don't work for you, remember?" I snipe.

"No, officially you don't. Yet. But then nor does Angel, or Picasso, or even Brios," he presses, "but they know better than to argue with me when I pay them for services rendered." He motions with one hand. A waiter glides over. He orders. "I'll have the roasted duck breast with Romanesco, wild mushrooms, and lemon pepper."

"Of course, and for the lady?" The waiter's voice and manner is so smooth it's irritating.

"She'll have the caramelized black cod in a Malabar black pepper sauce with pak choi." The bastard orders for me.

I think about it for a second. I wouldn't know where to begin, so I let it slide. He probably planned this too … *you don't eat unless I feed you.* I can see him thinking that.

"And to drink?" asks Mr. Smoothie the waiter.

Wolf pauses. "Have the sommelier bring out a selection for each dish."

"Of course, sir." Smoothie is dismissed and slinks off to do his job.

I silently admire the way Wolf just blew through a lot of money. He looked really good doing it too. Bastard.

"So?" he asks.

"So what?" I counter. "What do you want to me say?"

"You can say no." Wolf sips more water. "I hope you don't, but it's your call."

"How much do you know about me, Wolf?" I ask point-blank. Maybe he doesn't get that the hustle isn't for fun, that I have expensive tastes and need a bigger budget just for bills. To say nothing of my side projects….

"Please," he says, "while we're in polite society, call me Basillio."

"Seriously? That's your real name?" I choke on my laughter. "Your mother hated you or something?"

He glares at me.

"Okay, Basillio, what's in the package for me, what do I get?"

"Coverage for your extensive mental issues." His voice is like stone sliding on stone. Perhaps my choice of target this time has backfired.

"Screw you." I go to stand. I'd put up with him for the money, but I have standards; only my friends get to call me out on the crazy.

"So leave my mother out of it and we call it even." His voice rises just slightly. "Sit down."

His tone ends my anger. Spaniards.

I sit. At least I know we're even. "So what else?"

"You get paid." He pulls out a fancy kBit reader and slides it over to me. I push the chip he gives me into the slot and thumb the bio-lock. A really big number rolls across the screen. I stare at it.

"You did good work. It was hazardous." He lists off items. "It caused psychological trauma, only part of which was prior existing, and which is now ongoing. The list of other add-ons is extensive, including—"

"Shut up and let me think," I snap. I down the glass of ice water in front of me as I stare at the display.

He waits.

The wine guy arrives. Basillio samples each bottle. He nods, points to a couple of bottles, and waves the others away. Wine guy pours us a round and leaves us to our meal.

"Okay," I say. "I'm in."

"Wait," he says all forceful-like.

"What? Hurry up and wait?" I look at him. He is the most frustrating person on Earth. A trickle of juice catches my breath. "You have to stop this push-me-pull-me shit, Basillio, or I'm just gonna hate you."

"Good to know," he says. "I just want you to understand that by saying yes, a full confidentiality agreement comes into immediate effect."

"And what happens if I say no?"

"That man by the door sends a signal to the men outside, and you don't reach the curb alive."

I know my color comes up.

"I'm joking," he says. "You take your pay and go off to live whatever life you can build."

"And saying yes?" I breathe out. He's pushing make-me-angry buttons all over my dashboard. My pleasure-tap keeps me nailed to the chair.

"Yes means that you agree to take etiquette classes. I can't be seen wandering around at high powered functions with only my bodyguards." He sips wine. "You in essence become my armed escort."

"I'm not having sex with you." It comes out by reflex.

"Okay." He shrugs. "It's not like I suffer in that regard in any case."

"Do I have to move?" I ask.

He shakes his head. "If you like your old place that much, stay. It has a great view of AlphaPlaza."

Our food comes out. While we eat, we settle the details of my not-working-for-him to my satisfaction.

He meets my unspoken expectation and pays for lunch with hardfold, a lot of it. I guess credit is for slobs like me.

Brios meets me outside.

For now, I'm just glad to be free of the wood paneling, the white tablecloths, and the quiet music.

I get on his bike.

"So?" he asks as we pull away from the curb. The nighttime air in TopSide is fresh with a hint of coming rain.

"I'm not working for him." I press my face into his jacket. He looks good tonight.

"Huh." He pushes up the speed. "Me either."

"That's good, right?" I ask, "Neither of us working for him?"

He nods. "Yeah."

My dv chimes. The number looks familiar.

I answer it. "Hello?"

There's a click. I almost hang up because it sounds like an automated sales call. My datavice is supposed to screen those, but sometimes one gets through.

I recognize Larus' voice as my finger is poised over the disconnect button.

"If you are receiving this message, it is because something terrible has happened to me, and I am, in all likelihood, dead. If you are in any position to owe me anything, I now ask that your efforts to repay me be converted into seeking vengeance for the sake of any friendship we may have shared while I was alive. Thank you for listening, and goodbye."

1.21

The Ties that Bind

We sling off Brios' bike, pushing our way to the mouth of the ally. People flow along the sidewalk without noticing anything odd. My eyes dial in. The homeless guys are all just lying in their crap-shacks and squats.

They aren't moving.

"Wolf said he's sending a containment team," Brios says as we creep along.

"Gas?" I look over at Brios. He slides a scanner ball out of his hip pouch, tears it out of the airtight packet, and rolls it down the alley.

He's accurate. The device goes almost the whole length to the steel door at the end.

He looks at the readout glowing on his wrist. "Yeah." He shows me the display. The red numbers spike as the sensor array in the ball analyzes everything.

The numbers are declining as the gas dissipates.

I can see the steel door is ajar and a light is flickering inside. "Screw this, Brios. We can't wait around. I'm going in." I dig out my filter mask and shove it onto my face. I haul up my guns as we leapfrog cover to cover to the door.

I ease the door open.

Char marks and divots lace the concrete entryway. Vicky was busy with her shotgun and its flamethrower rounds.

The room's too big for a snake cam to do any good, so we simply duck inside. I find Vicky's body near the first choke point of shipping crates.

Her head is a short distance away. For them to be as far apart as they are, she was either moving fast, or someone punted her head after she dropped. The sight of her blood on the concrete floor unlocks something primal in me. My vision goes crystal clear.

There's movement from deeper inside the room, a light quickly panning back and forth. I signal to Brios, and we creep around a stack of hardware crates.

I see Larus first. He's twisted and bent on his back over his workstation. Blood is still dripping off the table edge. Two evil looking plugs jut out of where his eyes should be. The plugs connect to a black box humming on the counter.

At Ishacc's desk, a tall muscular guy has his back to us. His dark blue clothes are skin tight. He's wearing a belt with all kinds of expensive looking gear pinned to it. He's busy jamming plugs into Ishacc's computer rig.

Ishacc himself is propped in his extra wide chair. He's been gut shot. He's breathing and moaning softly. A set of eye plugs have been shoved into his head. Neither Larus nor Ishacc have artificial eyes, so it's nasty to look at.

I can see the back muscles of the tall guy tighten just so. I know he knows we're here. I have just enough time to tip Brios to that fact, when the guy turns and throws something at him. The bastard is really fast, probably faster than either Brios or I.

Everything is decided in an instant and happens in the place between. I start popping off rounds as I reach for my backup gun. The guy's not my target. The rounds hit, and Ishacc's computer rig explodes into useless smoking wires and spinning trash. I take out the guy's black boxes before my next heartbeat. I've changed the conditions of victory.

There's a flash of blue lightning and Brios yells, his expression snapping from intent to blank surprise. All the armored jackets in the world can't stop his flesh-and-blood arm from shearing off in a spray of blood.

The severed end of his limb is garroted by a set of pulsating bolas. His augmented arm is still up and firing, but I see the moment his military grade implants lose the fight against his shock.

Brios is on his way to the floor.

I drill the guy in the pelvis with Little Tommy.

The guy grunts and whips his hand back to fling something at me. I'm already throwing myself flat.

I count one second.

There's a wet ripping sound as the micro rocket unspools.

Then echoing silence.

The tall guy falls over. He's a jelly blob inside an armored sack of expensive rags. Only his shoulders, head, and lower legs are in okay shape.

I scramble over to Brios. His face reminds me of a lost little boy. His mouth moves without words. The damage is horrible to look at: cut muscle, shorn bone.

I flip on my com-link. "I need medical in here now. Right now." I roll Brios onto his side. "Brios?"

His eyes swim.

My panic at so much of his blood everywhere makes me scared for the world, for where I'll end up on the day he can't be recovered. I pull in a deep breath. "Brios. Where are you at?"

He slowly nods at me as an AlphaTek Recovery Team rushes in.

~~~

I watch Brios through the glass. He's below me in an operating theater getting a new cyberarm grafted on. Two guys oversee a pile of robots doing the work.

It's been six hours since we got to Ishacc's place.
~~~

A young med-tech is watching from the seat next to me. He's eating popcorn. I guess that's why they call the place a theater. There are seats for twenty, but we're alone. Silently, he offers me popcorn. Silently, I refuse.

Wolf comes in and drops into a chair next to me. The med-tech doesn't look up. He just extends his popcorn. Wolf takes a handful and pops some into his mouth.

"Ishacc isn't fat," he whispers to me between pieces.

"What?" I look over at him.

He turns slightly away from the glass. "Ishacc isn't fat. He's alive because at some point in his life he had a bad graft. Internal torso armor plate. He's a mess, but he'll live."

"Damn." The things I didn't know about my friends.

"Something Ishacc was looking into found its way back to him. So far, all we got out of him is a garbled warning about Neo Detroit. Does that mean anything to you?"

I shake my head, trying to hide my frustration. I warned Ishacc not to dig too deep into anything PharmaComp. This can't be a coincidence. I'd counted on Larus' paranoia to keep his new partner in check; I should've known better.

We watch for a moment. Brios' new hand twitches. His fingers open and close faster and faster, then stop.

"Vlasta has reported that the guy you took down is a gene modified clone. He has no machine implants. But he does have muscle augmentations, lungs, vision, the works. It's all optimized and tweaked right into his DNA."

"Well, that's illegal as hell," I mutter. I watch Brios' arm flex from the elbow and rotate at the wrist.

"There's an arcology in Neo Detroit." Wolf is watching me. What he doesn't say is as important as what he's said.

Cloning isn't illegal in arcologies, nor is gene tweaking.

Crap.

"You think this guy's from an arcology?" The idea of a world within our world, so separated and closed off, makes me uncomfortable.

I frown.

"I had someone look into the information Ishacc gave us. Turns out PharmaComp has strong ties to the Neo Detroit Arcology. Your boys stumbled onto that connection and triggered something."

They were poking around because of me. Now Larus is dead, and Ishacc's kids are going hungry.

I fume. "Can we use that as our reason to go in and wipe them out?"

"Not officially." He shakes his head. "All of the arcologies together form what is essentially a dispersed single country. They function like a mega-corp in that regard. The different locations share mutual agreements. Those agreements cover support for one another during external conflict. We attack one, we attack all."

"Like we haven't gone to war before." I snort.

"We've had all kinds of fighting in the last hundred and fifty years, but never a war like the old wars." He wipes his hands on a tissue. "No one does that. It's too expensive and too unpopular to fight like that for more than a few months."

Politics.

"Carpet bombing an arcology will only make things worse," he adds. "They research things in there that are illegal, maybe even immoral. No one can say what kinds of weapons they'd unleash globally as a counter attack."

The med-tech looks over at us and then back down at the surgery. Brios is getting prepped to be wheeled into recovery.

"Fine, I get it. Not total war. Can Vlasta get anything out of the guy we brought in?"

Wolf raises one shoulder noncommittally. "She's working on keeping him alive. It'll be a while before we get anything." He stands and turns to the tech. "Hey," he says.

The med-tech looks up.

Wolf nods at him. "Good job on the robotic software in there. You have my permission to take your project to the next level. I'll approve your budget tomorrow. Thanks for the popcorn."

"Thank you, Mr. Ferdinand." The young guy is all smiles as Wolf leaves.

~ ~ ~

"So why can't I see him, Vlasta?" I harass her as she bustles along the cafeteria counter placing fruit and yogurt cups onto her dinner tray.

"It is not a good time," she says.

"When is a good time?" I ask as I load a greasy burger onto my plate and help myself to a mountain of fries. It all smells so good.

"Never." She slides an employee card into the reader. Her food is gratis as part of a healthy living incentive.

She walks away.

I scramble to dig out my ID and shove it into the slot. The card reader demands fifteen credits for my tray. I leave the food as I see her making what looks like an escape. "Wait, Vlasta. Just tell me why."

I catch up to her as she sets her dinner next to a trash receptacle.

"It will damage your psyche. That is why." She hunts around in the trash with disdainful tsking sounds. I pace until she comes up with her prize: a half-eaten burger.

The meat goes onto one corner of her tray.

"Damage my psyche?" I trail after her. "You mean because he works for Phillip?"

She arches a brow at me and proceeds down the hall to a narrow steel door marked private.

I follow her in, hoping she'll change her mind. I regret the action almost immediately.

A single oak dining table and three chairs occupy the center of a room whose one wall, floor to ceiling, is glass. The view is completely obscured by the tangle of her plants. The tallest one sways in what must be excitement.

I swallow and pick a chair farthest from the jungle.

She ignores me. "Hello, my darlings."

I wait. This much at least, I can learn from Wolf.

The White Witch spends several minutes hand-feeding her pets bits of recovered hamburger. When she comes back to me, I have to shake myself out of a half stupor from the exotic smells that the plants give off as they eat.

She sits across from me. "I strongly believe you will be at risk if you meet him."

"So what? What's it to you?" I look at her. She refuses to meet my eyes. "Come on," I say, "I can handle it."

She finally looks up, but it's with a killer's gaze. "I will get no peace from you, will I?"

"None." I smile and start picking fruit off her tray. "I will follow you every moment I can until you tell me why, or let me see him."

She frowns in annoyance as I eat her food. She sighs and says, "Genetically, he is your brother."

I drop the fruit. "I have a brother?"

Her eyes follow the fruit. She looks angry at me for disrespecting her food. "Technically he is your brother, yes. But you should consider yourself widely estranged."

She slaps my fingers as I reach for a different piece of fruit. She hands me back the piece I dropped. "He lives only on full support. He is a killer sent to hunt down fugitives. Your tiny rocket severed connections that would have made him explode. He is very upset that he is not dead."

"Oh." I ponder the facts. "So he was looking for me?"

She leans back; her eyes narrow as she chews. "You are smarter than you look. Now will you leave me alone?"

"Nope." I smile and stand up. "Now I really need to talk to him."

"I knew you would not be happy with my answer." She shakes her head. "This is why I should never have answered you to begin with. My answer is no. If you go to him, you will find all the doors are locked. Understand that your behavior in this has been less than exemplary. I am done talking to you. Away from here." She makes a sweeping motion with her elegant white fingers. "Away. Now. Go."

~ ~ ~

I slip along a hallway in AlphaPlaza's medical center. It's after hours and way past midnight. The big AT never sleeps; it only slows down. This time of night is as slow as it's going to get. Lucky for me, the secure wing of the medical center moves at a dead crawl.

I'm watching the ECM unit from the airship adventure as it accesses cam and sensor feeds and loops them while I pass. It's a nice piece of gear. I liked it so much I decided to keep it after the drop. The guys doing the recovery never asked for it back, and I didn't offer.

If the plaza is as wired up as I think, I'll be glad I took the time to prep for this run.

I've brought my best B&E gear, and I know exactly where I need to be. I'd grin, but I keep mentally tripping over feelings that well up from simple things like the chemical cleaner smell and the subdued overhead lighting.

This is so similar to what has come before. Not just recently, but from years ago.

The flowing memories have me clenching my jaw. Was the man I killed back then a prince, or had he been a president? I got in, got out, got paid, but my mind draws a blank on names, dates, or who hired me. I'm used to the not knowing. Better than that, I tell myself that I don't even care. The flashes of memory are proof that some cages are missing their bars. I'll have to deal with that mess at some point, but now is not the time.

I get to the security door that marks my point of entry to the emergency stairwell. This door won't be locked, but it'll send a signal through the system the moment it's opened.

I pull my multi-wave scanner off my belt, link my optics, and run it over the wall to the right of the door.

Ghosting lines of blue show me exactly where the alarm sensors are buried in the doorframe. It's a simple magnetic switch that activates when the door separates from the frame.

I do a quick check to make sure there's no accelerometer to complicate things and slide a magnetic dummy chip into place.

The ECM unit indicates an all clear.

I ease the door open. No alarm.

I scoot up a flight of concrete steps and stop at the floor I need. The secure wing has a far better security door: heavier gauge materials, better sensors, nicer lock….

Hooking the scanner back into my optics, I crank the range and resolution to max. The skeletal image shows me a cart, a corner of the hallway, and, to the right of the door, the back of an armed security guard. He's seated at a desk watching the maglifts.

I flirted with this particular security guard as he was coming on duty, skimming his personal ID code from the standard RF chip embedded in his wrist and grabbing nice clean images of his eyeballs. It was a piece of cake; he was staring hard enough I may as well have been cake….

I'll be putting all of that to use in a minute, but first I have to get through this lock.

It would be a challenge to crack this door on my own, but I've got a most interesting solution.

I bring out Shadow's security tap.

AlphaTek's active trace aside, now is as good a time as any to give this thing a go.

I figure if Basillio wants to raid his own tower, let him. It'll be funny. For me, it just means I'll have to move fast. At worst … well … at worst I'll end up cooling my heels in a holding cell until Brios can convince Basillio to let me out.

I adjust the ECM output settings and shrink its sheltering effect to about six feet. The guard and his desk are just outside that range. I don't want him jumping up if his world view goes blank. But I don't want any stray signal setting off an alarm either. It'll have to do.

After a careful breath, I hold the tap up to the keyhole of the deadbolt. A tongue of silver liquid shoots out, touches the opening, and morphs into the right shape. It slowly pulls itself from my fingertips and sticks itself into the lock.

A muted click later, and the multi-wave scanner confirms the bolt is open. The ECM unit stays green. Time starts now.

I crack the door a finger's width.

No alarm, nothing.

I tug on the tap, and it falls freely into my hand. Damn, color me impressed.... Shadow had some sweet gear.

Inching the door wider, I lower the barrel of the dart gun through the gap. I tag the guard above the collar. He stiffens and then slumps.

Now I'm moving quickly. I take the guard's security keys.

Together, the keys and his ID, spoofed through a signal generator, get me through a checkpoint in the hallway. Not having both would send a hefty stun-shock jolt in my direction and trigger the section's alarms.

My brother's room is the second entrance on the left. I hustle to the door I need and find that Vlasta is as good as her word. This one's locked too, and there's a retina scan feature. My illegal aftermarket upgrades come into play as I load up the guard's retina scan on my Ripperkins.

A second run with the security tap, and I'm in.

Locking the door from the inside won't be enough. Slapping a bar on the door is next on my list.

The extending metal bar I pull out of my kit spans the door from one side of the frame to the other. I tighten it into place with a twist. Prying open the wall switch plate lets me access the wiring. I pull the switch out of the box partway. Clipping gator clips onto the power supply, I watch the capacitor and the electromagnetic anchors latch the bar securely onto the doorframe. The building's own power magnetically locks the bar in place.

I check the time. I've got a couple of minutes and that locking bar will buy me a few more. Finally, I make my way to the curtained-off area.

It feels weird having to break in to see my own brother … and the fact that I have a brother at all … I take a deep a breath and duck past the curtains.

Pipes, hoses, wires, and a ton of scanning equipment lace together and feed into stacks of machines meant to replace missing organs. All of the gear runs in and out of a severed upper torso. It's gruesome and cool to look at.

My brother's arms are strapped down with a couple of heavy restraints.

Vlasta mentioned he wanted to die.

There's a rumor about arcologies. It's a rumor because no one ever gets in or out and is alive to prove it.

If anyone escapes the arcology, they send out a seek-and-destroy team. Once the target is dead, the whole team destroys their gear and then kill themselves. No one in, no one out.

I step closer and stare at his face. He's handsome enough for me to be okay with the idea of him being my brother.

"Are you here to gloat?" He doesn't open his eyes. His voice is thin; the pumps that push air into his throat whine as speaking demands different volumes of air.

"No." I study his features, trying to imagine a father and mother for us both. "Should I be gloating?"

"I failed." His chuckle is painful to watch. "I would gloat if I were you."

"I'll take that under advisement." I'm disarmed by him. I want him to be my brother. "Why are you out here?"

"It wasn't my first choice of assignments." He keeps his breathing steady. "Simply put, I was given a task."

"I think I need something more specific than that." I look around for a chair. There isn't one.

"I was sent to locate specific data. The data was inside the offices in that slum."

"You killed my friend."

I feel bitter about what happened. Maybe I could've done something different to warn Larus and Ishacc.

"Am I supposed to say something placating to you now?" He tries to shake his head, but the medical gear hinders the movement. "Your friends were part of my target group."

"Who else was in your target group?" I have a good idea, but I ask anyway.

He opens his eyes. Now he really looks like my brother. "You are, Raven."

"Who sent you?" My frustration comes out. I lean over him. "Why are you here?"

He throws out his answers. "The arcology's High Council sent me. I'm here to help you choose better friends by killing off the ones who are slowing you down. That way, when you meet Phillip again, you'll have no choice but to follow your destiny. Is that what you wanted to hear?"

"You're full of shit. Phillip is dead. I killed him." My first sibling fight, and I'm losing to a blown off torso.

"Of course I'm lying, Raven." He glares at me. "Except for the part about you needing better friends. That part is true. You really do need better friends. The skinny one told me everything. I didn't even have to threaten him. He rolled over like an old dog. He told me everything he knew about you."

I stop myself from slapping him. I regret my pleasure-tap as I lose my patience. It's creepy.

"I don't understand you, Raven." His respirator pushes more air. "Phillip took a look around and realized that without a strong governing State, businesses were going to fuck everyone over. He just wants to level the field."

"By turning everyone into drooling zombies?"

"You never cared about the plan. About the greater good. He told me you've always had problems focusing on reality."

"Screw you."

It occurs to me that I'm busting his chops without even knowing his name. My own brother's name is a mystery.

"What the hell is your name anyway?"

"Why, Raven? So you can build some delusional little world about your family?" His snort of contempt is mechanical. "Don't you have enough problems with your memory without having to toss in more irrelevant garbage?"

~~~

Wolf finds me and sits on a couch across the lounge space. "Do I have to tell you how angry I am at you right now?"

"Only if it makes you feel better." I hardly look at him. "Maybe you can channel your Spanish outrage into erasing the past. I can't undo what I did."

"You drugged a guard, broke into a secure area *inside my building*, and you beat a restrained patient."

I shrug.

I would've killed him if Picasso hadn't dragged me away. I turned on Fire-eyes, ready to kick his ass too, but his eager response spun me back to the reason I slept with Angel instead.

We're too much alike, too dangerous for each other.

Wolf surges from his seat and prowls in front of me. "Vlasta tells me she's not speaking to you right now. Is that true?"

"Yeah." I lean back and close my eyes.

"She's pissed at you. You know that right?"

I take a deep breath. "Yeah."

He continues, "And just to confirm. You let him get to you and you beat him? A restrained patient? One who is little more than a head and a pair of shoulders?" Wolf spits out his questions.

"Yeah." It wasn't my proudest moment, but I'm not saying that to him. "Like I said, I can't undo what happened. We all get to live with it."

"How can you be so…" He sighs. "Do I even want to know why you did it?" He sounds tired.

"Hey, he started it!" I rouse myself. My honor is weirdly at stake.
~~~

"Oh really? And how did that happen?" he asks.

"He's my brother." I try the only defensible thing I can think of: I get angry. "Did you know that?"

"I'd heard that, yes." He frowns. "Genetically, he has markers that would indicate a relation to you."

"You sound like Vlasta." I glare at him. "And when were you planning on telling me?"

"So you slapped him around because he's your brother?" He doesn't even address my question.

"Yeah, well, that and he was being stubborn, and flippant, and full of shit."

Red flag.

There's a sinking moment as I realize my brother knew, and then masterfully used, every button I had. He reflected me perfectly. What does that say?

Wolf nails me. "Did you stop to think that maybe your brother knew about your past psychotic breaks? And did you think that maybe he would want to trigger one so you would kill him?"

"No." I hate having to put it out there.

"Ah ha. I thought so." He stops in front of me. "You aren't allowed to see him."

Regardless of what he thinks, I'm not gonna let him dictate what I can and can't do. "He's my brother. Aren't there rules about you not being able to stop familial visitation?"

"Yes, there are rules." He nods. "But I make my own rules when I need to, Raven. This is one of those times. Don't even go near his rooms." He turns to leave.

Here's my moment. I throw it all out there. The real reason I'm moping. "There's another Phillip."

He'd started to walk away. I've drawn him back.

Wolf turns back around. "Phillip is from inside?" His eyes are hard under his brow.

I nod. "The real Phillip is alive inside the Neo Detroit arcology. The one I killed was a clone sent out here for some kind of experimental study."

I know Wolf well enough to see the news has messed with some plan he has going.

"What do you want me to do about that?" he asks.

"Brain hack this guy." I meet his dark grey eyes. "Hook the bastard up and strip everything out of his head that we can use."

"This is your brother." He cocks his head at me.

I don't know if he's testing me or telling me that my humanity has just slipped away.

"No, Wolf." I stand. "He's the tip of a larger incursion force that's going to fuck up everyone's shit." I use his trademark look back on him. I pin him, and don't look away as I speak. "Yours, mine, everybody's shit, all fucked up. Brother or not, we need what he has, and if he isn't willing to give it to us, we need to bust in there and take it. Period. End of discussion."

"I'm glad we agree on that point. I had Vlasta start the process half an hour ago. It'll take time. Even in this condition, he's tough." He sounds spent.

He tosses his hand in a tired gesture of dismissal. "Go home, bunk here, I don't care, but it's late and I'm turning in. When I have some solid information, we'll act."

As I watch him go, I realize all I've done is confirm his course of action; he was planning to go into Neo Detroit before I nailed him.

He takes even that satisfaction away from me.

Crap.

I'd kill him if my pleasure-tap didn't make being mad at him and not killing him so much fun.

1.22

On the Moro

When they let Brios out of recovery a day later, we decide to celebrate with an expensive sushi order for delivery. I've never had sushi delivered.

The delivery bot cracks some pretty good jokes and isn't programmed to beg for a tip. I tip the programmer through the machine anyway. Programming humor is a job that sounds like it would suck.

Brios actually digs out the ceramic plates I bought and not his favorite brand of disposables.

"This is really good food for having come out of the side door of an automated kitchen vehicle," I say as I fill my plate.

"Yeah." Brios drops onto the couch. "Looks good." He cracks open his chopsticks. "So what do you think of the whole arcology thing?"

I know he wants to talk shop. He's trying to keep my mind off all the shit going on, and I love him for the effort.

I've always hated the hurry-up-and-wait crap right before a job. This felt worse.

I might get to shoot my ex again … that's a plus … maybe.

But finding out I kind of have family, when I always pegged myself as an only child…. Yeah, there's a lot there to process that I don't want to. Instead, I focus on Brios, the food, and trying to be patient.

Brios starts levering pieces of sushi into his mouth. He eats like a machine when he's in recovery mode and his glucose fuel cells are low.

At least sushi is classier than eating a bowl of raw sugar.

I load him up a second plate. With his new arms, he's going to be eating a lot more, but I don't think he's processed that part yet.

"Look, since South Am I've thought about this. When shit happens, the corporations who can act just don't use enough violence the first time around. So the problem keeps coming back." I whip some wasabi into my soy sauce. "Finding the line between enough violence and too much violence becomes nothing more than political posturing. The corporations don't want to piss off their clients and customers, but they're not really looking to solve problems."

"Blasting the crap out of the bad guy of the week is your solution?"

"It's *a* solution." I join him on the couch, handing him the fresh plate. "If you hit someone hard enough, they never come back to bother you. That's all I'm saying."

"It's an unpopular concept, because there's a backend cost." He shovels a roll into his mouth, talking as he chews. He gestures with his chopsticks. "Look at the Middle East. Their leadership was a private family business who knocked around their own people until they fell in line."

"That's my point." I eat. "The guys who challenged them got slapped so hard they didn't come back. Problem solved, so far as the business is concerned."

"But that private business went under because the world got wise to their bullshit and stopped dealing with them." Brios shakes his head. "Wolf always asks what the real price is, and who has to pay it."

"If the arcologies are messing with things out here, big things like this nanobot project, they need to go."

Larus was in this because of me, and now he's dead. And so is Vicky. If Brios hadn't dodged that bola, it would've been him too.… The real price, as far as I'm concerned, has been paid up front, and I'm just looking to get what I paid for.

"I say we go in, find Phillip and the rest of PharmaComp, and we slap them down. Slap them so hard they don't ever come back." I slow down and pick at my food. Either way, I'm unhappy about the prospect of this job.

We've stuck with the theme and chosen Asian beers for the night. Brios pauses to have a drink. "Doesn't it bother you that You-Prime, your base level, un-cloned you, might be in there?"

"Hell yeah, it bothers me," I say. Brios nailed it, and I can't help my anger. "I want to know what the hell she was thinking, getting herself cloned. And how the hell did I get out?"

"Maybe she didn't have a choice." Brios looks up from his food.

"Huh. I never thought about that." Suddenly it isn't all about guns blazing.

Crap, it's my favorite business model too.

Then it hits me. "Hey. What happens if everyone in the whole damn arcology is messed up like the people on the airship?"

Brios frowns. "We'll be going into a whole city full of people who'll want to kill you. Pack your zip gun."

We eat in silence as that thought settles in.

The shitty antique cell phone rings, interrupting our this-isn't-going-to-work-the-way-we-want-it-to bitching session.

"Go." I answer the call and keep it short.

"This is Moro," the polite Russian controller says. *"We have the intel we need. Wolf is calling you in."*

Brios looks at me as I stand. Our eyes meet, and I nod. We're on.

While I'm on the line, Brios and I are moving. We grab our jump sacks; everything is prepped.

My heart rate climbs, and I push aside concerns about the job. Wolf wouldn't have us going if he wasn't ready.

"Anything else?" I ask.

"Ten minutes," Moro says. *"Bring any personal equipment you might need."* He cuts the line.

~ ~ ~

Well inside the ten minute mark, Brios and I watch a needle-shaped air car drop onto the pad. As we approach, the gull-wing doors open. Angel nods at us from the pilot's seat.

A tall figure climbs out of the passenger side. "Hello." He extends a hand. I recognize Moro's voice.

I realize I've seen him before. He's the hunky blond with the razor cut hair and the expensive Leopold Geiger suit from Vlasta's place.

He introduces himself. "I am Morochevsky. It is good to meet you in person."

I desperately want to ask how long he and Vlasta have been going out. I barely manage to hold off as I shake his hand.

"Please." He motions for us to get in. "Wolf is no longer patient."

"Good." I smile and catch Brios' look. "Pissing off Basillio might be my new favorite pastime, but I'm done waiting."

We climb into the air car, and the doors swing closed.

"Are we heading to the drop point now, or do we meet Wolf first?" Brios asks.

"Wolf is waiting to speak with you directly. More a personal confirmation I am sure. After that, he will be joining us," Morochevsky says.

The car exits the city through one of the huge side ventilation openings. It's the first time I've flown through the side of the Stack. I try not to gawk too much.

"Is he out in Rafter country?" Brios asks.

Morochevsky snorts. "He is with his anarchic boat people, yes. I will be waiting on the outskirts."

The sore spot isn't something I miss. I file it away. A girl never knows what might be important later.

Wolf meets us out on the docks near a line of PBRs that are sheltered from prying eyes by a collapsed bridge and a sharp embankment.

As we arrive, a guy with Maori facial tattoos is handing him what looks like a parts list. "This will finish the conversion to nanoflow fuel cells on all of these craft," the fellow says. "They'll be easier to maintain and quieter all around."

"I'll get these parts out to you in three days." Wolf skims the list and hands it back before he joins us on the dock. He motions for us to walk with him.

We climb up along a brush covered ridge that looks past the floating Rafter village and toward the Gulf.

As we walk out of earshot, he begins the briefing. "We have a map to a relatively unguarded edge of the arcology. We also have a contact who can get us to some kind of entrance. The same contact has the names of people and their societal positions inside the Block. Reports indicate that Phillip is a researcher inside the arcology."

I keep my expression bland as Wolf watches me for any reactions I might have to Phillip's name.

Apparently, I pass.

He continues, "What he'd been working on was deemed by their council to be too risky to test on their population. He was given permission to send clones of himself outside to run the tests and report. They've been operating outside for about a decade. They infiltrated the outside, starting small with one lab in the PhillyMetroplex. Now PharmaComp is a world leader in electro-organic pharmaceutical hardware integration."

"That's a mouthful." I look at Brios. He's being all serious. I ask Wolf, "Is that title on their shareholders' reports?"

Wolf points us along a wide trail through the trees. "They've made a fortune. All the things they put patents on are things that are supposedly basic technologies from inside the arcology. Out here, it all looks advanced. In there, it's common knowledge, common practice. Phillip and his friends inside are now major players on their council because they're importing new raw materials which they buy with the company's profits. They've also been combing our technology for things they haven't developed on the inside and importing them. They control all the access to that technology coming and going."

I'm done talking, but just to be polite I say, "So they're business dicks?"

"Yeah," he says. "Dicks."

"Okay. So? What?" I fidget. I regret asking because it only starts him off again.

"They've been manipulating people on a global scale. People in key positions across dozens of business sectors." He pauses again, probably for effect. "At this point, they're ready to start phase three."

I blurt out, "Which is when they take over the world?"

"Don't make too big a joke out of it. It's bad." Both he and Brios have military-serious faces on now. "Key hardware manufacturers have been compromised for at least the last five years. A large percentage of everything with a chip in it, or any kind of remote computing capability, can be flipped into performing roles outside of normal function."

Damn. I have to admit it. "Okay. That's bad."

The path we're on opens up to a view of the bridge and the waiting air car.

Wolf stares at the light dimpling on the water as we near the air car. "I've managed to find someone who is originally from inside the arcology. He's willing to help us. He's part of a group that tried a rebellion a while back. It was suppressed, but he and a few others survived the purges. He escaped."

I look at him. "You trust any of this intel?"

"Not as far as I can throw it, but it's what we have to go on. Vlasta is confident that it can't all be crap." He shrugs. "Somewhere in there are facts. Once we get inside we can go forward."

Now we get to the inevitable, the whole reason I'm here. "Who's on the team with me?"

"How do you know I have you on a team at all?"

"I'm the only clone you know. We don't know jack-shit about how things run in there, but my being a clone can't hurt our chances. I may have a better chance at blending in. That buys me a second or two of hesitation. That's enough time for everyone who comes with me to do their thing."

He flashes a smile of approval. "Glad you thought about reasons why I'd send you instead of saying something like 'because I want to be on the team.'"

"When do we go?" I'm anxious now. If I have to wait any more, I think I'll lose my shit.

"Now." He matches my grin and points to the vehicle. "Any equipment you need will be available at the entry point, and we'll be monitoring from the outside. Moro will be your controller."

Wolf nods toward the tall blond Russian who opens the gull-wing doors as we approach.

~ ~ ~

It takes three hours by air to get to our staging area.

There was a city here, once upon a time. Old Detroit. From the air I can make out pockets of nomads in scattered enclaves between the rubble, tilted ruins, and wild forest regrowth.

Wolf and his regular troops have negotiated a clear zone for a forward base and then covertly secured a mile-wide corridor all the way to the walls of the arcology.

There's still some sunlight when we arrive, and I have a moment to actually see what autumn looks like for real.

I've seen pictures and tourist ads about places like this. Trees that drop their leaves, and leaves that change color, all that hype.

It's pretty to see it in person.

When it's dark, we crowd into our fortified building and watch satellite and drone footage of the area we're going to.

By the sixth time the same drone footage plays on the screen, I've had enough.

"Look, guys," I say. "I'm not saying this is a waste of time, but this is like planning to rob a jewelry store and pouring all of our preparations into understanding the sidewalk outside the door. Do we know anything about what's inside the Block. Does it have levels? Interior walls? Oh I know, maybe they live in tents on the ceiling and wander around in magnetic boots."

"GPR shows us interior spaces to a depth of one hundred feet." Wolf taps a still frame onto the display.

"Jesus, that's it?"

Our lives are at stake and we have one hundred feet of ground penetrating radar for our visuals.

"The Block is referred to by that name for a reason, Sweetie. This isn't New White Sands where there's eleven hundred feet between floors. This place is built up like a hive on the inside. We have effective top down maps of the upper ten stories and around the perimeters all the way to the ground."

Wolf flips through shots rendered into usable schematics. "Sections closest to the rooftop look abandoned, others look as though they are in use by tribal types, or possibly act as locations for a variety of illegal activity."

I try to wrap my head around what he's saying. Gangs, tribal types, even organized crime. Maybe the Block isn't as different as I thought.

"What about lower levels and infrastructure?" Brios asks.

"From the side profile, we picked out service and utility floors every twenty-five stories. The central stories are hydroponics, primary sewage, and water treatment. The lower floors are geothermal pumps and power."

I tune out the blah, blah, blah.

I'm breaking into a sealed arcology with intel that's little better than bathroom gossip, and my backup amounts to resources that I can't even take with me.

Fucking Phillip. He's the real reason I'm here. The rest of this is just window dressing and crap.

A lot of good people I knew are dead because of him. Otherwise, why should I care?

Because someone in the arcology is threatening to unleash a little bit of extra chaos onto the earth? Because it might actually cause it to split open and force normal people to deal with a little bit of extra hell?

Yeah, I'm not that kind of girl.

I should be shopping, or writing articles about the latest color palettes in fashion trends or living room decor. I should be going to clubs, taking side jobs playing good-time girl and bodyguard to famous citizens, or mugging people for trinkets.

I leave the briefing, find a pallet of beer at the rear of the cantina, grab a six-pack, and stomp up the hillside. I sit on a rock and stare at the Block in the distance.

It's a few miles long and windowless. The whole thing has a faint glow to it. I wonder if it's throwing off the same kind of radiation that made John infertile on my show.

It's full dark when I see someone else come out of our ops building. It's Morochevsky.

He's the only other person in the camp that I know besides Brios, Wolf, and Angel.

He looks around and makes his way over to me.

"May I join you?" He's so polite. I would've just sat.

"I've heard this area of the country isn't in a Corporate Control Zone. I guess that makes it free."

I pull out a beer and offer it to him.

He accepts the can with a nod. His movements are precise. There's no wasted effort in his actions. He moves with an economy that screams danger-boy.

When he sits beside me, he instinctively assumes a pose I know he will stay in until he gets up to leave. He could sit like this for days if he needed to.

I try small talk; it's something my etiquette instructor says I need to work on. "So, what part of Russia are you from?"

"I am Russian only as my place of birth. My parents were forcibly immigrated into Russia after the Crimean Incident.

They were deemed to be high value human assets." His face is grim as he drinks his beer. "I was born in Siversky. It was a small city outside of Saint Petersburg."

I watch him shake off some mental demons.

He asks, "And you? Where are you from?"

I tip the edge of my beer toward the Block. "I'm told there's a good chance I started my life in there. I can't say for sure though. I don't remember much of anything before I became a barely-restrained-psychotic-fashionista-assassin. Or much after that either."

"Hmm. Interesting baggage," he comments.

"Yeah." I finish my second beer and pull out a third. "I don't talk about it much. I have really big memory lapses."

"How did you end up working for Basillio?"

He doesn't need to ask that. As my controller, he probably has my 201 profile memorized.

I opt for the short, safe answer. "It just kind of happened that way." I deflect further questions with, "Besides do any of us really work for him?"

He chuckles. "No, I suppose none of us here in camp work for him in a traditional sense."

"So how long have you known Vlasta?"

He seems surprised by my question. "Long enough to know I should not be talking about how long I've known her."

I laugh. "Okay. Knowing Vlasta, that's probably the best answer you could give. I didn't mean to pry."

I'm not going to get any goods on her from him.

"It is all right." He smiles. "Very few people know about our relationship. We try to keep our work lives separate from everything else."

"What did you do for work back in the motherland?"

"I was Spetsnaz doing high-orbital operations," he says. He finishes his beer and sets the can down. "I specialized in command and control, covert EVA, and demolitions."

I laugh again. "Damn, you're the first real space marine, from anywhere, I've ever met."

He performs a gracious half bow.

I get it now, why he's my controller, why the airship was so thoroughly destroyed by his explosives, and why he moves the way he does.

The wind rustles through the trees.

"What do you think of the mission?" Why the hell did I ask that?

I brace for an answer I know I don't want to hear.

"The neurochemical mind manipulation system has profound and dangerous implications. Therefore, this mission needs to happen. Will it succeed? I have high confidence in the members chosen for the team. Some of them, like you, are very motivated to see a successful outcome."

He stands. "Will all of the team survive? No, I don't believe so. My best outcome for the mission is that one of you will survive long enough to get to an extraction point before succumbing to injuries."

He doesn't flinch or look away as he finishes presenting his assessment. "Recovery of a body would be calculated based on the factors of casualties to the recovery team, monetary cost, and the degree of provocation a recovery might incite. Provided there is limited pursuit, the body may be recovered for a postmortem debriefing. I also believe your knowing the truth about your odds is better than you having delusions of your own safety."

"Way to keep it real, Moro."

"Get some sleep," Moro says as he turns to go. "You leave before sunrise, and it will be a cold walk to the entry point."

I stare after him and remember the last thing my brother said to me just before I hit him. *You'd never survive a day inside the Block, Raven. Your attitude might serve you well out here, but inside they'd cull you like an animal.*

What's left of my single six-pack of beer isn't going to be enough to blunt my worries before the mission green-lights in the morning.

I wish the cantina had stocked something stronger.

1.23

The Block

There's anecdotal evidence from local gangs that suggests the building has some sort of anti-vehicle weaponry built in. Control has opted not to test it, so we walk, and it's cold; just like Moro said it would be.

There's frost everywhere. It's a new thing for me, and at first I'm excited. But the novelty of a world covered in a skim of frozen water gets old quick when I'm moving cover to cover. The frost takes its sweet time melting, especially from the places where I have to hide.

Autumn rapidly becomes another oversold concept for me. Cold, wet, rotting leaves cover chilly, slimy, swampy soil. The leaves are packed into jagged corners of busted up roadways and slabs of ruined buildings.

I'm covered in wet cold filth when the group finally stops.

I wish I was at a day spa.

At least in South Am, the leaves had the decency to be warm when they rotted even if they were freshly wet. At least, that's how I remember it.

We initialize our Horatius perimeter security system and wait in our chilly bivouac for our contact to meet us.

We're camped near our rendezvous point and within sight of the Block. The jutting lip of a collapsed parking garage ramp offers us shelter from a light rain.

Someone brings out a deck of cards. In between hands everyone stares out at the massive structure.

Because I hate cards and have never seen a Horatius unit before, I leave the group and take a look at one of the automated sentries.

Brios told me stories about fighting auto-turret emplacements in South Am. Dug-in defensive positions that could take out ten men just getting to them. That was back when postmortem revival was voodoo magic. If they managed to bring you back at all, you were lucky if you were the same person when you woke up.

Back then, auto-turrets were just big-ass guns, a couple of poppers, and a basic targeting computer.

I call up the AlphaTek mission file on my left eye and select our equipment inventory. Specs scroll across my vision as I examine the unit. Wolf hasn't gone cheap. These are the best that money can buy.

The Horatius I check out is currently linked as part of a series, but each tripod can be set up as a single hard point defense unit. They're self-contained autonomous killing machines, using sealed communications to talk to one another. These ones are kitted out with a mix of weapons systems, various grenades, smoke launchers, micro-missiles, an assault rifle and a heavy weapons canon all guided by a multiple-sensor array.

Non-cybered infantry twenty years ago would've needed a mule or a vehicle to move their auto-turrets around. But these units fit into a large man-portable pack specifically for field carry.

It's an impressive piece of hardware. Basically if anything moves downrange, Horatius checks it against his ID software and kills it if it doesn't match parameters. He also counter-battery fires; locating and counterfiring at individuals or groups near instantaneously. I get giddy just thinking about it. I can't wait to see one of these unleashed.

I have one of the Horatius units on the list of goodies coming inside with me.

You never know when a girl might need a secure doorway, or a bridge.

I turn off the visual overlay and glance at the Block looming behind me. From this vantage point, the arcology looks way bigger. Not New White Sands big, but it's imposing just by the fact it has no openings or features on its skin. It looks like a solid block of polished stone.

The whole thing could've been floated in by aliens and set down onto the terrain. Ruins of buildings, sidewalks, and streets run up to the glowing wall and then stop. Everything vanishes under its bulk.

Another creepy thing I notice is that, even at range, my com-link puts out a low hum on all channels.

I duck back into our bivouac and ask the communications guys about it. They quickly adopt a stoic nothing's-wrong-at-all set to their shoulders. Their expressions and non-answers make me moody.

I find Brios hulled down on a chunk of tumbled concrete, and drop beside him. I offer him an energy bar. He takes it silently. I can tell he's as unhappy as I am with the current circumstances.

"You think this clown is going to show?" I ask. All this waiting has me itching to run a hustle.

Brios shrugs his reply.

"We should start a pool," I say as I scan the overgrown ruins. "You in?"

"Nope."

When Horatius pings his warning, our contact is still eight hundred yards out and on foot in the rubble.

A com officer lets us know of the contact's approach, and we get a view of a Null in grubby looking clothes stumping his way closer to camp. We sit and wait for him to arrive.

He stops a hundred yards away. I dial in my Ripperkins.

There's something not right about how the Null stands, how he holds his head, and his posture in general.

"This is our guy?" I ask.

Brios nods.

"Okay then." I tighten my armor vest. "Let's reel him in."

We start walking and keep our hands where he can see them. He returns the courtesy.

As we approach, Brios asks, "What's the password?"

"Ferdinand the Bull." The Null shuffles a bit and pulls back his canvas hood. "It's a stupid name. The story is only satirically funny if you get the historical context."

I try not to stare at his massive deformities. His eyes are lopsided, his head misshapen; cysts of yellowing flesh protrude in random places everywhere.

He notices me staring and glares back.

"An educated Null, that's a first," I say as Brios looks him over as well.

"My name is William." His attitude is intense but oddly casual. "The gangs out here don't care what I look like or what name I use. They respect me for what I can do and have done, for myself and them."

"You're from the inside?" Brios asks.

"Yeah, but I've been out for eight years now. The people of the Block don't like to keep anything around that reminds them that the system can fail."

"If they chop up their failures, how'd you happen?" I ask.

I catch Brios' mental wince.

My insulting tone and fight'n words run off William like water on a banana leaf.

"Only the DNA modified elite get to spawn." He turns miscast eyes toward the Block. "Everyone else gets rendered infertile through harvesting and then cloned and educated as needed to fulfill specific roles. My parents decided their act of rebellion would be to mix their bodily fluids and shove the result into the production line without screening of any kind."

"Wow," I say. "That's messed up."

"I'm told my surrogate womb pled to have me destroyed, but the attending medical technician was also a counter-culture rebel. He kept me and raised me secretly to become a symbol. A living symbol of what it means to stand against elitist social oppression."

His voice becomes bitter. "The rebels themselves rejected me as abnormal. I got tired of playing Cassandra and hiding from both sides when I was always proven right. I escaped."

"There's definitely a story in there," I say.

Brios looks lost. He may have thought William dressed as a girl named Cassandra for his disguise. I'll have to explain Greek mythology to him later.

"I wrote a book: *Homogeneity, the Successes and Failures of the Culture of One*," William says. "It was self-published on an IndiePress."

"Never heard of it." Brios shrugs.

I sure as hell am not going to tell him I only ever read booklists and reviews just so that I can use them as filler in conversations at parties. And I only do that to get gigs.

Besides, who reads nowadays, I mean other than headlines on Infotainment marquees? Okay, Brios read Robin Hood, but I know that was part of a play to get in my pants, so that doesn't count.

"I'm not surprised." William shakes his head in resigned disgust. "The book was suppressed by corporations out here because it echoed a lot of their dreams for the future. It upset them that someone figured out their game."

"Makes sense. The savings for having homogeneous demographic points would be substantial." I think about the chaos of people, cultures, and ideas mixing on every level of New White Sands.

He points to the glowing slab of wall. "Inside, people who express differences of opinion undergo re-education. It's a source of intense frustration to me that everyone forgets that institutions are built by man to serve man. When the institution fails to serve, we're entitled to dismantle it. Replace it."

I stifle an impulse to fidget. Brios understands me well enough to know that I'm doing my best to be polite, trying to win this guy's trust.

William continues, his voice becoming driven with passion. "Peaceful, internal reforms are only sloppy cosmetic displays, not real change. Wholesale ground-up restructuring can't be done peacefully because the people in power like the system and protect it. It serves them. So they actively promote a fear culture. The great unwashed masses simply follow along as a reaction to that fear, or out of complacency and ignorance."

"I get it," I say. "I get the idea of Sheeple." I've been one. Still am one? It doesn't matter.

"Out here, people have guns," he says. "Push comes to shove, people start dying. Institutions and businesses are quicker to change. Refusing is too messy and the people out here hold grudges. But everyone inside the Block is oppressed. They're waiting for a sign. They want a mystical tipping point in the tide of societal norms, something that will promote a leader overnight for their cause who will guide them to freedom." He shrugs. The movement momentarily pulls his frame straight.

He's actually taller than I am.

"The Godot they're waiting for is not coming," he says. "In this case he's not coming because he's been murdered. Their own inaction killed him, and no one is brave enough or desperate enough to replace him."

"Okay, Bill." I've had enough standing around listening to this.

How am I going to function inside if this kind of monologuing is what I can expect? Maybe I need to pack in a lot of coffee.

I holster my gun, nod to the bivouac, and start walking. "Let's get a coffee and you can tell us what we need to know." I'm hoping a change of venue will get him back on track.

"Real coffee?" He drops in behind me. His steps are shuffling, but he's nimble enough to keep up. "Or that freeze-dried stuff passed off as coffee?"

I make a face at him over my shoulder. "I'll eat a bucket of stims before I drink that stuff. Come on."

We drink a pot of fresh coffee while holding an informal interview. I glare at a few gawkers when Bill isn't looking and word spreads quickly not to react to the grungy Null's deformities.

Bill relaxes when he figures out I'm the one running the process. Not because I'm a woman, but because I'm not military.

A different attitude yields different results.

William is a rebel. He was born and raised to be the very symbol of the rebellion, a living martyr.

Everything he says is peppered with layers of rebel philosophies, indoctrination, metaphors, parables, and examples of Block Elitist oppression.

He keeps pushing to overcome objections to the rebellion even though we haven't raised any. We have to vet everything that comes out of his mouth to get what we need.

He doesn't get it and we don't tell him: We aren't here for their rebellion.

I only want our mission objectives achieved, even if that means rendering the Block an uninhabitable ruin. Apply enough violence…

1.24

Arcology 101

We have to wait another two days for the weather to shift. When it does, it's an early morning snowfall. It comes down in a writhing mass.

William assures me this kind of weather is wreaking havoc with the Block's sensors and is going to make our approach on foot possible.

"And you're sure the snow is jamming their sensors?" I ask again as we creep forward.

William looks at me. "I like my life. I wouldn't be here if the sensors could pick me up."

I peek over my shoulder. Brios is nearby. I feel safer knowing he's on my flank.

Our team was rounded out that morning, solidifying as Brios and I, two gunslingers including one heavy, and a late arriving nettie. We have a lot of gear because none of us are sure what we'll need, but even still we make good time.

We get to the entry point.

Years of rainwater from an eroding watershed has plowed up against the structure and undercut one edge, hollowing out a low cave. One after another, we duck out of the snowfall and under the smooth material of the arcology.

William leads the way. We follow along behind the dim light of the chem-stick he's carrying.

The passage is filled with debris carried in by spring rains and decades of runoff. We pick out a path in silence.

The cave drops and opens into an old sub-basement. It looks like a high-rise of some sort stood here once.

William stops and sits. "Someone from inside will be here to take us the rest of the way."

"You don't know the way?" asks Portia. She's our heavy weapons operative and built like a fireplug.

She hasn't said more than two words to anyone. Her voice is what I imagine a sweet old grandma sounds like, or at least, a grandma with a chainsaw in her throat.

Maybe she's a rebuild. Her records show she knows how to use the minigun she's hauling and has a really high verified kill count with it. Everything else I don't care about.

I can't care.

If Moro's appraisal of our survival is on target, then my only concern is Brios. He's only here because of me.

The second gunslinger is named Spyker. His profile lists a bunch of minor conflicts across south and central Africa. I know better than to call him Dutch. He looks competent on paper and that's good enough for me.

I look at our two gunslingers. Wolf put me in charge because I'm the clone. As I sit there waiting, a dark part of my mind comes to a decision. If either of them screw up, I'll just kill them. I would rather risk the mission by going it alone than risk the mission by having incompetent people watching our backs.

Of the three, only our nettie is vital.

James Leroy Takashi. His tag is 'Jimmy the Slip.' His profile lists a number of big hacks, a few nasty viruses, and some solid adaptive antiviral programs. He looks young for someone who's twenty-two, and he has no experience under fire that I could find.

Jimmy doesn't look like anyone Wolf would send on this drop. If we get a moment alone, I'll pry him for information on that front, but for now he's here and we're moving.

"To answer your lame question," Bill whispers, "I know a bunch of ways in, but only the people on the inside know for sure which of those ways is least guarded, unguarded, or being watched at any time. We sometimes can bribe the guards if they aren't outright sympathizers."

Minutes after we arrive, a light bobs out of the darkness. My Ripperkins adjust to my best advantage. I see the passageway clearly. The entire thing from here back has been dug out by hand.

A woman makes her way toward us. I sign to the team. I don't want surprises of any kind.

"William," the attractive looking woman in her early thirties greets our contact. Her clothing is all one shade of tan and simply cut. Everything else she's carrying looks like it hangs off her belt. She hesitates as she sees us crouched like demons in the shadows. "I see you brought friends."

"Lynnette, these people want to help us." William nods at me. "One of the council has had operatives on the outside making mischief and they tracked the source here."

"Phillip has made more than mischief." I step out from the shadows.

The woman's eyes flicker what looks like quickly contained surprise. "Phillip? I have heard of him on the council. He's a worthy target."

"I have the supplies you asked for," William adds as he pulls foil wrapped bundles out of his grungy coat. "Will you take these people inside and introduce them to your cell?"

"Aren't you coming?" I ask. I look at him. The referee pulls out a red flag and gets ready.

"No. What good would I be?" He gestures to his face. "Look at me. I can't move freely with you. I'm still hunted as an abomination. Besides, Lynnette has cleaner, current information and knows people who will be able to help you."

Brios meets my eyes with his talk-later look. I nod once as we part ways and follow Lynnette deeper under the Block. I fight the feeling that William has set us up.

I know everyone on the team is feeling it, but we all keep our opinions to ourselves.

"Are you here to kill Phillip?" Lynnette wastes no time.

"If we *were* here to kill him," I banter back, "would that upset you?"

She looks over her shoulder. "Only insofar as I couldn't predict who might succeed him. So are you here to kill him?"

"We're here to see what's feasible, what can and can't be done," I say.

She leads us toward a series of wide geothermal pipes running vertically from inside the Block into the ground.

My Ripperkins let me see that the floor of the Block, our ceiling, has been hammered away to make a man sized hole beside the pipe itself. A rope ladder hangs down from above.

"Are we meeting anyone at the top?" I look around as we approach the ladder.

"Paranoid?" She smiles at me.

"More like dangerous and twitchy," I reply. I meet her eyes. "I'd hate to kill all of your friends because of a simple miscommunication."

My words bring a pause and consideration. "There's one man up top who's mine. There are two guards and an engineer in a side room. Those last three are being distracted and shouldn't bother us."

"Go up slowly." I don't ask. "Let your man know we're coming."

Lynnette does as she's told, climbing nice and slow.

"I fucking hate choke points like this," whispers Spyker. "One goddamned grenade is all it would take down here."

We all feel the same way, except Jimmy who's been busy with his handheld rig since we crawled below ground.

I look at Brios who I know is listening in.

He signs an all clear.

"Spyker, Portia, Jimmy, me, then Brios." I lay out our team formation.

Everyone just moves.

I wonder what they've read about me in my profile to make them so complacent.

When I get to the top, I have to clamp down on my first reaction. The guy with Lynnette looks a lot like my brother but with all of his limbs. My gun hand twitches.

I suddenly get it. These people are knock-offs of better gene sets.

There's an uncomfortable moment as I stare too long and he notices. I wonder what he thinks our silent exchange is about.

I look around, setting my Ripperkin implants to take still frames of everything I see of interest.

The facility is clean, but it's showing its age. How do you fix something as major as a power-tap with limited supplies and no large equipment? Yeah, they could run like this for another hundred years but then what? Evict everyone and start over? Try to swing a full overhaul?

"We should go." Lynnette gives us a rundown for our path of travel, the room we need to sneak past, and where we're supposed to wait for her. She gives us a head start so she can deal with the guards on duty.

We move carefully down the hallway.

None of the offices have doors on them. The sensors that run the system are automatic and don't seem to care that the engineer has abandoned his post. Maybe it's a union job. Do they have unions in here?

Lynnette said the men were being distracted, and as we slip past the last door we get a glimpse of what she meant.

They are definitely distracted. …Taking turns with a still struggling girl barely out of her teens.

I swallow my knee-jerk reaction and have to push Jimmy past the doorframe.

We get to our meeting point, stay in cover, and wait. Brios reaches over and sticks his finger on my mastoid bone.

"Anytime you want to go out again, just bring us another one of these treats." He's amped-in on the conversation between the men and Lynnette.

"You always have the nicest stock," a second man says.

"Yeah, you could even come by more often," adds a third.

Lynnette sounds upset. *"Aw come on, guys. Do you know how hard it is to get one of these girls off the line? I have to come up with a reason that's good enough for her to be listed as defective. I have to wait for her to be removed to medical and have her certified as defective before I can requisition her physical removal. Then I have to manually delay her reassignment. It's a lot of work. The failure rate on the line can't be too high or the computer starts poking around."*

"Yeah I guess, but she's cute," the second man says. *"I'd take this model over the last one anytime."*

Lynnette replies, *"Again, too many failures of a specific model and they start looking around."*

"Just, you know, keep my preferences in mind."

"See you in four weeks," Lynnette says. *"Or less if the sensors get static."*

"Good to hear." The third man chuckles.

Lynnette and her guy hurry over to where we're waiting. They bring the girl along with them. She's still naked and filthy from her encounter, walking along in a daze.

Spyker throws his jacket over her shoulders. "Bloody animals," he mutters.

The girl doesn't notice the jacket. Lynnette and her friend seem taken aback by the gesture, but we don't have time to explore social niceties.

"Come on, while they're still dressing," Lynnette whispers. "We don't have much time."

We move in single file behind her. Eyes bright and guns up.

A few doorways, a couple of stairwells, and a hallway or two later, Lynnette opens a door that looks onto a well-lit metal gantry. Below us, some kind of recycling facility churns along. A few staff seem engaged with their control panels. Thankfully the gantry has welded side plates that can hide us from casual glances. At Lynnette's nod, we crouch and follow her out over the running machinery.

We get across and find ourselves at an intersection.

"We wait here a minute," Lynnette says.

Her guy grabs the girl by one arm and steers her toward a wide double door.

"Where is he taking her?" Portia asks.

"Where are you going, buddy?" I ask him directly. He ignores me.

"Is everyone outside like you?" Lynnette asks. A frown crosses her brow. "Paranoid?"

My gun flips up under her chin. "If you answer my questions, we'll get along so much better, understand?"

She nods. I decide Lynnette is either fearless or ignorant of what a .45 can do to her head.

She answers, "She needs to be reassigned."

"What is that? Brainwashing?" Portia asks. "Re-education? "

"No. I needed her body to bribe the guards. Citizens inside the Block can't reproduce. Even sex is forbidden. Everyone has an implant that renders it impossible to become aroused with another citizen. Since that model isn't mature enough to have an inhibitor, sex becomes possible with her. Being with somebody that way is a powerful bribe. I listed her as failed so I could take her off the line to use."

"Being able to commit rape is a bribe?" My blood is up, and I can't stop it.

"Rape? I don't know that word." Lynnette stares at me. "But look, there's nothing going on in her head yet. She's a clean slate. I'm pretty sure she can't remember anything anyway."

"Pretty sure?" I grit my teeth.

Lynnette is looking a little concerned now at my reaction. "Since she's listed as failed, I had to have the examination system find an appropriate reason to explain why she failed. In this case I created a mental instability in her brain that would make her unable to learn anything. It's the only way to get past a computer controlled investigation."

"You scrambled her brains so you could have her raped as a bribe?" Portia seems as pissed as I am.

"I don't know what you mean when you say rape." Lynnette stands her ground.

"So now what happens to her? What do you mean by reassignment?"

"The Block is a sealed ecosystem." Lynnette is trying hard to explain everything calmly, but I can see she's starting to fray. "Nothing can go to waste."

"What the hell does that mean?" I ask.

"It means her raw material goes back into the system for later use." Lynnette is matter of fact about it.

It can't be all bad, I tell myself. I keep repeating that thought over and over.

"Later use?" Portia asks angrily. "Like an organ donor?"

"That's disgusting." Lynnette makes a face. "Who would want organs from a failed line doll."

I'm about to ask what the hell a line doll is when the bomb drops. Lynnette is still matter of fact as she says, "She'll be converted into a food surplus."

I find myself sitting on my shoulder. Brios tries to get his arms around me. I might be yelling, I don't know.

Our shit slides sideways off the pan and into the fire.

1.25

Clone Culture

I recover sometime later as I'm being carried into a low wide space that turns out to be a living room. Brios hustles me to the sofa.

"What is wrong with her? She could have gotten us killed." Lynnette sounds panicked. "As it is, everyone in the facilities room knows something is going on that shouldn't be."

Brios checks with me to see if I'm okay. He answers her as he does. "Sometimes a switch in her head flips when she gets angry at people or situations."

Lynnette's eyes narrow at the explanation. The rest of the team comes into the room. Portia slings the hard case that holds Horatius off her back and looks around the room. I watch Spyker give an all clear as he poke-checks the other rooms and secures the main door.

I know I've screwed up. No one is going to listen to orders from me now unless I get control.

Lynnette points at me. "She has a cut on her arm. I have something for that." She leaves to get medical supplies from another room.

With a glance at Brios, Portia shadows her down the hall; it's common sense, not paranoia.

I hadn't noticed the gash. I look it over. It's not bad. Just bad enough to look worse than it is. "How?" I ask Brios.

"My bad," he says. "It happened trying to get you here."

Jimmy comes over to me. "You okay? That was crazy. I've never seen anyone move as fast as that in my life."

I'm not going to tell him I have no memory of what I did.

"I'm starving. You got ration bars on you?" I ask.

"Yeah." He hands one over.

"Brios and I need a second alone to figure this out." I scarf back the energy bar. "You cool?"

"Yeah." Jimmy nods. I can see he's still coming off the adrenaline spike. As he moves away I think he may even be a little shocky.

Is it odd that I feel fine?

I realize, whatever just happened, this has to be Jimmy's first real exposure to active violence.

Crap. I've scarred him for life.

Well, it was bound to happen, and it was Wolf's idea to have him along, so he can shoulder the blame.

Brios sits down beside me, his look asking his question.

"I'm fine." I look to the door where Lynnette went. "The people in this place aren't human. Sure, they're clones, but I mean they have no humanity. Who fucking does what Lynnette just did, on a monthly basis?"

Brios shrugs. "It explains a lot about Phillip's behavior."

"Yeah, everyone is expendable." I look at him. "What the hell did I do?"

"Not much." He watches the others. I can tell it was bad by how he's acting. "Aside from almost killing Lynnette and destroying the equipment in the reassignment room." He pats my leg. "That guy? Yeah, he had it coming anyway."

I sigh. "You mean her partner?" I hope Lynnette isn't one to hold a grudge.

"Yeah." Brios sits perfectly still. So it must be bad.

"Okay, I get it's bad. How bad?" I ask.

"Well he was in flagrante delicto with the girl's corpse." He pauses. "As it was going into a giant meat grinder. So I guess pushing him in crotch first is fitting."

I stare at him. "He was in what?"

"It's Latin." He looks smug. "You don't know Latin?"

"I know it's Latin." I arch a brow at him. "What I want to know is, why is it coming out of your mouth?"

"I upgraded my language base." He grins. "I need to keep up with you somehow."

"That's cute, Brios. You didn't need to do that." I ask for clarification, "So he was…?"

"Full on necro." He grimaces. "I've seen Nulls less into it than he was."

"See? These people aren't human," I say. "Wolf should have gone with my plan A and carpet bombed the shit out of this place."

"Maybe." He shuts up as Portia and Lynnette return.

Lynnette gestures. "Can I tend that arm?"

"Yeah," I say to her.

Lynnette cleans the wound, applying a type of skinseal after wiping it clean. She leaves to put stuff away. Portia trails along behind our hostess once more.

Spyker comes over. I know what's coming next. "What the fuck was that?"

I say blandly, "It's a party trick I do when I get excited."

"Fuck you." He looks at Brios. "If she's a nut-can, are you in charge?"

"She's fine." Brios is deadpan. "What you witnessed is what we need in here."

"We need crazy like we need dead," Spyker snaps. "Meaning not at all."

"I meant the speed, the aggressiveness, that surety of action." Brios is mega-calm. "If you needed to do what she did, could you have pulled it off?"

"No. But I wouldn't let my emotions drag me in to begin with." He paces "Where I'm from, what we saw in there was nothing. People do that kind of thing to their own kids if it'll get them ahead. So either she toughens her skin, or we'll have a problem."

I'm on my feet. My knives are out and pressed against his vitals before he can blink. "No more talk of problems. It ends here. Choose, Spyker. You end now, or you settle the fuck down."

"Fine, I'll do my job, no talk of problems." He's frozen. "Shit turns south again though, and I'm only listening to him." His eyes flick to Brios.

To make my point, I'm back on the sofa, knives sheathed, before Spyker exhales.

He draws a breath. "Bugger. Crazy or not, you're quick. I'll give you that."

Lynnette's cries of protest are mixed with the chainsaw of Portia's yelling. Brios and I crowd past Jimmy, down the hall, to the door where the sounds come from.

Portia has Lynnette in an armlock on the ground. Lynnette is pleading innocence to something and trying not to cry.

Portia looks at me. "She took your blood off the bandage and shoved it into that machine." She points with her chin. "It doesn't look like a fucking trash can to me. So I call her on it and she starts bullshitting."

I squat down. "What the hell are you trying to do, Lynnette? Get killed? Because if I think we can do what we came for without you, I'll drag you back for reassignment."

"You aren't from the outside," she hisses through the pain of Portia's armlock.

"See?" Portia growls and twists a bit harder. "Spouting that kind of shit."

"You're a clone. Where are you from?" Lynnette asks around a grunt of pain. "Paris? New Elgin? Berlin?"

"Shut the fuck up with that crap," Portia snaps.

"Get her to stop." Lynnette has a wild look in her eyes. "Please. She's breaking my arm."

"Let her up." I tap Portia's shoulder.

Portia drops Lynnette's arm and steps back. Her hands go to her gun. "Say the word, and I'll put her back into the food chain right here."

Lynnette lies on the polished concrete floor, rubbing her arm and shoulder.

"Brios?" I nod.

"Clear out for a minute." He sidesteps and motions Portia and Jimmy out of the room.

"It's shit, right?" Portia asks Brios as she moves. "That stuff about her coming from in here?"

"She's not from around here," Brios reassures her as he moves them both farther down the hall. "Not from in here that's for sure."

I wait until I figure they're far enough away. "You have ten seconds to explain yourself, Lynnette. I can get to Phillip without your help. It's just faster if you cooperate."

"I ran your blood through a scan." She sits up. "You know don't you? That you're a clone like the rest of us in here?"

"My knowing anything about any of this doesn't change why I'm here," I say as I look at the machine she fed my blood to.

"But where did you come from?" Her voice is tinged with an urgency I don't feel. "You must be from New Elgin."

"Maybe, but I'll say it again." I toggle the screen up and down over the symbols it shows, I grab still frames of what I see. "It doesn't change why I'm here."

She nibbles her lip and stands. She's hedging now. I can see her thinking about her options.

"Phillip," I prompt. "He's relatively new to the council isn't he?" I'm not sure about her so I figure I need to milk her for intel now while she's still upset and too off balance to lie convincingly.

"Yes. He's been on the council for the last four years." She stays warily away from me. "He invented a new way to recycle our resources."

"That's crap," I say as I lean on the console. "He's been buying resources on the outside and shipping them in."

She's surprised. Then she's angry. "He can't do that. It's forbidden."

"Golly, there's a first, someone in power behaving in a corrupt and self-serving way." I sigh. "This is a big enough deal that everyone on the council probably knows about it. You should just tell the masses. And then see what happens. You'd need proof of course. "

"He's been given special dispensation to have clones outside working on some council project."

I nod. "I can tell you what he's been doing. He developed a type of neurochemical mind control. Your council thought it was too risky to test in the Block, but hey people outside are just lab rats. They told him to test it outside." My bitterness leaks out a little.

Her voice drops. "Everything is so regimented in here, we may as well be machines, why would they need to implement something like that?"

"I don't know, maybe Phillip is looking to subvert opposition on the council," I say.

She nods. "I think I've seen that already."

"How many Phillips are there?" I ask.

I have visions of shooting and stabbing hundreds of identical Phillips. It makes for a fun daydream about exs, until I remember the airship passageway and the crush of people. That many Phillips rushing to kill me wouldn't be much fun in real time.

"In the block, there can only be one Phillip," she explains. "The rest would be diluted versions. And they would be assimilated and terminated if they returned from the outside."

I frown. "What does that mean? Are we going to run into an army of knock offs or not?"

"Elites are clean and gene modified. The Phillip you are looking for has been alive for over one hundred years and he will live for another hundred or more unless something happens."

"He must be in good shape for a centenarian." But I guess the lifestyle of Elite pure blood gene-mods inside the Block is pretty easy.

"Diluted clones have a functional lifespan built into them for control purposes. After a specific number of years, their cells accelerate the aging process." Her tone matches my earlier bitterness.

I begin to understand her urgency as she looks at the backs of her hands.

"How long do you have?" I ask.

"I'm well past my half-life." She pinches some skin. "I know that I'm close."

I wonder how old I am, and if, somewhere inside me, an expiration date is closing in. I know what my ID says. But that number could have been pulled out of a hat based on how old other people thought I looked.

"Your friends don't like clones, do they?" she asks. She meets my gaze.

"Cloning is illegal outside. Clones have no rights. They aren't legitimately considered a version of their Prime because only the body can be copied."

As far as the world is concerned, experiences and memories can't be copied or implanted. The tech doesn't exist outside. In the Block, memory is handed down like an inheritance, or a ball and chain. Outside, cloning is linked to horror stories of rich people keeping fresh versions of themselves for replacement parts.

They couldn't keep the clones in stasis because it takes too long for the bodies to develop muscle tone and reflexes. When the original needed parts, a clone was medically dismantled. Someone discovered there were secret communities of kids who would get randomly black-bagged.

Free range clone farms.

It must have made for great Infotainment.

It all became illegal pretty quickly after that. The populace lobbied with bullets and voted by pulling the trigger. It's the American way after all.

"You said I might be from New Elgin. Why?" I ask. I'm sure Brios is listening in.

She looks at the scanner. "These markers here indicate a European origin."

I can't remember anything clearly before the South Am lab. New Elgin rings no bells because there are none to ring.

I can see Lynnette hedging around her next question. "Will you help our cause?" she asks.

I struggle to see past the broken society. I'm trying to see what could possibly come after a cock-up this large.

"The man who sent me in here hates the idea of this place flying apart for good. Change for the sake of change might only be replacing one pile of shit for another. He's going to want a system that would benefit you both. And he'll want payment for our help. He'd want access to trade with the inside," I say slowly, trying to imagine what Wolf would do.

"We have a plan that can be used that way." Light springs to her eyes.

"Oh good." I wonder if she gets my sarcasm.

Friggin' revolutionaries: always so full of self-righteous anger and entitlement.

Brios and I killed dozens just like her in South Am.

"I don't want to know your plan. If it turns out we helped you along, okay. But I'm not going outside of my mission parameters unless I slip."

"Like you did earlier?"

I can't tell where she is mentally or emotionally over my 'incident.' I *did* shove her partner into a giant sausage maker.

"Yeah." I look at her. She's focused now. Which I guess is good. "I need to go back to my people and give them something. You need to show them I made the right choice. Me not ordering them to kill everyone in here has to come with a reason they can understand."

I let her brain wrap around that for a second, and then I say, "Because as far as they're concerned, it's on the cusp of that. And they'll do it anyway if they think I made the wrong call."

"I'll get you the information you need," she says. Her eyes are still blazing.

I go back into the other room.

"She's going to get the intel we need, and then we can roll out."

Portia walks over to me and slaps my shoulder. "Crazy or not, the Wolf put you in charge, so unless you fuck me over I'm good with you staying in charge."

Jimmy chimes in. "I'm good with you in charge too."

"Umm, thanks guys."

I look at Spyker by the door. Since I've reached a working agreement with him, we have nothing to say.

He glances at me and goes back to watching the corridor.

Some kind of com-link chimes from the ceiling. We tense. Lynnette answers in the other room.

Brios drops hand-sign with us. *Authorities are searching.*

We need to get moving.

Lynnette rushes in a second later, but we're geared and ready.

"We can't stay here. Someone in the reassignment area filed a complaint. The main computer has locked all my access codes. The Enforcers are on their way here now."

1.26

Unexpected Protocol

"You have thirty seconds to gather what you need into a sack, and then we're leaving." I look to my people. Everyone is by the door in good formation. "We'll leave with or without you, Lynnette. Make it fast if you're coming."

I'm impressed when she runs to a closet and yanks out a jump bag.

"This is everything I need. Let's go." She shoulders her way to the front of the line-up, and we're on the move.

We check every corner as we go.

There's navigation signage at every turn indicating the directions to different aspects of the facility, and the floor has remnants of colored paint lines that match the signage.

The low ceilings, the narrow concrete hallways, and the lame strip lighting serve to make each space look the same as the last. Without the signage, I would be lost.

No GPS, not even a simple magnetic compass works in this place.

At least we don't have to worry about snipers. Wolf was right. It's the biggest friggin' apartment block in the world.

"We're going that way." Lynnette points. The sign indicates a transit system.

"Is that safe?" Spyker asks. He's become a nervous ball of brandished weapons as we've crept along.

"We don't have a choice," she mutters. "If we walk, we'll hit fifty checkpoints between here and where we're heading."

"Which is where exactly?" I ask. Spyker glares at me and then hustles to the next inset doorframe.

"The central computer power supply and its backup run through a junction point very close together."

"The plan is to drop the central computer?" I ask.

She nods.

I look at Jimmy. "Talk to me, James. Tell me good news."

He grins. "That … that I can help with."

Lynnette looks at him. I can see her confusion. I'll deal with that in a second; James' report is more important.

"I have their main system up and on my rig. We can cap it from here with a few minutes' work."

"Cap it?" Lynnette asks.

"Yeah." Jimmy's voice fills with pride. "I can shut down the entire arcology central computer, or I can feed it any information we want."

"And here I was wondering why Wolf sent you along." I pat Jimmy's cheek. "I see that I have underestimated you."

"No offense taken. I get that reaction all the time." He nods at his handheld. "I've been working on getting into the Mains since we crawled in. I'm sure I can do whatever you need."

"How can you control the central computer with that little box?" Lynnette's expression is one of shock. "No one knows the machine language except the central engineers."

"No hackers live in here." Jimmy shoots me a sly look. "and the computers pretty much fix themselves, right?"

Lynnette frowns. "Several specialized clones are granted the knowledge required for maintenance and repairs. They are the central engineers. They are incapable of anything else. Any other skills have been restricted to eating and personal hygiene. It is all they need for their flesh to perform the tasks as assigned."

"That's really fucking creepy." Portia voices the expression we all have on our faces.

For all her disgust, Portia's huge gun never drifts off the far end of the hallway we're parked in.

I turn to Lynnette. "Outside, lots of people know code, hardware, software, built-ins and externals. Jimmy here is one of the best."

"So what's it gonna be boss?" He fires me an impish grin over the edge of his handheld.

"Tell security we aren't here anymore." Finally, things start to feel like we can get ahead. "Lead them off in a different direction."

"Done and done," he whispers as he drops into an over-focused trance.

We head out, and things are quiet as we move through the corridors. We clear three city blocks in a straight line before trouble hits. Volley fire from a dozen electronically actuated razor guns whistle toward us as we round the corner.

Spyker, on point, turns partway and shoves a confused looking Lynnette against the wall. Brios pulls Jimmy clear. Portia and I suck wall.

Razor thin discs ricochet everywhere, scoring the concrete and making the air thick with grit.

A hot line stings across my cheek.

We fallback around the corner. Spyker's armor takes a beating. I can't tell if he's bleeding, but the vest is pretty much only a front plate and tattered straps by the time he pushes Lynnette into cover.

"Spyker, you good?"

He nods, and I rattle off orders. "Brios, hold six. Spyker, get me a cam. Jimmy talk to me, man. What the hell is going on?"

Jimmy the Slip stares at his handheld. "Well, that's craptastic. They have redundancies running almost continual comparisons to a sealed baseline system."

"What the-fucking-ever, Jimbo," I bark over the ricochet. "Kill all internal communications. Kill the lights for two sections around here. Work the rest on the fly."

I hear an Enforcer yelling instructions.

Officers sound the same in here as they do outside in the rest of the world.

Spyker slaps a sticky cam to the wall around the corner. I toggle a command link to my left optic and get a view of a staggered line of men rushing down the hall toward us.

I nod at Portia. "Do it." I clap her shoulder as she steps past me.

She leads with the barrel as it spools up to speed. The concrete walls, floor, and ceiling make it almost impossible to miss them. Divots gouge out of all the surfaces as rolling thunder erupts.

The lights die. The muzzle-flashes pulse. It's like a dance floor light show.

There is no failsafe power.

Jimmy is thorough.

Portia lets off the trigger as random people pour into the hallway from suites on either side. Citizens mill around in the dark, yelling about the power failure. Their yells become screams as they trip over the fresh corpses.

The mayhem in the hallway spreads.

We mix with the population, taking full advantage of our night optical gear to push our way through. I keep Lynnette ahead of me. I have one hand on her shoulder and maintain a running dialogue of where we are.

We clear the area in what feels like record time and make our way to the transit hub. It has a separate power grid for its lights. We approach the glowing platform.

More Enforcers meet us there. A monorail has stopped partway down the outbound tunnel but people are streaming out of both tunnel openings.

I had thought the civvies present would provide us cover.

I thought wrong.

The Enforcers don't yell a warning. One unit sees us and opens fire through the crowd.

Spyker's chest armor takes a slash from a razor round. He drops to the floor and returns fire.

The platform clears really fast after that, people run around us screaming. The only cover on the platform is the growing jumble of bodies.

Lynnette is yelling something racist about the Elites. She's unarmed, unarmored, and more concerned about protesting than surviving.

I shove her behind me. "Stay the fuck down."

Brios keeps the hall clear at our backs.

Portia lobs a frag over to the nearest security group. It makes a meaty mess of their left flank. The rest dive for cover in the slot the train runs through.

I see a large guy lying there dead. He looks like any one of a million people from New White Sands. Just a guy on his way home from a crappy job he probably didn't like but had to do. I meet his lifeless eyes and know this is not my time.

"Cover me." I sprint to the row of corpses and haul him up. Razor guns spit to life. A thousand knives a minute slide through the dead guy's ill-fitting suit. The muted sound of each popping cut fills my head.

I push to the far end of the security unit on the right.

My com-link pips with Jimmy's voice. *"Train inbound."*

Jimmy returns power to the monorail. The cars surge silently out of the tunnel. The unit of men sheltered in the trench are crushed.

The second unit of security, most of the men I'm rushing, hear the screams of their comrades and turn in horror.

Only for a second.

I don't miss a step.

What's a dance in Paris without a little butter?

"Not a tango."

I'm among them before they can bring their guns back on target.

My hands fly, blades slicing flesh, tendons, muscle. I don't clip bone unless I need to reverse direction fast. I dance. I can hear the music in my head. Syncopated bass line, high clear vocals, crescendo of guitar riffs merging.

The guys in front of me move in slo-mo as my adrenaline overclocks. Then it ends, I'm done. The music is replaced by the groans and whimpers of the dying.

The anticipated climax rushes through me, and I draw a deep breath to slow down my racing heart.

I wait for my team to board the cars behind me. Their faces are bleak as they pass.

Portia nudges Jimmy forward. The kid has stopped in the midst of my carnage. "Keep moving, Slip. Staring'll let it grow in your head later."

His face is chalky as he steps around me.

None of them meet my eyes.

Except Brios. He's the last to come aboard as I cover him, a zip gun aimed at the corridors.

"You still have the best blade work," he says with a grim smile. I know he, at least, likes what he sees when he looks at me. Flushed cheeks, wild JF'ed hair.

"Yeah, and don't you forget it." Maybe, if we lived through this, we'd get back together.

Maybe.

"Good times." He chuckles.

When I'm on board, Brios reaches up and slaps a strip of sticky tape to the ceiling and pushes an ECM unit onto it.

The light on the end of the flat metal box switches from blue to bright green.

"Jimmy, get us moving." I sit next to Lynnette. "I'll get you a stop number in a minute."

As I get the information we need from a subdued Lynnette, all of the team, except Jimmy, slam power bars to keep themselves moving. Me, I hate it, but I dump three packs of raw sugar into my mouth. The food bar on its own isn't cutting it.

The monorail glides forward and chimes for attention at the next platform.

"Stay down," Brios orders.

We take cover below the windows and roll through the next three stops.

With the electronic countermeasures running, our cars will be invisible to the rest of the system. At least, until we overtake the next train in line and plow into it at speed.

I glance at our stunned-looking nettie. "Slow us down, Jimmy."

Lynnette counts and nods. "We're a few stories below the council rooms and a little ways off. The next platform will be the closest."

"All right, everybody out," I say.

One at a time, we bail out the rear door into the tunnel as the monorail continues on its path.

We run after it, chasing it down the tunnel and vaulting out of the trench onto the platform. No guards meet us, but citizens stare and more than a few rush to speak into security helpline com-boxes. Jimmy reroutes the calls into a dummy line that takes complaints and does nothing with the data.

Lynnette directs us to an emergency staircase, and we climb as quickly as we can. Jimmy pops the lock on the door we need for a fraction of a second, and we pile through almost on top of one another.

We need to avoid holding the doors open and using extended hacks. Jimmy's made it clear that speed will limit the system's ability to find us.

If it wasn't so serious, it would make a great college dorm drinking game. The guy who sets off the alarm has to drink.

I'm just getting into the spirit of things, when we enter a section where the lights are already off.

We freeze; the reverse of Nulls trapped in headlights.

Spyker signals from point position, and we drop into a crouch, staggered along opposite walls, waiting for the gunplay to start.

I whisper harshly, "Jimmy? You do this?"

"No," he replies. His voice has a lost-in-a-dream quality to it. "No, there's some sort of executive over-ride in place. Working on it."

"Shit, shit, shit," Spyker mutters.

"Stow it," Brios snaps, his head cocked. His tone would've been enough to have me pulling up my weapons, but I already know he's locked onto something. Something not so good.

There's the sound of a door latch being worked open. Spyker is already moving.

The lone Enforcer eases through the doorway. The last thing he says on his chunky looking com-box is, "Lights are off. I'm in position."

Spyker throws an arm across the guy's neck and pumps his filament edged stiletto into the Enforcer's torso five times. The blade thrums softly as it zips through the layers of body armor.

"Fuck," Spyker mutters as he lowers the corpse. The stench of punctured viscera builds in the stagnant air.

I know why he's swearing. The guy he killed is a point man for a bigger unit searching for us in this zone.

"Raven?" Phillip's voice eases gracefully out of the overhead announcement speakers. *"I know it has to be you, love."*

My team stares at each other. It's only a second more and then they're staring at me.

My turn. Shit, shit, shit.

I wonder if Vlasta actually got all of his invasive software out of me.

"I knew you would come home on your own." His voice echoes along the corridor. *"Did you really think you had killed me? I'll die a thousand times if that's what it takes to get you back."*

"He's looking for you?" Lynnette whispers.

"Yeah," I say into the silence. "That's my ex all right. He sounds as desperate and deluded as ever."

Portia snorts. "Men."

"Hey, I happen to like men." I look at her. "Just not this particular one." I wonder if she might be getting sweet on me. Or if she just hates men. "Phillip's on my short list of least favorite people that are in need of a good killing."

"Let's see if we can help you with that." Portia hefts her cannon and stands.

We move out with a rising sense of urgency. It's not going to take long for the strike team to realize their point man is dead, if they don't know already.

Jimmy keeps popping doors in front of us and locking them tight after we go through.

"I have the locks scrambling on my own algorithm," he says. He's not grinning anymore. The last round of fighting has broken it through to him. We are in shit, and the shit is for real. "It will take a long time for a system to jack those doors."

"Nice," Spyker says. "Until you die from a stray round and we die locked up in this shit hole."

"Good point." Jimmy doesn't hesitate; he shows me how to unlock his doors. "I think you've got the best chance to get out alive."

Spyker glares and says nothing.

Phillip's voice goes on and on overhead.

I tune him out and focus on business. We need something to throw off the hunting party. "Lynnette, if Jimmy sets you up with a systemwide com-link, can you mobilize your people elsewhere in the Block?"

"You would use rebel lives as a distraction?" She looks to where my voice is in the dark. "Just to achieve your aims?"

"You were going to throw a rebellion anyway. Now's a good time to start the party … but if your people are cowards, tell me now so we can make another plan." I know she can't see me in the dark. Her heat and fury blossoms in the eerie glow of my optics.

I grin at Jimmy. "Get the girl a mic."

1.27
Risk Analysis

I hate the feeling that I'm not on the cat team in this cat-and-mouse game. Feeling is the same as knowing, at least it is when you're in the shit.

We've covered what feels like half a city block heading toward the last set of stairs. Jimmy's initial reports of disruptions by rebels are nice, but there's no action close enough to us to offer cover or distraction. Phillip's voice continues to blah, blah, blah, from the ceiling. My attention is solely on keeping us alive long enough to find him.

We need to be smart mice.

Jimmy taps my shoulder.

"What?" I turn to face him in the darkness.

"He just said you're a clone." There's no hint of surprise in his voice. "Is that true?"

"Well, here's the thing, Jimmy. I might be." I watch his reactions. I hope he isn't some kind of neo-puritan. "If you can find out for sure for me, that would be swell. I'm sure it'll make a huge difference to all of us in our next firefight."

"Hey I'm just asking." He lifts his hands. "Personally I think that's cool, and for the record, I don't give a shit."

"Sorry, Jimmy." I frown. "I just keep expecting a certain bias. I'm serious though, if you can find out for sure that'd be nice."

"Okay." He nods.

Spyker yells as he's on his way flat. Portia crouches against one wall and spools up her cannon.

It happens fast.

Portia drops dead in a spray of gore.

This set of Enforcers are carrying real guns. Outside tech just like ours.

We're still diving every which way. Enforcer counterfire hammers the concrete around us. They're blind-firing, but it's bad enough.

Brios rolls over to Portia. Incoming slugs make her body bounce inside her armor. He pries the grip from her gun hand and squeezes the trigger, panning the heavy weapon side to side. His upgraded arms handle the recoil with ease.

Fire to suppress.

Buy time to secure your position.

Evaluate, probe, re-evaluate, and counterattack as needed.

"Spyker, mobiles, two of them. Roll'em when I stop."

Brios pans the gun across and I've timed my movement; I pump my muscle augmentations and lay on as much speed as I've got. I hit the recessed doorway closest to their position.

Spyker calls, "Outbound."

Two mobile bombs, grenades on wheels, speed past. They take off wildly, careening around the corner and detonating two seconds apart. Concrete and flesh mix somewhere out of sight and billow out toward me.

I count two and rush the corner.

Three men survived the grenades and are farther down the hall, tucked into a recessed doorway. I don't slow. I'm on them, firing single shots as I come. All three drop with stunned expressions.

"Clear," I com-link back to my team.

I walk through the Enforcer group. They're all either dead or dying. I haul the least injured survivor into a sitting position.

"Where's Councilman Phillip?" I have to repeat it a few times as his head lolls around.

Suddenly his eyes brighten and his head snaps up. He looks at me and smiles with a moment of clarity. "It's all right, Phillip still loves you. No matter what happens here, he'll find a way to fix you."

I hurl myself away. The explosion slams me against the wall. My reactive armor stiffens with the initial blast, goes slack as I fly, and springs rigid again on impact.

Blood runs from cuts on my cheeks and forehead. My ears throb.

I sit for a second holding my ears and trying to make sense of the new information I've just received.

Brios drops beside me and checks me over.

"Motherfuck," I say.

Brios cleans off my cuts and blasts me with a stream of skinseal.

"Did you see that?" I ask him.

My CPU politely informs me via scrolling marquee that I'm yelling. I modulate my voice lower and ask again, "Did you see that? The guy was internally wired. He had an implanted explosive."

Just like my brother.... A queasy wave hits me at the idea of thousands of suicide bombers mindlessly rushing us, detonating in bone, meat, and flame. I imagine it'd be a worse game than the Airship Extravaganza that Brios and I just got through.

Brios purses his lips. We're both thinking the same thing. We haven't brought enough ammo. Moro's words slide across my memory. *...only one of you will survive long enough to get to an extraction point....*

"Get everyone up." I shove my way into a standing position, sliding up the wall at my back. "We don't want to wait around. More of them will be coming."

Brios gives orders as he moves. Jimmy awkwardly keeps an eye on our flank. Spyker strips everything useful off of Portia. I note grimly that he's rigging her body with a couple of grenades. Our eyes meet. His hands slow.

"As you were." I nod at him.

He continues with his task. I make my way over to Jimmy.

I watch the young man's lips move as my hearing achingly works on its recovery.

"What the fuck was I thinking?" He quietly repeats it a few times as he stares into the darkness behind us.

Something clicks, and I realize what's been bothering me about our nettie.

"I know you're good at hacking, Jimmy. I can see that. But I've figured it out." I step up to him and whisper in his ear, "You hacked AlphaTek and got yourself assigned as our nettie, didn't you? You aren't supposed to be here."

"I don't know what you're talking about." His expression is flustered. "I definitely don't know what you're talking about."

"Wolf wouldn't send someone like you on this incursion, James. Risk analysis said that none of us are getting out of here alive. But you didn't know that when you hacked in and put yourself on the list, did you?" I keep my voice low. "In fact, this is probably the first time in your life you've even held a real gun isn't it, James? So why would a seasoned tactician like Wolf send you? He wouldn't."

I watch Jimmy's twitching.

Brios, behind us, is giving Lynnette the basic ten-second-rundown on the use, care, and feeding of zip guns.

I ask Jimmy once more, "Why are you here, Jimmy? You better tell me because the only answer I come to is that, for some messed up reason, you want to be here."

Jimmy stands there a long moment.

Finally, he whispers, "I thought I'd gotten lucky, you know? I got hired as a freelance contractor for AlphaTek. I'm the one who traced back the Ripperkin's client list. I made my reports directly to some woman named Jen. She signs off one day, and I kind of follow her back into the company mainframe. I goofed around a bit and found an operations file with a lot of activity. I hacked in, just to see if I could do it. I saw the Block listed as the objective.

"I've heard crazy rumors all my life about the whack tech they build in here. I wanted to see it in person, maybe learn some stuff, steal a few ideas and make a killing back on the outside."

Something flickers in the darkness at the far end of the hall we just came from. I cut Jimmy off. "Brios, incoming on our flank," I yell as I shove James toward the others. "Go."

Our time's up.

We head out following our original direction of travel, splitting our attention between firing at targets that appear behind us and finding our way forward. In a moment we find ourselves with sizable groups of Enforcers on either end of the hall we're in. They've brought in their heavier guns and the sound in the narrow concrete space is deafening.

The situation's untenable and deteriorating.

We're hiding, crammed into a single doorway recess. Brios and Spyker are popping suppression fire in either direction, keeping our opposition pinned down.

Lynnette tries the door. It's locked.

"Jimmy." I send his name out on the com-link. Jimmy doesn't move.

Brios yanks the young man sideways and shoves him toward me.

If the system is tracking us by watching which doors we go through, we need to strip that advantage from them....

"Jimmy." I yell his name twice more before he looks at me, hands shaking. "Jimmy, pop all the doors in this section. Do it."

~ ~ ~

"This is a fucking dead end." Spyker looks around at three solid walls in a panic.

We've spent more time than I like fending off the fresh opposition, and we've led them backward through a number of rooms to do it. We need to keep moving, but we've been backed into a corner.

"Lynnette, where do we need to go?" I turn to Lynnette. "Which direction?"

Her face is a mask. Jimmy's not the only one getting an education today.

She points at a wall. "That way."

In silence, Brios and I slap on a wall-breaker, and he yanks the go-cord. The muffled sizzle and whump sends a cloud of concrete dust billowing. I poke-check our new door, and Spyker dives through.

Brios rigs a chain explosive to our new line of retreat and off we go.

We make our way into what passes for an administration area. We see a sign pointing to where the council room is.

The first detonation echoes behind us.

"How long a string did you leave back there?" I ask.

"Six mixed loads," Brios replies. "We get to see how determined they are."

"Or how stupid," Spyker adds.

We duck along, following the sign. Our destination can't be far. We slow as we approach an arched entrance that opens into one end of a wide, high vaulted hall. It's pretty in a retro art deco kind of way.

I motion an all-stop and peer into the elegant hall, trying to keep to where the shadows are deepest.

The doors to the council chamber are on a second-floor balcony. Stairs curve up from either side near the far end. Between us and the doors, the massive space is full of civilians. They stand in an even rank and file.

Red flag.

If they see us, they don't show it. None of them are armed.

"Brios." I motion him to our front. "Spyker, watch our six."

Brios starts the barrels spinning on the cannon and steps into the arch. At the sound, the people in the room rush forward in orderly waves.

About halfway through, I toss my last two frag grenades into the back ranks. I hear Jimmy puking behind me.

Lynnette is in shock. She stares at the carnage, her face blank disbelief. Jimmy's got nothing left to puke, but he keeps trying as the smells of death, and the sounds of dying, spread until the floor is a writhing carpet of blood and parts. Brios lets the minigun fall silent.

I hold up my hand to tell everyone to stay put.

"Why are we waiting?" Spyker nods at the distant, upper doors. "Those are the ones we need?"

"Yeah, but that was too easy." I have my optics dialed all the way, and I'm scanning the room. "Jimmy? James. I need you to pull yourself together. James."

"What?" His voice is bleak.

I meet his eyes and hold his gaze until I can see he's mentally ready. "Block every incoming or outgoing signal from this room."

He hooks back into his handheld. "There's a lot of the same signal coming out of here."

"Jam it all." I keep my eyes focused on the new abattoir. "Inbound and out."

"Done," he replies.

I wait.

Spyker boils over. "Screw this. It's a bunch of dead bodies."

He shoves his way past Brios and gets two steps before he's flung flat by the first explosive. The bodies are rigged.

Spyker crawls back to us. Brios pulls him through the doorway. As he checks Spyker over, I debate the merits of waiting longer.

A few more bodies detonate in the center of the room.

"Random explosions. Maybe individual timers?" Brios glances at me.

"Maybe. There's no signal now. They could also have some kind of motion sensors. You know, shake them and they pop." I really don't know if that's the case, but we can't wait here forever.

Lynnette grows pale as more corpses of citizens explode up to the base of the stairs.

"I got this." Spyker stands and fires rapid single shots into a handful of bodies.

None of them detonate.

"I'm going to say they don't have motion switches," he says.

"Okay. Random it is." I scan the room and pick out a path of least resistance. "We can head for that side and boost over the railing onto that landing." I look for confirmation of understanding.

Single file, we start moving along the edges of the room. By the time we get to the top of the stairs, we're covered in gore as bodies explode near us. We're all sporting minor cuts but thankfully no impaling injuries.

The overhead speakers cut in, and Lynnette's people come on the line exhorting the population to rise up. The voice reports multiple sections in revolt and hundreds of acts of resistance.

It feels too little too late.

"About fucking time," Spyker mutters.

I can only nod as I check on the rest of the team.

Jimmy has officially become the most miserable looking thing I've ever seen. He keeps wiping sticky blood and fleshy bits around on his face. He might be silently crying.

"Let it dry," Spyker advises him as he moves to point position. "You'll scare more enemies that way."

Corpses still pop behind us. A sick reminder of how messed up Phillip and his cronies are.

Spyker tries one huge handle and finding it locked puts his hand on the second door. He completes the circuit for the trap. His arms char off from the elbow down as a couple thousand volts rip him apart.

His body drops steaming and sizzling.

Jimmy flinches away, doubling himself over. His stomach has nothing left to give. Lynnette's shriek is cut off in her throat. Brios and I just grimace.

The landing smells like fast fried death.

Brios clenches his jaw, tosses me the carbine, and then rolls Spyker's blown open torso onto its front. He pulls the Horatius unit off the body and settles it onto his back.

I need Jimmy to open this door, but he's taking too long to recover.

"Brios, plant this." I hand him our last wall-breaker charge. I point. "Over there."

He gets to work.

I heft Spyker's carbine and turn to Lynnette. "You win the lotto," I say as I push the gun into her hands. I give her a once through. "Safety, mag release, slide, shot counter. Just like the zip gun but a little heavier, got it?" I stuff more magazines into her new web belt. "If it jams, it's faster to switch guns. We can clear it later."

She nods. I can see she's still in shock, but I don't have time to coddle her.

"Brios?" I check where he's at.

"Everyone duck and cover," Brios says.

The wall blows open. He and I step through the dust.

1.28

The Loneliest Number

The council members are all seated around a beautiful circular table. There's a huge holographic display projecting from its center: a transparent image of the Block slowly spinning. Most areas of the structure glow red. Two sets of numbers float below the image as it turns. One number is increasing, the other is decreasing.

"Hello, dearest." Phillip stands from his seat opposite us.

No one else at the table moves. From my position along the wall, I dial in my Doc Ripperkins. No one else at the table is moving, because they're all dead.

"Jonestown," I whisper to Brios.

"What?" he replies.

"Never mind," I say as we split up, moving around the table on opposite sides, widening the angle of fire on Phillip.

It's obvious Phil isn't concerned.

He's older than the version I already killed. He's well-dressed, also unlike the last him I killed.

Cages in my head rattle; this Phil looks like *my* Phil, my husband, the one I loved, married.

Feelings unlocked at Bastion Medical swoop in multiplied by a hundred. I'm screwed. Out of the corner of my eye, I look at the other people with me, at Brios.

It worries me as much as pisses me off.

"Phillip." My fight for control has me reaching for bravado. I toss my chin at the display. "What's going on here?"

"Raven." He smiles.

For an older guy, he's still attractive. I try to hate him. For all I know, there's a program still dictating my responses.

"You and your friends actually managed to get to me. Impressive." He smiles and leans with both hands onto the table. "You came to kill me, I presume. I had hoped you were happy with your earlier revenge."

"Your mistake was sending my brother to hunt for me." At his expression, I push harder. "What, Phillip? Did you think he would explode before I could take him alive? He talked. That's why I'm here."

"I see." He sighs and shakes his head in disappointment. "Then he failed. Twice over."

"I'm not going to give you a chance to regroup and find some other way to fuck me over. Fuck the world over. No, I'm here to take you out of the picture for good."

"I suppose I was rather abrupt in how I pursued you. That may have been more off-putting than I'd intended…." He lifts his hands from the table and turns slightly to face me, his eyes softening at their corners. "I was just so surprised to see you alive, after all those years."

"Off-putting?" I snap. "Really, Phil, that's all you've got?" I need to keep my anger; it's all I have. "I remember flashcard memories of you. Of Adel. Of wanting to be dead and not getting my wish. Off-putting? As for what we had, you … you tried to kill me. So, no. Never. I'm not listening to your shit."

"If you kill me, you kill all of your history, your past." He narrows his gaze on me. "We don't have to fight about this, Raven. We could be happy again."

"I don't need you, Phil." I tighten my grip on my gun. I can feel my anger fading. Not good.

"Your real memories don't interest you?" I sense his desire to torment me under his tone. "Your parentage? Adel? None of that sparks in you a hint of curiosity?"

I feel Brios' eyes on me. "Nope," I say. I kick myself for my second of hesitation.

"I could always tell when you were lying. Ever since—"

"Fuck you, Phillip." I cut him off around clenched teeth. My finger hovers on the trigger. I strain to finish the action, to set myself free. The bottoms of my feet sweat. I'm falling. I'm failing.

"You don't want it to end like this. We've both changed. It would be like starting over. It only takes a yes," he says softly.

"No. It ends just like this." I have to kill him now.

My desire rushes through me like a pulse, now, now, now.

But I don't.

His smile is quiet. In that moment, I know he knows I can't pull the trigger.

My heart pounds in my ears, and I try to imagine clocks and hot pink cue cards. I remember Brios slapping my ass and saying, *Nice ride, how much?*

But nothing changes, because I'm not fighting third-party programming.

This time, I'm fighting myself.

"Those numbers, what do they mean?" Lynnette asks. She's moved forward to the table edge.

"Hmm." Phillip acknowledges her for the first time. "An old Lynnette model. I thought we'd purged all of you. Oh well. Only a little time left for you, either way."

She stiffens.

Brios has kept up his slow advance, waiting for a signal from me to act. I know he'll do what I can't.

Part of my mind stumbles forward, calculating strategies and trajectories to stop him if I have to. I hate that it happens.

"To answer your question…," Phillip gestures. "The increasing number is the concentrations of poisonous gas filling the Block in parts per million." He looks from her to me. "The other number is, of course, the surviving population."

Crap.

"You're insane!" Lynnette screams at him.

"I'm pretty sure I mentioned that, didn't I?" I say into her echo. I'm stalling.

Maybe I'm wrong about all of it.... Maybe the life I've locked up is the one I want.

"No." Phillip frowns. "I'm not insane. I'm a megalomaniacal perfectionistic self-serving egotistical narcissist with plans for world domination. There's a considerable difference."

"It plays the same," I say. I need to buy time, look like I'm in control for Brios' sake. "Jimmy?" I wave for him to step up to the table console.

Jimmy starts clicking away, checking his handheld every couple of keystrokes. "Sections of the system are cutting themselves off ... but I'm working an angle...."

"That is a remarkable talent you have, young man. Pity I didn't find you outside, you'd be rich."

Jimmy grits his teeth. "Shut up, Phillip."

"There's nothing you can do." He gestures to the rapidly changing numbers on the holo-projector. "This is just a matter of time. I suppose, Raven, that I could arrange for you and I to escape. And I guess I could make an exception and send your friends out a different way. Just say yes, Raven. I can still make it happen."

I watch Brios' eyes narrow.

Phil looks at Lynnette. "I'm sorry though. Poor, pitiful thing. To have survived this far. I can't make an exception for you. Inter-Arcology treaties and such."

"You bastard." Lynnette yanks her carbine up.

My world slows.

My boost system overclocks. I'm stepping forward and jerking my weapon around.

Lynnette's high-powered rifle rips Phillip to shreds.

"Whoa!" Jimmy flinches away from her, right into my line of fire. I pull my barrel up, sending my rounds chunking into the ceiling.

Jimmy stands paralyzed, Lynnette has no idea how close she just came to death, and Brios....

Brios stays where he is, his face a mask.

I'm the only one moving. I rush to Phillip, my heart pounds in my throat. It's hard to breathe. No, no, no....

I know it, feel it with every fiber in me: my regret is real.

I drop to my knees beside Phillip, fumbling for a dose of Suspend that I know won't make a difference. There's too much blood. Too much damage. We're too far from an exit. By the time I drag him out, he'll be cold, unrecoverable, gone.

"Raven...?" I feel Brios approaching me warily. "You good?"

I ignore him.

"I knew you would come home." Phillip smiles at me. "You always do. Now we're together again." His body shudders as he chokes on blood. "I never wanted this for us. If only you had said yes...."

Any resistance I had vanishes, washed away by a tide of loss.

I bow my head to his as the tension in his frame eases. I can't stop myself: I lean forward and whisper the word that I know will change everything.

Time distorts into a blur ... ... Jimmy's shouted warning, Brios' sudden movement, and memories flooding back. So much of what was before ... happy family life, a seaside house, and Adel. Adel in the sunshine.... So many things about my life. ...My life before it burst into flames....

Brios finishes his leap. He tackles me hard.

Phillip detonates in a crimson sheet of flesh and bone.

Brios and I slide across the polished floor; the concussive force leaves me breathless. The ringing in my ears is replaced by the hammering of my pulse.

"Raven?" I feel Brios' question through the rumble of his chest. I can smell the blood in the air, taste it. I know I'm crying. The last food bar I ate swirls heavily around my guts.

For a moment, the room is filled with empty silence.

"I'm good." My head's reeling, but I can feel myself pulling back, withdrawing, dissociating from the mad panic losing Phillip had unleashed.

But the memories cling. Cling with renewed life.

Brios unfolds his arms. He runs fingers through the hair at my temple, his thumb catching the tears on my cheek. "It's over," he says.

I look at him, my brain sliding around the events of the last seconds.

"Yeah." I wipe my eyes, trying to sort feelings that threaten to overwhelm me.

"You're not going to find answers here. Not anymore." He says it matter of fact. I can't tell him I said yes. I can't tell him I have my answers.

He's right about one thing. It's over.

Brios has always had my back. We've jumped into the fire for each other more than once. Right now, we're not just standing in the fire; we're rooting through the coals.

I sit up straighter and look at the gore. I look at Brios. His expression is worried.

For both our sakes, I manage to come up with some words. "Motherfucker, he always was a selfish prick."

"You got that right." Brios chuckles and says, "We gotta get going."

I know I can't stay here. Stopping equals dying. I can't process everything that's happened unless I live long enough.

I hang onto that thought like a girl with a discount card in the Milano's store.

"Yeah. We have to get the hell out of here."

Brios pulls me to my feet, and I turn to Jimmy.

"Holy shit." He stares at me. "That was fucked up."

"Are we good?" I manage to ask him.

"I guess. I mean…." He looks up at the ceiling and then nods. "I'll be okay. Are you okay?"

I give him a tight nod. "I'm good." It's a lie, but no one needs to know that.

I catch Brios' sidelong glance. We look away in the same instant. If we get out of here alive, we'll mutually avoid talking about it, like always. It's a cold comfort, but I'd rather that blanket than a shroud.

Lynnette is frozen in place, knuckles white where she's clutching the carbine.

I struggle to contain my anger. It's done now, and there's no way to turn back.

I stomp over to where she's standing.

"Can I trust you with that?" I point at the rifle. "Or are you just going to shoot anything you want to from here out?"

"He had to d—"

"Shut up." I glower. "You point that thing at anything other than what I tell you, I'll shoot you myself."

Brios is cleaning off some of the bigger mess from his head and shoulders. "Jimmy, where are we at?"

"Some kind of meta program fired up before we got in here." Jimmy looks at his handheld with a blank expression. "I can't tell what it is, only that it's running flat out. It's trying to lock me out…," he mutters.

Brios has been moving as Jimmy briefs him, poke-checking doors that lead out of the council room. "Jimmy, anything like a door or a hidden passage, secret rocket-ship? Phil had a way out. He said so. We just have to find it."

"I don't know, man." Jimmy grimaces at his hand-held and says, "Personally, I think that we'll die if we stay and look for it."

After a moment, Jimmy stops and shakes his head. "I can't access much. It's throwing me off of every system. I barely managed loading a backdoor into engineering—"

A soft repetitive chime sounds and then stops.

Jimmy blinks and says, "And … now the main system is completely dead. I can't reset this. Everything has switched over to an alternate system."

"And the gas?" I ask.

Even now, I'm desperate not to be alone with my memories.

I had a daughter, and she's dead. I had a life, and it ended in fire. Mentally I run from the hurt. Back into the cold. I find shelter in the disconnected feeling which is eating me. It's familiar, familial. I throw myself at it.

"I can't stop the inflow of gas," Jimmy says. "But I can try to seal a few passageways to the main door by messing with the environmental controls. It won't be a direct path."

Brios glances at me. He can see that I'm struggling with the new normal.

"Jim," he says. I know he's made a decision. "Get us a path to the nearest ground floor exit."

The decreasing number on the holo-display hits one and stays there. The single digit flashes red.

"What does that mean?" Lynnette's voice is small in the big room. She points at the number.

I stare at her. "It means you're it, Lynnette. The last citizen of the Block still alive."

1.29

Protocol Resolution

We left the council room an hour ago, and the situation out here is grim. Dead citizens, curled around themselves, are scattered along hallways and in open rooms that we pass.

I'm inured to the scenery. It's the same and yet different from other battle spaces I've been through.

Jimmy has his eyes locked on his shoes. Portia's lesson has stuck with him.

For me, far worse than all the bodies everywhere, is the fact that my filter mask is driving me crazy. The gas in here is nasty; the mask doesn't even cut it. I know because we dropped down through a gas filled stairwell. Unpleasant is an understatement. But partial protection, a developing rash, and a burning throat is still better than being a corpse with ugly red blisters on its face.

"We have all this tech. You think somebody, somewhere, would've come up with a self-sealing mask that doesn't feel like fire ants on your face."

"I'm guessing you actually know what fire ants feel like," Jimmy comments. His voice is distant.

"Hell yeah. Not nice. Exactly like this mask." At his look, I add, "You ought to get out more. Experience the world."

"The mask thing must just be you," he replies. "I'm okay with it."

"Our nettie handles masks better than you." Brios chuckles. "We'll make a merc out of him yet."

"Fuck no," the young man chimes in. "I'm not doing anything like this again. This was just a random act of stupid. Never again."

"Back to grandma's basement?" I joke.

"What?" Jimmy's face goes blank, and he glances between Brios and I. "Is that supposed to mean something?"

"Just keep moving." Brios chuckles.

Lynnette looks sullen, and I can't blame her.

To be the last of anything, and know it as fact, has to suck.

We cover off a hundred more yards when Brios raises a hand, then clenches it and pulls it down.

We all freeze, crouch, and then slink to the walls.

"What's up?" I sidle near.

"I thought I saw something moving up ahead." He points into the darkened hallway with the heavy multi-barrel.

"Everyone's dead," I whisper to him. Then I see it too. Whatever it is, it's big.

Brios taps his lenses to zoom. He mutters, "Well, that's shit."

I dial my eyes, still thankful for having spent the money on quality optics. There's not one, but three large humanoid robots. They're busy tossing bodies into a wheeled unit that bounces as each corpse goes into the hopper on its lid.

"Jimmy," I whisper. "We got robots. Lynnette, you know what those units are?"

She peers down the hall using Portia's old single-sight.

"No." Her surprise breathes into her face mask. "I've never seen anything like them."

Jimmy, ever the proficient nettie, is fiddling with his handheld. "One second. I've got a lot of data cached from before the system went down, so—" he stops. "Oh damn," he says in muted awe. He looks at me. "They're part of the Arcology Purge Protocol. They recycle the corpses for the next run of parts … and food."

I clench my jaw and nod.

Lynnette's face is pale. I wonder what she thinks about the whole reassignment thing now.

"Will they ignore us?" Brios whispers.

"I don't know," Jimmy replies. "The main computer is prepping to reboot the entire place, people and all." He shrugs. "If their sensors pick up on our movement, it might trigger a subroutine. You know, something that'll try to complete the objective in the event of a failed purge…."

Brios watches the robots. "What are we looking at for processing function? I mean are they independent units or are they just manipulator bots for the whole system?"

He wants to know if we can get around them by accessing the new system and mucking with the command inputs. That'd be a sweet deal, if it worked.

"They run semi-autonomously," Jimmy says. "It looks like they jack in periodically for updates and orders."

"Jimmy," I ask. "Any chance you can access the new system the same way they do?"

"Maybe. I'd have gain access to one of them, see how it's coded, run a cutting program into its onboard system, find and change the command lines, then jack in someplace to spring it on—"

"No time," Brios says.

A robotic unit at the end of the hall drops an armature into a wall mounted com-port. As it steps away from the wall, I get a bad feeling. "Brios?"

His name is just out of my mouth when Jimmy pipes up. "Here they come."

The robots turn as one and begin marching toward us.

Exterminate, exterminate, or, *intruder alert, intruder alert,* that's all I think they should be saying as they advance. The metallic whirring and clicking against the silence is threatening enough.

Brios runs the cannon over them, sending fragments of metal scattering as the three bots get chewed up and collapse one by one.

He lifts off the trigger, letting the gun wind down. He throws the heavy weapon aside.

"Out of ammo," he says. He slides his rifle around to firing position. "Let's go."

We skirt the pile of twitching metal limbs and scoot to the far intersection.

I take point and access Jimmy's map as an overlay as we move. Brios keeps an eye on our six as I check the intersection.

"Clear," I say. "Going left. Straight through hallway with a door at the end."

We round the corner and keep moving.

"We're so close," Jimmy whispers.

Just as the words leave his mouth, the hallway behind us fills with bots, the sound unmistakable.

"Contact. Six o'clock. Lots of them," Brios says. "Run."

The sprint to the end includes hurdles over bodies that haven't been cleared. Brios follows behind us, back peddling and shooting as he moves surefooted through the dead. He's switched to selective fire to conserve ammo. His shots drill robots in their knees since headshots aren't stopping them and their pelvic areas are too heavily armored.

"Jimmy. Door. Now," I say between aimed fire of my own.

"On it…." Jimmy works the lock, trying not to stare at the advancing bots or the corpses slumped against the wall beside him. Popping the lock takes a lot longer than before.

"What's the delay?" I'm starting to feel the strain, fighting with the recoil. Brios and I keep buying time, but it's a losing battle. More keep coming. Striding around the corner, locking onto us, and advancing.

"Remember the part where I said the whole system reset itself…?" Jimmy replies, his handheld is in a death grip. "Well, the system tracked what I did, and how I did it. Now it's rewriting its code on the fly. There's only so many ways to crack a lock. As soon I try them all, it'll have the advantage."

"We're counting on you to make this fucking work, James." I say to him as I punch another magazine into my weapon.

"I know that." Jimmy's voice is detached; he's gotta be close. "For the record," he says, "You suck at motivational speeches."

Bots begin to pile up in the choke point as Brios and I mark targets and finish them. They're coming quicker as more are rerouted to our position. I hope this isn't a new trend.

"When Jimmy gets this open, which way do we go?" Brios asks me.

"Straight fifty yards and then a right at the intersection."

Brios cracks off a few more rounds. Bots claw over the wreckage of their companions.

"Got it," Jimmy says as he steps back, pulling the door open.

A mechanical arm lunges through the gap and grabs Jimmy's elbow. It yanks him in.

I'm firing past Jimmy's head while he's screaming. His body is forcing the door closed as the robot on the other side keeps pulling. More crowd forward behind this one.

Jimmy's scream becomes a thin whistling sound as his arm is torn off.

I keep firing as his body drops.

Brios steps close with a flash of movement. "Grenade out," he yells over my gunfire.

The crumple and metallic destruction sends components flying, clearing the hallway we need.

I rip my medical pouch off my webbing and shove it at Lynnette.

"Six injectors," I say roughly as I start wrapping a pressure patch around Jimmy's skinny chest, covering his gory shoulder. "The shots are numbered. One of each color at the location pictured on the label."

"We should leave him. He's dead." She looks at me.

"Brios could kill you and I'll do it all myself." I seal the wrap onto Jimmy's torso. "Or you could fucking do what you're told."

I swing my rifle back up and cover the far side of the door.

She clenches her jaw and goes through the injectors, pushing medication into Jimmy's body. Her tone is angry, "Done."

"Start a clock," I say to Brios as I haul the body over one shoulder.

"*Understood,*" he subvocalizes, his face grim. He's focused on pegging bots in any exposed joint he can as they surge toward our position.

Brios strips off the last of the ammo Jimmy was packing as we hurry down the hall.

If we can survive, get out, and get Jimmy medical attention inside the next forty minutes, he might come back from this. The kid's got a talent I can respect, and if I can get him out, I'd work with him again, but he's also just a kid. One who should never have been in here in the first place.

We go right at the intersection. The next hallway is older looking, empty of civilian bodies, and just as full of bots. We pour through ammo, knowing that we have to be close. The outside must be near.

Brios checks a corner and then steps wide around it. "Here. It's here."

The cramped-feeling passage widens out, and the ceiling climbs three stories. The ancient looking main doors are sealed at the far end. Freedom and the outside world are on the other side.

Before we can move, a familiar rattle and clack echoes through the massive foyer. Side passages boil over with moving metal. More and more of the robots are coming in armed. Fire axes, guns, and tools of all kinds are ranged against us.

Brios hauls Horatius off his back. Lynnette and I churn out rounds as he locks the components together.

"Get ready to run. Stay along the left wall," Brios says.

"Initializing," the Horatius unit chimes.

"Move, move, move." Brios gives the order.

We break for the wall. Jimmy slung over my shoulder limits my arc of fire to a wide zone on my right. I'm behind Lynnette, and Brios is pulling up the rear.

The Horatius unit unleashes its full fury. Volleys of auto-cannon shells burn past us as we advance.

I risk a glance at the sentry unit. Bullets fly out of him in every direction. Lancing lines of fiery light sketch paths to soon destroyed targets. Thickening plumes of smoke build in the air from the volume of micro-missiles spewing carnage downrange.

Horatius' counterfire HEAP rounds rip the gun-wielding bots to shreds. Chunks of metal, flying debris, and parts scatter on the ground and then become a tripping hazard.

"Pick it up, Sweetie," Brios yells.

I move faster.

Lynnette is now our biggest liability. Without augmentations, she doesn't have our speed. I gauge the distance. We aren't going to make it. I outpace her, twist mid-step, and shoot her in the head.

She drops.

It's over so fast she doesn't even know it's happened.

Brios snags the carbine off her tumbling corpse, and we keep running.

We get to the doors. There are no handles, no manual override buttons or levers. I drop Jimmy and grab his handheld. I pull plugs out of the rig and waste precious seconds hunting for ports by the doorframe.

Robots close in.

I find the control panel and spend a lot of calories ripping off the steel cover. I shove the plugs into the available ports and then panic when I realize they don't fit.

Thankfully James has expensive hardware. The plugs reconfigure after a moment. I run the lock program like he showed me, not even sure it will work with the system actively countering his hacks.

Horatius lobs smoke grenades for our protection. His fire rate is high and he's still ripping bots apart, but they're rushing his position. He's fighting on all fronts.

Come on, come on…. My heart pounds in my ears as I wait for the doors to cycle. The handheld sits there, blinking.

Jimmy's program fails.

Behind me I hear the ratcheting *clack clack clack* of empty hoppers and magazines as Horatius runs out of ammo.

There's a roar of screeching metal. Through the smoke-screen, I catch a glimpse of the sentry unit disappearing under a tangle of metal limbs. Horatius uses the moment before he's torn apart to self-destruct.

Brave Horatius.

Flaming components cut through the smoke, hissing and crackling as they fly.

The robots marching toward us lurch and pause as if the main computer is trying to figure out what happened to so many of its workers.

Brios takes full advantage of the stationary targets, clearing us some breathing room. His single shots are quick and precise as he pushes his augmentations to the limits.

I run Jimmy's program again. I hope I'm not enacting the definition of insanity.

Nothing. The main doors stay sealed.

Insane once shame on me, insane twice…

I slap my webbing and pull up the only thing I have left.

Shadow's security tap.

As I lift it toward the control panel, it exudes its tendrils of silvery liquid. The tendrils grope the air and then form into a match for the access ports. I jack them in and pray. Whatever happens now, this is it.

I turn and stand next to Brios. My gunfire joins his.

Robots fall under our combined fire, but more and more of them keep crawling forward.

Brios uses his last few shots and yanks my zip gun off my belt. He drains the magazine three shots at a time, then starts blocking blows with his armored limbs, tearing into robots as they reach for us.

I'm running through the last of my own ammo when I see Brios drop. Metallic bodies fold over him like a tide rushing to take him away.

I draw my knives. I won't let them take him.

I dance. Twisting, slashing, severing. Vibrating monomolecular edges separate weapons from wielders, limbs from torsos.

It doesn't matter how fast I move, I'm overwhelmed.

A fire axe raises in metallic hands. Hemmed in by jabbing metal limbs, I can't dodge, and I'm out of position for a block.

Cold autumn air washes over me as the doors cycle open. I close my eyes and feel the blow.

Epilogue

I hear a chair rolling on smooth floor. My nose tracks a hint of expensive cologne.

"Wolf," my throat burns as I try to talk, "Brios?"

"He's in another room." Wolf keeps his voice low. "He'll be fine, a bit more metal but basically the same."

"Jimmy?"

"Jimmy's condition is sketchy. He was dead a lot longer than either of you." Wolf clears his throat. "The doctors are giving him even odds. He's brilliant, so it's worth it if we can fix him."

I pull my face into what I hope is a grimace.

Wolf continues, "He grabbed a lot of data from inside. He ripped it all to an external. The instant the door breached, his system dumped all the data into a secure core at AlphaPlaza. It'll take a long time to sort through it. One thing I know for sure is that he planted a massive virus on the arcology main computer. It'll give us a backdoor if anything else happens."

"The Block?" I need to know. I'm still connected to an arcology somewhere.

"We got you three out. The gas was a nasty surprise." He sighs. "We have a number of men under treatment and a longer list of deaths than I counted on. But we can worry about a debriefing after you recover."

"Thanks boss." My legs feel like they're twitching, but I can't tell.

He squeezes my arm as he stands. "Vlasta says it'll be at least another week."

"What do I owe you?" The amount is so high it's a running joke now as far as I'm concerned.

"Nothing." He replies with his standard answer. "AlphaTek and its subsidiaries will make money off the data Jimmy pulled out."

"He gets a cut?" I feel a certain loyalty to the kid for all he managed to do. I owe that kid a lot.

"He's a thief who shouldn't have been there." Wolf chuckles. "I was planning on giving him a job."

~ ~ ~

I'm standing in the sunshine outside the MetroCafé. I'm glad it's sunny. It keeps the streaming holo-ads faded and hard to see.

Traffic rolls past, motorbikes, lowriders, and convertibles all trying to outdo each other with color, flash, and music. It's classic TopSide. On a day like today, no one wears anything but the newest, best, next biggest thing.

It's stuff I stopped wearing two months ago.

A threatening low rumble echoes down the street. Brios pulls a u-turn across traffic. No one honks or complains; he looks too good doing it. He waves at a few cars that stop to let him by.

His new B&V looks faster and meaner than his old one. It's this year's LX model. He still likes the high-gloss black paint.

I watch him slide off the bike and come up the sidewalk. He's wearing the classic cut suit and shirt I bought him. It shows off how wide his new chest and shoulders are.

I like the look and steal a glance, admiring the view.

My palmscreen chimes to let me know there's a deal on men's shoes not far from here. I double-check my bags to make sure the pink panties are at the bottom.

I set the bags down as he steps close. "You're late," I say.

"Had to pack a few more things at my old place." He checks me out. "You still sure about this?"

I slide my arms around his neck and kiss him. He kisses back. His lips on mine unlock a tangled mess of emotions, but his skin is warm, and he smells like sunshine….

No complaints. He's good at more than just kissing so I've kept him around longer than two weeks.

"Yeah," I breathe against his cheek. "I'm sure."

We go inside and skirt a few booths of wannabes with their heads down whispering about biz.

The waitress greets us. "Hi, Raven."

We make our way to a table on the patio. I signal for a couple of coffees as we go.

Suits and business-types hustle past on the sidewalk, heading to whatever big score they think they've got lined up.

Life on the edge of the Corporate Core isn't like UnderCity at all. Here, it's all about eat first, eat often, or be eaten.

"I added you to the security list for my, *our*, apartment." I sit under the striped sunbrella, cool air gently blowing out of the table's center.

I've been splitting my time between decorating the apartment and Brios' safe house. If I'm ever going to hide there again, I may as well be comfortable.

A woman walks onto the patio leading a bunch of men in suits. They're all carrying white construction hats. A new subroutine in my processor throws out a local news update about a ceremonial groundbreaking that just ended down the block: a new CitOne art commune is going up.

"You know Wolf bought our building?" Brios says as he sits next to me.

I'd frown, but it's too nice a day. "Our not-our-boss is our new landlord?"

"Yeah." He flips through the menu screen. "He says he may have a gig for us. He's waiting for intel to develop, and we're in."

That cocky bastard. Fingers in everybody's pies. At least I'm getting paid.

I catch my reflection in a car window as it glides by. I look great.

Brios stretches out on his chair. "If it doesn't come through, we could always take a trip."

I realize that the memories Phillip unlocked are a gift of luggage. They imply coming from someplace while hinting at freedom. But it's luggage I didn't buy and can't weigh, even though I carry their weight.

It's a good thing I like to shop; I know where to buy new bags and some locks for the old ones.

I smile at Brios.

My palmscreen chimes.

I turn it off as our coffee arrives.

* * * * * * *

Thank you for reading.

Share your experience of this book with other readers by posting a review on Amazon or GoodReads. **Please turn the page for a sneak preview of book two.**

Get a **FREE New White Sands City Cyberpunk e-book novella** by signing up for the **INSIDERS mailing list at www.thecyberdeck.com**. And stay tuned for the return of Raven and Brios in future books….

In Book Two:

When a high-profile vigilante gets diced up on New White Sands City streets, it's just another day in UnderCity Precinct Three. But when the case is pulled and handed to a mega-corp to deal with in private, it's just another day for everyone but Rico.

Rico Suarez is a good cop walking a fine line. He knows this corporation. It's the same one that buried his partner's murder eight years before. The cases might not be connected but the players are. This time Rico's not going to let it go, even if that means he'll have to break all the rules in the name of justice.

Back on the streets, there's a gang war brewing, and everyone's looking for one missing witness: the niece of a local oyabun and a yakuza clan paragon. If Rico hopes to find his answers and save the innocent lives caught in the ensuing firestorm, he'll have to go against the very organization that gave his life purpose.

One thing is clear: walking the line
was never enough....

STREETS of FIRE

NEW WHITE SANDS CITY CYBERPUNK
Book 2

2.01

Corps-a-Corpse

"Listen to me, Suarez," the Capt. says as he leans onto my desk. "The whole precinct has been ordered to let this one go. The corporate guys are in charge now. They'll sort it out."

"A citizen gets gutted and prepped like a piece of sashimi, and we do nothing?" My disgust comes out a sneer.

"No." The old man clips the word short. I know he's pissed at me for pushing. "We do what we're told. Now the ball is in someone else's court. It's finished for us, case closed. Like we had time to work on a dead-end case anyway. The guy must have been an asshole to get diced up like that. So one less asshole and no mess for us, paperwork's done. Hell, they even took possession of the body."

"Sure. Okay." I pull my suit jacket over my body armor and straighten my tie.

I'm not ready to let it go. I have more than a gut feeling.

The corporation pulling the case is one I'm familiar with. They were the ones who pulled the case that got my partner killed. I've been waiting eight years for something to link back to them.

"I'll let it go, Capt."

"Goddamnit, Rico." He glowers. "You are one terrible liar. But you already knew that." He stands as tall as he can and looks me in the eyes. "I mean it. We. Are. Off. This. Case. This isn't worth fighting for. Now give me your files and get the hell out of here."

I hesitate. The Capt. plucks the mem-chip from my fingers.

I'm glad I ripped a chip copy for myself. It burned all guilty-like against my chest, hanging beside my grandfather's Saint Michael medallion.

"It's been a long night, Suarez. Go home." The Capt. is smiling at me now. His idea of working with local corporations is flexible and includes bending to hold his own ankles. "The shift is over, and you're not allowed anymore O.T. this week."

"Home."

If my situation were different, I'd consider hot-bunking in one of the holding cells upstairs like some of the other guys. Trouble is, I like my place even though I'm only there a few hours a week.

I have to be the only cop in New White Sands UnderCity with a TopSide apartment. It's in a rent controlled tower on the sun-side of the Corporate Zone. My abuelita inherited the place from her mother's family, and it was passed to me when she died.

"Yeah, good idea, Capt."

"I know it is." He gestures magnanimously. "Now, go on, get outta here. Next shift needs your desk."

I pull my pistol out of my thumb-locked drawer and make my way into the back hall leading to the maglifts.

An officer comes out of booking. It's Williams. He and I butted heads when he first joined, but we're solid now. I suspect we had trouble because he's the only cop in the precinct almost as tall as I am.

He always looks pissed off, and tonight is no different. It's his game face. By his own words he uses 'bald, black, and angry' to intimidate the CitOnes who slink around in UnderCity.

If he really was upset, it would show around his eyes.

I nod and head toward him.

"LT," he rumbles as I join him. We fill the passageway side to side as we walk, both of us twisting to let other cops go by the other way.

"How's it going?" I ask.

"It's my kid's birthday this weekend. She wants a clown at her birthday party."

"A clown? Really? Jesus, better you than me. But hey, swing past the Corporate Council, I hear they have lots."

Williams snorts. "You could come by if you want."

"That's funny, Williams. You know I'm not great with kids."

We get partway to the maglift.

"Lieutenant." I know whose voice it is. "Lieutenant Suarez." I pretend I can't hear her. Williams arches a brow and follows my lead. He pushes his way into the lift's cabin, making sure he elbows just enough room for me.

"Rico, I know you can hear me." She's coming at me from behind, moving fast.

It's late. Why the hell is she even here?

I step into the maglift as the doors glide shut.

I'm about to grin, but I'm not so lucky. Her hand scissors into the closing gap, and the doors bounce back open. She steps in and nods at the other officers in the lift.

"Lieutenant," she says.

I stare at my shoes, doing my best not to look at her. She's practically standing on my toes.

Maybe in a different time and place she'd have been attractive. As it is she's just cold, from her looks to her attitude.

"Doctor." I force myself to be polite.

She says, "We had an appointment earlier today, and you never called to rebook." Her tone is winter frost. I wonder if she's ever been in a relationship. I can't see it.

"I was busy solving crimes." I roll back on my heels and shrug my reply. My blunt flippancy causes snickers from the men behind me.

I hear Brady undertone, "Way to save the city, LT." The laughter grows, but no one looks up from their feet. They cut it off after a struggle and a loud clearing of throats.

Doctor Hildebrandt's eyes narrow into hard points. "You are required to rebook if you can't make the meetings."

"Doctor." I do my best to look disappointed with myself. "I was busy. I apologize."

"You said that the last five times, Lieutenant, and I've been lenient with you so far."

My temper slips. "What now? Huh, Doc? You gonna tell me I can't go back to work in the shittiest place in the city, a rat-hole so bad cops are *drawn by lottery* to work it? I stop coming in, bad guys get away. Simple."

"You overestimate your role in the UnderCity hierarchy." She's cold all right.

"Ouch," comes a chuckle from someone behind me.

"Yeah, I took a bullet that time." I feel a vicious grin on my lips. "My point is, the scum out there is always rising. Rising up to the sunshine. You live TopSide don't you, Doctor Hildebrandt? Should we just let'em boil up to your doorstep?"

"I'll suspend you." Her voice drops, but it's a clue I register way too late. "I check off the boxes that agree with the common consensus: Lieutenant Suarez is a better shot than a cop and refuses to accept treatment for what is obviously a severe mental condition resulting from traumas experienced *before* he joined the NWSPD." She stresses the word 'before.'

I get the hint now. The union won't cover any prior mental issues. If those issues are bad enough, I'd lose my pension and health coverage, be relieved of my badge. Everything would be open to review and someone would find reason, whether there were one or not, to have me dishonored, every collar I ever made called into question....

I clench my fists.

"Let it go, LT. She's just pushing to get a rise outta you. Let it go," Williams says over my shoulder. The chorus of murmurs behind me is sympathetic.

She sneers up at Williams and then passes her gaze across the other occupants in the lift. It's an unconscious movement on her face, only there for a fraction of a second. But now I know what she thinks of cops in general.

"I want a rise out of him, do I?" she snaps. "Why would I provoke a murderer with a badge in a maglift filled with his fellow officers?"

The whole car falls silent.

I unclench my hands. She said the magic words. My friends are all around me. They're on my side. And as for calling me a murderer… "Suspend me. I'm talking to a union rep and a lawyer as soon as I'm out of the building: breach of confidentiality and slander. You guys witness for me?"

"Yeah, LT. All the way." William's voice is louder than the others, but he's not alone. The men behind me have my back.

"We got you, man," says Omar quietly from the corner.

Her eyes flick from face to face as she realizes she screwed up. The maglift opens.

"Excuse me." I push my way past her.

As I leave the offices, I'm followed by a thin blue line, all of whom are hitting the streets.

I get to my car and sit just as the suspension goes through.

I look at my datavice.

"Huh. That was fast. Who'd you blow to get that signed and stamped in less than five minutes?" I know the answer to my question even as it leaves my mouth.

The Capt.'s name appears next to Hildebrandt's at the bottom. That's who she blew.

He's pro-corporate control and a 'friend of the council.' It figures. A corporate type who panders to corporate loving types. A guy who loves kickbacks from corps so much, he'd screw his own mother if it paid enough.

The doc and him, they'll make a nice couple.

The Capt. has to know I bullshitted him about dropping the case. This is his pressure, keeping me down. Hell, he might even think he's doing me a favor.

"Well, now what, Rico?" I lean back in the seat and slip the dv back into my breast pocket. The edge of the copied mem-chip hanging next to my medallion jabs into my skin like a calling from beyond.

"Okay. I'm in."

I leave the precinct's bunkered parking garage and let the car push me into the traffic flow going up. By the time I hit the TopSide ramp, there are only three cars around me.

I buzz through the automated checkpoint and take control of the wheel.

2.02

First Light

The routine I have programmed pulls the curtains aside and alters the opacity of my bedroom window. The morning sun struggles through the low layer of clouds outside.

I know what's coming next.

I hate modern J-pop. I roll out of bed at the first strains of speed metal overlaid with a helium drifting underdeveloped starlet wavering through incomprehensible lyrics.

"Okay. Okay, CeeCee, I'm awake."

CeeCee is part of a software upgrade that rolled out half a year ago for the entire building. Half a year to get it almost right, but it's better than nothing.

I reach for my pack of synthacco sticks, tap one free, and flick the end alight. Vaping is for pansies. I pull in the heavy smoke and let it sit in my lungs for a second before I exhale. The stick stays hanging from my lip as I make my way to the kitchen.

I push the empty scotch glass into the sink. "CeeCee. Do I have what I need for a breakfast?"

"How big a meal would you like?"

"I'll be out late." I frown at my lack of a plan. It's not my usual style.

CeeCee scans a few months' worth of my breakfast data. *"Baconkelp, four slices, and four shots of egg?"*

"Good." I look in the cooler for juice and drink the last of it from the carton.

"Would you like toast?" she asks.

I can't help my smile. The mother-in-law subroutine has finally stopped bitching at me for my habits.

"We have any bagels?" I look through the window. The rain might be slowing. It's hard to tell from up here.

"You asked that bagels not be purchased," CeeCee reminds me.

"Right." I'd forgotten; that's a good sign. It's good not to remember her. This is the first morning I needed to make an effort to remember her name. About time. "Three pieces of toast and get more juice along with coffee."

"Would you like real coffee?" CeeCee asks.

For a second, I wonder if the most recent software upgrade added a hidden comedic subroutine.

"I can afford real coffee?"

"There are funds available through the offshore accounts," she replies.

"CeeCee." It makes me wonder how much I've drawn out for my scotch. "Do not access the information or money in the offshore accounts, understood?"

"Yes."

"Is there enough inside the food budget for real coffee?"

"Just. But you will have to restrict your purchase of alcohol until the next pay period."

"Then no coffee, order the scotch." I shove the empty juice carton into the recycler and head for the main room. The idea of real coffee with my stick has me swallowing saliva. I take my next drag and chase it with the last of yesterday's bottle. I slide into my jogging shoes as the treadmill folds out of the wall.

I unhook the mem-chip from my medallion chain and plug it into the drive. Wireless links connect it all to the treadmill. I load up the area around the crime scene. The wall opposite lights up with the course for the most recent drone through the area.

I set my stick into a tray next to the empty, step on the mill, and trigger the holo-projectors. "Start program. Run the file from external drive...."

I string a cable and plug my head in. I like that my eyes are still hardwired: don't have to worry about getting my optics hacked remotely. I watch the world dissolve into the landscape of UnderCity.

...UnderCity on the morning the body was found as seen through the eyes of city drones and utility vehicles.

The jog through UnderCity is a custom streaming VR program provided by the department. It's supposed to prevent cops from getting turned around and killed in the mazes of crap and temporary shelters. Since the footage is only a few hours old at any time, it's a handy tool. It gets erased regularly, but I kept this copy for the case file.

I'm ten minutes in when I stop running. The projectors auto pause. "CeeCee, back up the footage by ten seconds without the mill running." I step off the machine.

"That violates the purpose of the training," she replies.

"Override. Play it." I recover my synthacco stick, light it again, and lean against the treadmill.

There's a mugging to my left. I ignore that and zoom into one corner of the image to watch a food trolley grinding along. "Slow the footage to one quarter speed from here."

I see a well-dressed kid jump off the trolley, black ponytail swinging. The Cram 'N Jam vehicle slides quickly past her even as she bolts through the crowd on the sidewalk. A guy splits from the crowd and chases after her.

I've seen people running for their lives. Their faces get a certain expression of fear, shock, and disbelief. She has that and more.

Something drops in my gut. Timmons told me they'd pulled a girl in with the dragnet, and they'd let her go just as fast. I skim the contents of the case file. She isn't mentioned anywhere, just his verbal side-comment. I check the location and timestamp and wonder if this is the same girl.

I start the loop again, comparing the timestamp with the one on file from the murder; twenty minutes after the crime and three blocks away.

The guy chasing her follows her down a service passage. The footage I have ends there.

I watch it four times. The fourth time through, I record the specifics I need onto my optics' short-term storage. The passage number and the trolley license get loaded along with a clip of the footage as a just in case. I pull off a still frame of the kid. It's a perfect three quarter profile. I can't get a clean still frame of the guy because of the hood on his vinyl cowl and the wide filter mask he's wearing.

I get back onto the treadmill. "Resume program."

I run another eight blocks before CeeCee informs me breakfast is ready.

"End program." As the unit retracts into the wall, I mull over the mystery of the kid.

There should've been record in the file if she was pulled in by the dragnet next to the John Doe crime scene. She doesn't even show up on the footage from inside the crime scene command vehicle. She had to have been in the van for less than two minutes before she got dropped out the back door, but why?

I trust my instincts. The plan for the day makes itself. It's time to see Timmons about the case.

While I eat, I log my Internal Affairs complaint with the union. That leads to more paperwork. I'm out of scotch so I decide to wait on filling it out.

My badge and service pistol became non-functioning the instant the suspension went into effect. Swapping them for my personal 12mm and Gyroc9 is bittersweet.

I stand over the floor safe under my bed, watching the thick steel door slide closed. The encroaching darkness consumes the light flickering along the edge of my badge. My abuelita would have said it was an omen. I loved my grandmother and her crazy stories.

The bed drops back over the access as I put on my full-reactive body armor, get dressed, and strap up my armaments. I'm better off wearing my personal gear anyway. The department provided kit is bulky and still uses inserts. My stuff I can wear under my clothes with twice as much protection.

The new suit looks good, not too bulky even with the armor. A fedora, pulled low in the front, fits the look and will keep the brown water off me. I load a large stack of hardfold into my wallet, and I'm good to go.

My wait in the foyer outside my suite is short. I try my police key in the maglift. It still works, and my ride to the parking garage is given priority. I drop the two hundred and thirteen stories without a pause.

I drive my car on manual into UnderCity.

Somewhere a bunch of computers track my ID, VIN, registration, insurance, and speed. I'm on file as having gone down here. Normally that would mean nothing. Except today I'm down here as a citizen, not a cop on his way to work. Worse, I'm a cop on temporary suspension. And to whoever watches that kind of thing, maybe it's an important part of a new pattern to be scrutinized.

There aren't many tourists in UnderCity, and most CitOnes who make the trip do it with fake ID, or a hacked bypass, or bribe.

Hard business types and desperately poor live down here. The rich come to hire, be hired, or buy something illegal. Elitist punks come looking for kicks. I remember coming down here with my friends. It's a dangerous mix, as old as the idea of cities themselves.

The summer rain TopSide makes things crazy all across UnderCity: bodies wash out of culverts; homeless, CitFours, and unregistered citizens come out of their trash piles and wander around; and the crime rate, in general, goes up.

It'll make it easy to find Timmons.

My promotion to lieutenant left Timmons short a partner. Good partners are hard to get, harder when the precinct is strapped for honest cops. He's the only partner I had in the years after Axil.

You tell your partner everything. Everything, that is, until it gets too big or too close to home. You talk because you spend almost every waking moment joined at the hip. If you aren't completely human to your partner, they might hesitate, or fuck up, or drop the ball in some critical moment and bang … you're dead. It's a lot of pressure, a lot of weight. These days, I prefer to work solo.

When I got my promotion, Timmons admitted that he initially thought I was a player, part of the Blue Code. I wasn't offended. I learned my style from Axil.

Axil had been good at his job, but he had his demons. After his murder, I spent a lot of energy making sure he was remembered as a good cop. It strained things when I found out I knew Axil better than his wife, Marion, did. But that's how things go for cops. Trust. I never found out who couldn't trust whom between Axil and Marion.

A good guy who made bad choices, that's what Axil was.

Paul Timmons isn't anything like Axil.

The scanner chatters about a multiple homicide. Detective Timmons will be there, and now, so will I….

I find a patch of streetside parking and take a moment to look around before I get out. This area is made up of gutted buildings, a few local shops, and a tarnished looking bodega with wares crowded on the sidewalk behind a wire cage. The flashing rain-soaked signage is the only thing that breaks the gloom. The Major Crimes Unit truck, all folded out, eats a lot of curb space. Aside from my car, it's the cleanest looking thing on the block.

I get out and shoulder my way through the crowd of gawkers. I duck under the glowing projected tape. Breaking the beam without an active badge would get me stun-shocked.

The senior patrol officer watching the line turns. He recognizes me and tips up his short-barreled machine-pistol.

"Hey, how you doing, Cortez?" I clasp hands with him.

"Better than you, LT." He tries to keep a serious look on his face for the sake of the gen-pub behind us. He can't hide his grin. "I heard you were suspended."

"I'm having technical difficulties communicating with that headshrinker from Internal Affairs." I scan the crowd as I talk.

"I hear she's crazy because she doesn't have any cybernetics. You think that's true, running with trodes instead of a plug, can that mess people up?"

I shrug, my bitterness playing on my face.

"I know her, and true or not," Cortez says, matching my shrug with sympathy, "she's got a mean heart." He flicks his eyes to the crowd behind us. "Why the hell are you down here, LT?"

"I'm looking to talk to Timmons." I glance up at the derelict building covered in anti-corporate and gang related graffiti. "He inside?"

"Yeah, careful though, they're still sweeping for evidence. They may even make you suit up. Third floor."

I nod my thanks and make my way in, snapping on gloves. I greet more cops as I go. The place is crawling with Blue. Whatever happened here, it's big.

I step onto the third floor and spot Timmons.

CSI in their white paper spacesuits are crisscrossing the room with tiny vacuums, pulling up eyelashes, and other bits of crap. I stay close to the door and out of their way.

"Citizen Suarez," Timmons says with a smile. "What brings you back to the bottom of the toilet?"

I look around at the bloodbath covering the top half of the walls. The gore is thickest in a two-yard-wide disk across the ceiling above the bodies that are oddly clustered in the middle of the room.

"What happened here?" I ask.

"I can't say, Citizen. Ongoing investigation; I'm sure you understand. Why are you even inside the perimeter?"

"My bad, Detective." I catch his drift. The CSI team aren't friends of ours. "I was hoping to have a word with you?"

"Sure." He comes closer. "Just get outta here before this case gets compromised and we lose a collar over bad containment of the scene."

"Meet me by the rope?" I turn to leave.

"Yeah, give me five?" he replies.

I watch CSIs watching us. "Sure."

I head back down to the street. I know both Cortez and Timmons took a risk letting me in there to begin with. I don't want them hurting because Doctor Hildebrandt can't see eye to eye with me. I watch the crowd casually ebb and flow along the marker tape. I pull out another synthacco stick and wait in the thickly humid air.

A guy who doesn't fit the neighborhood is hovering near the edge of our truck. I eye him. He spots me. After a second he turns to go. Something about how he handles himself is off. He shoulders his way past a homeless guy who barks an incoherent obscenity at the contact. My gut tightens up.

"Shit," I mutter. "Cortez, come here a second."

"Yeah, LT?" He glowers at some citizens farther along the rope. They back up, and he joins me.

"Get a com-op in the truck to drop a discreet drone on that guy over there." I point him out with my chin. "See him, in the blue long coat, the one who's walking away?"

"The guy who looks like he's holding in a shit? Yeah I see him." Cortez watches the guy's progress. "Why him?"

"I got a hunch, that's why," I say. "Just do it. Okay?"

"Sure, LT." Cortez goes and does as I ask.

Timmons comes out of the building as Cortez is jumping into the rig.

I watch the guy vanish down the block. I'm running a full body language scan on him as he walks. Blue coat comes back 'guilty' by a fifty-four percent probability. He's not local to the area, and he's suspicious enough that Cortez won't get in trouble over the drone.

My gut is telling me he's involved somehow. I hope the drone query yields up more than that.

Paul follows my gaze, glancing down the block. He's a detective after all, trained to pay attention. "Anything I should know about?" he asks.

"A strong hunch." I know Timmons would need better than that to put on a drone deployment report, so I say, "Some pasty guy who bailed when I made eye contact."

"Maybe he thinks big guys in expensive suits are scary?" Timmons crosses his arms. I get it. He was my partner before my promotion; with my suspension and him on the job, he has to at least appear uncooperative.

"Cortez is hopefully gonna have him followed."

"Nice. You bust into my crime scene and then bully a senior patrolman into following through on your hunch? What's next, Suarez?" he says. "I mean I know you're suspended. The Capt. was very clear about what'll happen to anyone helping you, okay? So don't make things worse."

"Fine," I sigh. My berating for anyone listening is over, and we get to business. I lean in and say, "You pulled this kid into the dragnet during the John Doe investigation outside Nu Hong." I hand him the still frame of the girl. "She doesn't show up in any of the records, and I'm curious. Why did she get cut loose so fast?"

"Shit, Rico. We're supposed to have dropped that case." Timmons shakes his head. "It's not ours anymore. The corporation who owns the building is on it now."

"I know." I meet his gaze. "But I need this information."

"We picked her up on the same block as the body. She didn't have ID." He hesitates.

I look at him. "And?"

"I dropped her out the back door because she's covered in yakuza ink," he says. "I mean I've seen lifers with less artwork on them than her."

"Yakuza ink? What the hell is a little girl doing covered in irezumi?"

Even progressive clans only just started letting women get serious irezumi, but a kid, a girl?

"That didn't set off any alarms with you?" My failure to train him properly comes out as a tinge of frustration. "Maybe, strike you as kind of odd?"

"Sure it did, Rico, why do you think I jumped on it and let her go so fast?" He grimaces at me. "Smart people know better than to piss where they aren't supposed to. And we're both smart people, aren't we, Rico? I put her out because of the flack we would have gotten if we'd kept her. As it was, we fielded discrete inquiries from two different law firms, and then someone else opened a Missing Persons on her as well. All of that inside twenty minutes."

"Twenty minutes?" Given it happened at two in the morning and lawyers never got out of bed before noon unless someone put a gun to them....

Timmons nods. "That was my reaction too."

That kind of speed means someone in the department is a funnel, sending out specific information.

I keep to the facts of the case. "A Missing Persons?"

Yakuza kids don't run away from home let alone have files opened on them.

"Yeah. Apparently someone high up in the clans is missing a niece."

"You did a DNA poke, right?"

He hesitates again.

Timmons is a good cop. He won't chase any of the leads he isn't supposed to. But I'm also a friend.

He doesn't meet my eyes. "We did a routine DNA poke before we figured out she'd be trouble." He looks past me. "She went out the door before the results came back."

"What the hell are you not telling me, Paul?"

"Just.... Damn it, Rico. Don't even go there with this one. This isn't shit I want to see you step in. These kinds of cases get cops killed."

"Do you have access to the girl's DNA poke, or not?" He's a good cop, but it doesn't mean his way is right, or better. "I'm serious. It's important."

"Fine, but you've been warned." His voice drops quiet as he says, "The corporation cleaned out the case file, but I know where to find it." He frowns at his PD System Access strapped to his forearm. A moment later he nods. "It's on file under the 'At risk' section of the Juvenile Identification Database. They didn't think to look in the JID because it's manually linked by the officer at the time of questioning."

"I didn't know that," I say as he pulls up the data packet and forwards it to me.

"Yeah. I started life as a young offender," he says sarcastically, "I figured it would be the backdoor to a promotion."

"How'd that work out?" I snort.

He looks at the crowd that ebbs and flows around the police tape. "I made full detective at twenty-eight, so you tell me."

I laugh. "You haven't made lieutenant yet. Your baby face keeps you from bullying information from people. You want a decent promotion? Get a new face."

He scoffs at my comment. "That's what I had your ugly mug for. But do me a favor?"

"What's that?"

"Don't let that file eat you up, Rico. As a friend, I'm telling you, just let it go."

I push a smile onto my lips even as I wonder what the hell he's talking about. "Sure. Sure, Paul. It'll be okay." I clap him on the shoulder. "Let me know if that drone pulls anything in, will you?"

"Yeah," he says. "I'll call you."

"Here's the alphanumeric for a burner dv. Reach me there for the next few days." I hand him the slip of rice paper with my temporary code on it.

"Okay, Rico." He fires me a grin. "I have to ask, is that IA doctor on you for not banging the crap out of her, or what?"

"I'd rather pound a sack of ice cubes. It'd be warmer. Better conversation too." I figured word of something had to be spreading, and now I know what's going around. "I missed a few meetings over the pistol discharge on that serial rapist."

"That's such a bunch of crap." Timmons looks at the number on the slip I gave him. "The money and connections he had, even with the evidence, he would've walked."

"That, between you and I, was my point," I say. "I gotta go."

He folds the rice paper around a stick of gum and pops it into his mouth. "Well, enjoy your time off."

"Yeah." I wave once over my shoulder as I head back to my car. "Right."

I climb in and pull my handheld out of the center console. A quick search for Timmons' badge number in the JID and I find the girl's file. I skim it, then read it, and read it again.

I get it now: why Timmons didn't want to say anything.

"Axil, you bastard."

As a cop, his DNA is on permanent record. With a one percent margin of error, this girl is his kid.

I knew Axil had a mistress on the side. I never met her.

He never mentioned there was a kid.

* * * * * * *

Other Titles Available in the New White Sands City Cyberpunk Series

SNITCH

Forces are moving in the high-tech rat race of New White Sands City and one low-level transporter has an opportunity to make it big if he can survive the dangerous backwaters of corporate espionage.

This novella takes place before the first book and lays the groundwork for the larger scope of the series.

Read this e-book for free by signing up for the mailing list at www.thecyberdeck.com.

JIMMY the SLIP

After dying in the arcology incursion, Jimmy's finding it hard to cope with his new reality. College classes don't seem to matter anymore, yet he's avoiding his new boss because he's pretty sure he never wants to work in the field again.

Unfortunately for Jimmy, being a hacker prodigy with a reputation means, sooner or later, someone's going to make that choice for him. The question is, what's he going to lose this time.

This is a novella in the New White Sands City series that spans the gap in the run-up to book three.

Book one is required reading and this novella contains minor spoilers for book two.

* * *

This page redacted.

* * * * * * *

AlphaTek Global Publications,
at the request of the *Corporate Council*,
is happy to comply with the *Corporate Advertising Directive* regarding subversive CitFour content.

AlphaTek Global Publications

a division of AlphaTek Global Security

New White Sands City
Florida

"Future Forward"

For all inquires please contact
publisher@thecyberdeck.com

About the Author

Ron Bender has been an international business consultant, business process trouble-shooter, and marketing specialist. Besides consulting for the Canadian government and the private sector, he's had thirty-seven years of RPG storytelling experience. He spent the majority of that time running and designing games using the customizable GURPS system while focusing on gaming as an interactive storytelling forum. Today, he's happy to present his science fiction cyberpunk series: the New White Sands City series.

Ron enjoys watching formula one racing, tracking a wide array of burgeoning trends and technologies, and researching obscure time periods. He can sometimes be found taking in the occasional pint of beer while sitting in one of Calgary's local pubs.

For more information about the New White Sands City series, or to get in touch with Ron Bender, visit the official website at www.thecyberdeck.com or connect with him on twitter @AuthorRonBender.

2.5.0

Somewhere in New White Sands

Coordinates in the message lead her to a maze of ruined stairwells and crumbling passages under the old city. A high-security door has been installed at the end of the final corridor.

It unlocks at her touch and opens into a circular chamber made of burnished concrete.

Cold air spills out. It smells of bleach, ozone, and running electronics. It's meant to be unsettling. In that regard it fails. Every place she works eventually smells like this.

She knows that the world is an ebb and flow of dominance and submission, of power and control.

This place has been designed to subvert dominance and demand submission.

Light panels spaced around the perimeter glow a dim crimson. Most of the room is in shadow. A high-backed chair stands in the center, lit by a single pin-dot of harsh white light.

She acknowledges the feelings of pride and amusement that well up inside her. They were trying so hard. She knows this game well, and knows that she plays it better than they do.

She walks in and sits. The chair is stiff and uncomfortable beneath her. She arranges herself on it as though it were a cherished piece from her own collection.

A holo-projection materializes. It shows a narrow, unmoving field of view: a night-vision cam fixed to a ceiling. An unlikely looking group of people move down a cramped hallway.

She's seen teams of mercenaries, corporate paramilitary, and police forces in operation. It's obvious that some of the group are untrained: their movements panicked and clumsy. Even the trained members move as though they've never worked together.... A contracted team, possibly selected to be expendable.

The cam footage freezes. Its crisp resolution enhances even further and switches to a full daylight filter.

"This individual." A male voice echoes around her as one of the figures expands to fill the projection. Her audio processor indicates the voice is manufactured, a simulacrum of human speech.

The enlarged image shows a male in his mid teens.

A second holo-screen opens; lines of data race upward faster than her enhanced vision can track. Flagged keywords mark points of deeper analysis throughout the text. She studies the young face, tracing its smooth lines with her eyes.

She wonders who the young man is. What made him so important that she needed to be called? She's secretly delighted by him, by what he represents.

Her processor indicates an Intelligence file is waiting for permission to download. She accepts the contract by permitting the file access.

The holo-screens vanish. The light panels begin to fade.

She leaves the carefully constructed space. The door closes at her back, and she hears a sleeting hiss of movement as nano-disassemblers devour the room. Her hair tightens across her scalp in a primal reaction. A smile ghosts across her lips. What a curious thing.

She opens the INT-File.

SUBJECT: (M) Takashi, James Leroy.

KNOWN ALIASES: (1) Jimmy the Slip.

* * * * * * *

Printed by Amazon Italia Logistica S.r.l.
Torrazza Piemonte (TO), Italy

17591893R00194